Also by Michael Mail

Coralena

EXPOSURE

Michael Mail

Scribner

First published in Great Britain by Scribner, 2003
This edition published by Scribner, 2004
An imprint of Simon & Schuster UK Ltd
A Viacom Company

Scribner and design are trademarks of Macmillan Library Reference USA,
Inc., used under licence by Simon & Schuster, the publisher of this work.

1 3 5 7 9 10 8 6 4 2

Simon & Schuster UK Ltd
Africa House
64–78 Kingsway
London WC2B 6AH

www.simonsays.co.uk

Simon & Schuster Australia
Sydney

A CIP catalogue record for this book is available from the British Library

ISBN 0–7432–3913–X

Typeset by M Rules
Printed and bound in Great Britain by
Bookmarque Ltd, Croydon, Surrey

To
Karen & Raymond
Andrea & Steven
Debbie & Danny
&
Keren

Acknowledgements

I'm very grateful to all the people who helped me with this novel. Among them, I want to particularly mention: expert photographers Naomi Ellis, Gavin Jack, Colin Jarvey, David Koppel, Jan Lawrie, Rosie Potter and John Zammit; Sharon Abudara, Rob Berg, and Simon Morris of Jewish Care; Charlotte Dawkins, Nina Goswami and Mark Ross of Queen Mary Westfield; Chaim Neslen and *Di Fraynt Fun Yiddish* at Toynbee Hall; Keren Barrett, Ronnie Mail and Sara Zimmerman for their general comments.

Special thanks also to my agent Giles Gordon, and Tim Binding and Rochelle Venables at Scribner for their support and guidance.

'The photographer is like the Zen archer, who must become the target so as to be able to hit it.'

Henri Cartier Bresson

The incident provoked mild curiosity in the media.

Attention was far more on the results of the local elections formulated as a massive vote of no confidence in the Thatcher government. One newspaper cartoon had a vampire-imagined Prime Minister rapidly deflating, skewered by a 'poll tax' stake. London papers focused special concern on the *rise of the Far Right*, highlighting the unprecedented capturing of ward seats in the East End by the British People's Party.

This was another East End story. It peaked on page seven in the national press – run under the headline EXPRESS EXCLUSIVE despite its appearance with virtually identical detail in several other newspapers. What was written was actually very little, simply a rendition of the facts, the briefest of backgrounds on the victims, mostly on how they were found. On its causes there was hardly any speculation. Yet speculation was to become the surest legacy. And of course there were the photographs.

The *East London Chronicle*'s coverage led with photographs. There was something utterly compelling about these portraits, far too fabulous for their awful context, propping up a headline that declared, SUCH WASTED LIFE! – the concluding sentiment of a hurriedly released police statement. In the end, it was all that the police were required to do. The local student newspaper edged its next edition in black.

The official summation was provided by the Coroner at the Inquest that summer of 1990. She spoke with moving eloquence of 'the grievous tragedy of inexplicable death'.

Whatever happened was locked inside the photographs. The photographs remain.

PART 1

AUTUMN

1

It began with a flash, a stinging in the eyes, her head jerking back with the surprise of it. —

Suzy was feeling anxious enough, making her way into Room 206 behind a cluster of chatting students who appeared far too at ease with this novel university life.

The burst of bright light accelerated an urgent swing towards the semicircle of shiny orange chairs laid out across the room, confronting a desk with whiteboard beyond. She made her seat selection judiciously, declining the prominence of the circle's middle, while avoiding what could be perceived as the indifference of the periphery. From somewhere centre left she now allowed herself to absorb fully what she had just experienced, watching entering students being similarly photographed by a man she presumed was their lecturer. He was using a Polaroid, each picture disgorging from the camera's rear being carefully applied to a growing collage of images along a bare white wall.

Suzy glanced at her peers presently forming the semicircle. Her eye settled on one woman struggling to disentangle herself from an impressive display of camera equipment. She was older, perhaps mid-twenties, and was wearing a long flowing dress that could easily have been a fashion-page feature. Her face was strikingly emphasized through make-up application and Suzy wondered if she realized just how incongruous she looked. Suzy herself had flirted with the idea of wearing a skirt, still trying to seek out occasions to justify an extravagant summer purchase. She had enjoyed the flirtation all through wriggling on her trusted jeans.

'I'm Mister Terence Raymond.'

The lecturer's own choice of clothing was an unrelenting black; baggy trousers accentuating a tight-fitting T-shirt over disappointingly thin contours. Suzy wondered why he had bothered.

'That order *is* important!'

He was speaking from the edge of the desk, legs dangling just above the floor. There was a northern-sounding accent, but not her own brand.

'Please try to get it right. It's really not that difficult. And when we get to know each other better, I might allow *some of you* to call me Terry.' He smiled. It was the first time and Suzy was grateful to witness a peculiarly intense expression relieved. His eyes softened their scrutiny and his whole face seemed to open up, presenting a more rounded aspect. As a reward, she decided to knock several years off his age, dropping to mid-thirties. Suzy was pleased that they shared the same darker hair colouring, although she presumed his straightened locks, side-parted to launch a wave across his forehead, were effortless.

Mr Terence Raymond set off a roll-call of names meandering along the semicircle. Suzy listened carefully to these first clues as to the identities of her classmates, enjoying the rich mix of accents. The grandly presented woman, now revealed as Nina plus too quickly said surname, was forgiven her appearance being evidently exotically foreign. So was the floppy-haired man curiously squatting on the next seat, who chose to announce himself simply by his first name – Salvo – as if he needed no introduction at all. When her own turn came, Suzy let rip with acutely flattened *A*s, fully exposing her distinguished Yorkshire roots. She had also *journeyed* to this place.

There were sixteen students arrayed in the class. Two anticipated students were missing, and one unanticipated present, resolved after a brief interrogation. 'Fine Arts is in heaven upstairs!' said Terry, pointing a finger ceilingward. 'Wait!' The student's embarrassment was cruelly sustained while Terry sought out her photograph from along the classroom wall, finally presenting it to her. 'Do remember us fondly!'

Terry remained before the collection of wall images.

'The London New University BA Honours in Photographic Studies. Entering class of 1989. Gruesome!' Someone near Suzy giggled. 'No. You're not so bad,' he conceded. Terry then walked across to Nina and picked up her glamorous camera. 'See this!' He revolved it clumsily in one hand. 'A box with a hole in it. That's all it is.'

He returned the camera to a relieved Nina, 'How many photographs will be taken today?' – restoring himself to the edge of his desk – 'Hundreds? No, thousands and thousands, millions. All over the world. Tourists, families, outings, events, occasions of every kind. You name it. All those picture albums, wallet photos, frames on the mantelpiece. People who've never done a

BA Honours in Photographic Studies. Not any sort of course. It doesn't bother them!'

Terry stood up again.

'So why are you lot here?' He was looking straight at Suzy and she prayed the question was rhetorical. 'Because you don't just want to snap pictures. You want to become photographers. In whatever area that interests you – art, journalism, fashion, advertising, documentary – whatever it is, *first of all*, you have to become a photographer. And that's the hardest thing in the world.'

Terry returned his gaze to the pictures along the wall. 'Now I want you all to stand up. Come on! Quickly.'

There was much scraping of chairs. Suzy had the sudden queasy sensation that she had been transported back to school.

'Come forward!' Terry waved a hand.

In the process, Suzy accidentally nudged the woman next to her, who took this as a prompt, introducing herself as Jo. Suzy just had time to admire the remarkable fountain of bleached blonde dreadlocked hair contained within a luminous headband before they merged with the flow of students.

'Apprehensive, self-conscious, pompous, nervous.' Terry was reciting rhythmically. 'Shy, angry, arrogant, confused, self-assured.'

Suzy sought out her own picture, immediately confirming the worst – a mop of curls falling forward from her forehead, a surprised expression enhancing too ample cheeks, her brown eyes lost behind a squint and, worst of all, the twin spots on her chin that had been stalking her for days far too visible through the seam of foundation. Could she ask for another go?

'Yes, it is yóu, dear. Hard to handle, I know.' Terry's words delivered to her side provoked immediate embarrassment. 'Why don't you have a look at the others?'

Suzy shuffled along, interweaving with her classmates, avoiding the effrontery of eye contact while carefully scrutinizing their reproduced personas along the wall.

'Cooperative or antagonistic, conventional or eccentric, comic or grave.' Terry continued on, the boom of his voice swirling above the melee of his charges.

Suzy discovered through her picture that she hadn't noticed Jo's three silver loops neatly aligned down her left ear lobe. Nina was so composed in hers, an expression of gratitude as if she had long prepared for this moment of celebrity. Suzy wondered if she had been forewarned, which would explain her overall appearance. The photograph alongside Nina revealed a bizarre hangdog expression, which Suzy could confirm was a faithful replica. In yet another, someone had successfully launched a lunging tongue.

'What d'you think?'

Suzy was suddenly confronted by the original – person and tongue. He was tall, looming over her, chin shaded by the early shoots of a beard. Suzy returned to the refuge of the picture. His mouth dominated the shot, although she also took in bright eyes under emphatic eyebrows. Long brown blond hair framed his face.

'Big tongue?' she replied, turning back to him. His baggy sweatshirt was awash with sporting insignia.

'Suzy, isn't it?' He put out his hand in an oddly presumptive way. 'I was paying attention!' His expression turned sheepish, which did serve his cause. 'I'm Nicholas, or Nick.'

He looked like a Nick, but sounded like a Nicholas Suzy thought, polished vowels masking a Mancunian core.

'First impressions!' Terry struck up again. 'We so quickly make up our minds about people. Look at the photographs. I want you to *think* carefully about what you *see* in them. Think about *first impressions*.

And Terry had successfully made his own.

2

It annoyed Suzy that she had always been made to justify her interests. Playing an instrument, hockey, dressing in a tutu all appeared the acceptable face of youthful passions growing up in Leeds – photography was certainly not.

Her mother frowned on it, categorizing photography a masculine pursuit, something akin to football or rugby. It was as if Suzy had embarked upon an act of sisterly betrayal. And her mother despised the fact that it was such a solitary affair. She wanted Suzy involved with groups and teams, not removed to her room playing with old dolls and lighting effects. In what her mother presented as an act of compromise, although it felt more like a weaning away, she had even tried to steer Suzy into more 'mainstream' artistic appreciations – taking her to the city galleries, stiff lectures on art – activities they could share.

Most of her friends were similarly suspicious, as if Suzy was a member of some secret society from which they were being excluded. Suzy appeared to be needlessly adding to her teen anxieties, yet she knew it was precisely the opposite. Photography was her very protection from them.

Suzy could recycle justifications now by rote – photography was an art form, freezing moments of life, creating a record. She loved its immediacy, and intimacy. But these were words largely for effect. She hoped that she sounded clever. Not as some sort of swot heaven forbid – more in a mysterious kind of way, perhaps worldly, maybe even special.

What she would not reveal was the actual truth of it. What had happened on that fateful day as an eleven-year-old being handed a camera for the very first time. After some fumbling, her father had helped her align her eye with the correct orifice. The effect was instantaneous and sensational, releasing a rush of emotion. It wasn't what she saw through the lens, some windswept English beachfront scene long forgotten. It was how she felt being behind the camera – so completely *safe*.

And it was her father who presented Suzy with her first proper camera – a Weston TT in glistening red and black. Suzy could recall the moment with utmost clarity, it being her last birthday celebrated as a family. The shots she took in the restaurant that evening were her inaugural assignment, capturing a family swansong – her mother tight-lipped and sombre, blaming a cold, her father ridiculously expansive, cuddling his growing girl – and Suzy miraculously handed the precious means to extract herself from it all.

The Weston TT launched a march of photographs that in time came to consume every available wall space in her bedroom – Mum clambering on the roof, Leeds town hall at night, leery football fans, horses parading through a sunny Spanish village, her grandfather Abie asleep in the garden, Roundhay Park Butterfly House, great barges of the Union Canal, her friends Beverley and Rochelle at an Easter fair. And there were her experiments, like the twenty-three images of an Ilkley Moor sunset, each taken with a different combination of light and speed. It was a template to possibility.

Suzy was quite brazen when it came to her choice of career. There was always an expectation that she would go to university. It was the instilled aspiration of every self-respecting Alwoodley child. However, her choice of study was most definitely a singular decision.

Her mother came round to accepting the inevitable. It could even be said that she colluded in its outcome. She had, after all, allowed herself to become vital subject matter for Suzy's project, 'Home Truths', that clinched her university place – a series of unconventional black and white vignettes of domestic life that involved Suzy cajoling and bullying her mother with increasing unpleasantness over several days. Suzy was most proud of the transposed image she had pulled off that had her mother's face spinning with washing-machine laundry.

The project had facilitated her escape from the very life she had portrayed, sending another provincial in search of her destiny to London town. Suzy became hugely excited by the anticipation of this new student life, even to the extent of engaging in various acts of preparation. None of the portrayals of the great photographers she encountered in the photography tomes appeared anything like what Suzy saw in the mirror. She began buying clothes, experimenting with formulations of hairstyle – largely hopeless – and she even embarked on a diet. She wanted to remake her appearance and, in the process, also to *feel* different.

Her mother had wanted Suzy to study locally. 'Who will you know down there?'

That was the point, Mother dear!

Suzy was making space. Her amazing Prague holiday that summer had confirmed it. The trip provided the final photographs applied to her bedroom wall, and the very first of her new bedroom in the student hall of residence. Suzy was ready for a wider world – apprehensive, but also longing for it. And she had her own unique way of taking it all in.

3

The afternoon boat trip down the Thames was unashamedly an exercise in class bonding. The fact that it rained for most of the journey, forcing the group to stay largely in the lounge, clearly helped the mission, if not the mood. And there were even little games to facilitate the mingling. The name stuck on Suzy's forehead was eventually revealed to be Wise, and her activity partner, Morecambe, proved to be the glamorously maintained Nina. Explaining the subtleties of Morecambe and Wise to an

Argentinian made the assignment far more demanding than no doubt intended.

Of all her new classmates, Suzy stayed closest to Jo. She was the first person to introduce herself on that auspicious first class and, having been later reunited in the same hall of residence, they had already shared several conversations and large milky coffees. Jo had a relaxed and engaging manner that compelled Suzy to forgive her idyllically thin shape. Although from Bristol, Jo had family in London and Suzy was enthralled by the authoritative way she could talk about the city. It was a mastery Suzy was eager to acquire.

They were joined by a woman called Megan from a village near Norwich, with tightly cropped hair upstanding in impressively irregular tufts, dressed in combat trousers and jean jacket crawling with badges that shouted various causes. Megan was keen to express her dire assessment of the males with whom they were destined to spend the next three years. The specimen receiving most opprobrium was one particularly severe-looking student called Marvin, who appeared to be dedicating his time in search of his own company. Jo wondered if he might be Salman Rushdie. 'It's a great place to hide. Enrol on a course. Might as well learn something while you're hanging about!'

It was noticeable all along the boat that there was a parting along gender lines. The exception was Salvo, who had been determined to ensure everyone on the boat appreciated his Italian provenance, including the crew, and who then settled on trying to convince Nina that they were soulmates. Suzy felt his case somewhat weakened by the way Nina had to bend herself for their conversation. Jo and Megan speculated loudly about whether Salvo would have been so keen if her skirt had had a less generous split. Suzy had aligned herself with a formidable pair.

The keenest mixers were undoubtedly the university staff, serving up a forced bonhomie as they circulated among this latest batch of initiates. Terry, being not only the class's lecturer on photographic theory but also overall class tutor, led the charge. He was being supported by a beanpole of a woman called Clara designated to run the practicum, and two part-time technicians, Maurice and Mandy, affectionately referred to as Mork and Mindy.

Every so often, student clusters would brave the wet conditions of the deck to marvel alfresco at the familiar London landmarks being paraded from this less familiar angle of the river. Suzy emerged for the Houses of Parliament, joining what she now realized was a preponderance of dedicated smokers. She managed to remain all the way to Tower Bridge until she felt the first trickles slithering down her back. She chatted with Gareth, originally from Jamaica and now a Londoner for more than ten years, dressed in a flamboyant orange shirt with substantial cuffs. And there was Barry, large and freckle-faced, who was taking the course on sufferance because no one would employ him in the field of fashion photography without experience. The London New University was anyway 'his local', and Suzy delighted to find an authentic East Ender among them. Nina, with Salvo fixed to her side, insisted on learning more about Morecambe and Wise.

While personal cameras had been forbidden, one did make its appearance as part of a later group activity. Turns were to be taken capturing 'one moment only' that could suitably serve to mark the occasion. True to the persistent ethos, students were yet again split into pairs, each having to provide the other with a rationale behind their choice of shot. Suzy found herself in a second conversation with Nick – this time more resolute on his name. She called him Nicholas and he curiously corrected her. Suzy had registered his manoeuvrings at various points, a task made easier by the bright red of his Manchester United shirt, which also served to confirm his origins.

'I shouldn't be speaking to you,' he said. 'You're from Leeds. You know. Manchester and Leeds!' Nick tugged his shirt.

Suzy didn't know. 'You've shaved.'

'Yeah.'

'It's better.' Suzy wondered if giving up on the beard was connected with his now decisive Nick persona. He stroked his chin uncertainly while she reflected on the tragedy of progress on the face front being immediately reversed by the clothing. Nevertheless, there was something definitely attractive about him. Undeserving of Megan's blanket judgement on the men of their party, Suzy decided. She was also trying to determine if she was being chatted to, or chatted up. It was the way he was looking at her, so attentively.

Nick tackled the assignment first, at Suzy's insistence. He proved an eager conversationalist, regaling Suzy with a detailed account of six months 'bumming around the Far East'. 'I wanted to build my portfolio,' he said in a way that sounded suitably intimidating. Suzy hadn't so far dared to employ such a term for her own work, yet she noted how appealing it sounded. She trialled the word when she talked of the images she herself had amassed from her summer trip to Prague – Wenceslas castle, the old Jewish synagogue, Gustav monastery, Terezin concentration camp. She had accompanied her friend Beverley on a thrilling visit to her Czech cousins.

Nick hadn't been, but wanted to go, 'before it all changes in Eastern Europe'. Speculation on the future of communism had dominated Suzy's conversations with the young people she had met there. And then Nick had them back in a rainforest in Bali, and some technical problem with light metering and filters. There was now an arrogance in the way she felt he was lecturing her, although she found this not unduly unpleasant. She had her own aspirations in that respect.

They stepped out on deck during a rare moment of rainlessness and, much to Suzy's surprise, Nick took a quick shot of the first company of students they happened upon, a composition of bodies draped in various languorous positions along a railing.

'So what were you thinking?' Suzy posed the assignment's question.

'I liked the way they were standing.'

Suzy waited for something more commensurate with a student who had a Far Eastern *portfolio*.

Her picture was taken at the prow of the ship. She had managed to entice Jo and Megan out of the lounge, locking them into position until the next bridge. Suzy felt she caught perfectly a mood of foreboding through the way the darkly enveloping bridge framed the picture, and how she had arranged Jo and Megan in each other's arms.

'Think of yourselves alone at sea . . . in a life-raft,' Suzy announced as she took the shot.

Nick vehemently denied that he had sniggered.

Suzy had her longest conversation with Terry towards the end of the journey, delicately raising an aspect of the course that was filling everyone with varying degrees of dread – the project over the full academic year that accounted for a whopping 60 per cent of the final mark. The course material had included a project timeline with an expectation of initial ideas by the end of that month.

'A year sounds a long time but, believe me, it goes just like that.' Terry snapped his fingers.

'And the theme is set?'

'Community. It's a very broad one, don't worry! I'll be explaining all about it in class.'

Community. Community! Suzy couldn't begin to think.

Terry brought up her 'Home Truths' course submission – 'Your poor mum!' Suzy was delighted with the compliment that rounded off the recollection. He spoke about work that addressed similar themes and recommended that she seek out Faye Goodhart and her 'eccentric tableaux of raging domesticity'.

Suzy had never heard of Faye Goodhart, nor could she imagine what 'eccentric tableaus of raging domesticity' could possibly entail. Yet it made her feel excited. Having established infamy in Leeds for her idiosyncratic pursuits, she had landed herself among a hearty band of fellow enthusiasts. It was a world to which Suzy would gladly commit.

And so she could forgive Terry his unrelenting black costume, curious as to how he would maintain the look throughout the next three years. Indeed, Suzy considered him altogether far less intimidating in close-up, and resolved to defend her mid-thirties assessment despite Jo's vicious insistence that he was well over forty.

4

Her mother didn't hate her father. Suzy knew that they were well past all that. What lingered was simply *the hole*. It was what Suzy worried about the most. Typically, her father had a new woman in his life right from the separation, indeed, was now married to Charlotte. Whether he was happy or not, she couldn't really say. He had the ability to regale her with tales of all sorts of doings that ensured Suzy was up to date with the various compartments of his life, while skilfully managing to obscure any sense of an overall. Maybe she could identify with the technique because it was something she recognized in herself. Whatever problems her father faced, there wasn't that hole, not as far as she could tell.

It was her mother that worried her. Suzy kept waiting for her to change, for something to change. She had become somehow frozen into a routine of measured limited living. She had her school secretary job, her small circle of friends. And of course Suzy had been around, and now she was gone.

Yet Suzy was discovering the irony that this university life might actually create a whole new re-engagement with her mother. In a flurry of concern that revealed her at her most archetypally Jewish, she had dedicated herself to ensuring that her daughter was suitably nested in her new environment. She had driven Suzy down from Leeds, the car packed with all manner of supplies; had spent a morning giving her room in the student hall a thorough cleaning – 'you'd think they could have made it at least inhabitable!' – fitted a special allergy protection sheet to her bed; stocked her tiny fridge to bursting; and then, as a *coup de grâce*, presented Suzy with a wodge of materials providing information on area transport services, swimming pool openings, local library policies, and every other amenity the East End could possibly provide this Leeds exile.

Her mother looked at Suzy with such pride and expectation, yet it seemed to accompany a hint of dissatisfaction that was carried with a strange purposefulness. It was an ambivalence that Suzy struggled to unravel not just for her mother's sake, but also for her own.

'I know all about the *East End*!'

If moving to London was a disappointment, locating to its East End was evidently a calamity. Her mother made it sound like a penal colony. The fact that London New University, reduced by all to 'the LNU' for ease of reference and to test the wit of students in devising crude alternative denotations, ran one of the few undergraduate photography courses in the country, and for every place there were over thirty applicants, did not alter her mother's stance. When Suzy challenged her apparently substantial knowledge of the area, she made a surprising revelation – that her late father, Suzy's grandfather, had actually been born in the East End. It was a discovery that thrilled her.

'They got out as fast as they could. Everyone did. *Those that were able to.*'

'Does that mean we were once Bengali?'

Suzy's own view of the area was unreservedly romantic. She instantly sensed its rich history and traditions, a far more earthy London than the pretty West End, the coldness of the financial district oddly termed 'the City', the bland swathes of suburbia. The very term *East End* conjured up a host of exotic shapes and images to which she was longing to give form.

Suzy spent the first days familiarizing herself with the more immediate geography of the university itself, more a succession of buildings clustered along the Mile End Road than a definable campus. The only attempt at creating an internal space was around the Student Union building, unrelentingly white and shaped like a ship's funnel, standing virtually opposite the Tube station out of which Suzy disgorged each day having journeyed from her student hall two stops further east.

However, the station was far less convenient for Suzy's classes, which sent her on a march some way down the Mile End Road to a place called the Hanway Building – 'the London New University's Centre for Art and Media Studies' to give it its full bulging title – a grey squat structure that manifestly resented its designation, affectionately referred to by its inhabitants as H-block. She soon learned how much her mood was determined by the conditions experienced on that dreary daily expedition from the station. Then, at lunchtime, she faced the choice of a return journey to take advantage of the Union's eating facilities that still basked in the glory of winning a 'best university restaurant of the year' distinction some time in the early 80s, while evidently failing to appreciate the move towards continuous assessment. Or she could make do with the Hanway canteen designated 'The Granary' as if it was some rural idyll, supplying a daily diet of cheese, chicken, egg or tuna sandwiches, presented in ruthlessly alphabetical order for ease of recognition, served up by aged rasping women clearly unschooled in rustic charm.

The compulsory orientation tour culminated in a dismal address by the Vice Chancellor on students 'being at the crossroads of life' and 'facing the challenges of transition from child to adulthood', a speech relieved only by the huge cheer that greeted his reference to 'the importance of experimentation'. It took place in the campus's oldest building which also housed the LNU's vast central library and which, appropriately enough given the proclivities of its current clientele, had originally been a brewery. Suzy's relationship with that particular building had so far been one of abstinence.

There was something crazed about the myriad Freshers parties using the promise of cheap beer to corral the first years together, largely as it turned out for the benefit of marauding second and third years sizing up new quarry. It all served to heighten Suzy's anxieties over that awful and frenetic enterprise called 'making new friends'.

It was a concern her mother focused on most, including the inevitable question about whether there were other Jewish people on the course. Suzy could never tell her how often she had been in tears during those first days. Indeed, it was her mother who had precipitated them.

'You realise what's happened,' she had announced as she prepared to drive back to Leeds. 'You've left home. You're never coming back!' It was her mother's tone, so definitive, and with such large sorrowful eyes.

Suzy's Freshers tactic was to attend every event going, but to experience it from her own special perspective, securely behind her camera. It became her very first photographic foray into this new university life.

The most effortless social plans were made as after-class arrangements. There was a relaxed rapport with her fellow classmates that grew with each encounter. Having a boyfriend provided a safe haven. And Nick was different in every way.

5

There were exactly seventeen shots of the river excursion along the corridor wall outside class, each one corresponding to a specific student. Yet no one was prepared to own up to the *mooning* shot, providing the most striking portrait from the event. Terry did suggest a simple test to uncover the culprit, involving a degree of general uncovering, which caused much amusement. What he actually accomplished was to turn the issue into a discussion on the power of provocative imagery. It was how he had handled outlandish behaviour in the earlier 'first impressions' exercise, as if an expectation of mischievousness was integral to the syllabus.

Suzy discreetly spent considerable time along that particular corridor. She had become acutely self-conscious over what she now viewed as a competitive exercise. She was deep in 'compare and contrast' mode, sizing up the competencies of her colleagues against her own through these inaugural works. She was convinced her shot was inferior. Were her classmates already talking about her? Nick's only comment had been that she shouldn't try so hard. It was so infuriating. What did he mean?

Rhythmic ticking announced Terry's next class. He had set some kind of device in motion on his desk while he leaned back against the whiteboard behind, his black polo neck providing the customary contrast.

Suzy's favoured chair was on the far side of the semicircle, a position shared with Jo and Megan, if the three arrived early enough. Salvo was making a point of squatting on different chairs for every lecture, and Suzy had so far been twice displaced to the salute of his malicious grin. Nick had initially placed himself closer to the door, next to Barry, now revealed as a disturbingly incessant nail biter. Nick and Suzy had earnestly discussed the implications of their relationship in terms of seating, quickly agreeing not to relocate next to each other. In fact, they soon established a routine of barely speaking to each other in class, which Jo later declared was the telling behaviour that confirmed for everyone that they were indeed a couple.

Having successfully secured her chair of preference, Suzy began to inspect Terry's contraption.

'What is it?' she whispered to Jo.

'A metronome,' Megan replied. 'Didn't you ever take piano lessons? You know, that tick-tock thing.'

Megan had slicked back her hair, and Suzy was convinced it was even blacker than before, certainly with a more formidable sheen. It reminded her of the toecap of a finely polished shoe.

'So what's that bit of paper stuck to it?'

'Who recognizes this?' Terry leaned forward, easing his chair off the whiteboard.

Nina, in unprecedented trousers, shot up a hand. 'Is it by Man Ray?'

'Good! Very good!'

'How does she know that?' Jo gasped. Suzy reflected on Nina's confusion over Morecambe and Wise and instantly decided she should give her more respect. Suzy had never heard of a man called Ray, or whatever.

'Who was Man Ray?' Terry followed.

'A guy with a funny name?' proposed Salvo.

'You can talk!' Megan bit at him. The previous day the two had argued at regular intervals over Salvo's assertion that Margaret Thatcher had stopped Britain becoming a third-world country. Megan's vehemence had suitably intimidated everyone else.

'I'd say quite a cool name,' Terry went on. 'Man Ray is part of your heritage.' He wrote out in large capitals 'MAN RAY!' with exclamation mark, across the top of the whiteboard.

'He was a surrealist photographer, and you can't get cooler than that. Before you is a replica of a famous work. Now does anyone know what it's called?' Terry paused. The class uniformly turned to Nina, but she was a spent force. Suzy stared at the relentlessly ticking creature with growing irritation.

'*Object of Destruction*.' Terry repeated it. '*Object of Destruction*. I want you to think about that title. Can everyone see what's fastened to the front of the metronome?'

Salvo slid from his chair and walked forward to analyse. 'It's an eye,' he nonchalantly declared on the expedition's return. Suzy leaned forward, fixing on what was indeed the picture of an eye swinging lazily back and forth, each motion checked by the beat. It was extraordinary.

'The eye belonged to a woman called Lee Miller. Also a photographer. She flew all the way from New York to Paris in 1928 to ask Man Ray if she could study under him. Which she did . . . in more ways than one.' Terry smiled. 'She became his muse, his inspiration. So what d'you think of it?'

'Spooky!'

'Freaky!'

Challenging, was Suzy's first thought, although she was struggling to formulate a clever justification.

'Intimate,' Nina suggested.

'OK. Why intimate?'

'Because the eyes are the most intimate part of someone.'

Salvo lifted himself as if poised to question the assertion.

Terry picked up the metronome and carried it forward, the eye now clearly delineated. Suzy had the odd sensation of a sudden reversal of roles – that it was the class being inspected by the object.

'This is a portrait, unconventional yes, but as much a portrait as all the others you'll see. It's the reduction of a whole personality to the simplicity of an eye, decontextualization taken to an extreme! But we also know it's the portrait of a photographer. She's looking out at the world as all photographers do – inquisitive, searching, penetrating. And it's called *an object of destruction*. I want this eye to haunt you throughout the course. This is your eye.'

Terry was holding the work high above the class. It felt like an anointing. Jo raised her camera and captured Terry dramatically composed.

'Why is it on a metronome?' Nick asked.

'Because photographers are always working against time.'

6

The rain chased the train all the way to Yorkshire.

Suzy was returning to Leeds for Rosh Hashanah, the Jewish New Year. She had hardly had the chance to bask in her new London identity before being thrust back to the homeland by maternal command.

Yet they would be beginning the festivities apart. Suzy had

been the intermediary in a delicate three-way conversation, the result of which was an amicable apportioning of her time. Suzy would start the New Year with her *new* family.

Charlotte, *Charlie*, opened the door to Suzy that evening.

'There you are! Come in!'

And how did this Mrs Green mark 2 look? Her outfit reminded Suzy of Nina, trimly presented in coordinated jacket and skirt with pinks to the fore, make-up carefully applied. Suzy was the only guest and she couldn't understand why Charlotte had gone to such trouble. Yet the sophistication of her appearance was compromised by her hair, pulled back in a childlike ponytail, a roundness of face exaggerated, as if she might also want to demonstrate youthful solidarity.

The emphatic manner of her welcomes always made Suzy immediately uneasy. She wondered if they would ever get past it. 'Have you been on a diet?' Charlotte was keen to talk about her own 'battle' to lose weight following the birth of Jennifer, their daughter. It was Jenny before whom Suzy was next ushered, quietly taken into her bedroom to witness her scrunched up sleeping form, an army of teddies and dolls on guard.

'Is Beatte in?' Suzy found the idea of employing an au pair bizarre for several reasons. She was certainly discomfited by the thought that they had a teenage girl living with them and it wasn't herself.

'It's her night off. Isn't Jen just the image of your father?'

Suzy pondered the intriguing concept of her father as a baby girl. She herself had long been claimed by her mother, and the physical evidence was ample. It was precisely for that reason that Suzy had taken to dressing herself consciously in opposition to her.

Her father entered the bedroom behind them, mischievously pinching Suzy while simultaneously placing a finger to her lips lest she squeal out. 'My three girls all together!' They returned to the living room. Suzy conceded the main sofa to Charlotte and her father, settling on an armchair next to the mantelpiece crammed with photographs suggesting a substantial heritage for this new coupling. Suzy picked out the ones that were her own contributions, including several from their wedding. It was her first commissioned work, and the perfect role for her.

'So, how's our Sooz?'

Yet it was his news that dominated. A latest tale from the shop interweaved with a golf match as if their conclusions were linked. Suzy watched Charlotte search out her father's hand while he spoke. It was over that summer that Suzy had noticed the growing vigour of the march of grey assaulting his hair. What was most different about him was yet another pair of glasses, large square brown ones that made his whole face appear similarly shaped. He looked like a television presenter, and she told him. Suzy had always felt disappointed that she didn't need glasses herself, thereby cruelly failing to reap the benefits of an optician father.

Suzy helped Charlotte serve the meal, her father's role for the event being principally that of food critic. Charlotte enquired about her new life in London, which she followed with comment on 'wonderful shopping' and 'wonderful theatre', as if she was more concerned to demonstrate her own interests. And she was obviously oblivious to the economic circumstances of students. This was a particularly sensitive issue given her recent difficult *allowance* discussion with her father.

'Have you managed to find a job?' he slipped in, resurrecting it.

'I've started looking.' It was true. Suzy had made a tentative visit to the employment bureau in the Student Union, because she now knew in no uncertain terms that she must. Suzy wasn't objecting to the principle. She had worked weekends and holidays in her father's shop for long enough. However, she did wonder whether he would get round to asking *dear Charlie* the same question. Her mother had worked all her life – running a home without any assistance from Scandinavia! Suzy managed to stop herself replaying that well-worn tape in her mind. This was Rosh Hashanah, the New Year, after all.

It was Charlotte who asked after her mother, but her father more keenly followed the reply.

Suzy talked about the course. She described Terry, and her classmates, realizing as she spoke how familiar she made them sound. Suzy had a new gang.

'I'm looking forward to coming down some day,' her father said.

'It's so difficult with the baby,' Charlotte added, effectively neutralizing the thought.

How perfect for him! Her father was at his most comfortable when he could blame forces beyond his control. There were other women now ruling his life. As Suzy listened to his pompous endorsement of the dessert, she considered how self-contained he always appeared. It was clear from the photographs along the mantelpiece, her father presenting himself under the same impenetrable sheen. The greying of his hair was revealing him as human after all.

'Any nice boys?' Charlotte enquired through a wide grin.

'No,' Suzy lied, resisting her chummy tone.

'Suzy doesn't have time for such nonsense!' her father proposed, rather strangely. 'She's going to become a famous photographer. Just remember who got you started!'

Suzy would have found photography without him. Her camera was the surest family member of all.

The meal ended with Jennifer screaming her existence to the street. Seeing her father holding his baby still looked faintly ridiculous. It prompted Suzy into first photographs, capturing this family twosome, then threesome. They insisted she took a turn with the baby and Suzy spent some moments following the flow of facial contortions, concluding that Jennifer was irredeemably fickle.

Her father took her picture with the baby. For the longest of times she had been desperate for a sister, but not now. Jennifer did look like her father.

The next morning, Suzy accompanied her mother to the supremely social occasion of synagogue at New Year. When her mother came out of the bedroom in her striking blue and yellow suit, pillbox hat perched cutely to one side, Suzy was reminded how beautiful she could still look. And Suzy her escort – it was so unfair.

Suzy traditionally pilgrimaged to synagogue on sufferance twice a year, for Rosh Hashanah and Yom Kippur, usually arriving towards the end of the service, swiftly abandoning her mother to seek out friends and diversion far to the back.

As she passed through the familiar glass portals of Oakington Road Synagogue, she recalled that, surprisingly, she had made a recent foray into this world, visiting the ancient Altneu synagogue during her summer trip to Prague. The contrast between these two buildings could not have been more striking, and Suzy considered how the Altneu, with its medieval arches and thick atmosphere, seemed so much more *authentic* than this remote outpost of Jewry.

Against the drone of prayer, Suzy settled herself high in the women's gallery, staring down at the men in the sanctuary below. Suzy had hoped to sit with Rochelle and Beverley; however, the former had managed to exploit study commitments to stay on at university, and the latter had, even more unforgivably, been allowed to sleep in. Marcus was there, crushed between his brothers, but she was not particularly looking forward to meeting up with him. He would no doubt still be brooding over their summer fall-out. Marcus encapsulated all the reasons why she felt so pleased to have left this place – the small-mindedness, the suffocating intimacy. This was a community that could congregate in its entirety inside one building! Suzy longed for anonymity, to be whatever self she might find.

She followed the service through the numbing routine of stand ups and sit downs, sufficient engagement to mask her complete boredom. How could she mumble in a language –

Hebrew – which she could not understand, towards a deeply suspect destination? Suzy didn't believe in God, and it never ceased to amaze her how unimportant that was to her mother, as if that was never the point. It was a conclusion Suzy had re-affirmed with her grandfather's passing. He was the religious one of the family, and yet had suffered so much.

To pass the time, Suzy resorted to the routine of the 'identify the face' game among the pews. She could unravel most, young and old, the people she had grown up with rolled forward another year. Her father would once have been somewhere down to her left, but he now used the excuse of work to avoid an awkward presence. Suzy caught herself searching for her grandfather. He would be waving at her and she would smile. She really couldn't do this any more.

What about the service from the perspective of theatre? Ranks of men swaying in supplication, their uniform white *kippot* astride heads, striped prayer shawls, all bent towards the imposing shiny steel Holy Ark in which rested the Torah, the word of God. She evaluated the quality of light in the sanctuary, and the various ways she might angle the shot. This was her language.

Suzy also accompanied her mother on another Rosh Hashanah tradition – the cemetery visit.

Suzy considered herself as close to her grandfather as her mother. His loss created their firmest bond.

They drove through the cemetery entrance, marked by an awesome Holocaust memorial that portrayed great hands soaring skyward. The sun was out, but there was a cool breeze energized by the open space.

'D'you remember where they are?' Suzy asked as they trudged through an army of low-lying headstones. There was only one other set of visitors, quietly making their way back from a remote end of the site.

'They haven't moved!' Her mother was still irritated that she was returning to London that night. It was a half-visit.

Soon they were standing before the graves of Abraham and Sarah, the briefest of details presented in a mix of English and Hebrew. Suzy hadn't known this grandmother, who had died when her mother was in her twenties.

'Next year I'll be the same age that she was when she went,' her mother noted grimly.

'You've still got a few years left in you!'

'Sometimes I don't feel like that.'

Suzy squeezed her shoulder hard in annoyance. It was becoming too typical a comment.

Her mother moved closer to Sarah's headstone and used her fingers to sweep around its top.

Suzy began to do likewise with her grandfather's, carefully brushing flakes of grime from the letters carved into the massive stone that spelled out this resident – ABRAHAM LIEBOVITZ.

'Such a great name,' Suzy said. 'Perfect for a photographer. You must have heard of Annie Liebovitz?'

Her mother shook her head.

'Just the coolest photographer. American. She toured with the Rolling Stones. Suzy Liebovitz. Doesn't it sound great!'

'It sounds terrible! I hated that surname. *L for lemon, I for Ink, E for England* . . .' she listed in a childlike voice. 'I never met anyone who could spell it in under ten tries. Giving it up was the happiest day.'

'Is that why you got married?'

Her mother scowled at her.

'There's no one keeping the name going. And what's so great about *Green*? It's so-o boring!'

Suzy photographed her mother's perfectly formed frown, then positioned her between the headstones for the next.

'Do you think Grandpa's bossing everyone around up there?'

'They'll be sick of him by now,' her mother replied. 'They'll be sending him back!'

And she caught her mother as she placed the customary tribute of small stones on each grave.

'I don't think a day goes by when I don't talk to him.'

'I know,' said Suzy.

'Yeah, but he listened to you!' Her mother put her arm around Suzy. 'We were his two girls.'

'I must be living near to where he was born . . . in the East End. I wonder what he'd think about that.'

'He'd think you were mad!'

Her mother stared at her and Suzy knew what was in that look. Why did she have to feel so protective towards her? If she started Suzy off, they'd both cry for ever.

7

The East End was beginning to make its own first impressions on Suzy.

She was becoming familiar with two distinct locales. The Bernard Centre, Suzy's hall of residence, was named after some long-forgotten philanthropist, Sir Aubrey Bernard, whose bust monitored all comings and goings by the entrance. It was universally referred to – with assured historical accuracy – as 'BC', being a heavily weathered tower block plonked on the edge of a housing estate off Leyton High Road. She had walked up the High Road, and down it, and had even repeated the exercise for fellow resident Jo's benefit. She couldn't imagine what might induce her to return.

Her daily two-stop migration to LNU via that unique twilight world called the Tube brought her to the Mile End Road, which she viewed far more benignly. She had used the thoroughfare as her platform from where she had launched her first photographic excursions into what was the East End's truest hinterland.

What astounded her was the sheer variety of environments it contained – garden cottages plucked from some quaint country village, sweeping Georgian squares, glass and steel riverside developments; Victorian mansion blocks giving way to vast 60s legoland housing estates; two up, two down terraced housing leading to the latest red-bricked and gated apartment complexes. Add to that the rich diversity of people, the crush of shops and warehouses, the myriad markets, historic pubs, eateries of every persuasion, and the East End was indeed a profound patchwork – not really one place at all, more a collection of identities each competing for space, with every passageway an invitation to adventure. It was photographic heaven, with the camera as ever Suzy's trusted protector.

Terry himself was leading this latest charge down the Mile End Road.

The much-feared year project and its theme of *community* had led that day's class, with explanation turned into intense debate. In a noisy brainstorm, Terry filled the whiteboard with every form of definition – geography, ethnicity, religion, gender, lifestyles, occupations, hobbies, interests, conditions, kinship, values, and on and on.

Terry stressed that the only expectation initially was in respect of selection, how he would then work with everyone individually to develop the more comprehensive project brief.

'It's fundamentally about identity. The richness of people!'

Yet he was failing to shake the mood of quiet panic. Finally, he ordered everyone out of the classroom – destination unknown.

In entering Mile End Station, the assumption was that they would be journeying on. Instead, Terry corralled the students along the side of the entrance hall.

'Exciting field trip,' Nick remarked to Suzy. Salvo slid down the wall to his familiar crouch. Suzy noticed how he was using the back of a hand as a notepad, filling it with scribbles like an intricate tattoo.

The hall was busy with commuters. A ticket office queue

snaked from the left. Terry stood silently for some moments. He was watching the heave of people scurrying in, purchasing tickets or clutching passes, launching themselves through the ticket barriers into the abyss of the descending stairway, as if abandoning themselves to an insatiable underground god. A more minor wave surged upwards, belched from the great below.

'What are we doing?' asked Salvo in the form of a sigh. He had evidently already included Tube stations in his sightseeing of London. Suzy followed the trail of a mother steering a small child who was insisting on inserting her own ticket into the barrier, fumbling over the task.

'Don't look at me,' Terry announced. 'Look at them!'

He turned his back on the group in order to align their gaze with his own. In staring, there was also much staring back. Suzy wondered what the perception was of this band of students beached along the wall. Early carol singers?

Terry looked round and Suzy promptly returned to the task in hand, simply to watch what was occurring around them. A youthful father had entered with a bundled-up baby on his shoulder. There was a casualness in the way he negotiated his progress, yet one never sensed that his attention was on anything other than the child. Two older men were swinging a large holdall between them. There was a feeling of deep familiarity in the way they ignored each other, yet were perfectly in step.

'So what do you see?' Terry finally broke the silence.

'Skeletons,' suggested Megan, true to that day's especially bleak appearance.

'OK.' Terry wasn't grateful, and there were several titters. 'I think we'll leave that comment for our tutorial, if you don't mind Megan.' He smiled painfully. 'Anyone else?'

'People looking at us,' said Nick.

'How does that feel?'

'Uncomfortable,' Nick replied.

'When you look at people, they look back. Looking is an uncomfortable business,' said Terry. 'But it's our business. What else?'

The challenge hung in the air. Suzy watched an elderly woman inspecting her reflection in a glass-encased advert.

'Observation and imagination,' Terry declared. 'Observation and imagination!'

He waved his hands in the direction of the bustle around them. 'I want you to observe, and use your imagination. Do you think you could do that? What's going on here? Think of people as stories, as texts. Everyone here is in some way *heroic*. Think about how that could be true. I want you to try to see more than what you see.'

Nick and Barry exchanged baffled expressions. Terry began pacing like a frustrated sergeant major.

'What each of us sees is different, because our imaginations are unique. It comes out of our own backgrounds, and sensibilities. Imagination is all up here.' He tapped his head. 'We each lock on to different images and shapes that engage us. Attract us! We're compelled to capture it. Taking a photograph is like love at first sight!'

Suzy kept up her scrutiny. Three Asian girls entered wearing the same blue school uniform. Each wore a sombre scarf carefully wrapping their hair. As Suzy followed them, she detected that one was unusually distinctive. She was the only one wearing lipstick and, having noticed it, her lips began to shine out from her. Suzy felt a rush of excitement.

'The world is continually on the move. Look at these people. Tomorrow will always be different. That's what makes photography so challenging. Hundreds of thousands of pictures will be taken today, and none of them can be like tomorrow's. That's what drives us on. These people are extraordinary. Can you see that? Could you capture that?'

8

Suzy had insisted to her mother that she wouldn't return to Leeds yet again for Yom Kippur, the Day of Atonement. Her return for Rosh Hashanah had been premature, simply re-establishing the sense that she was in limbo, which was unsettling for everyone, most especially herself.

In a strange way, Suzy could relate to Yom Kippur, being totally at ease with the premise that one should be judged for one's deeds, with or without a God. Anyway, she was committed to fasting for the full twenty-five hours. She had accomplished that feat ever since she was twelve, and it had become something of a badge of honour that each year she would carry out this most challenging central ritual, if not much else.

She assured her mother that she would seek out a synagogue

locally, plugging in at some point over the course of the day. She knew that the East End had once been a Jewish heartland, the home of her grandfather no less. She also had that lingering memory of Prague, where she had surprised herself by feeling emotionally drawn to the city's Jewish story. Suzy joked to herself that, having given up on the idea of God in Leeds, she was entirely open to Him having an East End address.

Hearing herself spell out such attitudes to Nick made her feel profoundly self-conscious. Nick had not come across Jews before and, having thought of them as essentially Christians with a twist, he was struggling to master the distinction. It reminded Suzy of those regular playground conversations where she was continually made to explain herself, with the ever-present hint that something was wrong. Why couldn't it simply be her own affair? That was why she wasn't keen to get into it all with Nick. That wasn't his purpose.

Her mother's eccentric collection of literature on local services finally proved useful as Suzy searched under religious organizations. Disappointingly few synagogues were listed, but there was the 'Sharei Shalom', helpfully translated as 'the Gates of Peace', making it sound more like a centre for alternative therapy. And Stepney was adjacent to the university.

Suzy did go to class that Yom Kippur morning. It was a session on darkroom procedures led by technicians Mork and Mindy, who clearly revelled in their moment of authority, detailing the various operations – chemicals, trays, temperatures and timings – with the enthusiasm of mad professors. It was more than Suzy's head could take. Nick suggested that she at least down a glass of water but Suzy was determined to maintain her martyrdom. She left by mid-afternoon with Nick promising to take notes for the remainder, and to endeavour to make them legible. She also insisted he not reveal where she had gone, which he found bizarre.

The fast was due to end at sunset and Suzy had decided to make her synagogue visit for the concluding service, representing as it did the climax of the occasion, and her struggle. In the aromatic H-Block toilets, she changed from jeans into her 'course interview' pleated blue skirt. She also placed her faithful Weston TT camera in her locker. Suzy was travelling alone.

'The Gates of Peace' synagogue wasn't far from the university in terms of distance, but it did require a number of turns through backstreets that made her less than certain about finding her way back. Even when she arrived at what she understood to be the synagogue's location, it was hard to have that confirmed. Roseberry Crescent was deeply ordinary in appearance, consisting of parallel tracks of two-storey terraced housing. And there was nothing particularly remarkable about the exterior of number 43 that might be indicative of sacred purpose. It did occur to Suzy that she might have recorded the address incorrectly, or perhaps her information was out of date and 'the gates' of the Gates of Peace had permanently closed. The only clue suggestive of anything unusual was the fact that its blue door was ever so slightly ajar, and then she spied the mezuzah at its side. It was sufficient to propel Suzy onward.

In the darkened hallway, the first thing that caught her attention was a noticeboard. Next to a sign that promised

'Friendship Club News' she identified a Hebrew calendar, a Sabbath hospitality announcement, and a forthcoming event for Yiddish speakers. Suzy had arrived! On the opposite wall she admired a memorial board dedicated to various dearly departed. She skimmed the display with its panoply of legendary Jewish surnames – Cohens, Levys, Greenbergs – her grandfather's own august Liebowitz surname disappointedly unrepresented.

'Can I help you, dear?'

Suzy swung round. Before her stood an elderly bespectacled women in a large hat with dangling feathers that blocked out much of her face.

'Looking for the service are you? Come with me dear.'

The lady turned and marched down the narrow corridor with Suzy adjusting her stride behind. Soon, they were tackling tightly ascending stairs.

'So late!' Suzy heard her mutter. The stairway gave way to space at its top. 'So late!'

Half a dozen or so women were assembled in the small gallery. The murmur of Hebrew prayer simmered. Suzy peered into the sanctuary below where scattered men were rhythmically swaying.

'I'm Gloria, Gloria Tobias,' the woman whispered.

She had tipped her hat backwards, enabling Suzy to identify more of her features. She was certainly older – much older than her mother! – a slim face with gentle criss-crossing lines marking her cheeks like a fading crossword puzzle. A certain liquidity about the eyes was accentuated by thick glasses, their string supports drooping oddly behind her ears.

'And your name?'

'Sorry. Suzy. Suzy Green. I'm studying at the LNU.' Gloria screwed up her face. 'The London New University?' Suzy elaborated.

'A student!' Gloria exclaimed, abandoning her reverential whisper as if she had just discovered a new species of being. The noise turned the heads of the full complement of gallery women, all of an age in multiples of Suzy's own, each one as aggressively hatted as the next. Suzy felt like a different species.

The hum from below suddenly swelled, suggesting the arrival of a key moment of prayer. This prompted Gloria to lift two prayer books from a side shelf and assume a seat, tapping one adjacent in summons. She proceeded to find the page with authoritative speed, handing the book over to Suzy while she repeated the exercise with the second.

Suzy was curious to discover that she was among a group of prayers as opposed to the more familiar constituency of talkers. She was also relieved by this, because she was beginning to sense that she would not be up to extensive conversation. Suzy prided herself in having the sort of constitution that usually enabled her to stride through the fast, but she had never anticipated it before on curry, and promised would never again, if only that East End God would save her now.

As a distraction from her growing queasiness, Suzy concentrated on her surroundings. The synagogue was the smallest she had ever seen, narrow yet long, presumably by way of a rear extension to the original house. Ceiling and walls on ground and upper floors were of an unrelenting magnolia occasionally relieved by unfortunate patches of discoloration, and windows of coloured glass whose effect was obscured by protective wire mesh. Well worn furrows could be identified in the brown carpet that led up to the *bimah* at the centre of the sanctuary below from where the service was being conducted by one of the more lively-looking congregants, a large rotund man whose voice ebbed and flowed in a rich baritone sound. Suzy was struck by its passion, confounding the somewhat frayed setting. Around the platform were arrayed several rows of wooden pews among which sat small clusters of ancient men.

Suzy began thinking of her visit to Terezin concentration camp outside Prague. There had been an exhibition of photographs illustrating Jewish life in Czechoslovakia between the First and Second World Wars. The taut textured faces of that doomed generation had deeply affected her. She had made a point of attending synagogue services in Prague the very next day, sitting in a similarly sparse congregation, wondering about the people who would have once filled the seats.

'Live locally?' Gloria had turned to her.

'In Leyton. In a student hall.'

Suddenly, the congregation got to its feet and Suzy followed, returning her gaze to the scene below. The Holy Ark positioned on the far wall was being opened to reveal elaborately decorated scrolls of the Torah, God's Law, the sustaining text of the Jewish people. Suzy noticed how ornate the Ark itself was; carved in wood, shaped like a restless flame.

Suzy was entranced. The leader was belting out the final prayers with great drama and gusto; the last pleas for forgiveness before the Almighty as the 'Book of Life' was sealed for yet another year. It was a rousing conclusion, thickly operatic in its force. A fulsome cheer marked the end, and he quickly became the centre of much adulation.

'There'd have been a lynching if Eli hadn't finished on time,' announced Gloria. 'God, do I need a cigarette!'

An outbreak of kissing and hugging marked the finale upstairs. Wishes for the year ahead were exchanged and Suzy was effortlessly incorporated into the celebration, as if just another regular. A tiny woman asked Gloria if Suzy was her granddaughter.

Feeling somewhat delicate, Suzy was eager to return home to replenish and recover. However, Gloria had other plans – 'Do you see *anyone* leaving?' She was being invited to what was the long-standing tradition of post-Yom Kippur refreshment – 'in the Club hall'.

'What Club?' Suzy asked.

'The Friendship Club!' Announced as if Suzy must surely have forgotten. 'We're all members!'

Suzy tagged behind Gloria as she pursued the others down the stairs and through the sanctuary. Suzy was now in male territory, free to admire the detailed biblical imagery on the panels that encased the *bimah*, and the carving of Hebrew letters that soared with the flame-shaped Ark.

A rear door led into the hall. Suzy was prepared to concede the term only because of the small stage at its rear. It was more a classroom, made even smaller by the crush of gaily covered tables laden with all manner of food – fish balls, tubs of dips, crackers, bagels, herring rolls – around which groups of elderly congregants were salivating. More significant for Suzy was a series of impressive photographs along one wall. She scanned the row of images recording long-ago synagogue events, wondering which of those featured could still be found among this class of '89. Suzy had never been with such a concentration of aged beings before. Yet it didn't bother her. In fact, what she was sensing was a definite attraction. It was their incredible faces – rippled textures, mottled tones, the curiously unselfconscious expressions – that seemed so suggestive. It made her feel somehow honoured to be there.

Suzy was certainly being treated with honour. Of the forty or so people in the hall that evening, she was approached by most. Gloria appeared to be deriving great pleasure from her 'discovery'. She remained close to Suzy throughout the reception, as if nervous that someone else might stake a claim.

However, it was celebrity shared. The man who had led the service so magnificently introduced himself.

'You say it just like belly. Eli!'

Eli's belly was an unfortunate reference. He was a plump man, yet with a frame that enabled him to carry his weight comfortably. His face was large and eager – cheeks brushed with red, bushy eyebrows above attentive brown eyes. He appeared younger than the others, helped by a lush silver-grey head of hair.

'I'm Suzy, or Suzanna,' she replied. She wasn't clear why she had mentioned her extended name. Perhaps she was viewing Eli as some sort of rabbi figure who warranted a degree of formality.

Eli held out his hand. 'In Hebrew, we say Shoshana. Better, no?'

She took his hand. Suzy had just been renamed.

'I hope you enjoyed the service. I have a little cold.'

'You were fantastic!'

'Thank you!' Eli was delighted, and it emboldened him. For he started talking about his long association with the synagogue, at length. How he had 'been asked' to lead the Yom Kippur services every year for the last twenty. His East European accent was most obviously revealed in his handling of his *F*s and *W*s. Suzy assumed the effervescence was a post-performance high.

'Once the synagogue was full to bursting! After ten in the morning, not *one* seat to be had. Hundreds of people. But now!' He shrugged. 'You see now!' He looked around him. Now was a paltry forty souls.

Eli's relative youthfulness was compromised by what Suzy now recognized was a somewhat dishevelled state. It didn't help that, in keeping with religious tradition, he hadn't shaved that day, but it was in his overall appearance – the suit in a long-forgotten style, his strangulated tie, shirt collar well worn.

'Do you like music?' Eli asked.

'Let her eat, Eli!' And Gloria her guardian.

9

'So you and our Nick!' Jo was successfully feigning surprise.

Suzy had confessed the relationship to her. She could hardly have done otherwise. They were in her room at BC currently dominated by a magnificent display of flowers that had greeted Suzy on her return from the Yom Kippur service. In contrast to the exuberant bouquet, the note from Nick conveyed a simple 'well done!'

'Isn't he something?' said Suzy. 'A real star!'

Suzy and Jo were dressing for the Student Union's infamous Sports Night. Wednesday afternoons were reserved for the LNU's many sporting activities, with students so inclined shunted off to assorted pitches, courts, courses, rinks, pools and waterways, all to reconvene that evening for one massive party, the main thrust of which appeared to be the abandoning of every inhibition.

'Hand me that lipstick,' Jo demanded. She had parked herself in front of the room's only mirror, with Suzy waiting with increasing impatience at her rear. 'And tell Auntie Jo all about it. How rich *is* he?'

Jo's comment wasn't based solely on the flowers. There was his Electra 1000 camera, causing much envy and resentment. But it was the car that sealed it – a BMW no less. Its presence had been revealed with the story of its theft, later discovered to have been a prank by Nick's housemates who had managed to pick the car up and move it round the corner. News of the car's existence had surged through the class like wildfire. Megan distinctly cooled. Salvo clung to him. Suzy dared not mention the television set in his bedroom.

Nick was the very antithesis of her previous boyfriends. He was her first of the non-Jewish persuasion, although that was more by accident than design, Suzy having been made victim throughout her youth to her mother's discreet social engineering. And he was the first to share her enthusiasm for photography. Indeed, he was far more technically proficient, to the extent that he had constructed his very own darkroom by his early teens.

But while photography was a primary passion, it was not his only one. Nick loved food, not just the consuming of it, but preparation as well, something he put down to his father. Suzy would not have believed it if she had not experienced it at first hand, his fish cakes followed by chocolate brownies being the courses of an early date. Suzy routinely took to gazing into his fridge.

Was Nick handsome? He had well-proportioned features – relatively square jawed – and soft green eyes. She liked how they looked out at her when they spoke, the way she knew she had his full attention. He was considerate, a bit of a gentleman in an old-fashioned sort of way, which Suzy still wasn't sure about. His hands were big and expressive, and he was tall, which made Suzy feel taller. Regular workouts in the gym gave him a muscular toned bearing. Nick looked great in a T-shirt, sexy even, yet it highlighted what Suzy firmly viewed as an interest too far – rowing!

Suzy had landed herself with what she giggled to admit was some sort of athlete. She wouldn't have minded so much if it was not so all-consuming. It felt as if he needed to be on the go all the time. He trained in the gym two nights a week, at least, and was in water every Wednesday, and on Sundays – by nine a.m.! Suzy was at her most sceptical when he became so dreamy about the whole thing. She had to interrupt him when he began describing the bliss of chasing rainbows down the Thames.

If Nick represented several firsts for Suzy, there was another first that she wanted to add. She didn't consider herself a virgin although, technically, it was her status. Perhaps she was a semi-virgin. She might have got there with her previous boyfriend, Marcus, if he hadn't made it into such a *thing*. He just couldn't let it be something ordinary. Suzy had left home, and simply had to get that 'it' out the way.

None of the above was actually conveyed to Jo. Suzy made vague remarks that suggested pleasure, yet also a calculated ambivalence. She had made a pact with Nick that demanded absolute discretion when it came to classmates. He was hating the teasing over the car. And Suzy wasn't yet sure how discreet Jo herself could be.

'He likes my smile,' Suzy added, providing the evidence.

Jo frowned. 'He's young. He'll learn!'

Suzy was accompanying two of her tops to Sports Night that Wednesday. The one she was wearing and the tight-fitting v-neck Jo just *had* to borrow in what she declared was an attempt to recreate Suzy's curves.

A wall of raucous noise assailed them as they entered the Union bar, wading through every specimen of student to locate Megan, Salvo and Barry who had arrived earlier to secure a table and soak in the benefits of 'happy hour'. Nick turned up soon after with dramatic river tales, displaying blistered hands before a profoundly apathetic audience. Salvo spoke with matching enthusiasm of an afternoon in bed.

Drinks were consumed amidst remarkably coherent conversation. The year project featured prominently, with notions of *community* shared. Megan was contemplating the merits of a refugee hostel in the East End, while Jo's inspiration had come in the form of a canvassing Hare Krishna on Oxford Street – '*so* friendly!'

'Terry's up his own backside!' was Barry's considered view on the course so far.

It was Nick who began the drinking games, the object being to remember in correct order an increasingly complex sequence of numbers. 'Three fingers' length of beer was set as the penalty for failure, with the first to finish responsible for a round of drinks. Jo took to interrupting with her own dubious contribution to the entertainment, screaming 'dead ants!' which required everyone to wriggle spontaneously on their backs on the floor.

Salvo somehow wangled himself on stage for the karaoke. The table stood in salute as he careered through a most singular rendition of 'Tainted Love', which he kept up long after the music had stopped.

A sound of trumpet blasts soon followed, heralding the arrival of the evening's main event. It was the signal for each of the teams involved in that day's sporting endeavours to congregate in their respective categories. Nick navigated towards his rowing mates while Suzy and Jo played spot the sport. All eyes were to the stage now occupied by a bizarre pantomime figure announced as 'Lady Lena', complete with high heels, ball gown, and white powdered wig.

'Be humble, you rabble of buffoons!' she, or he, scowled in a grotesquely posh accent.

Lady Lena then commenced a roll-call of the triumphs and tragedies enjoyed and endured by the various teams. Selected players were invited on stage to receive the adulation or otherwise of the crowd. Losing teams were required to abase themselves before her, their fate forgiveness, or punishment.

The disgraced men's hockey team was set an assignment to appease Lena's teetering wrath. Suzy joined in with the encouragement as they feverishly scavenged among the audience for bikini briefs, sanitary towels, condoms, jockstraps, love bites and other essentials of student life – a yard of foul-looking drink awaiting them should they fail.

Jo was the first to lose it that evening. She was giggling uncontrollably, then went completely silent. Suzy had been priding herself on being able to match Nick's prodigious consumption, until she couldn't lie to herself any more. She couldn't bring herself to reveal that she had never in her life drunk even close to the amount she had managed that night. She remembered dancing with Jo and Megan, and Nick being annoyed with her for taking a cigarette. She remembered going back to his flat, ridiculously babbling about how gorgeous he was. She remembered being with Nick that night.

10

Suzy was about to experience her first one-on-one tutorial with Terry, and she was nervous.

He had ended that morning's class with a rant about students abusing the Department's equipment. Nina had managed to snap a tripod in circumstances that were still not fully understood, although the rumour mill placed her photographing a building from an islandless middle of a busy street. 'Some people treat this place like it's Santa's grotto!' Suzy was hoping he had got it out of his system.

Terry's tiny office was a mess, his desk filled with papers, contact sheets and assorted journals. Placed on the wall immediately behind was a film poster of the notorious *A Clockwork Orange*, a thickly eyelashed eye menacing its viewer. The remaining walls were given over to a rich array of photographs, some original, some extracted from magazines. They were mainly portraits, although there was also a rectangle of industrial landscapes. On the bookshelf, space was made between large photographic tomes for Man Ray's *Object of Destruction*, so dramatically introduced to the class, its enigmatic eye resting to one side.

Terry was standing when Suzy came in, clutching a phone to his ear. The topic was plainly the student Marvin who had failed to turn up for the last three classes and was presumed by most to have left the course. 'Moved on,' was Jo's view, expressing sympathy for Salman's predicament.

Terry ushered Suzy to one of the two seats in front of his

desk, then impressed her by rounding the desk to take the second at the conclusion of his call.

'So! How are we doing?'

He was close to her now. She noticed that the T-shirt under his shirt had bright flecks of yellow intermingled with the grey and she wondered if that constituted a breach of colour code.

Suzy felt she was doing fine, although she was perfectly open to being advised otherwise. The first written exercise had been handed in two days previously. She had agonized over the assignment: 'Is the news a presentation of facts or a set of meanings determined by social and institutional forces? Discuss.' Of course Nick had managed to discuss it fully in a mere day of scribbling!

However, it soon became clear that Terry had in mind a more general conversation on her 'settling in'. He was keen to find out about her living arrangements, and whether she was fully familiar with the 'special charms' of the LNU campus. 'Full of students, I know. I'm sorry!'

'It's great being a student!' Suzy instinctively defended her kind. It was truly how she had come to feel. She was living a life that was giving her freedoms she had never experienced before. She was washing her own clothes, cooking her own meals, making all her own decisions, while having the opportunity to pursue her dream career. She belonged to a wild tribe that warranted its own restaurants and bars, preferential pricing on travel and entertainment. And there was Nick. He was definitely growing on her. Suzy carried her student card with pride.

To how she was finding life in the East End, Suzy eagerly

declared her recently discovered roots in the area, as if her grandfather's association might imply a genetic rapport.

'So you're basically happy?'

Suzy nodded.

'Your assignment.' Was Terry about to make that all change? she wondered. 'I apologize for not having got to yours yet, but I should do so soon.'

Suzy breathed out. Student life was good, at least for a little while longer.

Their next topic was the extensive and intimidating reading list. Terry reassured her that he wanted students to pace themselves and Suzy reassured him that she had now ventured into both the departmental library, and the vast central library. What she didn't reveal was her wrestle with a current book, being completely stymied by *modernism* and its evil twin *postmodernism*. Nick had promised rescue.

Suzy moved the conversation along by anticipating Terry's enquiry on her proposal for the year project. She had found her community. 'The JFC,' she announced firmly, enjoying the tease of minimal disclosure.

Terry was suitably baffled. 'A football club?'

'No! The Jewish Friendship Club. I thought you knew your East End!' It was a fleeting reversal of roles, but no less pleasurable. She *could* relax with him. 'It's a social group of elderly Jewish people who regularly meet up.'

Terry rubbed his chin. 'OK. Tell me more.'

Suzy described her Yom Kippur visit to the synagogue, the singular atmosphere, the fabulous, intriguing faces.

'So what about them?' Terry asked. Suzy wasn't clear what he meant. 'So they're old, and they're Jewish. So what? I'll need more than that. Do you have an idea of where you want to take it?' Terry leaned forward while Suzy struggled to contain a blush. 'I want an angle! I don't need it right now. You can see what comes out of the research. But the brief *must* have a clear focus.'

They discussed how Suzy should approach gaining permission. Terry stressed that learning how to handle people was a key aspect of the exercise. 'And a big responsibility!' How she should 'always, always' be respectful. Suzy had already noted the special relish he derived from repeating words.

'They're old people. Be sensitive to that. Remember, a photographer is by definition a violator.' And, of course, there was the drama of his language.

'Don't rush to use your camera. Hang out with these people, get to know them first. You'll be conducting interviews. Use the tape recorder. Please don't break it! Look. Listen. Smell. Bring *all* your senses to your work.'

Terry paused. 'Well, well, well. The JFC!'

He liked it! Suzy had received her calling on Yom Kippur.

Terry leaned back. 'So. Have we anything else we need to talk about?'

Suzy pursed her lips doubtfully. He perused his watch.

'We still have a few minutes. Let's take a look at that assignment of yours.'

Suzy froze.

57

11

Suzy thought it might cheer her.

It was Sunday morning. Suzy was dutifully parked by the payphone at the designated time, revealing to anyone who might pass at such an ungodly hour the tragic truth of her pink elephant dressing gown, with her mother full of morbid reflection. She had been to see Shirley Valentine at the cinema that previous evening. 'Should I run away to Greece and have a fling, or stay and talk to walls?'

'Mum, I'm going to a Yiddish discussion group!'

Her mother went completely silent. Suzy sensed her struggling to absorb the announcement.

'But you don't speak Yiddish! No one speaks Yiddish. What could anyone possibly . . . discuss!'

And the idea that this was some sort of exercise linked to her course simply fuelled her mother's confusion. Suzy recalled how her very first mention of the Friendship Club had elicited a curious lack of curiosity from her mother.

'So you've joined an old-age home!'

Her mother's reaction was in sharp contrast to Gloria's. She had promptly replied to Suzy's letter of enquiry, the title Club Secretary typed grandly under her name. Gloria had been effusive. The project was on.

Suzy could now visit the LNU's main library with renewed purposefulness, which in the event could only be partially satisfied. In attempting to find books on the Jewish East End, all she had discovered was their absence. Nevertheless, she could read up copiously on the East End in general – how it had developed in contrast to its more affluent geographic mirror burgeoning West; the importance of the docks to its evolution; how it absorbed successive waves of immigration from the Huguenots in the sixteenth century all the way to the Bangladeshis and Somalis of the present day; how cheap labour attracted industrial development of every sort including the dreaded sweatshops; the growth of political radicalism both communist and fascist; a host of social ills – poor housing, unemployment, poverty, drink, crime and prostitution – and their discovery by an appalled Victorian England who turned the area into a vast rescue mission involving religious salvationists, temperance advocates, political campaigners, university intellectuals, all bent on saving the East End from itself.

Suzy especially enjoyed coming across the early photographic record – the spirited faces of Irish dock workers, children playing alley street games, crowds spilling from the Music Hall, mothers on knees scrubbing the step, bathers splashing in Victoria Park Lido, trams chasing carting horses clomping down Commercial Road.

The Jews did warrant their place in the great tales of migration and settlement, but never centre stage.

'Moishe was reluctant to go. A seance! But. He was missing his *Zeide*, his grandfather. So why not try it!' Eli was once again the focus of attention, this time in the Club hall, his hands theatrically palms out as he spoke. Suzy noticed how, despite getting to his feet, his crumpled suit faithfully maintained its state.

'So Moishe went to the medium, who worked herself into a trance, you know.' Heads nodded round the circle as if everyone did. '"Moishe – is that you?"' Eli growled the words for effect, conjuring up his medium. '"Zeide, can you see me?" said Moishe.' Eli whispered this part. '"Yes, Moishe my boy," came the deep voice. "What's it like where you are?"' Eli paused. '"It's good," said the voice. "Moishe, I'm fine. Very happy up here. I'm with all the family. We play cards. Very peaceful."' Eli leaned into his audience. '"And Zeide, you've learned English!"'

Suzy watched these creviced cackling faces all around her and was seized by a tightening apprehension. What had she done? She had escaped the confining world of a small Jewish community, only to find herself committed to spending a year with another, whose average age she couldn't begin to guess. It all suddenly seemed a huge mistake.

Suzy recognized most from the Yom Kippur service, despite the change in dress code with cardigans and sweaters now to the fore, tweeds and checks, but still a bow tie and a beret. Of the fifteen present, women dominated. The fact that she had attended the service had established her Jewish credentials, which Suzy emphasized by revealing her Liebovitz heritage, although several still seemed doubtful that Jews and Yorkshire could intersect.

The seats had been laid out by the wall that supported the photographs of earlier episodes in the synagogue's history. Gloria took it upon herself to present Suzy formally, explaining her project with a flourish that suggested Suzy was on a vital mission. For some reason, Gloria made her stand up, despite the fact that everyone in the circle could see her well enough, merely serving to heighten Suzy's discomfort. She spluttered words of gratitude.

'You're *welcome*!' came an acute accent from somewhere.

Gloria then launched a procession of introductions around the circle, and Suzy did her best to absorb the names that so perfectly reflected this world to which she was committing a year of her life.

'Will we become famous?' asked one brightly attired woman by the name of Becky, distinctive for her bulging reptilian eyes and chunkiest of earrings that hung like chandeliers.

'You're famous already!' said the man next to her called Monty sporting a striped bow tie, dark glasses still fixed to his face despite having been inside for some time.

'Eli's more famous for his terrible jokes,' said Becky, causing Eli to bark back at her.

A particularly sullen figure called Lionel, the only one of the group who for some reason couldn't look Suzy straight in the face, began tapping his watch. In turn, Gloria glanced sternly at Becky who, mustering a degree of unlikely gravitas, proceeded to call the event to order. In so doing, she deployed the language that was its very purpose.

'*Lomir zikh tsuzamen kumen.*' Chandeliers gently swinging to the sound.

Suzy had never heard Yiddish in full spoken form before. Of course she knew what it was – the lingua franca of Eastern European Jewry, a language largely wiped out along with its practitioners during the Second World War. And she also had managed to acquire some words from the limited patois of her Jewish upbringing: chutzpah, schlep, schmooze, mentsch, schlemiel – beautifully descriptive words that defied translation.

'*Kont ir farshteyn Yiddish*, Suzy?' Becky was peering at her.

'Shoshana,' corrected Eli.

'*Kont ir farshteyn Yiddish*, Shoshana?'

'How can you ask someone whether they speak Yiddish – in Yiddish!' said Gloria. 'She just wants to sit in. She *knows* she won't understand.'

Several faces scrunched in bemusement.

'Pretend she's not here!' Gloria added.

Suzy nodded keenly. 'Please just carry on as before.' She sounded like a school inspector.

'*Krasavitsa*!' said Eli, receiving an emphatic 'Sssh!' from Gloria.

Lionel was now furiously tapping his watch. He was completely bald, and with the flattest of faces as if someone had taken an iron to it. Suzy longed to catch him sideways to examine his appearance in relief.

A large woman called Esther strained to get to her feet. She was clutching a well-worn book, patting down the slipping pages before venturing to open it. '*De Shnayderke*,' she announced, then turned to Suzy. 'The Tailor's Wife. It's a story by Isaac Bathshevis Singer.'

'Gloria said not to do that,' Becky murmured.

Suzy spent some time extracting the tape recorder from her bag, turning away from the group in the hope that she might prove less of a distraction. It was her only piece of equipment that day. She had taken Terry's advice to heart and had resisted the temptation of her camera.

Suzy began following Esther's face as it orchestrated itself through this unfamiliar yet famously expressive language. The subsequent discussion was conducted largely in a tone that was either characteristic of Yiddish, or heated, Suzy couldn't tell which.

Other members presented further works, each bringing their own personality to the renditions. Suzy was completely fascinated. It occurred to her that knowing their meaning might actually be a distraction.

Inevitably, this man Eli had his own contribution to make, getting to his feet in a mannered way as if this was *the* moment, shooting a glance at Suzy to ensure she was paying full attention. While others had used a text, he presented from memory, his gaze locked above his audience. The words began rhythmically, like a poem, but then grew more melodic, fully exploiting the richness of his voice that had been so extravagantly on display at the Yom Kippur service. It appeared to be a well-known piece, because several members joined in at times, adding soft echoes. It was a lilting, plaintive recitation that conveyed, in the very mystery of the words, such overwhelming sadness.

Suzy looked towards the old photographs along the wall of the Club, and she thought of that book by J. F. Cooper she had studied the previous year for her A levels. She was among the last of the Mohicans.

12

It was to be breakfast in bed. Suzy had been ordered to remain under covers while Nick concocted in the kitchen. She had no difficulty complying. The prodigious energy Nick displayed in the mornings never failed to amaze Suzy. It was another demonstration of how opposites attract.

Friday mornings were lecture-free and, for this second time, Suzy had slept at Nick's following an evening together in the Union bar giving Jo moral support as she pulled her first pints from behind the bar.

There were many practical reasons why staying at Suzy's hall would be out of the question. There was her single bed, the need to sign in guests, her teddy bears – knowledge of which remained strictly under wraps – and the thriving gossip of the place. A fire alarm had been accidentally set off the previous week in the wee small hours, and stories of the combinations of people forced from rooms filled BC for days.

Anyway, Nick's flat was closer to the university. It contained a television, and that awesomely bountiful fridge.

An added allure of Fridays was the disappearance of all three of Nick's roommates to assorted classes – Chemistry, French and Political Science in order of departure times, which Suzy pointed out also corresponded to their geographic origins if you went West to East, as in the chemist was Welsh. The cat, Margaret, who had started out as Neil in honour of the Labour Party leader until its sex was correctly identified, remained to supervise.

Being in a boyfriend's bed filled Suzy with all sorts of warm feelings mainly centred on intimations of maturity. This certainly could never have happened at home in Leeds! It made her feel like an adult, *womanly* even. Nick was making her breakfast, she was propped up in bed, and they could even be a married couple!

Most of all, Suzy adored the sheer anonymity of it all. She had arrived in the East End as a complete unknown. There was no one to report to, nor to report back. She had broken free of every witness to her previous life and, while not particularly planning to reinvent herself, the fact that she could do so excited her.

With Nick still preparing somewhere offstage, and despite the chill of his room, Suzy decided to sneak from the bed to return to the extraordinary wall display of his Far East photographs. She lifted several off their bluetack supports to confirm the coding on the reverse that Nick had explained was linked to a battered red jotter in which the circumstance of every single picture – depth of field, shutter speed, exposure times, special filters etc. – was intimately detailed covering the whole six months of his travels. It was the sort of dedication that deeply disturbed Suzy. She was considered, and considered herself, a photography obsessive. And now she was meeting people like Nick.

Suzy tried to imagine herself in Nick's shoes, standing just as he once had before these landscapes, processions, the astonishing faces. He saw himself as a photojournalist, yet his images communicated so much more than mere description. What would her eye have made of these scenes – the whirl of dancers in their blurred blue costumes, the fisherman picked out against a low-lying sun, crowds besieging a glistening temple? What captivated her most were the portraits. Suzy was drawn to a series of faces, each elaborately decorated in a way that dramatically accentuated character.

So what did Nick, that renowned Mancunian chef, serve up for breakfast? Fresh orange juice, the real stuff with bits; sausages, poached eggs and grilled mushrooms with toast; fresh pineapple quarters in a creamy yoghurt, all finished off with a strong aromatic brew of freshly ground coffee. Suzy was seriously impressed.

'Was this a takeaway?'

She pulled Nick to her and kissed him, but that wasn't his only reward. Suzy reached for her bag, soon setting in motion a strange indecipherable lament.

'What's that?'

'*That* is Eli!'

Suzy turned up the tape recorder's volume, releasing the full force of his creamy baritone voice. Margaret padded to the bedroom door and stared through. Nick furrowed his face.

'What's he saying?'

'How do I know? It's Yiddish!'

'So what's the point? Switch it off. It's awful!'

'Don't say that!' Suzy nevertheless turned the volume down. Margaret sauntered away. 'It's a dying language.'

Nick was unimpressed, nodding as if he could appreciate

why. Suzy responded by expressing her surprise that Terry had, according to Nick, 'wholeheartedly' endorsed his own proposed *community*, namely his fellow band of rowers. He had won Terry over on the basis that he planned to subvert the classic sporting imagery. Suzy felt that could easily be accomplished over the course of one Sports Night.

Nick retaliated by bringing up Suzy's proposed employment, yet again. 'Fabulous Faces' was a firm specializing in offering free makeovers to clients, essentially women, who were then photographed for a fee. It meant Wednesday afternoons, occasional Monday evenings and, most crucially of all, £30 per session.

'It sounds absolutely appalling!' Nick wanted her to hold out for studio work.

'As if first-year students could walk into such jobs!'

'I thought you wanted to be Richard Avedon!'

Nick himself had no interest in finding employment because, with an affluent background that embraced breakfasts of fresh orange and quartered pineapple, he evidently had no need to. Jo was now behind the Union bar three evenings a week, Megan's weekends were spent in a photo processing shop, while Nick's concept of working went as far as the gym and splashing in the Thames.

There was also the strain of regularly polishing his BMW, in which Suzy had so far made one glorious outing up, and then down, the Mile End Road. She reached for the tape recorder and revived Eli to his full Yiddish splendour.

13

Suzy was going back to school. It was only when the high wall shadowing her walk relented to provide a gate that she realized that behind it lay the Northbridge Primary of her destination.

Walking across the hard surface of the playground, austere blackened red buildings towering on every side, made Suzy ill at ease. It felt like an evocation of an earlier Victorian East End, and she wondered if she might be absorbing echoes of generations of childhood dread. Perhaps her grandfather had attended this very school.

In keeping with the atmosphere, Suzy was met by a severe-looking school secretary who greeted her as if the police had already been called. Suzy had wanted to express her solidarity with a woman who shared her mother's profession, but immediately thought better of it. Her demeanour worsened with her bewilderment over Suzy's disclosure that she was with the Jewish Friendship Club. Suzy was quickly deposited.

A number of JFC stalwarts were already in the classroom. Suzy thought how odd they appeared, surrounded by the glittering wall paintings of children, plonked on their diminutive chairs. It felt as if the room had just been zapped by some strange power instantly ageing this unfortunate class.

Suzy received several friendly nods of recognition. Eli made a point of standing up. He was tidier than usual. She noticed the haircut, bringing calm to a previously edgy bouffant. 'I've got more jokes for you, Shoshana.' Suzy was returned to her *yiddishe* persona. 'When are you taking my photograph?'

Was this the cause of Eli's improved appearance? she wondered.

'Soon. I promise!'

Eli lowered his voice. 'I can help you with your project.'

Suzy sensed that he probably could. Eli was a project all on his own.

Becky also approached, clasping Suzy's hands. This time she was wearing more reserved earring studs compensated for by colourful wrist bangles. Becky asked about her family in Leeds and then, without pausing, whether she knew any single men. Suzy's only 'problem' was with the enigmatic Lionel. She caught him staring at her, delivering a cold grimace as he sat hunched on an undersized seat. He was the only one who made her feel like an intruder.

Another JFC member by the name of Wolfie hobbled in, waving one of his walking sticks in triumph, somewhat compromised by heavy puffing and the way his glasses were lopsided on his face. Gloria was just behind, entering in the company of a tall graceful woman whom she introduced as a teacher, one Mrs Henderson – 'an old and dear friend of our Club'. As Mrs Henderson herself spoke, Suzy marvelled at the crush of teeth that overfilled her mouth, as if capacity far exceeded demand. Suzy followed the formulation of her words, wondering how she managed the logistics.

'The children are all so excited that you're here. As am I!'

She went on to explain the school project, which was exploring the waves of immigration to the East End – how different year groups had been assigned to different tasks, how Year Six had been working on personal testimonies, examining specific ethnic and religious groups. It was a perfect event for Suzy to witness.

'We're going to put you into small groups so that every pupil will get a chance to speak. They've been working extremely hard on their questions!'

'I hope there aren't any difficult ones,' Becky whispered to Suzy.

The large hall was decorated with what Suzy soon identified were maps of different countries out of which grew dramatic East End-bound arrows. There was France with the beaming features of Louis XIV above the expulsion of the Huguenots. Ireland illustrated the potato famine, while Eastern Europe served up pogroms for the Jews, and there was the Indian Subcontinent, the Caribbean, the horn of Africa.

The mix of nations that had come to claim the East End was extraordinary. It was as if the area existed between Britain and these lands, an extraterritorial no-man's-land that signified transitions. That was true for Suzy's own family. The East End was a place to come through. Remaining meant being in a state of limbo, locked into the stigmatized status of immigrant, newcomer. It was what explained her mother's reaction to the East End, for she was a daughter of that generation. Suzy was far enough away to return.

The room was set out in circles of chairs, each with their complement of nervous, giggling children, cute faces staring expectantly as their elderly guests filed in, representatives no less of those arrows on the map, *ancient mariners* with tales to tell.

Eli insisted Suzy join his group consisting of Becky and Monty, the man permanently in bow tie beneath dark glasses. From the way Eli escorted him, it was evident that Monty had impaired sight. His suit spoke of a long-ago fashion, far baggier than its incumbent, and Suzy thought how sad that was, suggesting he was no longer able to fill his former self. He smiled generously at her when introduced by Eli. 'I can see you,' he assured.

They had been assigned a lively group of children. Becky made a point of introducing herself to each one, asking their names, conveying her own. Suzy followed suit, grasping these miniature hands, feeling she was part of a trade delegation, saying hello to Shaminder and Lowell, Peter and Katie, Mira and Gavin. She then helped Eli steer Monty through the ritual.

'Such lovely names,' said Becky. 'We've chosen well!' They grinned. Suzy took out the tape recorder and Eli nodded his approval.

Peter began, explaining with impressive authority for one so young that each pupil was going to take it in turn to ask a question and they would all be writing down the answers.

'No arithmetic,' Becky solemnly requested.

It was Monty who swiftly took the floor for the first question. He talked of arriving in the East End as a baby. How his father had come from Russia because it became impossible for Jewish people to remain.

'What is anti-Semitism?' asked Lowell.

Eli guffawed. 'In Eastern Europe, it's taken in with their mother's milk. They hate Jews, have done for centuries, killed them for centuries.' He was talking with bizarre relish.

Becky interrupted, flashing him an angry glare. 'Sometimes people are not liked just because they're not the same as everyone else. They have a different religion, or look, or speak different.'

Small heads nodded. Mira fired off a next question. It was on occupations and Monty seized the chance to wrest back the conversation. 'A lot of them went into the tailoring trade. I was in it myself for forty-six years. I gave my eyes to it, see!' He raised his glasses in a manner suggestive of a routine party trick, and the children leaned forward in morbid fascination. His colleagues had been decisively outmanoeuvred.

Monty went on to give a detailed description of the various roles within the trade – cutters, lining trimmers, machinists, buttonholers – marking his own progress through each, culminating his address in the 'world famous' garment workers strike of 1931. As Monty drew breath, Becky launched into a depiction of her father's bakery. She described the smell of freshly baked challah, the special bread made for the Sabbath, and how every week her father made her a tiny version of her own. Eli, who came to the East End after the war, added exploits in the life of a hairdresser, including a listing, completely unappreciated, of the once famous whose hair he had allegedly trimmed. 'Kid Coleman was European champion!' he pleaded in a desperate attempt to inspire awe.

As the event continued, Suzy found herself emotionally alongside the children. The easy authority with which Eli,

Monty and Becky spoke, especially their entertaining squabbles over detail, created a spellbinding effect. Suzy wanted to intervene with her own questions. Why did the two bagel women of Monmouth Street never speak to each other? How could so many people live in such small homes? Why was the ghost of Spitalfields a Spanish sailor?

Suzy had anticipated moving between groups, but had become far too engrossed.

At one point, young Katie, who had by now commandeered several of Becky's bangles, asked Suzy why she wasn't answering any of the questions. Becky found this highly amusing.

'Don't you live in the East End?' Katie asked.

'Yes. I do!'

'Just off the boat,' Becky explained.

The afternoon ended with what Mrs Henderson described in a resumed dental display as a 'very special thank you'.

The JFC cohort was now seated before the hall's stage on which Year Six had re-formed into two long rows.

'Songs of the Music Hall!' Mrs Henderson announced with an enthusiasm that suggested she had been struggling to hold back the good news. She raised her hands, and the cherubs let rip with 'Roll out the Barrel!' sung with spectacular gusto, Mrs Henderson flaying her arms as if trying to keep up. This was quickly followed by 'My Old Man's a Dustman' and even 'Maybe its because I'm a Londoner'.

The Club members loved it. In no time, it was hard to distinguish the voices of the children from their audience, Eli unsurprisingly to the fore. There was much cheering and clapping. Some were on their feet. The applause had the children beaming with delight, and Suzy marvelled at how music could establish such a rapport.

However, as she continued to watch, Suzy began to consider more the profound difference between these two groups. Here they were, sharing the same songs, yet could the two be of greater contrast – one basking in the naive joys that marked life's - beginning, the other sliding inexorably towards its end? Here were the extremities of a lifespan squaring up to each other.

The thought made her deeply uncomfortable. Weren't the schoolchildren flaunting their youth, taunting their audience with it? Suzy suddenly wanted to intervene, put an end to the cruelty of it all.

14

Megan was furious. Salvo was defending Margaret Thatcher again and she was swinging a Granary tuna sandwich menacingly in front of him.

'Why be part of Europe?' Salvo cried. 'Believe me, you're better off without us. I like a country that's proud of its identity. What's wrong with that!'

'She's a bigot and a fascist. That's what's wrong with that.'

'You call everyone who doesn't agree with you a fascist. So who's the fascist!'

Now Megan was really furious. Suzy picked up her chair

and moved to the more relaxed environs of Jo and Nina, who had dedicated their lunchtime discussion to the far gentler pursuit of tattooing. Jo had made Nina pull down her shirt to reveal a firebird soaring across her shoulder. Jo touched it and Suzy followed, patting the exotic creature.

'I'm going to do it!' Jo declared. 'For Christmas.' Her issues centred on logistics – size, location and, most crucially, design. She made it sound like a project.

Jo turned to Suzy. 'Will you come with me?'

'No way! Yuck. Needles!'

Suzy had her own question for Nina. 'Does it make you feel different?'

'Of course! Isn't that the point?'

Terry had set up a projector, and was playing with dimming the lights as the class went through the ritual of locating seats. Nick arrived precisely on the hour, taking his seat next to Suzy, now permissible after having their relationship announced over the Student Union tannoy by Jo, who justified it on the grounds that she had to test the equipment.

A ghostly 'Woooo!' was Salvo's reaction to the ambience as he entered. He also managed to induce Megan into walloping him for some reason, the force of which no doubt reflected the intensity of their previous conversation.

A huge image of the New York skyline suddenly conjured itself before the class. The city was portrayed as dark and ominous, like an alien spacecraft, its towers great spiky weapons of terrible destruction.

Terry began flicking the projector's controls, commencing a roll of astonishing images – an ancient mother breastfeeding a baby, shoulders wrapped in a fraying shawl, her expression one of aggrieved exhaustion; a politician thrusting a fist skyward before an adoring crowd; a pole vaulter, face fierce with intent, charging down a track; dazed survivors of a car crash being helped to the side of a road; a child soldier swathed in military fatigues marching in parade.

'Do you really believe you're so special?' said Terry, letting the intrusion of his voice settle.

He continued on with the imagery – a handcuffed prisoner being forced from a cell; children aggressively running through a swirl of birds; a woman staring mournfully from a window. He stopped at one striking picture, composed in the style of a classical painting. A bare room was lit by a petering fire in the hearth. A family cluster stood around the bed of a sick woman. Was she dying? Children, four girls positioned neatly in order of height, displayed various expressions of distress. A severe-looking older woman – doctor, sister, mother? – was clutching the sick woman's arm, holding it in a way that conveyed pointlessness. Everyone in the picture was female, the setting non-European, South American perhaps.

'Whose emotions engage us here?' Terry asked.

No one answered, opening the way for Salvo to expound on a detailed analysis of each face, their strengths and weaknesses in terms of some sort of calibration of resonance, concluding that the fearful smallest child at the shot's corner was the most expressive.

Megan argued the case for the sick woman 'dying or whatever' at the picture's centre because she was the narrative's focus. Nina agreed; however, her reasoning became quickly entangled as the sophistication of her answer took her beyond the parameters of her English.

Barry explained various technical aspects of the shot – lighting effects, use of vertical and horizontal lines, the way the figures had been situated in order to draw the eye of the viewer.

Suzy herself thought it was the older woman holding the sick one's hand. There was something powerful in her very reserve. She was looking towards the sick woman, yet beyond her, suggesting a spiritual motif. Gareth backed her assessment.

Terry listened, giving nothing away.

'You know what I loathe?' said Terry. 'When people say things like, "Let me take *your* picture." Whose picture is it?'

He moved to his traditional perch dangling from the desk.

'It's the photographer who sees, right? But if you're only seeing with your eyes, you're not seeing at all. I'll repeat that. If you're only seeing with your eyes, you're not seeing at all.'

Terry turned to the image on the screen.

'We've talked about imagination. But we need to take that further. Photographic seeing has at its core the willingness of the photographer to become *emotionally involved*. This involves risk, but it's what defines this profession. That's what's in every one of the images I've been showing you, taken by real photographers, the people who live this profession. *Emotion*. It's *your* emotion that fills that tiny inch of negative. And it's your most important tool. You must dedicate yourselves to honing it. Those of you who don't just want to snap pictures.'

Suzy re-examined the projected photograph. *It was the composer, not the composition.* It now seemed such an obvious observation. And she had just one thought – how magnificent Terry was.

Terry picked up a book. 'This is something Bertie Albricht wrote: "I walked past a blind man on the street. There was something about him that drew me. I suddenly realized that I didn't want to ask his permission to take him, or ask him anything at all. I silently photographed, and the man was completely oblivious. It was the purest photographic moment I had ever experienced."'

15

Everyone was gathering in the Student Union to watch. The Berlin Wall was being torn down after days of mighty protest. Nick wanted Suzy to join him and she stayed for a while taking in the amazing scenes – a huge sea of people chanting and dancing, great slabs of concrete broken and humbled. There was something truly monumental and mesmerizing about it all. However, Suzy had to leave to prepare for her own more modest event that day. Mother was coming.

Suzy dedicated that afternoon to a frenzy of cleaning – tidying shelves, arranging cupboards, wiping surfaces. She even tackled the shared kitchen, although she didn't feel inclined to own up to any particular seam of layered grime.

Suzy had a far longer Tube journey than her usual two-stop hop. She amused herself by thinking about her education in train travel etiquette, the way such close proximity to strangers threatened an encounter, which meant everyone tried with such quiet determination to avoid the most minimal of interactions. She noticed eyes meeting then rapidly averting as if to deny any inkling of acknowledgement. How dare you look!

Her mother arrived at Kings Cross Station weighed down by the next batch of foodstuffs, including a freezer-bagful. This was despite Suzy's previous protestations that food supplies *were* getting through to London. However, Suzy also recognized that she was unlikely to thwart her mother playing out her motherly role.

'I've missed you so much Sooz!' Her mother hugged Suzy tightly. She did want to reciprocate the sentiment, but resisted. It sounded too confessional, as if Suzy might be admitting to having wronged her, and then she felt ashamed that she hadn't.

Suzy had managed to find a reasonably priced hotel a mere one Tube stop east of BC. Nevertheless, the hall was their first destination in order to dispatch supplies.

On their journey, Suzy mentioned the winter holiday her father had brought up. How he had invited her to join them. *You know how much we'd all love you to come!*

'So are you going?'

Suzy had turned him down because, with the absence of the au pair, she couldn't help but consider the invitation more an attempt at babysitter recruitment. It became an uncomfortable phone call.

Her mother amusingly described recently bumping into 'Madame Charlotte', clutching her new baby tightly lest she make off with her.

'I really feel sorry for her. But she knew what she was getting into. I wish I'd have known!' Her mother straightened herself. 'I just hope this time he makes a better job of it.' She put her hand to her mouth in mock regret. 'Oh, I'm not supposed to say things like that, am I? Your father's a wonderful man!'

Suzy delivered her usual half smile. Her mother had been making that particular faux pas for a long time. Fortunately, she had never asked Suzy to take sides, which she presumed was for the simple reason that her loyalty had never been suspected. Her mother considered the apportioning of blame a straightforward matter. It was her father who had left – end of story. But Suzy recognized that other truth – that it was her mother that he had left. Her truest feelings were deeply ambivalent. And she was careful to keep her own counsel.

'Your room is so tidy. I thought I was coming here to work!' Her mother kissed Suzy, a gold star for effort firmly planted on her forehead.

Suzy rummaged through the food parcel, picking out a bottle of tomato ketchup. 'How could you!'

'You're so busy!' her mother said. 'You don't have time to shop. You're a student, concentrating on higher things.'

Discreetly, Suzy was delighted, spying several of her favourite foods including a lethal M & S fudge cake dessert. Stores were replenished while her mother straightened the family of teddy bears on her bed.

Her mother soon moved on to the photographs on the wall above the bed, and Suzy felt the first pangs of concern. There wasn't one image of Nick. There were two. In the first he was suitably disguised within a crowd of students, but the second had condemned him through solitude. It was like watching a lit fuse.

Her mother was already familiar with her striking images of Prague, giving them a cursory review. 'How can you put pictures of a concentration camp above your bed?'

Suzy pointed to her striking first depictions of the East End. Her mother was far more occupied by the photo of herself. She had dressed for a school parents' evening and was suitably *glammed up*, her hair unusually released to fall to her shoulders. 'I don't look like that any more,' she muttered. And she most definitely refused to share in the joke of her ex-husband's hearty laugh in the next image, re-engaging for Grandpa Abe, hunched over a chessboard.

'Poor soul. Why is he beside your father?' Suzy wasn't doing well. 'And who are these?'

'People on my course.' Should she own up now, or wait?

'And him?'

'Him.'

'Look. I'm not stupid. Do you think I don't want you to have a *him*? I went through the 60s you know. My stories are far more outrageous than yours, I promise you.'

Suzy prayed that she would never have that borne out. The vision of her mother scurrying for jockstraps on Sports Night was too awful to contemplate. Anyway, as usual, her mother was missing the point. It wasn't that she was worried what she might think, not completely, so much as that she simply didn't want her getting involved.

'That's the outside of the synagogue I went to on Yom Kippur.' Suzy shifted her gaze back to the East End in the hope that her mother might follow. 'It's called the Gates of Peace.'

'Are you going to become religious? I don't know what's worse – marrying out, or becoming Orthodox. I take it he's not Jewish.'

Her mother's visit reacquainted Suzy with the pleasures of shopping, familiarizing herself with the stores of the West End that Charlotte had presumed were a regular fix. Meals were in proper adult restaurants, which was a definite treat. Suzy also enjoyed witnessing once again her mother's many endearing traits, like when she asked the waiter if the milk in her coffee was fresh, twice.

Suzy was deliciously in the company of someone who wanted to spend money on her, although she was careful not to abuse this. She knew all too well how financially difficult life was for her mother, even with the divorce settlement supplements.

'Nick cooks.'

Her mother nodded. 'Will I get to meet him?'

'No!'

But she was allowed to hear his voice. Suzy telephoned him when she knew he was out, permitting her mother to listen to his answering machine message with its forthright conclusion – '. . . and if anyone has my ironing board, please give it back!'

Her only word of relationship advice was the vague expression that conveyed utmost clarity, 'Be careful!'

And they went to the theatre. They purchased half-price tickets on the day of the performance and, this time, it was Suzy's treat. 'On Dad!' she corrected herself, having recently received a cheque from their common paymaster. Coming out of *Jeffrey Barnard is Unwell*, Suzy wondered how Peter O'Toole would have coped with Lady Lena's Sports Night brews.

Just as memorable was an incident on the Tube journey back, her mother sitting opposite Suzy. The train drew into a station and, in coming to rest, succeeded in totally filling the window behind her mother with a field of lush grass, complete with cow, supplied by some advert on the wall behind. They had been magically transported far beyond Holborn Station, with her mother completely oblivious. The train moved off, and they were brutally wrenched from the countryside back to a tunnel deep under central London.

However, the climax of the visit, certainly for Suzy, took place in the heart of the East End.

Mother didn't appreciate walking at the best of times. A keen wind was nagging at them, and Chamberlain Crescent was far longer than the map suggested.

As Suzy had requested, her mother had dug out Grandpa Abe's birth certificate, which crucially disclosed an address. Suzy was on a mission.

'You go on!' Her mother sounded as if they were stranded on an ice cap. Suzy enjoyed ignoring her. Chamberlain Crescent was lined with parallel terraced housing, at least all the way to number 126. From then on one half of the street – the wrong half – had been gouged out, replaced by a squat tower block set back from the road, strangely painted bright orange as if that made all the difference.

Suzy was by now fully acquainted with the havoc wrought by the Blitz in the Second World War, explaining the abrupt shifts in much of the area's landscape. She was open to whatever she would or would not find. From 126 she simply began measuring, following the count of houses across the street in order to arrive at her best estimation of number 138.

'It was here!' she shouted back to her mother, who was yards behind staring mournfully at her shoes. 'This was where your dad was born, Miss Liebovitz.'

Her mother shuffled up.

'Look at the house across the street. It would've been exactly like that. Can you see your dad coming out the door? He's in shorts, wearing a school cap.'

Her mother looked at her in bewilderment. 'I really worry about you!'

Suzy took out her camera and began shooting, first the house across the street, then into the space of what would have been 138 Chamberlain Crescent – the residence of family Liebovitz, her ancestral home. She then asked her mother to take the final picture, Suzy herself in front of the plot, posing in triumph.

'I can see him!' Suzy insisted.

16

Suzy arrived to a blazing row.

Eli was to one side of the synagogue hall locked in a ferocious argument which only ended when a red-faced Lionel turned on his heels and marched out.

'*Ikh hob dir in drerd*!' Eli shouted at his back, accent thickly to the fore. Suzy didn't need Yiddish to understand. Gloria was furious, chastising Eli for his behaviour. He maintained his tone in justifying himself, finally calming down when he realized Suzy was witnessing it all.

'Shoshana!' He approached in an oddly rapid manner. 'That man is an idiot of the worst kind, an idiot with an opinion! He thinks you knock down a wall in Berlin and people will kiss and hug all over Eastern Europe. I know the truth about these people, believe me. *Az es kumt fun a catz zogt ses meow.* If it comes out of a cat, it's saying meow!'

The dance instructor's voice suddenly boomed, rallying her pupils from the four corners. Esther rushed to claim Eli for a partner, leaving Suzy to take in the full assembly.

She prided herself in being able to put names to practically all the faces, as well as by now a few of their stories. The couple gliding forward with elegant poise was Beatrice and Eddie – the former towering over the latter – who considered themselves true cockneys, having lived all their lives in the East End. It was they who had introduced 'Come Dancing' to the JFC calendar, having once been Latin American ballroom dancing champions. 'Of the Hackney Empire,' Becky had added sniffily.

Miriam was a small, mouselike woman with hair in little girls' braids, whose topic of conversation was inexhaustibly the exploits of her children, grandchildren and great grandchildren. Izzy, who had an unusually brief face, which he enlarged from both ends via a beret and goatee beard, had been a London cabbie and claimed to know every street and every secret in London. Gloria had advised Suzy never to play him at cards.

Around the sides sat the more infirm or cautious members including Monty, dapper in his characteristic bow tie, clapping regularly lest he be dismissed as a mere bystander. Suzy enjoyed how such outbursts repeatedly woke Wolfie sitting to his right, whom she had taken to calling *two-gun* from the way he skilfully manoeuvred with his twin walking sticks.

Standing out most acutely was the youthful teacher herself, squeezed into a fluorescent stretched leotard, a figure of such exotic incongruity. She was goading the dancers into two opposing gender distinct lines. With significantly more women than men, a squabble broke over which of the ladies would form the all-female couplings. As a result, one hurried off the floor, which meant her partner Miriam also had to retire, with glares exchanged.

'OK! We're going to start with the waltz. I hope you all remember from last time.' The instructor paced around the outside of the group. Suzy imagined whip in hand. 'Get into starting positions. Remember, we begin with a left turn. Man's weight on the right foot, lady's weight on the left.'

Soon, the music had struck up, and each couple was released to the floor. Suzy found herself witnessing a true spectacle, and was especially pleased that, for the occasion, she had brought her own partner. Her Weston TT camera was eased from the bag.

'Count the beats! Left foot forward, Izzy. Then turn to the left. Izzy! That's it.'

Suzy captured the instructor barking her orders – youth besieged by age at the floor's centre, Izzy's fumbling as he strove to master cornering, Esther drowning in a billowing dress as she pirouetted with Eli, Beatrice and Eddie gracefully waltzing themselves into a Hackney Empire sunset. But most of all it was simply the faces, her eyes kept fixing on these craggy, textured, intense, incredible faces that burst through her lens.

Breaks were taken at a drinks table, with lines of paper cups pre-prepared with watery orange juice. Becky told Suzy about her late husband, how much she missed him. 'It's hard to go on, but you have to. That's what this Club is for. We're the survivors.' Miriam's husband was housebound, and the JFC events were the only occasions she left his side. Izzy proudly announced he was a minyan man – one of the ten men committed to attending synagogue each week to ensure there was the necessary minimum to constitute a service. 'It's like the film. You know. *The Magnificent Seven*!' And Suzy drew them all into her camera.

'The Slow Foxtrot!' was proclaimed by the teacher like it was a special treat to entice a somewhat dwindling flock onward. Suzy took a drink over to Monty, taking a seat next to him. Wolfie was gently snoring on his other side.

'Are you having fun, Monty?'

'Aren't they great dancers?' he replied.

Suzy felt the presence of a figure looming above her and looked up. It was Eli. He had taken off his jacket, revealing bright red braces extending over a substantial paunch.

'Aren't you going to ask Shoshana to dance?' As he spoke, Eli touched Monty's arm. 'Come on! Let's get you to your feet.'

Eli evidently caught Suzy's alarmed expression. 'Don't worry, we've done this before. Shoshana, you've not just come to watch, have you?'

He eased Monty to his feet and Suzy moved to help. He did appear to be smiling.

'Take her hand.'

Monty held out his right hand and Eli took hold of Suzy's, connecting them as if positioning two dummies. Monty's hand felt warm.

'We know this one inside out by now, don't we?' whined the instructor. 'It's so easy!'

Ballroom dancing hadn't figured at any point in Suzy's life up until then, and she was about to dance the foxtrot with a blind man.

'Don't worry,' Eli assured. 'Follow our lead.'

Eli squared Monty's shoulders, placing his left hand round Suzy's waist. She was now inches from his face. Monty's mouth was gaping in apprehension, and she could just make out the outline of his eyes behind the smoked glass of his spectacles, how they were bobbing in a jerky to and fro motion.

'Are you OK?' Monty asked her, sounding as if he was asking himself.

'Are you?' replied Suzy.

'Yes.'

'Well, so am I!'

The music struck up and, to Suzy's complete surprise, Monty moved off in a sprightly manner.

'Use your toes, Izzy!' the instructor pleaded from somewhere. 'And your hands. Let me see expressive hands!'

Eli stood immediately behind Monty, whispering instruction, adjusting his posture like a puppeteer, counting steps under his breath. They made a most unusual threesome, gliding across the floor, Suzy doing her best to follow her men.

'You've done this before.' Suzy spoke loudly to be heard above the music, but Monty was too busy steering to respond. It was his shadow Eli who was looking directly at her over Monty's shoulder, and Suzy had the strange sensation that it was really the two of them dancing, with Monty merely the facilitator. Suzy noticed how unmarked Eli's face was, its round shape serving to enhance a sense of youthfulness.

'He was a great dancer,' Eli answered on Monty's behalf. 'The best of us all!'

They were coasting along now. Beatrice and Eddie, sashaying in the vicinity, studiously avoided eye contact. Suzy could hear them being clapped from somewhere and she felt a quiet elation as she realized that Eli had actually pulled the venture off. He was grinning at her, a smug expression in contrast to Monty who was looking increasingly distressed.

'I'm tired now.' Monty pre-empted Suzy's enquiry, then simply stopped as if all energy had suddenly drained from him.

He released Suzy from his grip and stumbled. 'Please take me back!' His voice had a tone of urgency.

With Eli and Suzy on either side, Monty was eased to his seat. Wolfie congratulated him, slapping his knee, while Suzy quickly went for orange juice.

'You were really great out there.' Suzy rubbed Monty's hand while he gulped down the drink. 'Thank you for the dance.'

Gloria approached, her face intense. 'Are you all right, Monty? You didn't let Eli push you into it, did you?'

'No!' Monty shook his head furiously. 'I wanted to dance.' Gloria glanced at Suzy, then backed away.

'He should join in. It's good for him, no?' Eli said, inviting Suzy's confirmation.

There was something undeniably special about this man, something truly exotic.

'Where does that accent come from?' It was a question she had been meaning to ask for some time.

He peered at her as if she was being impertinent.

'Hell!' came his answer.

17

Terry had returned from Berlin brimming with excitement. On a whim, he had decided to fly there for a weekend of photography. 'How often do you get to witness an event like that? The end of the Cold War. Who'd have believed it? Incredible! Incredible!'

And it showed in the pictures. He devoted a whole class to them – a *peace chain* standing atop a section of Berlin Wall; the faded photograph on a memorial to a border crossing victim; bemused East German soldiers being handed flowers; chunks of wall greedily collected up by souvenir hunters; and a whole host of exuberant faces, wild dancing, flags, kissing and tears. He had even managed to place a photograph with the *Guardian* newspaper, causing huge jealousy and mighty respect, featuring in that day's edition under the headline, 'BERLIN'S ODE TO JOY!'

Terry steered his experience into educational instruction by way of a discussion on the classic role of photography as provider of record. Suzy just had to find out once and for all if he was married.

Suzy was delighted that her tutorial was following such a bravura performance. He was bound to be nice to her.

In contrast to Nick's jovial sneering, Terry was fascinated by Suzy's new job. He adored the 'Fabulous Faces' name. Suzy described her work. Clients were prepared by a professional make-up artist in one room, then sent through to her in the next for portrait shots. Having been initially anxious, Suzy soon came to realize how routine the procedure was.

'It's a bit like a factory. I don't touch the lighting. It's all set up. Head and shoulders. Five pics and it's done.' Suzy did play up gaining experience with a medium format camera.

'So who are these people?'

'Women, wanting to launch modelling careers, or just feel good about themselves, show off to friends, boyfriends, husbands. We get a lot of Greeks. The owner's Greek. It's all harmless.'

'Sounds great.'

'They've promised to do me,' she added.

'Me as well!' said Terry firmly. Suzy hoped she was being laughed *with*.

'Now talk to me about the Jewish Football Club.' Terry smiled. Being laughed *with*, Suzy continued to hope.

She described the JFC events so far attended, some of the key personalities – Gloria, Eli, Becky, Monty. She was continuing to read up on the East End, although she shared her frustration over the paucity of material specifically on the Jewish aspect.

'Maybe it's a good thing,' said Terry. 'You're doing pioneering work.'

'At its peak, there was a Jewish community of a hundred thousand, mainly around Whitechapel and Shoreditch. Now its down to just twelve hundred.'

'Twelve hundred and one,' Terry corrected. Suzy was puzzled.

'You!'

'Oh!'

Terry suggested she examine material that covered the Jewish experience in other parts of the world. 'Look up the work of Gus Fielding on New York.'

Suzy also reported her tape recordings, including a few preliminary interviews. She then presented first photographic evidence, her pictures from the evening of ballroom dancing, which Terry pounced on with an eagerness that ignited a rush of anxiety. He was like a child devouring chocolates. Suzy couldn't figure out what he thought. He had suddenly turned so serious.

'These are just some very early rough shots.'

'Ssssh!'

Terry reached the end of the pile, then started again, this time laying out selected ones on his desk as though they were playing cards.

'Tell me what you see?'

Oh shit. Oh shit! Stupidly, Suzy hadn't prepared herself for this. She frantically scrutinized her depictions – Beatrice confidently splayed backwards in Eddie's arms while he grimaces under the weight; Becky and Gloria caught in feverish conversation by the refreshment table; Wolfie's sleeping head slipped onto Monty's shoulder while he stares out oblivious; Eli and Esther striding forward on the dance floor, faces taut and purposeful.

'What's going to be your story here?' Terry amended the question. 'Have you got any ideas yet?'

Suzy hadn't.

'Don't worry! You've still got time. But you must be thinking about it. You'll only have maximum eighteen or so prints in your final display, so you must find a focus. I'm telling that to everyone. That's what a brief is all about – focus.'

Terry gazed over the images on the table. 'The potential is here. I really see that. You've got good strong characterizations.'

He picked up one of the pictures. 'Who's this?'

It was Eli. He was sitting alone, hair dishevelled and braces askew, caught in the immediate aftermath of a dance. Sweat had given his face a sheen, and he was staring into the camera with an oddly formed enquiring expression.

Terry leaned back on his chair. 'The camera loves this one.'

Suzy quietly gasped in relief.

18

'Him over there!'

'Why?' Nick enquired from under his lucky bright red baseball cap, which was an intrinsic part of his photographic look.

'He's so miserable.'

Suzy and Nick were spending a Saturday *hunting* in the East End, and were now encamped in Victoria Park on a bench close to the pathway, their weapons of choice – Suzy's trusted Weston, Nick's flashy Electra – both carefully to hand.

However, the day was not going well, for two reasons at least.

Suzy was still smarting over the way that, whatever they decided to do, Nick managed to excuse the service of his car. The night before, he couldn't understand why they should drive to the cinema when it was so accessible by Tube. Suzy couldn't understand the point of having a car at university if there was no benefit to it, except to show off the fact that he had one! That last opinion had launched Nick into one of his moods that ensured an evening's end as chilled as the recent autumnal weather.

He was fine again by the morning, although neither weather

nor Suzy were. It was Nina who was most damning over the *boys* of the class. Suzy was discovering that this was a woman who had seen something of the world, and she and Jo had taken to sitting at her feet. Nina was currently teasing them with ever-so-indiscreet references to a blossoming liaison with one of the Fine Art lecturers based in the mysterious world of the H-Block top floor.

'What about them over there?' Nick proposed.

Their other dispute was over methodology. Nick had the infuriating habit of asking permission before taking a shot, thereby immediately draining the subject of whatever naturalism that was the original attraction. From behind her camera, everything and everyone was fair game as far as Suzy was concerned, and she resented Nick's timidity.

A mother with two children and four dogs, all six on barely indistinguishable leashes, was approaching. So yet again, Nick politely enquired if she would mind having her image plundered for booty. He concentrated on the children, while Suzy focused in on the mother. She expounded to Nick afterwards on how she had contrasted the mother's ethereal face with the domesticity of the scene, suggesting her charges had her on a lead rather than vice versa.

In photographing a group of youngsters, Nick droned on about how he had caught 'the supreme self-consciousness and angst of adolescence, the terror of approaching adulthood,' until Suzy realized what he was up to and pushed him off the bench.

'Hey! Watch the camera!'

As Suzy helped Nick to his feet, an elderly couple drew near.

They were laughing together in a relaxed, self-contained way. Suzy stopped Nick from making an approach, capturing them herself with several shots as they passed.

'You're at your most free when you're old,' Suzy said.

They left the park at Queens Gate. Nick pointed to a commotion across the road, cars depositing gaily attired guests, a crowd assembling in a church forecourt. 'This is what we'll be covering soon!'

Suzy was fascinated. She watched the procession of colour ambling along the grey street, streaming in to the church – gelled hair, flower pins, aged and young. The trophy of an authentic East End wedding was irresistible.

'Come on!' She grabbed Nick's hand and pulled him across the street.

'What are you doing?' he protested.

'Is there anything more natural than photographers at a wedding? Don't be a wimp all your life!'

Suzy led Nick into the church, weaving among the guests by the entrance.

'I just wish we were properly dressed,' she teased.

'You're not going to get away with it!' Nick whispered loudly, his anger all too apparent.

'We will. We're photographers, remember. We get away with everything!'

Suzy turned to a cluster of guests and began marshalling them into formation. 'That's it. Closer. Thank you.' she whined in best imitation of every function photographer she had ever had the misfortune to meet. Through the lens, Suzy was startled and impressed with the contrasting bearings of the people she had happened upon. The two youngsters in the foreground were deliciously malevolent, a woman's plunging neckline plunged far beyond the call of duty, an older man was relishing a last ciga-rette before the agony of abstinence. Suzy realized the enormous possibilities of wedding photography when it didn't need to be played straight. 'Thank you everyone,' she whined again at the conclusion of the shot.

And so Suzy began. She took bride Sonia's Auntie Christine parading with a latest boyfriend. 'Seven years younger,' she had whispered with pride. Sonia's workmates from the hospital insisted on lining up in order of who was deemed to have the best pair of legs. And she caught the bridegroom's cousins fol-lowing the football on concealed radios.

By the time the bride and groom walked down the aisle, Suzy knew most of the details: Andrew had met Sonia through his brother Clive who had taken her out first; they had been together for six years if that didn't include the infamous three-month break about which nothing was said – beyond Clive's behaviour; they were going to the Italian Lakes on honeymoon. Suzy was tempted to stay for the reception, but she presumed Nick was waiting for her outside.

'How could you do that?'

Nick's mood had swung again, and Suzy's thoughts were of Nina.

19

The scale of the vast mural covering one whole side of the building overwhelmed Suzy.

'The war is over. Chaim finally returns to his shtetl in Poland from where he had been marched out to the camps three long years before.' Eli paused to ensure he had Suzy's attention, then continued. 'He wanders through the village recognizing familiar sights, and familiar people.'

The giant mural faces were grim and determined, men and women standing behind a fierce red banner declaring *Mosley shall not pass, bar the road to British fascism*. Immediately in front, a tumult of horseback policemen bucking before the crowds, milk bottles being thrown from windows, a Hitler-styled figure in his underwear falling comically to the ground.

'Chaim goes into the cobbler's shop and tells the owner how he recalled being a regular customer. He was always coming in with his worn shoes, had even left a pair the day he was taken. The owner stares hard at him, then says, "They'll be ready next Thursday!"'

Suzy took Eli as he laughed, his mouth gaping, eyes fiercely alive. At the last JFC event, he had offered to give Suzy an East End tour. Even Terry had singled him out. How could she resist?

'Everyone over sixty in the East End will tell you that they were personally on Cable Street that day fighting the fascists. Don't believe any of them.'

It was for that reason that Eli didn't want to be photographed in front of the mural. 'I wasn't here. I was in Romania living *under* the fascists.'

Eli also showed her the modest plaque on the front of the municipal building commemorating the 'Tower Hamlets International Brigade' – those from the area who went off to fight in the Spanish civil war. Its letters were partially obliterated, but the text was still legible. Suzy was struck by the final line – 'They went because their open eyes could see no other way.'

'Don't think this is just history. You're so young, Shoshana. The local elections are in May, and it's already started. They're crawling out from the sewers again, handing out their filth. People still listen. It's incredible! It's never over.'

Suzy took this next shot in such contrast to the first; Eli the comic replaced by Eli the angry prophesier.

'Why do you think they put up the mural?'

Eli walked at an energetic pace that took Suzy by surprise, and she was soon rapidly adding to the day's photographic catch. Eastchapel market was crammed with stalls covering every permutation of merchandising. Eli's only stop was at a second-hand record shop where he chatted at length with the owner – evidently there hadn't yet been a sighting of a hoped-for record. A garish tavern was declared to have various gangster associations, with Eli taking Suzy inside to point out dubious looking bullet holes along the wall. And there were the colourful Asian stores and curry houses around Brick Lane, some last surviving prefab homes from the war, the Jack the Ripper pub with the gruesome tally of victims proudly etched on its windows, the Royal London Hospital where the so-called Elephant Man was discovered.

Suzy however was more intrigued by that fading, less distinguishable seam of area life – the Jewish story. Eli provided her with the very street corner of the Odesser steam baths which, on a pre-Sabbath Friday afternoon, had been the centre of every form of gossip; the bagel shop that had reinstated a special rye variety after protest by Eli himself – the result of his effort sampled in the process; the ornate building that had originally been a Huguenot church, then a synagogue, and was now a mosque; the Yiddish theatre where Eli himself had once performed in amateur productions, now a bingo hall.

Suzy told Eli about her visit to Prague – how, in similar fashion, she had gone in search of the Jewish remnant of that city. He appeared very interested.

'The Altneu synagogue was the home of the great rabbi, the Maharal of Prague,' Eli said. 'The rabbi invoked God's name in a special way, and created the Golem.'

It was a story that Suzy had learned of, the Frankenstein-like monster that this rabbi mystic had created to protect the Jews. The guide had talked dramatically about the creature living on in the synagogue's attic.

She also mentioned Terezin concentration camp, and the display of striking photographs on Czechoslovakian Jewish life that had made such an impact on her.

'Where was the Golem when we needed him?' Eli stared at her as if she might have found out.

Eli featured in many of her shots that day. Suzy was keen to capture him at his most vigorous, which meant in full descriptive flow at various of their stops. In return, he demanded that Suzy demonstrate how the camera worked, which became a precursor to Eli taking pictures of her. Eli as professional photographer proved amusing, watching him wobbling the machine in front of his face, and he even obtained the services of an obliging policeman to take one of them both.

Suzy couldn't help but notice how attentive Eli was throughout their visit. He would take her arm whenever they crossed the road, repeatedly enquire if she needed a break, or was getting cold. It felt like a first date. And so many stories. A favourite was one concerning his Romanian mother whose advice to Eli on restaurants was to sit by the window, because you would be serverd bigger portions!

As they returned to his flat, they passed the hairdressing salon where Eli had once worked. He was happy to be photographed outside, but she couldn't persuade him to enter. 'I'm retired!' Suzy had no such qualms, and a bemused hairdresser and gelled-up client became the tour's photographic finale.

'Hot hot coffee for two, no?'

Eli lived in an old terraced house that had been converted into flats, with Eli occupying the upper floor.

Suzy was taken aback by how formidably groomed his apartment was, suggesting it was a far from natural state. She wondered if she was the cause of this outbreak of orderliness. Two large armchairs bracketed a bruised leather sofa. A small dining table with an old typewriter as centrepiece rested in a window bay framed by lush velvety red curtains. Suzy examined the painting above the fireplace, which portrayed some sort of distinguished musical gathering. A cluster of energetic musicians supported a lone singer consumed in performance. There was something quite exceptional about the work, its impressionist style creating dramatic swirling ripple and eddy effects. She suddenly realized that the artist was depicting sound itself.

On the mantelpiece below, kitsch dancing *Hassidim* silently performed, while endeavouring to avoid a display of glassware. Ceramic plates commemorating historic towns of Israel were affixed in an imperfect row along a wall. Colourfully complete bookshelves to waist height buttressed another.

The most immodest aspect of the room was the serious capacity of the two wall-mounted speakers over an equally substantial music centre – record player, tape deck and radio at least, all smoothly combined in black. Indeed, the record collection stacked in long racks alongside would have put many a student household to shame. Perspective was restored when Suzy read the sleeves: Tchaikovsky, Schubert, Bruch; fantastical opera covers – Verdi, Mozart, Puccini, and there was Hebrew liturgical music, and klezmer. Not a Housemartins nor a Madonna in sight.

Eli came in from the kitchen with the promised coffees escorting unannounced cake and biscuits on a tray. Suzy was being settled in, which gave her a problem. The walk had taken far longer than expected, and she was due to meet Jo outside the Union building at seven p.m. She explained to Eli that this would have to be a *first* interview. He nodded certainly.

'Do you like music?' Eli was now heading to the music centre.

'Some.' She hoped he wouldn't pursue it. This would not be a meeting of minds. 'Are you going to start collecting CDs?'

He looked at her in disgust. Suzy took up position on one of the armchairs, stopping herself from being submerged while she pulled the tape recorder from her bag. 'It won't be too loud, will it?' Eli maintained his look. Suzy also located her list of carefully formulated questions. She thought of herself momentarily as one of the schoolchildren of Northbridge Primary.

Photographs! Suzy suddenly identified what was missing from the room. There weren't any photographs. Suzy couldn't recall ever being in a home that didn't offer at least one, however bland. She almost felt like congratulating Eli on his restraint.

He eased himself into the sofa opposite while Suzy caught the first simmerings of sound.

'Have you seen *The Great Caruso*? The film. Mario Lanza!'

'No'

'*This* is Mario.'

Mario made a plaintive introduction, a creamily smooth voice gently moaning as Suzy placed the tape recorder by Eli's side, taking careful aim with the microphone. Nevertheless, her planning was immediately thwarted as he abruptly got to his feet, disappearing into another room.

The bulging folder under his arm on his return signified the reason. 'This is what I wanted to show you.'

What spilled forth was a whole collection of material –

primarily leaflets and brochures, but also articles – from what appeared to be an assortment of grotesque extremist political groups. Suzy recognized the BPP – 'the British People's Party' – infamous for its outspoken racism, but there were others that Suzy had never heard of, with names like 'the White Knights of Saint George', and 'Patriots Patrol'.

'See!' There was so much of it to see – 'the Mongrelization of Europe', 'White Revolution is Now!', 'the Holohoax of the Century'. Along with the revulsion, Suzy did feel a macabre fascination.

'Why do you have all this?' she asked.

'Everyone should. Cable Street. I told you. It's not over!'

She thought of the Cable Street mural, and the falling Hitleresque figure, and the incongruity of such material being handled by this silver-haired old man.

'People don't realize. Don't want to believe. They prefer sleepwalking to facing reality.'

And then Eli pre-empted Suzy's great list of questions by starting to talk about himself. Suzy quickly redirected the microphone to catch it. She would have asked that he lower Mario's swelling rendition, but didn't want to disturb his flow.

His initial remarks centred on the East End as he first encountered it as a post-war refugee. He had arrived in 1947 'just down the road, at the East India docks. Not that they are there any more.' He talked about how hard life was then – shortages, rationing. 'Went on like that for years. But the people. The people were special. You always helped your neighbour. Never locked your doors. Imagine that today!'

And then, accompanying a thrust of the biscuit plate, Eli asked Suzy about her own background – where her family had come from, her parents' work, if she had siblings – all the questions she had so carefully prepared for him. In the circumstances, Suzy felt obliged to respond, as far as she was able. She felt embarrassed that she didn't know where her family had started out from, but this was more than made up for in her detailing of the contemporary chapter of family history. It was only when playing back the tape later that she realized how much of it was filled by interviewer rather than interviewee.

Eli was expressing sadness over her parents' divorce as if he was an old family friend hearing about it for the first time when Suzy made her bid to wrest back control of the conversation.

'You came from Romania?'

She couldn't even get a straight answer to that. Eli confused her by explaining that he was either Hungarian or Romanian depending on which year of the century you posed the question. Eli had experienced both, and liked neither.

'There will always be dictatorship in Romania, either left or right. communism or nationalism. Red or black. Either way, the Jews will get it. Not that there are so many left.' Eli had moved on to the turbulent events currently unfolding in Eastern Europe.

'Ceauşescu is a villain and a monster and I hope he burns in hell!' Eli sat forwards as Suzy sat back. 'Mark my words. *If* he goes, and he'll only go if they manage to—' Eli drew a finger across his neck in illustration. 'He'll be replaced by another monster, except this time they will kill people in the name of nationalism!'

A loud orchestral sound boomed as if endorsing his opinion.

To the extent that Suzy had followed these developments, she understood them as portrayed in the media, as Terry's pictures had endorsed – the beginnings of a democratic dawn. It was what she had understood from the vague political rumblings she had picked up in Prague that summer.

'I know these people, too well, believe me!'

It was his passion that was so engaging.

'Why do you get so excited?' she asked through a smile.

'It's how I talk. I'm not English!'

Eli got to his feet and assumed an air of distraction, as if he had said enough and now wanted to be left to imbibe his music. Suzy anyway realized that she really did have to leave. Already late for Jo, the downpour beyond the windows was inflating her sin.

As Suzy hurriedly dismantled the tape recorder, she asked if she could take away examples of the extremist literature. Eli nodded as if that was his intention. He was heading for the music centre, which he turned up while starting to sing along to the soaring melody. He was soon belting out the verse, matching Mario note for note. Suzy was thrilled. She leapt for the camera and took several quick shots, moving closer with each one. Eli then stopped abruptly, as if he had just made another point.

Suzy returned camera to bag, and had Eli and Mario as her two escorts to the front door. In thanking Eli with genuine profuseness for an incredible day, she felt a compulsion to ask one further question from the list she had so miserably failed.

'Just tell me about your family. I mean, for example, were you married?'

'Sure. In Romania,' he told her matter-of-factly.

'So what happened to your wife?'

'I killed her.'

20

Nick was *supposed* to have synchronized his boarding with Suzy's to ensure they caught the same Tube train. Anyway, she was using the journey as valuable reading time. It began with *Good Jews and Upstanding Englishmen – The Jewish Experience in Britain*, the latest work retrieved from the university library. Suzy had also brought with her very different writings that she was itching to re-examine. Soon, a British People's Party newsletter was sharing her lap.

Suzy did begin to wonder about the confusion she must be causing her fellow passengers, which rapidly turned to apprehension. She returned book and leaflet to her bag, and it dawned on her that she had felt self-conscious about both.

Nick miraculously materialized as she stepped onto the platform, having caught the correct train, but incorrect carriage. As they walked out of Charing Cross Station, Suzy produced the BPP newsletter for Nick's perusal.

'Are you on a recruitment drive?' he asked.

'Excellent!' Terry had counted off the class and found the expected complement had successfully navigated themselves from East to West End, even Barry who, according to Jo, had come straight from an all-night rave and was being propped up by whatever he had popped.

As the group stood inside the entrance to the National Portrait Gallery, Terry handed out the visit assignment grandly headed 'Portraiture; Identity and Identification'.

'So where are we?' Terry surveyed his student rabble.

A nervous-looking tourist moved swiftly past, as if uncertain whether obliged to reply.

'This place was founded in the mid-nineteenth century. Where was Britain in the mid-nineteenth century?'

'The Caribbean?' Salvo had dedicated his December to complaining about the British weather.

'Queen Victoria,' came Barry to the rescue.

'The British Empire,' added Gareth, giving due recognition to his Jamaican roots.

'OK.' Terry began his familiar marching.

'Portraiture is about giving visual expression to identity. So what's a *National-Portrait-Gallery*? It's the identity of a nation. But who gets in?'

'It's for heroes!' shouted Barry again, demonstrating a rare enthusiasm that was alarming everyone.

'That's right. Like what I am to you guys.' Terry grinned alone. 'This is a temple to celebrity. It was where the great masses came to marvel at the famous people of their day – politicians, soldiers, royalty, great thinkers. Photography hadn't happened yet. There were no pictures of people in the newspapers. This place is the *Hello!* magazine of the nineteenth century!' Terry was delighted with his analogy.

'Now, the works were originally understood to be simply objective portrayals. But! But they didn't reckon on us savvy students. We've started thinking about cultural issues, and semiotics. This place is bursting with hype and propaganda, right? So, I want you to go through these galleries with your critical eye.'

Terry pushed his own 'critical eye' forward. 'Before you head off, one last thing on the assignment. People like celebrities because they say something about what we ourselves are capable of. That's why I want comment not just on how identity is constructed here, but also on how the viewer responds. Good luck!'

Suzy, Nick, Gareth and Jo headed off together, starting at the beginning of the main exhibition, finding themselves quickly surrounded by a mafia of haughty monarchs and barons bedecked in great symbols of wealth and power, looking as bored as these latest admirers. There was one so grotesquely ostentatious that Suzy could almost hear him hectoring the artist, 'make me a god!'

Jo was struck by how props were deployed to strengthen the narrative aspect of the compositions. Nick was more interested in the techniques to make the figures more expressive – how subjects were positioned within the space of the canvas, the use of lighting effects to highlight and conceal.

It amazed Suzy that such a vast venue could be dedicated to what was essentially a single topic. The human face provided such infinite possibility.

At one point, Gareth asked if anyone observed anything unusual about the works they had so far viewed.

'They're all white,' he said. 'If there had been just one black face, you'd have noticed.'

Jo laughed.

Terry had stationed himself by the earliest photographs to ensure that photographic pioneers Daguerre and Fox Talbot received due abasement from this latest batch of followers.

The photographic and painted portrait received equal representation in the twentieth-century rooms. Terry drew the group together to discuss the difference between the two forms, and the problematics of the photograph being perceived as the more real. 'The photograph uses as much invention as a painting. It just appears more honest.'

True to his journalistic instincts, Nick disagreed, claiming that a photograph was a precise reproduction that was open to manipulation, but had truth at its core. Their argument became an uncomfortable stand-off.

'You're both right,' said Barry, the class's new peacemaker. He hugged Nick, and then Terry. 'You're both fantastic!' Suzy and Jo didn't know where to put themselves.

Towards the visit's end, the students were ensconced in the contemporary section, among the comfortable images of the most familiar. Salvo was hanging out with Mick Jagger, Barry was dating Twiggy, Megan was hissing at Margaret Thatcher, and Nick was kneeling before Bobby Charlton, no doubt regretting the absence of his Manchester United shirt.

'Have you chosen which one you're doing the assignment on?' Terry was alongside Suzy, having returned with Nina from a cigarette break. Suzy took him to a stunning head and shoulders shot of a 1930s actress. The photographer had placed her in a completely blank space, thereby focusing attention fully on the face, intensely formed and protruding forward.

'You like strong women,' Terry remarked.

'Which's your favourite?' Suzy asked.

'That's easy!'

Terry led Suzy over to a bright colour photograph, before being called away by Barry. It was a full body shot of a model against a bare wall caught in a taut pose, legs and arms out-stretched. There was high energy yet also control, the tightly fitted clothing accentuating a straining exuberance. It was the integrity of the image that was especially remarkable, enhanced by the use of natural light, and the way she was facing the camera – open and giving, in some inexplicable yet definitive way.

Suzy looked down to identify the photographer, reading off the caption, 'Terence Raymond, May 1984.'

'Terry! You . . .!'

21

For some reason, the kitchen was Gloria's location of prefer-ence. She struck a stately pose beside her steel hobs, patting them like they were children, dressed in the highly dubious kitchen attire of a chiffon dress.

In the living room, Gloria parked herself beside esteemed possessions – the glass cabinet with its prizes of silver and glassware; gleaming dining-room table alongside gleaming owner; her poodle, named Cary after her favourite actor, which she subjected to profuse adoration.

'You really must come over one Friday night!' She said it as she crouched by the dog, as if it was he insisting. This threesome was warming to each other.

From the mantelpiece, Gloria selected an ornately framed picture of her late husband Gerald, which she brandished to her front. Suzy caught the moment, and the next when she pressed the image to her lips. It was a glorious act and it made Suzy wonder what she thought she was doing. Did Gloria actually believe the picture represented a trace of her husband?

The interview was conducted with Gloria seated in one of her puffed armchairs, from where she spoke through a puff of cigarettes. The Friendship Club was created twenty years ago to provide a social group for 'senior citizens'. The leaders at the time were connected with the Gates of Peace synagogue hence the use of its building 'at no cost'. In fact, the synagogue made a modest contribution towards activities.

'We used to get many more people. Don't ask me where they've all gone! But there are still events every single month of the year,' Gloria noted with pride. 'Sometimes more. And we always celebrate the festivals. You're coming to our Chanukah party, aren't you?'

Gloria had ensured Suzy was now on the club mailing list receiving every precious announcement. She smiled. Chanukah was marked boldly in the diary.

Gloria also explained how most of the remaining synagogue

members lived out of the area, but kept up membership for sentimental reasons.

'Some had bar mitzvahs or weddings here. They like coming back to their roots, show the children, now grandchildren. Then they get into their cars and drive back to Ilford, or Finchley. I recognize them all!' Gloria waved a hand.

Her own family was widely spread; daughter in Israel – 'I worry about her all the time'; sister in Australia – 'How can she expect me to visit her?'; son in Edgware – 'That one can look after himself!' Her son had been trying for some time to move her into sheltered accommodation somewhere in Stanmore, which she deeply resented.

'At my age, there's only one way he's going to get me out of here, and that's horizontally.'

Asked what that age was, Gloria was only prepared to confess to being 'over fifty', which wasn't much of a confession. She had lost her husband to cancer some years before. 'He said I'd be the one to kill him. Well I wasn't!'

'A piece of advice for you.' Suzy suspected she would receive a number. 'Marry someone a lot younger. Men don't preserve well.' Gloria shook her head and leaned back. 'The Friendship Club saved me. That's why I like to give back something. Help out. You need something to do, otherwise you might as well be dead, or in Stanmore.'

'How does the synagogue itself keep going?' Suzy asked.

'By a miracle! Every year there's the same vote to close it down. And every year it's defeated, just.' Gloria smiled. 'He's not ready for us.' She cocked her head ceilingward. 'It's our destiny to keep Jewish life going in the East End. Do you believe in fate?'

Of course Suzy did, from the moment she put that camera to her face as an eleven-year-old on a windy English beach. Deep down, at the deepest level, she had never doubted that she would get into the course and come to London.

'So fate has brought you to the JFC. There you are! You'll *have* to come for Friday night dinner.'

Suzy had talked about fate with Eli. It had come up in his interview, which more accurately could be described as *her* interview. Suzy couldn't believe what she had spoken about when she played back the tape. She hadn't told her father about Nick!

Eli's parting remark that day was a last question Suzy had for Gloria.

'He said *what* to you?' Gloria was as shocked as Suzy had been herself. She explained that Eli had conveyed the astonishing comment about killing his wife in such a straightforward manner that she had been unsure how to take it. She had even wondered if she misheard him. Suzy was just glad it happened as she was leaving.

Nevertheless, she had become so anxious afterwards, especially over the thought that she might have in some way upset Eli, that she found a pretext to telephone the very next day. He was completely his usual self. Of course, his comment was also utterly compelling, which was why she felt compelled in turn to raise it with Gloria.

Gloria squinted at her, causing her cheeks' thin patchwork of lines to break free of their powdery cover. She had to be well over seventy.

'That man! I'm going to phone Becky right now.'

'Becky!' It was a forthright summons. This was a business call. 'Did Eli kill his wife?' Suzy leapt inside.

'No! Thank you very much.' And the phone was down. 'He's a rogue!'

22

The Jewish festival of Chanukah was strangely not to the fore on campus. Christmas was launched with the arrival of a massive tree positioned like a flagpole outside the Student Union, donated for some reason by the good people of Basingstoke. BC was also seasonally garlanded in various ways, with students ensuring that the Bernard bust by the entrance did not escape the festive cheer. Decoration began with a tinsel necklace, to which bauble earrings were soon added and, on last sighting, shaving foam had been impressively laid down the centre of his bald pate mohican style.

A whole host of invitations were soon flooding mail boxes, fixed to noticeboards, showering canteen tables – the Science Fiction Society, the Global Peace Society, something wonderfully called The Morons Society – every group that ever breathed on campus was trying to out-market the others in the garishness of their party promotions, and the allure of cheap beer.

For Suzy, it was Nick's rowing club affair that would inevitably take precedence. Somehow, the university swimming pool had been secured for the evening and, adding to her trepidation, was the insistence that the watery themed party was strictly fancy dress.

Nick, of course, had to go to the lengths of actually hiring a costume. Suzy couldn't exactly say that she *recognized* him, kitted out in an outrageous Toad of Toad Hall outfit, complete with bulbous head, waistcoat and breeches. What annoyed her was how her own effort – a vaguely nautical jacket and mask that was her best attempt at Donald Duck – was immediately enfeebled.

The poolside area was dressed as a tropical island, with rows of colourful beach umbrellas and deckchairs at both ends. An inflatable island had been anchored in the middle of the pool, complete with teetering plastic palm tree. Gentle reggae music was playing out as a final touch.

Toad went off to find drinks. Donald stood alone, realizing how few people she knew. To distract herself, she began admiring the costumes on parade. There was a party of mermaids practising assorted shrill noises across the pool from her. Suzy identified at least three sailors, and one of more senior ranking, an Admiral perhaps. A tin of tuna passed before her, with a slipping label that the woman had continually to pull up to maintain her modesty. One student wore a bizarre grin above stripy vest, flip flops and boxer shorts that had the words 'Moby Dick' menacingly across the front.

Toad returned with two umbrella-topped glasses that he

described as rum punch. Suzy confirmed the latter with her first sip. Numbers grew. The music raged. Dress inventiveness flourished. Toad ensured that the umbrella count mounted. Suzy was alarmed to discover that the grinning Moby had a second film released across his rear – 'Free Willy'!

When friends of Nick passed, he and Suzy quickly assumed an air of studious silence, enjoying their conspiracy of anonymity. It reminded Suzy of how she felt from behind the camera, her more familiar mask. Indeed, she had planned to take photographs that night, despite Nick's disapproval. It was too marvellous an occasion. 'Can't you just join in for once!' He still didn't understand. This was precisely how Suzy could.

Her marauding brought a brace of pirates, necking salmon, a dangerously swaying watering can, and the *Titanic* – pre-sinking. Final shots were of a headless Toad – Nick protruding from his inflated waistcoat, flirting with a mermaid.

'You're a complete toad!'

'Well. You shouldn't have left me!' his excuse, as he twirled the latest rum punch umbrella in Suzy's face.

Anyway, Suzy needn't worry. Nick explained the principle carefully to her. 'When a man looks at a woman, it means nothing. Men look at women all the time. But when a woman looks at a man. That's serious.' He started pointing his finger at her. 'I saw you looking at me. On the boat down the Thames. That's when I knew.'

'You're a pissed newt!' was Suzy's considered response.

Nick started searching his pockets. 'You need something. So

do I.' He extracted a thin plastic bag. 'Barry gave us a Christmas present.'

'I don't celebrate Christmas!'

There were four small coloured pills. Suzy couldn't believe he had them.

One of Nick's rowing friends started calling him over.

'I'm not taking one unless you do.'

'You're such a . . !'

Another of his teammates grabbed Nick. It turned out that he had been enlisted to represent the first years in the evening's games. Suzy counted out seven umbrellas in her hand while she watched the relay pint consumption contest – empty glasses placed upside down on heads on a turn's completion, soon followed by outrageous gropings in a race to pass a length of rope through clothing to form a chain. Suzy had forgiven Nick by the beer-keg rolling, the measurement of success being not just the speed of transport, but also the quantity of liquid still retained by its end. Nick had performed far better than his team, which meant he was included in the inglorious 'ginnings', a verb entailing the forced consumption of the spirit.

The final round introduced a new form of sentencing, namely banishment to the island at the pool's centre. To a deafening roar, first convicts were dispatched into the pool, enjoying a deliriously drenched celebrity. It wasn't long before more of the party was under way *in* the pool than out. Assorted aquatic life was returned to the sea, voluntarily and involuntarily. Eventually even the *Titanic* was forced to re-enact its demise. A huge Santa arrived, his Ho ho ho-ing! rapidly submerged along with himself. Some had come prepared and were soon in swimwear.

Suzy managed to avoid the pool initiation for some time. Inevitably, it was Nick who sought her out. He had already been dunked twice, his outfit clinging to him, flattening any vestige of vigour. She was shamelessly lured by a piece of mistletoe. Nick gripped hold of her and sent them both crashing to the water. Suzy swiftly propelled herself away from the frightful Toad only to return in similar fashion with the appearance on her horizon of the infamous Moby, circling in shallow waters.

The evening finale came with the arrival, incredibly, of a full-sized rowing boat somehow negotiated into the pool area. It was ceremoniously launched, with several bodies clambering on board, using their hands to glide in splendid parade. Everyone stood poolside to clap the boat's progress. The crew collectively rose from their seats, saluted to every side, then proceeded to execute a capsize, boat and men spinning into the waters in one enormous crash of noise.

23

The idea of attending another party on the very evening following such a raucous first was daunting. Suzy's only consolation for a sore head was the promise of a far more sedate affair, reflected in the return of her 'course interview' blue skirt.

'Shoshana!' The evening began at Eli's flat. He had insisted that he escort her to the club, yet logistics demanded that she come by his home for the purpose. Eli kissed Suzy on the forehead and she thought how apt that was. Suzy hoped the gesture had healing properties, meanwhile imploring him to lower the frenzied music.

Suzy was relieved to confirm that they were still friends, despite the eccentric exchange that had ended their last meeting. She had thought about bringing up the reference to his wife, but they had by now had several overlaying conversations and Suzy wasn't even sure how she might go about raising it. She sensed Eli would anyway elaborate in his own time, that their relationship was developing an implicit aspect of which this was part.

But such thoughts were not for that evening. Suzy had slipped the all-enveloping world of Christmas for another faith and another festival – Chanukah.

Eli was looking well spruced – hair swept back and shiny, a colourful handkerchief placed in the pocket of what appeared to be a freshly laundered jacket. Chanukah was bringing out the dandy in him.

Eli launched their walk to the Club with several jokes. Suzy concentrated on providing the grin at the moment of punchline. His tone swiftly changed on turning into one particular street, where he pointed out a boarded-up home that had been firebombed some months before. 'They've been targeting Asians all over the East End.'

Suzy sensed the presumption that she now appreciated who *they* were. *They* were the British People's Party, the White Knights of Saint George and the various other Far Right groupings whose literature now graced her bedside table. Her education included homework.

They stopped in front of the building while Eli explained in passionate detail how the family with three young children had made their escape. He then somehow carried off a seamless transition to latest events in Romania – the burgeoning protest and expected clampdown – as if they were two dimensions of the same event. 'Ceauşescu isn't about to go anywhere, whatever happens in Czechoslovakia!' Suzy had heard the news that the communist Czech president had resigned. The regimes of Eastern Europe were crumbling, and it was all so incredibly real for Eli.

He appeared to derive a sense of accomplishment from their entry together, firmly taking Suzy's arm as they swept into the Club hall. Various heads nodded in greeting – Becky, an armed two-gun Wolfie, and Miriam. Even her dance partner Monty seemed to acknowledge her from behind his dark glasses. The exception remained Lionel, shuffling out of her way, this interloper in their midsts.

The room was bedecked in festive streamers of blues and yellows. Two tables had been placed on the stage, with one supporting a large menorah. More tables fanned out in several rows below, and a couple off to one side clothed in white offered up refreshment – the ubiquitous Club orange juice sharing billing with sandwiches and the customary festival doughnuts.

In the manner of a rescue, Gloria snatched Suzy as she progressed with Eli down the hall.

'Please make it short!' Gloria said to him as she led her prize away. He tutted.

'Being a famous photographer doesn't stop you giving us a little help, now does it?' Gloria handed Suzy a box of multi-coloured candles and pointed to the onstage menorah. 'Remember, it's all eight tonight.' Suzy hadn't remembered for quite some time. Chanukah was for some reason a festival too far in the Green household.

There were now around twenty-five elderly souls in the room. Gloria mounted the stage to motion her flock. Suzy set the tape recorder into action and wielded her camera for first shots, capturing Becky unfortunately waving at her, Esther secreting a first glass of juice, Izzy's beret slipping down his face as he jumped to knock the streamers.

After brief words of welcome, Gloria summoned Eli to join her.

'Come on, rabbi!' Wolfie barked. Suzy captured Eli as he took up position above them, clearing his throat as if before vast crowds.

'Louder,' shouted Izzy before he had even begun. Gloria hushed him.

Eli's address was essentially a brief summary of Chanukah facts. Jews against Greeks in the Holy Land; the future of Jewish faith at stake; Jews win. Hearing it explained so simply made Suzy feel even more embarrassed that she couldn't recall any-thing of the story, although she was sure she must have been introduced to it. Eli then talked about a miracle – the fact that the oil in the Temple menorah lasted eight days instead of the anticipated one, hence the eight candles. He concluded on the meaning of the word Chanukah – 'dedication' – and how the Friendship Club itself was a symbol of that, dedicated to keeping the Jewish faith burning bright in the East End.

Eli then covered his head and began reciting words of blessing while, with a flourish, he lit each of the eight candles, his JFC audience bearing witness to the continuing flame.

Suzy's thoughts went back to the synagogue in Prague, as she had sat among similar aged faces, how she had strangely felt that her presence *mattered*.

Wolfie led the charge to the food. From somewhere the sound of fast-moving klezmer-style music started up, perfectly scoring the pace of the feasting now under way around the two tables of food. Miriam thrust a doughnut in Suzy's direction, while delivering a message on a granddaughter's ice-skating prowess. The doughnut was actually rather good, although contained within was a potentially lethal ingredient as Esther found to her cost, running to the bathroom with a great splodge of jam down her blouse. Suzy then caught Becky stroking her dress. 'What material is it?' she asked. 'Don't worry. I'm not a lesbian!'

While Eli hovered behind, Wolfie wanted to know what she thought of Petticoat Lane market where he had sold shoes for over forty years. He hoped she was disappointed. 'It's full of *shmattes* now. The quality's gone. There's no real shoppers any more, just tourists.' When Eli's inevitable interruption came, it was accompanied by a brief glare in Wolfie's direction, although he seemed more annoyed with Suzy for indulging him.

'How was I?' was his urgent question.

And amongst it all, Suzy attempted to remain true to her photographic mission.

The next part of the evening explained the rows of tables, and brought the Latin American ballroom champion, of the Hackney Empire at least, Eddie, literally centre-stage. A second area of expertise – bingo!

'It was called *housey housey* when I was young,' commented Esther, now wrapped in a coat as a result of the doughnut stain.

'Top of the house – number ninety!'

Eddie's partner in dance and marriage Beatrice sat next to him on the stage selecting numbers from a bag, but only he could call them, summoning every ounce of authority for the task, enunciating in a formidable quizmasterly manner.

Why was number ninety top of a house, Suzy wondered but, recognizing the life and death atmosphere, thought better than to ask. She had already been accused of distracting Wolfie with her camera, and Izzy had been booed for wanting a number repeated.

'Doctor's orders – number nine!' None of it made any sense. Suzy decided to stick to her photography. She cruised the tables recording expressions of fevered concentration.

'Becky's age – twenty-one!' Becky beamed up at Eddie in appreciation. 'Two fat ladies – eighty-eight.' Then swiftly buried herself in her card.

'Bingo!' Izzy leapt to his feet.

'He's only read out six numbers!' sighed Gloria. Lionel stared daggers. Izzy quickly resumed his seat.

Suzy drifted over to the old photographs on the wall. One

was of the original synagogue consecration in the late nine-teenth century – sombre men in top hats and tails, another a visit by a local Member of Parliament. A party for the Queen's silver jubilee was the most recent, and the only one rendered in colour. Suzy failed to recognize any of the faces. An older picture that caught her attention showed the synagogue full of people, the rabbi on the *bimah* in his austere canonicals, all faces compliantly towards the camera. It was odd because it appeared to be during a service, despite the strict prohibition against photography.

'Four and eight, forty-eight!' boomed Eddie from behind.

Suzy's thoughts turned to Eli's material and that bizarre and disturbing world of the Far Right. And here was the object of their venom, a group of elderly Jews playing bingo on Chanukah. Simply being true to oneself was an act of defi-ance.

'Bingo!' shouted Izzy again, to universal groaning.

Suzy had a sizeable escort back to the Tube that night – Eli, Monty and Miriam, although it was Miriam who was the first to be dropped off. Suzy took over from her on Monty's left, slip-ping her arm through his, while he gripped the bottle of shampoo that was his evening's takings.

'It was lucky Izzy didn't win the shampoo,' noted Eli. 'He'd be washing his beret with it!'

'When will we dance again?' Monty asked Suzy.

'Will you ask me again?'

'Sure! Why not?'

When they reached the station, Eli gave her a lecture about being careful at night. 'Watch out for crazy people!'

Suzy amusingly thought to herself that she had just spent an evening with them.

'You be careful yourself, old man,' she said.

'Don't you know your Bible?' Eli replied. 'I'm named after Elijah the prophet. He's the only prophet who never dies. He lives for ever . . . until the coming of the Messiah.' Eli shrugged. 'So what can happen?'

Suzy smiled. 'And who am I in the Bible?'

'Shoshana is a flower. A sweet desert rose.'

'Why can't I be a prophet? It's always the men who get the best parts!'

Monty laughed.

24

Despite some initial apprehension, Suzy was beginning to appreciate the joys of being locked away inside the unique world of the darkroom, where the photographic gods were assuaged with special chemicals and the application of that essential life-giving tool – light.

Suzy was familiar with those fanciful notions of photographs 'stealing the souls' of their subjects. If photography was indeed the practice of black arts, then it was surely in the permanent night of the darkroom that this was played out. She was working on the latest batch of JFC film, summoning from the ether her very own manifestations of Gloria and of Eli, of Monty and of Becky. She thought of all those Frankenstein films, with the mad Baron creating his monsters.

Then a dull thud at the door. 'Do you need any help in there?' Clara shouting.

Suzy sneaked into his room minutes before the tutorial.

Terry entered to Eli's Yiddish poetry filling his office, while Suzy presented him with a Chanukah doughnut.

'Are you trying to soften me up?' Terry peered at her, delivering one of his characteristically playful expressions. Suzy had been devastated when she found out he was married, and with a kid.

And she was most definitely trying to soften him up. Suzy had received sufficient intelligence on the savaging of her fellow classmates to have instilled in her the deepest of fears, made all the more terrifying for being on the brink of realization. He had described Salvo's docklands project brief as soap opera, Megan's refugees as weak agitprop, and Barry's fashion models as a 'schoolboy's masturbatory fantasy!' Her only consolation was the excitement she felt over her own concept, which she so hoped was shared.

Terry raised from his drawer Suzy's colourfully bound brief. 'All eight pages of it,' he noted, grievously. 'Thank you for the lesson!'

Suzy watched as he then managed to cover its first page with copious amounts of jam, for which, of course, he gave her the blame. 'Can we turn the sound down a little?'

Suzy switched off the tape recorder. And so Terry began.

How had Suzy brought focus to the project? Eli was her inspiration. The first inklings of an idea came as she had watched him sifting through the extremist material in his home. It blossomed as she reviewed her JFC prints. She was playing over in her mind the literature's gruesome language of hate, and here was the enemy – Gloria and Izzy dancing the two-step. It was such a brilliant contrast! Suzy suddenly realized that she could combine the two for her very project, exposing to ridicule the former, through her exploration of the latter. Inhumanity against humanity. The written language rebutted through a visual one. She was a genius!

'The approach is provocative,' were Terry's first words. 'I like it. A lot.'

Suzy was astounded. Terry asked about the genesis of the idea and she quickly found the words to elaborate, giving Eli his due credit. Terry listened intently, then returned to the brief.

'Your choice of text is going to be important. In a strange way, it's going to have to work lyrically to balance with the photography, you know what I'm saying? I hope this doesn't mean you're going to white supremacist rallies!'

Suzy shook her head. 'Eli has plenty of material.'

'It'll all be in the interplay between the two dimensions of the piece. It's an interesting idea. It's good!'

Terry was keen to know how she was being treated at the JFC, and Suzy reassured him that she had been warmly received. She didn't feel inclined to mention her only nemesis, Lionel. At least he kept his distance.

'I'll go with the collage bit at the beginning, but let's not make this *schmaltzy*, as they might say at the JFC.' It was an idea Suzy had come up with during the school visit, that she would incorporate childhood images of JFC members as an evocative introduction.

He flicked on to another page. 'Do you think the word *ghetto* is fair?'

'I meant it ironically.'

'It doesn't feel like an ironic project to me. You'll want to change that.'

And a next. 'There're too many characters. It's confusing. Remember how few images you've got. You need a small number of key narratives here.'

Terry handed the brief back to her. 'Read to me the Brassai quote.'

Suzy had headed each page with a quote from a renowned photographer. It was the brief's killer touch. '"It is not the sociologists who provide insights but the photographers who are observers at the very centre of our times."'

'OK, I can see you're observing. It just feels to me like you're doing it at a distance. You've got your facts. A dramatic scenario. It's clever. But I'm not finding enough of *you* here!'

It had been going too well.

'How do you *feel* about all this?' Terry was staring at her. 'Are you an outsider looking in, or on the inside *with* these people? And if you keep yourself outside, how are you going to get to the heart of it, the emotional truth here?'

Suzy couldn't disguise the wounded expression now filling her face.

'Look. The brief is fine,' Terry continued. 'It's a good basis. But you've got more work to do. I don't want this to turn into a clever school essay. Give me far more of yourself here!'

Terry began wagging his finger at her. 'I'm pushing you because I think you can do it. Take all this as flattery. And no, you can't have the doughnut back!'

Terry went on to ask Suzy to explain some technical specifics on presentation, which she responded to as best she could, while still grappling with his overall critique.

Terry had a final remark for her as Suzy headed out. 'Being a photographer isn't about being invisible.'

25

Nick was pressing Suzy to join him and his family in Manchester for Christmas.

'I've told you. I don't celebrate Christmas.'

'That's exactly my point. You'll *be able* to celebrate Christmas, and be with me!'

Jo hushed them both as the lecture-hall stage darkened.

The academic term was about to reach its climax with the LNU's Centre for Art and Media Studies Seasonal Review. Notices for it under the dubiously conceived title 'Have 'n 'Art, Guv'ner,' had the corridors of H-Block groaning under the strain for weeks. No one would be allowed to escape. Even the Granary catering ladies had become infected with fevered speculation as to this year's performances. 'Is old Reynolds going to dress up as Lady Di again? Wouldn't want to miss that!' The thought of them attending the show had sent Salvo into deep apprehension. He was orchestrating the sketch that was their class's contribution to the occasion, with the Granary ladies the central target.

There were no classes on the day of the Review. It was anyway one of the last of term. Most students spent that lunchtime in the Union bar fuelling up with festive cheer. Nick had joined teammates for a farewell row on the river. 'Parting must be awfully sad for you all,' Suzy had grinned.

Suzy, Jo, Gareth and Megan had decided to search out new territory down the Mile End Road to evade the student hordes. However, they quickly realized their miscalculation from the glares of the pub locals, and retraced their steps back to the student-friendly perimeter.

Drinks were consumed on a double celebration – end of term and Suzy's birthday.

'Where's Nick taking you tonight?' Jo asked.

'Probably a gym.'

Gareth had heard from Barry about a rave in a barn in Surrey, which he was eagerly promoting as a perfect way for Suzy to party on her birthday.

'I know exactly what you're up to,' declared Jo. 'You want Suzy to come, so Nick will have to come, so Nick will bring his car!'

Megan added another cause for celebration – Jo's haircut. She had shockingly shaved off her magnificent dreadlocks, swearing that it was simply for the holidays – a symbol of how she viewed being returned to her parents – and had nothing to do with her year project on the Hare Krishnas. Terry had been effusive over her brief, in contrast to his treatment of Megan, who had emerged from her tutorial committed, albeit briefly, to leaving the course.

Suzy gave an account of a somewhat mixed reception to her Jewish Friendship Club. 'Terry likes my approach but . . . he thinks I'm invisible!' It prompted Gareth to make a curious observation. 'Jewish people are invisible, right? You can hide your identity if you want. No one would know. I'm always black to the world before I'm anything else.'

Gareth had chosen an Aids hospice. He had befriended a young man called Stewart. 'I'm going to record him dying. He wants me to do it. I've never been with someone who's dying.'

Suzy had. She had witnessed her grandpa fade on a hospital bed, sitting quietly by him, listening to mumblings of Hebrew prayer, thoughts of moustaches made of sweetie wrapping paper, chess games and playful cheating, great fishing expeditions to the Yorkshire Dales. And she recalled one hospital visit towards the end. She had taken her camera, so she could make herself invisible.

The atmosphere in the lecture hall could most kindly be described as boisterous. Most of the students had already mentally departed to their various holiday destinations. Whistles blew. Poppers popped. A number of orange helium balloons were released to dance on the ceiling, offered up as target practice for assorted missiles.

Professor Braithwaite, the Faculty Head, suddenly materialized on stage to a tumult of friendly abuse. As the event's compère, he had the unenviable task of bringing the gathering to a semblance of order, which he did by acting in a forthrightly formal manner, sounding as if he was launching one of Her Majesty's ships. Fortunately, that tone had soon seen its last with the arrival of the first act. A group of third years had devised a mock hypnotist routine. It involved bringing up on stage 'random' students who were then 'hypnotized' into acting out a series of bizarre episodes that included the most comprehensive range of washing machine noises ever assembled.

Suzy couldn't recognize, nor work out the true genders of the 'Jason' and 'Kylie' bold enough to come down to the LNU to perform 'Especially for You', and to announce it 'especially for you . . . appalling students!' as they gazed out consummately gooey-eyed at a delirious audience. Their syrupy rendition ended with an extended snog that lasted for almost as long as the song. Knowing how partial Jo was to *Neighbours*, Suzy touched her arm.

Her own brave classmates had their moment of infamy towards the end of the show – 'Blonde Date'! Jo revealed a whole new self as an ebullient Cilla, cooing over a most dapper Salvo – 'Italian, aaeeh! How about that, ladies and gentlemen!' His multiple choice over the screen – Megan and Nina included – were all bewigged blondes, all delightfully dressed in the same thick tights and stark pink uniforms of the Granary ladies. The noise of the wolf-whistles drowned out much of the rest.

The staff contributions were the slickest, no doubt honed over many years of experience. Terry's arrival as a glittering Cinderella in rags was truly a sight to behold. 'If only I could go to the London New University Centre for Art and Media Studies,' s/he pleaded to Doctor Reynolds, formerly an animation lecturer, now a rather effective Lady Di fairy princess. Professor Braithwaite was Buttons, Mork and Mindy the Ugly Sisters.

Suzy gorged with her camera throughout.

The after-show reception was a crush of noise and bustle. Salvo, as he had feared, became engrossed in deep discussion with one of the more formidable of the Granary women. Suzy resolved not to share his food next term. Barry took to parading in a 'Blonde Date' wig, restoring Jo to her newly trimmed look. Suzy sought out Cinderella.

Terry was surrounded by a gaggle of admirers but she managed to push her way in, careful not to stand on his frock, adding her own congratulations to the swell. Suzy decided that she heartily approved of Terry's revealing his feminine side. 'I can't take the credit. It's all my wife's work.' For the first time Suzy felt they were conversing as equals. He asked about her holiday plans and shared his own – a cottage in Devon and a crackling log fire. Suzy took out her camera.

'Wait!' He held up his hand. 'Whose photo are you taking?'

'Mine,' she announced, anticipating the ploy.

Terry nodded approvingly. 'Now you'll want more of my left.' He tilted his head.

As she took the shot, Suzy heard her name being called.

Blond Barry was approaching, carrying a bouquet of flowers. Suzy assumed this was some humorous tribute to Terry for which she was being recruited. She didn't imagine that Barry had bought her flowers, yet he presented them to her.

'Some old geezer brought these for you. Didn't want to come in.'

'Roses,' Terry noted approvingly.

Suzy located the card, reading its simple 'happy birthday' announcement. She turned towards the exit, but Eli had gone.

PART 2

WINTER

1

Suzy returned to Leeds with bountiful washing, carefully wrapped seasonal presents and, most awkwardly, a bouquet that she saw no point in leaving behind.

She had parted from Nick on the Northern line, their travels north requiring Suzy to exit at Kings Cross while Nick remained for the next stop of Euston. They would be meeting up again soon. Suzy had committed herself to an expedition across the Pennines on Boxing Day, having secured the donation of her mother's car for the purpose – 'as long as it isn't snowing!' In return, Nick promised '*hungover* turkey, and *leftover* family'.

They had embraced and kissed, Suzy making a timely leap through the closing Tube doors. Nick had helped her through the angst of beginning this more adult life, helping her believe that an adult was what she just might be. Suzy felt his absence in the quiet of the train journey home.

Her mother met her at the station. 'Roses! He's really keen on you.'

'They're not from Nick.'

Her mother looked confused.

'They're from Eli. One of the Friendship Club members. For my birthday.'

139

'Roses?'

'It's my name, my Hebrew one – Shoshana. It means a rose.'

Her mother was more confused.

'Your dad rang. Said he's been trying to get hold of you. They'll see you when they get back from holiday.'

Suzy nodded. 'I wonder how they'll cope.'

'You cope! I know, believe me.' Her mother took the roses from her. 'I hope that baby of theirs keeps them up every night!' Her mother laughed, and Suzy joined in.

'Nothing like two bitter old women,' Suzy declared, sliding her arm into her mother's.

'Hey. Where did that *old* come from!'

Her first act of homecoming was to assault the washing machine, creating a relay of washing and drying. Suzy was pleased to confirm that her room was precisely preserved. She sat first at her desk, recalling the agony of A levels, and how seeing a magpie out of her window would bring all her studying to an immediate halt until she spied a lucky second. She sought out her reserve teddy bear collection, and her music tapes, spilling them onto the bed. She searched out her winter boots in the cupboard and slid them on. It was the mess she was making that made her realize what that missing ingredient to her room was, namely herself.

The exchange of presents was saved for after supper. Suzy had a blue sweater for her mother of the same azure tone that defined most of her clothing. It was her mother's second present to Suzy in honour of her recent birthday that proved the most noteworthy – a pair of beautiful antique silver earrings.

'My father gave them to me. They were his mother's. I was always going to give them to you. You're an independent woman now.'

Suzy quickly put them on, then paraded. Momentarily, she recalled Becky's chandeliers, but these were far subtler. Her mother was rewarded with a prolonged hug.

Over that first weekend, Suzy caught up with her old crowd of friends, all engaged in the same pilgrimage home. She had thought that they might have stayed in more regular touch, but each had become so consumed by university life. At the Cherry Tree pub, similarly exotic student tales from Exeter to Edinburgh were swapped. Studies hardly featured. The focus was firmly on the comparative strengths of the social scenes. Lawrence was ecstatic in describing one episode, being tied to a lamp-post in nothing more than his underwear. *They must really love you*, Suzy thought, and almost said.

Those at campus universities presented themselves as having the superior experience, but Suzy felt secure in extolling the virtues of the LNU. A girl called Lucy, also studying in London, was proud to declare that she hadn't visited the East End. Well, Suzy couldn't live in any other part of the city. She was a loyal East End immigrant, just like all the others, just like her grandfather whose earrings she displayed. Suzy was sure he would be pleased.

Her old boyfriend Marcus was at the pub, but they didn't say much. His hair was longer, and he appeared to be growing a beard although he denied it. She noticed him leaning in when she submitted her own stories to the circle. Suzy wasn't going to mention Nick. Why should she? She had left them all behind. That was her growing feeling after the initial frisson of reacquaintance had faded. They all had so much to say, yet so little to each other. They jeered when she took out her camera, but she wanted the moment recorded. She was attending a wake.

Suzy had no intention of exposing herself to anything earthly pre-lunch on Christmas day. The embrace of the soft covers of her old bed represented the rekindling of a romance she had most definitely missed. What she certainly didn't expect was a telephone call at an incredible eight o'clock in the morning. Why would Nick commit such a dastardly deed? Her dressing-gowned mother, similarly bemused and bleary eyed, handed her the phone.

'Merry Christmas, shitface!'

'Shoshana?'

'Eli? Eli!' Suzy tried to shake off her tiredness.

'Have you seen the news?'

'Thank you for the flowers,' she blurted.

'Never mind the flowers. Have you seen the news?' There was a bubbling agitation in his voice that was now distinct.

'What news?'

'Watch the news Shoshana. It's over! They've murdered him!' The last words had the most sobering effect. Her mother placed a steaming cup of coffee by the phone.

'Eli. I don't understand what you're telling me. What murder? Who was killed?'

'In Romania. They've executed that *mamzer*. Ceauşescu, along with that witch of a wife. It's over. communism is finished. All over Eastern Europe, even in the Soviet Union. The bastards are done for!'

The phone went silent, and Suzy listened to Eli's hard breathing.

'I don't know what to say, Eli. You must feel so . . . excited.'

'Excited?' Eli's tone calmed. 'I know what's going to happen. Shoshana, I'm scared. I'm so scared.'

Suzy returned to her room and bed. She eventually found a route back to sleep, waking late morning to the ecstatic sounds of the neighbours' kids. Suzy lay there for a while wondering if there was such a thing as quiet toys for boys.

Her mother raised the phone call over lunch, causing Suzy to scramble to the television set. She managed to catch the latest news report with images of wild jubilation in the streets of Bucharest, the burying of martyrs and, most gruesomely, the display of Ceauşescu's bloodied body crumpled across his wife's. Suzy thought of Terry's stunning pictures from Berlin, and this far darker affair.

'Why do you want to watch that?' Her mother was filling her plate with seconds.

'That's why he called. Eli. He came from there, from Romania.'

'Is he that man who gave you flowers?' Her mother was getting confused again. 'So why does he have to tell you?'

2

Her mother had the endearing habit of naming cars based on registration-plate letters, and Suzy had taken to 'Tiny' from the moment the shiny baby Renault first arrived home. Indeed, they had together endured a multitude of driving lessons interspersed by no less than three agonizing tests.

Her mother waved them off – 'Love you, Sooz!' – coming into the street as Suzy and Tiny sped away. It was her tradition to bid farewell for as long as possible, as if her affection was boundless, although it always made Suzy feel slightly odd, as though she was a soldier going off to the front.

Eli dominated her thoughts on that journey through to Manchester. He was such an unpredictable, almost Jekyl and Hyde character – one minute the expansive joker, the next morosely speculating on the politics of the day. And how had he obtained her Leeds phone number! They were in the phone book, but he didn't have an address. How many Alwoodley Greens would he have harangued that Christmas morning, she wondered.

And why did he call? Suzy tried to imagine the importance of such an event for someone like Eli. What it fully signified, she couldn't really say. It made her wonder if that was what Terry had meant about her lack of engagement. Suzy wasn't immersing herself in this world. And there was Eli so keen to offer himself.

Entering Nick's neighbourhood, Suzy drew just one conclusion. He was rich! Jo was right. Wide tree-lined streets. Grand homes set far from the road aproned by carefully tended gardens. She recognized her destination from Nick's BMW, before her in the manner to which she was most accustomed to seeing it – stationary. It was set perfectly against the bright red brick driveway, looking as pristine as its surroundings. Suzy concluded that the car chose to make so few outings around the East End simply out of disgust.

Nick greeted her with enthusiasm, skipping down the pathway as she parked. She was as keen to see him and they hugged. His parents and younger sister were stationed by the front door like a reception line at a wedding. What were first impressions here? His father made the most immediate, a surprisingly small man with a kind face enhanced by a Mexican-style moustache that hinted at intriguing unconventionality. He embraced her with definite vigour. His mother was harder to assess, a smartly dressed square-shouldered woman who displayed a *let's-wait-and-see* politeness. 'Stealing son' syndrome? Suzy wondered. His ponytailed sister was eager to whisk her away to her bedroom.

Instead, they were soon around a lushly-decorated dining table finishing off the remnants of a previous day's gorging, as Nick had promised. His mother warned that the sausages put to the side were rolled in bacon. Suzy picked one up and munched. She thought this would be an act of reassurance, but his parents looked disappointed, as if Suzy might not be the real thing. Nick was announced as the creator of the amazing pudding, demonstrating his culinary skills in the place of their birth. The dessert arrived with three colourfully wrapped presents all bearing her name. Nick's was a set of lens filters. She had permanently borrowed his own. It was an ideal gift.

Suzy felt uncomfortable having brought only two Christmas gifts herself – one for Nick of course, and a collective one for the family. But she felt even more uncomfortable having them shared publicly. She had no idea how her present to Nick, a selection of stylish underwear, was understood. The withered condition of his current supply had been a long-standing source of tension.

Suzy expected to feel under scrutiny. She tried to decipher exactly how Nick had described her from the questions and comments that emerged through the course of her stay. She did get the sense that they viewed her as a somewhat exotic creature. She was after all from Leeds! She felt most sorry for his sister who was quite unnerved when Suzy revealed that she didn't celebrate Christmas. It was received as if she had announced herself an orphan. Her father talked about once working with a 'Jewish chap'. Suzy wanted to say that if she was to be judged by the actions of another, could she please make the selection!

Sleeping in his bedroom felt odd. Nick had been transported to another room, on another floor. From the stern look of his mother, Suzy sensed he was under strict nightly curfew, probably patrolled. Suzy stopped his attempt at apology. While she was sure the Manchester United team were exceptionally nice men, she didn't feel inclined to make love under their persistent stare. It anyway created a tension between them that ensured sizzling stolen encounters.

Having previously indicated that he was having a quiet visit home, with Suzy's arrival, Nick all of a sudden had a number of events on the go – invitations round to friends, a pub night. Suzy was being paraded for inspection. However, she had brought her camera – she could inspect right back.

Nevertheless, Suzy did find herself tiring of it. There was his friends' constant teasing about photography not being a 'proper' university course, how the East End was 'full of criminals'. It was directed at Nick but inevitably she felt included. He evidently should have gone to York or Durham, like Eve and Howard, where he could have kept up his horse riding. Horse riding! Nick had never mentioned such a thing. It did make Suzy wonder just where she had landed herself. And there was also the way Nick would put his arm around her, in such a proprietorial way, as if to say 'wasn't she lucky'.

Her mother was glad to see Suzy's safe return, although she initially paid more attention to Tiny, giving the car a comforting stroke. Coffee in the kitchen turned into a debrief, with her mother as usual pressing Suzy to divulge far more than she was prepared to reveal.

'So they treated you well?'

'Locked me up in the cellar. That's Manchester folk for you!'

Suzy pleaded with her mother to retrieve the albums of the Liebovitz dynasty from their languish in the attic, from where the Green antecedents had long ago departed in the company of an errant son.

She hadn't waded through the collection of old photographs for some time. They were spread across the dining-room table, and she enjoyed prompting her mother into reminiscence mode. Fortunately, some pictures came supplied with brief commentaries on the back, providing a little insight into casting or context.

Her mother struggled to recall anyone in the family with such a distinguished name as Rupert. The Bernstein sisters were somewhere in Australia, or at least their descendants should be, if indeed they did marry which, legend had it, was the precise purpose of their visit. Uncle Maurice, more accurately a great, great uncle, died in Africa, or maybe it was Malaya.

'Is that the same thing?' her mother asked. 'You really should speak to your cousin Philip. He did the family tree.'

It was such a great expression. Suzy imagined herself as a small leafy twig gazing down at the far sturdier branches of her antecedents below.

'Where did we come from originally?'

'Russia, and Lithuania I think.'

'Any Romanian?'

Her mother shrugged.

Suzy particularly enjoyed reacquainting herself with Grandpa Abe, whose footsteps she had so recently retraced up Chamberlain Crescent. Her mother located his childhood image, five or six years old perhaps, legs dangling off a chair between the stiff uprights of older sisters. Her mother confirmed that it must have been taken in the East End. It was a picture Suzy swiftly claimed. She also 'borrowed' another of him in nascent adulthood, the boy now contained within a suit, moustached in a weak attempt at ageing his appearance. He wasn't so far removed from the person Suzy had grown up with, had loved so much.

'He was handsome.' Suzy declared.

'Don't sound so surprised! Remember when he went into hospital that first time. The way the nurses made such a fuss. He was a terrible flirt. Shameless!'

'Did he speak Yiddish?'

'All that generation did.'

'I never heard him.'

'Why would you?' Her mother picked up her parents' wedding photograph. 'Abraham and Sarah – straight out of the bible. Just look at the pair of them! Have you ever seen such morbid faces?'

Abraham was projecting a macho air, squaring up for the picture, reminding Suzy of a boxer at a weigh-in. Sarah was such a petite woman, standing demurely at least a pace away, sporting a blank expression that could have been taken from any bus-stop queue.

'They don't exactly look like a match made in heaven.'

'Was it?' Suzy asked.

'Probably not. Hard to know. They had so many other things to worry about.'

Her mother was now inspecting a picture of herself in her late teens. 'People didn't get divorced in those days. You stuck it out.'

She was alone in the shot, her head cocked backwards, and she was laughing in a wild, wanton sort of way.

'What a dress! You could wear that now, couldn't you? And will you just look at my face! Can you believe I ever felt like that?'

The New Year slipped into the Green/Liebowitz household in its usual theatrical way. Her mother had acquired the custom from some long-forgotten Spanish holiday of eating a grape for every chime of the midnight bells.

Suzy had gone earlier to a party hosted by an old school friend. She was back at her mother's before midnight. Nick was on the phone as soon as Big Ben chimed its last. He was in a friend's garage for some reason and acutely drunk, slurring his greeting, then telling her a strange story about an elephant that she presumed was the rendition of a joke.

'I love you!' he suddenly screamed at her down the line.

'You're pissed, my man,' Suzy coolly replied.

'Pissed and in love!'

'How was he?' her mother enquired after.

'In love.'

'That's nice. Anyone I know?'

3

Suzy found it hard to refuse. She wasn't *against* Nick coming; it was just that they hadn't discussed it. And now that she had experienced his hospitality, she appeared to be under an obligation to reciprocate. He kept saying how bored he was, as if it was Suzy's fault. But there was her mother to think of, and she was due to provide holiday cover in her father's shop. They finally agreed that he would visit for two nights only.

The highlight of his stay from Suzy's viewpoint was, unexpectedly, the time they spent touring the city. If he hadn't visited, she certainly wouldn't have undertaken the exercise, and would therefore not have discovered that her relationship with the city itself had changed, just like the other fixtures of her now former Leeds life. Suzy could adopt the status of city guest just like Nick and, from this new perspective came a surprising new motivation. She found herself actually enjoying taking Nick to the Armoury, Roundhay Park, Ilkley Moor – the commonplaces of so many outings, locations she would have dreaded just months earlier. When Nick took to baseball cap and camera, Suzy found herself just as inspired.

They even found a photography exhibition at the Spencer Gallery. It proved to be work by a Mexican photographer, the most memorable images being his haunting coverage of the 'Day of the Dead' festival. The occasion involved disinterring the deceased who were taken home by their families. The text explained that the event was held to placate the spirits of the dead, lest they return in their own time! Suzy was appalled and enthralled in equal measure.

The visit highlight for Nick seemed to be her mother's kitchen. Suzy was unnerved by the rapport he quickly established with her, which began with the issuing of an authoritative comment on her butternut squash soup. Each impressively held their own in the conversation on the intricacies of its preparation, the debate spiralling into the realms of crème fraiche and garnishes. A similarly conceived deliberation continued through the two remaining courses.

'Why don't you talk about rowing?' Suzy wickedly suggested.

Yet her mother was uncharacteristically reserved about Nick. She obviously liked him. However, Suzy came from a community where 'nice Jewish boys' were the precribed aspiration for allegedly 'nice Jewish girls'. Suzy had played that role while it was expected of her. In London she was free of every expectation.

Nick's last afternoon was spent in a sunny chilled Leeds city centre, surrounded by the splendid Victoriana of Mitchell Square, enjoying the chutzpah of an outside café table. Suzy explained to Nick that they should get larger portions, recalling Eli's mother's sensible advice on the tactics of table selection.

Suzy had the first go, pointing out the attractive waitress forever fixing herself in the café's full-length mirror, shifting her hair, touching her face. She routinely paused ever so fleetingly just as she finished her adjustments. 'That's the moment!' Suzy declared.

And they considered the merits of the older woman shouting at the car driver, her face pinned in a grimace, arms waving, a wounded dog limping off; the two businessmen striding past, the one following the speech of the other with a fawning gaze that spoke of awe, and hierarchy, and expectation; or the older man, perhaps a grandfather, holding a little girl up to peer through the glass of a hairdressing salon, wanting the child to marvel at the unfolding drama, yet she more interested in the doll she had let fall to the ground.

Suzy knew Nick was disappointed that he hadn't met any of her friends, and she was annoyed with him for not saying so. He was acting as if it had all become suddenly so serious between them, which Suzy suspected was more about his own boredom. That was how she regarded that New Year's phone call, and it was what she read into *his* face that afternoon as they sat in Mitchell square.

'What about them?' Nick identified an approaching couple lost in intimate conversation, arms determinedly entwined, the woman raising her head and laughing, the man following her every gesture.

'I don't believe it,' she said.

'If only you could have come with us!' Charlotte enthused, the whiteness of her teeth accentuated against a freshly ripened tan.

'Were you able to get around much? With the baby?' Suzy still suspected the motives of that particular offer, namely Suzy as stand-in au pair. Beatte was ensconced in her room, no doubt exhausted by her re-enlistment.

'It was fine. Really fine. She's such a good good girl, aren't you, Jen.' Charlotte extended the baby from its perch on her shoulder. 'Such a good good girl.' It was a gesture to demonstrate that she was mastering motherhood perfectly well.

'Don't pay any attention to the mess.' Suzy couldn't detect any. In fact she longed for mess that might make them all more comfortable.

As usual, her father made his own entrance. 'There you are, Sooz!' She hadn't been hiding. Suzy wondered if he could ever break the habit of bringing the routine of office to home – Charlotte still his assistant doing the meeting and greeting, he sweeping in to conduct the main business.

Charlotte's oozing suntan was perfectly matched by his own. He hugged Suzy, and she felt criminally pale against him.

'Have you changed your glasses again?' Suzy was sure he had.

'Don't think so. Have I, honey?' The secretary would know such things.

Her belated birthday card contained a cheque, which he was sure was the present of most use to her. 'What did your mother get you?'

Suzy pulled back her hair and rolled her head.

'They're lovely! See her earrings, Charlie. Trust your mum. How's she doing?'

Suzy paused before answering just to look at him. What struck her was his complete sincerity.

He was soon enquiring about her job, getting Charlotte to sit close to translate as Suzy explained the workings of Fabulous Faces.

'Women do that?' He turned to Charlotte.

'Why not?' Suzy indignantly replied.

'But does that really do it? Do you feel good just having a pretty picture of yourself?'

And yet here they were in a living room filled to bursting with pretty pictures to boost this new couple. Suzy resisted making the observation. Instead, she decided to add to the collection.

And what did she see through her lens? A self-contained pair;

hints of insecurity suggesting a relationship still resolving its dynamic; two people committed to believing in their own happiness.

And what about herself at that moment? What would be an honest self-portrait? Nothing too heavy. Suzy thought about that self-help book her mother had once shown her on families and 'surviving' divorce. She recalled the emotions she was *expected* to feel and ticked them off in her head – anger and jealousy, loneliness and displacement, and what was that other one? Oh yes, betrayal. Apart from those, she was feeling just fine.

4

Suzy was reminding herself about the odd manner in which Salvo chose to occupy a chair, the way he squatted on it as if either chair or himself had a design flaw.

Loud groans announced Terry's arrival.

'And I've missed you all too!'

He immediately launched into announcements, including another warning about equipment abuse. 'Whoever kidnapped the Hasselblad for their holiday snaps has got twenty-four hours to return it, or they're off the course. Do I sound severe?'

He sounded more severe when he held up a postcard depicting a quaint rural scene. Terry had received it from 'one Barry Collins, remember him?' saying he had been delayed returning from Devon because of 'family commitments'. 'Oh dear! Nice of him to write though, don't you think? Let's hope the sheep don't keep him too long.'

Terry had had his hair cut! That was what had been bothering Suzy. The drooping side parting had gone, and he was now pushing his locks backwards, topping his forehead with an unprecedented turret. It made him look younger, but not in a particularly appealing way. Suzy far preferred the former soft Cliff Richard style.

'So! Second term. And most of you are still here. Even you, Salvo. Never mind. It's a new dawn. I was thinking as I chewed on my turkey that I'm being unfair on you guys. I've been too nice. I'm sure you feel the same. We all need to get more serious, including *moi*. This term you're going to become photographers. That's how serious I mean to get. I know some of you are scared. Photographers . . . on a photography course I hear you say! But I chose this course because I couldn't get into a proper art college! I'm only doing this degree because I was told the LNU has the best sports facilities! Hmmm!'

Suzy wanted to laugh, but managed to resist. Jo was less restrained.

Terry spent most time on the year project.

'You've all got my comments on the briefs. Work to them. A good professional always works to the brief. I want to see real commitment from you. Get stuck in! And greater focus! Focus. Focus.'

He outlined the timetable to the end of the academic year, culminating in a show presenting the class's work before 'all sorts of important people'. A new development for that term was the group tutorial. 'We're going to start sharing our work, and receiving feedback.'

Salvo groaned.

'This isn't about slagging off people's work because you don't happen to like it, nor is it about being nice to people in the hope they'll be nice to you. Both approaches are not going to help anyone. This is about learning to give and receive *constructive criticism.*'

Suzy understood only dread.

'I want *lots* of pictures from you now. Be honest with your subject matter, and yourselves. Remember, it's all about *interiors*, not exteriors.'

Terry concluded on a rousing note. 'It's in your hands. Photographers are *gods creating worlds*. Ladies and gentlemen, it's time to work!' He clapped his hands to complete the effect.

'Nice haircut, Cinderella,' was murmured, with a noticeable Italian tinge.

'By the way. Have I wished you all a happy New Year?'

The Granary canteen was offering scintillating new fare. The tuna sandwich had gained a sibling with the introduction of a daring sweetcorn option. The salad selection had been enhanced by something beetroot based that ominously bled from its container pen, and a shredded carrot and cabbage dish was now dressed in a layer of fruits. Salvo was the first to congratulate the ladies for such splendid innovations, no doubt still nervous over the reception to his Christmas review sketch.

Views on Terry's hairstyle were split largely along gender lines – women against, men claiming not to have noticed.

On holiday chronicles, all attention was first on Megan. Her central revelation from her time in the Peak District revolved around her meeting an *older man*.

'You're eighteen. That's not too hard!' Salvo was deeply unimpressed.

'He's divorced,' she continued, with an enthusiasm that suggested a second criterion had been met. She then produced his photograph, which was soon circulating the table.

'He's gorgeous!' declared Nina. 'South American?'

'Did you take this?' The photo was now with Salvo. 'The lighting.' He pulled his face into a frown. 'What speed of film did you use?'

'Give me that!' Megan grabbed the picture from him.

Salvo proved unusually coy about his own seasonal exploits back in Rome. 'I have no photos, sorry my friends. Just blessings from the Pope.' What he confided much later was that he had also been with an older companion, and she wasn't divorced.

Jo's hot news involved lifting her shirt.

'What is it?' asked Nick.

'*It* is a swan.' Jo had acquired a graceful swan tattoo navigating its way across her lower back. 'Legs paddling in my knickers,' she added less than gracefully.

'Isn't it a duck?'

Suzy hit Salvo. 'It's beautiful!'

In the spirit of Terry's announcement, Nina made the first request for constructive feedback, producing a set of pictures from her new year on a Welsh farm 'with friends from fine arts'. 'Friends, or friend?' Jo casually asked. They were winter landscape imagery – a field of shivering cattle looking like lost old men, a river dancing beneath a dagger-shaped crust of ice, brightly adorned cottages adrift in a white-carpeted valley – and all stunning.

'You must show these to Terry,' said Suzy.

With Nick refilling on coffee, and Salvo explaining to Nina how to handle a reluctant sneeze, Jo wanted to hear from Suzy about her time in Leeds and, more especially, Manchester. 'Did he use his car?'

Discussion was postponed to an evening rendezvous back at BC.

'Is everything OK with you two?'

'Why d'you ask?'

5

Things were not OK between Suzy and Nick.

She felt it with their very first encounter back in London, his reserve towards her. Suzy made a special visit to his flat, sitting among the traffic cones being collected by his housemates to listen to his complaints which centred around her alleged coolness towards him in Leeds.

A frank conversation ensued during which their exchange visits were compared and contrasted, with grievances also exchanged. Suzy's case centred on the behaviour of his friends, mother, his presumption over the Leeds visit. It was a moment of crisis that might have ended their relationship except, the more they argued, the more Suzy realized that was not the outcome she wanted, and she hoped Nick felt the same. It was a bleak mid-January. Nick had been at the centre of her student world right from the first days.

Peace was restored over a hot curry, and they sealed the accord by having their picture taken.

However, Suzy was not over her relationship problems.

'Why haven't you been in touch? I've been so worried about you!' were Eli's anxious words when she returned his call.

'Why?'

Men weren't giving her an easy time.

Suzy assured Eli she was most definitely going to the next Friendship Club event. Gloria's latest event proclamation was her only London post. And could Suzy dare miss out on an evening dedicated to opera highlights, delivered by the maestro himself?

What she didn't reveal to Eli was his promotion. Just like the JFC, Suzy was moving him centre stage for the purposes of her project. Not that she was excluding the others. How could she ignore Becky or Monty or Gloria? But there was something so compelling about Eli. What she knew about him, but more especially what she did not. Terry demanded focus, and her focus was on hand.

Eli was waiting for her on the pavement outside his building, smartly dressed in jacket and tie as befitted the evening's theme, clutching a bag that contained his preciously selected opera tapes.

Suzy was restored to interviewee for their walk to the synagogue, being made to provide a full account of her holiday in
Leeds. And, yes, she had brought photographs of her family, as
he and several other JFC members had requested, repeatedly.

'Well, let's see!'

It was odd watching these Green family photos being shuffled
by Eli in the manner of a relative catching up with family. Her
father received only a cursory inspection. Eli spent more time
with Charlotte, most with her mother.

'Just like her daughter,' he concluded, sizing up Suzy to confirm the observation. 'Good faces,' he murmured.

Suzy took that as a compliment, although it was not one she
had heard quite phrased like that. Perhaps it worked better in
Romanian!

He was keen to hear about Nick when his name surfaced in
the holiday reminiscence. Suzy told him about their argument –
to the extent that any of it could be articulated – and subsequent
making up. Eli pressed her for more details, which she deflected
by mentioning her latest reading, '101 Questions on Judaism'.

'Make sure you get all hundred and one answers!'

Of course, Suzy was eager to renew her interrogation of him.
Yet, she was reassured by a certain knowingness in the way he
engaged with her. It was their unspoken agreement. It was what
made her so willing to indulge him. In time, she was going to
learn everything.

'Hello, stranger!' Becky was the first to greet her, with Izzy
quickly behind – 'happy New Year to you!' – wearing a rather

fetching tartan-style beret. 'How was your trip?' enquired Miriam.

The hall was laid out with rows of chairs, and a table on the stage held up two hefty speakers. Eli rapidly decamped to it, mumbling something about acoustics. Gloria was filling last plastic cups. Wolfie was asleep along a radiator, his sticks like crossed swords at his feet.

Suzy's circulation of her family photos caused a flurry of excitement that significantly enlarged the gathering around her.

'What a handsome fellow,' remarked Becky of her father. 'Any *single* men in the family?' she queried with bright-eyed innocence.

'Your mother's far too young,' Miriam insisted. Monty asked Miriam to describe her. 'She's got her daughter's kind face.' Monty nodded. 'She must miss you so much,' added Miriam, ending with the curious remark, 'Parents love their children more than children love their parents.'

'This is your stepmother, Charlotte, isn't it? With her baby Jennifer.' Gloria had a remarkable memory. Suzy wondered if, having reached the status of mailing list regular, there was now a file in some JFC vault detailing all her particulars.

Only Lionel remained stubbornly unimpressed. 'He thinks you're here to spy on us,' whispered Esther gleefully. He seemed to be making a point of situating himself in parts of the room that were farthest from her, which made Suzy feel as though he was circling from a distance. Was Lionel the spy?

Suzy was glad other people were noticing. She had thought about reporting Lionel to Gloria, but then had second thoughts.

It didn't seem right that she be the one sowing discord in the JFC ranks. And Terry himself had given a further warning about the importance of managing relationships. She would manage with them all.

The room was momentarily blasted with percussion. Eli was keen to remind everyone for whom they had assembled. Wolfie jumped from his seat, glasses leaping from his face in what must have been a painful awakening.

Suzy wanted Gloria to make her announcement, but she made Suzy explain it herself from the stage. 'Speak up!' shouted Izzy.

Suzy outlined how 'our project' needed old photographs of members for an introductory piece 'ideally from your teenage years, and please in good condition' to be copied and returned. 'Thank you!' She promptly scuttled off the stage. It was the primary reason why she had brought her own family pictures. This was to be an exchange.

Becky nudged Suzy when she sat down. 'Don't know why you'd want one from me. I haven't changed!'

Eli began the programme like a grumpy headmaster, demanding that his charges quieten before the lesson commence.

'*The Bartered Bride – Prodana Nevesta* – by Bedrich Smetana,' he began, pronouncing the words in a precise manner that immediately established his authority. 'It's the story of two lovers, Marenka and Jenik. Marenka's parents have decided that she shall marry the son of the wealthy Tobias Micha, whom she's never met, the son that is, as arranged by the local marriage broker, Kecal.' Eli was speaking rapidly, as if simply reminding people of a well-known story. 'The son turns out to be the simpleton Vasek. Marenka persuades Vasek to have nothing to do with her, but Kecal gives Jenik 300 crowns if he will finish with—'

Miriam was waving a hand furiously. 'Can you repeat that?'

'Just play the music!' shouted Izzy.

'You have to know the story first.' Esther came to Miriam's support. 'I'm right, aren't I?'

Others joined in the argument on various and no sides, until Eli brought it to a dramatic end by indeed starting the music. He plonked his finger on the tape machine with the panache of a pianist stroking a key, announced by the ascent of a thunderous noise that had Wolfie at his most alert.

'The dance of the comedians!' Eli barked above the sound, now a vigorous melody with violins prominent in the charge. The audience's grumblings swiftly subsided as all ears tuned into the fantastic noise.

Suzy was on her feet for the full excerpt. She captured Eli's imperious visage as he gazed down on the peasants he was inspiring to culture; Izzy with a sublime expression that suggested he was on the way; Miriam looking irredeemably glum, suggesting she had given up. Becky was determined to be taken with a suitably unselfconscious contemplative pose, which Suzy obliged. She even dared to capture Lionel, ever so discreetly, but with enough of him to reveal the full flat effect of his face. If Suzy was a spy, then she might as well not disappoint.

Smetana was followed by Strauss, who in turn made way for Puccini.

'Is a geisha like a prostitute?' Wolfie was getting into the music.

Eli leered back, no doubt regretting he had stirred Wolfie from his slumber.

Why would he agree to marry a prostitute?' Miriam asked.

'Why not?' barked Izzy.

'And you would?' followed Gloria.

With an urgent flourish, Eli pronounced '*Un bel di Vedremo*' – One Fine Day. One of the finest soprano arias in opera.' He turned ceilingward, as if there he might find his truest audience. 'Optimism that her lover will return, yet also hear the hopelessness! It's unbearable.'

'I recognize that!' Becky was excited. 'Isn't it that advert for cheese?'

Eli racked up the volume.

For his final offering, Eli strangely began talking about football. He announced that another Puccini aria had been chosen as the anthem of that summer's World Cup. However, Eli changed the context. He stood to make the dedication: 'To all those dying for freedom in Eastern Europe.'

Soon, *Nessun Dorma* was booming through the sound system, a beautiful plaintive piece of music that swirled and soared around the room. Suzy felt herself grasped by the passion in the performer's voice. Eli remained on his feet, swaying to the emotion, mouthing the words as if he might join in at any second.

As it built towards the crescendo, Izzy got to his feet. He was followed by Wolfie, and Becky. In an instant, everyone was on their feet, even Monty. The Jewish Friendship Club of the East End was standing tall and proud, a veteran army moved by this remarkable music to face down their former oppressors. It had all suddenly become something extraordinary. Suzy couldn't bring herself to take the photograph and break the intensity of the moment. That was also extraordinary.

Eli hummed the tune for much of their walk back to the Tube station, which ensured Suzy had it locked in her brain through-out that night, and the next days.

6

Suzy couldn't fathom how Nick had such energy. He was a deeply unnatural being, she concluded, watching him pull his Manchester United shirt on over a sweater. Suzy hadn't seen seven thirty of a Sunday morning for many a year. Even the cat Margaret was not to be found at such a malevolent hour.

Why was she doing this? This was Suzy's effort to 'make nice' with Nick after their recent spat. She was going to watch men paddle in a boat.

Nick was also playing his part in the restoking of their rela-tionship. The previous evening he had made a special dinner for them between the traffic cones of the living room, culminating in what he described as 'bruléed lime curd cream tartlets'. Suzy could hardly say it, but could most definitely eat it, and prac-tised mouthing the title in preparation for her next conversation with Mother. 'She'll be wanting the recipe.'

They had also foolishly signed up to a late film, which Nick had taken too much to heart. 'Seize the day!' He had now repeated that *Dead Poets Society* mantra several times, and loudly, over the course of breakfast and Suzy was pondering which bit of him she might seize if he repeated it once more.

There was an occurrence on their journey to the river that fed Suzy's fascination with Tube travel etiquette. A plumpish middle-aged man, his leg in plaster, entered the carriage, and no less than *three* people started up conversations with him. The fact of his disability had torn down the usual barriers of discretion. She eagerly pointed this out to Nick, who took it simply as evasion. He was busy delivering Suzy's orientation programme, ensuring she grasped the intricacies of rowing, convinced of his abilities to fire her interest. Once again, Suzy noted that major difference between them, also highlighted in their distinctive approaches to their craft – Nick's inability to master empathy. He reminded her of her father, a thought that filled Suzy with horror. What she was prepared to concede, strewn among the tedious jargon of equipment and technique, was the passion. His most poetic comment came in the summation. 'It's not about strength.' Nick described that 'moment of magic' when each of the eight rowers stroked in absolute harmony, and how the boat would lift and surge through the water. 'It's like the perfect photograph. Everything comes together and just feels so right!' It was precisely that sensation that had convinced him to choose the company of rowers for his project.

'I'm going to start going to synagogue on Saturdays,' Suzy announced. 'Will you come with me?'

'No!'

'Come on! It'll be a laugh.' From Nick's expression, she wasn't even close. 'I'll introduce you to *my* gang.'

Both ascending and descending escalators were empty, which launched their race, with Suzy given the advantage of the former. Even with that, she was still roundly beaten, arriving panting at the stair's top while Nick did a lap of honour round the ticket hall. She was going to hate this day!

LNU was taking on its mortal enemies, Southwark College, in various racing categories. This was Nick's first competition and Suzy's departing words of encouragement were on the merciless wrath of Lady Lena should her good name be tarnished. She thought about giving him a scarf or something, like he was her knight going off to battle.

A small crowd of groupies, or maybe just sad people, had gathered by the riverbank. The Thames was deporting itself in a dignified calm that hinted at the auspicious nature of the day. Nick emerged from the boathouse in Lycra and flip-flops, the boat transported to the river high above heads like a trophy. Suzy took first shots, catching Nick as he stepped onto the wriggling boat, settling himself towards its rear, then again when he waved as they pushed off.

'Good luck!' Suzy shouted, reminding herself of the dutiful girlfriend role. 'I'll wait for you!' Suzy didn't get the sense along the riverbank that many other girlfriends were. Perhaps, the only one that mattered that day was the lady on whose back they were now riding boldly into the river.

The opposition was in such garish green that Suzy couldn't

believe they stood a chance. She had borrowed from Equipment a 200 telephoto lens, and had decided to use the occasion to conduct an exercise in shutter speed permutations, the very topic of a recent confused lecture by Clara. The starting pistol went off just as she located a suitable surveillance post. Her shots were quickly taken and probably a blur, and then both boats disappeared round a bend. It was only then that Suzy appreciated the full absurdity of being a spectator at a boat race.

'Go on, Nick. Seize the day!'

The scene in *Dead Poets Society* which had lingered with Suzy was the one in which the teacher lined up his protégés in front of a school memorial board. He made them examine the photographs of the various sporting teams, the strong and arrogant faces of hallowed youth of yesteryear. Where are they now? he had asked. Pushing up daisies! What would it mean, she wondered, to achieve a perfect photograph? That had to be her dream. Would she even recognize one when she saw it?

Suzy captured riverside pubs being dusted down for the day ahead, the meanderings of early morning strollers, river craft of various types, resolute joggers, intriguing fellow spectators, like the leathered-up bikers picnicking with flasks and sandwiches. Suzy even took a flotilla of river swans, which she thought she might compare with Jo's tattoo. She was still undecided over her own. It would have to be something discreet. Jo was so much braver than she was!

And then Nick's boat finally veered into view. The race had two legs, which meant that, having been let down by the start,

Suzy could redress the situation with the drama of a finish. Except there wasn't one. Nick's boat was cruising many yards ahead of its green-smudged adversary by the time Suzy captured it crossing the line.

The obligatory rituals of celebration were her most entertaining images. The team collectively tossed the cox into the river. She might have felt sorry for him if it wasn't for the fact that he was the weird Moby character from the Christmas party.

Nick was jubilant. 'We were good, man, really good. Did you see us!' Suzy hadn't much. 'It was fantastic.' He kissed her, firmly, as if his zeal might yet prove infectious. 'Seize the Day!' It was Nick at his most boyish that she found so infuriating, and so irresistible. It made her wonder if there was another dimension to their relationship. Suzy had grown up an only child, bereft of siblings. Her complaint to her parents on the subject became her childhood's running joke. Nick was a boyfriend, but was he also that longed-for brother?

Whatever might happen to them in the future, she would enjoy this time. Seize the day!

Nick made sure Suzy, and as many of the class as he could cajole, attended that Wednesday's Sports Night. Everyone cheered as he and his comrades made their triumphant stage entrance dressed in togas. They had beaten the despised Southwark College. In kneeling before Lady Lena, they received her blessing. 'Be proud, but show humility, you wretches!' Each was then slapped across the face by what appeared to be a fish before being sent off in procession to the bar, led by a rhythmically challenged trumpeter.

7

'Mr Cohen. I have some news for you, his solicitor told him. Your wife has a picture that's worth a million pounds. A million pounds! Mr Cohen was shocked. No! I never realized she owned such a picture. I knew she liked to go to galleries once in a while, but this! It's amazing. The solicitor continued – it's a picture of you with your secretary!'

Eli let out a great guffaw at his joke's conclusion. Suzy was mainly concerned about his scissors' positioning at the moment of punchline, watching more of her glorious curls fall to the ground. Eli's radio introduced the next piece of easy listening.

'It mustn't be too short!'

He began humming. 'Relax, Shoshana. You're going to look like a real lady.'

It didn't sound like the sort of aspiration she had in mind. Suzy had mentioned in passing that she needed a haircut, and Eli had insisted on demonstrating his trade. 'Part of your research, no?' And he had after all offered a special free student rate. So here she was, squeezed into Eli's tiny bathroom, watching the subject of her project at work in the mirror, being soothed by melodic crooning. It was an impressive scene, yet Suzy was denied the opportunity of capturing it, having placed herself at its centre.

'Why do you keep calling me Shoshana? I've been perfectly happy with Suzy.'

'It's good to have many names. The more the better. It

confuses the demons. They might be coming for Suzy, and instead find Shoshana.'

She was suitably baffled.

'Anyway, you've got Shoshana hair.' Eli said.

Suzy didn't have to be reminded of that. Brown and curly was de rigueur among her Jewish friends. She had often been taken for Italian, or Spanish. Such hair could be tied up, or plaited, but you could never escape it.

The radio turned to news, with the lead story being speculation on growing revolt inside the Conservative Party.

'Margaret Thatcher made this country great again, and see how they're treating her. Her own ministers. It's a disgrace!'

Suzy thought about Megan's somewhat contrary view on the subject.

'The way she stood up to the Soviets. What's happening in Eastern Europe is because of that. You have to be strong with them!'

Suzy could imagine Eli as a strong man in his younger days. His physique suggested that potential.

'Thatcher was really popular,' said Suzy. 'When I was in Prague, I saw posters of her.'

And Eli could even provide authentic hairdressing salon banter – discussing world affairs and Jewish hair to Terry Wogan.

'Does Nick like your hair in any special way?'

Suzy shrugged. 'I don't know.'

'Romance is good, no!'

Eli was such a vital character, defying all the stereotypes of the elderly. Suzy had been startled when he opened his door to her, dressed in a somewhat trendy, blue open-neck sports shirt, making her wonder whether his body clock was magically working in reverse. It was the very vivacity of the JFC to which she was drawn, that she was committed to celebrating.

Eli held up a hand mirror, setting it at various angles to expose the full panorama of his efforts.

'Not bad for a gentleman barber.'

It wasn't bad at all. He had clipped back her curls giving her a far neater appearance, while keeping her hair vaguely shoulder-length as she had ordered. 'I'm a real lady,' she confirmed.

He stepped from the bathroom, returning seconds later with a rose, which he fixed in her hair with a flourish.

'*Bellisimo*,' he declared, stepping back to delight in his creation. 'A very good face, Shoshana.'

Suzy felt very good. It was a glorious finale. She grinned wildly.

With no charge made, Suzy nevertheless had a reward to give. From her bag, she presented Eli with two photographs, both taken from their East End walk – one of the two of them embracing by a stall in Eastchapel market, the other taken by Eli of Suzy alone – and she kissed his cheek.

'It's a pity they're now out of date,' she added, admiring her newly shorn look.

Soon the camera was once again being wielded, Suzy catching Eli tidying a row of elegantly shaped scissors, sweeping the bathroom floor of freshly mown locks.

'I'm going to keep these as a souvenir,' he said. 'You'll be a famous photographer one day. I could be rich!'

And she caught his wide generous expression, lifting his face, filling his bathroom.

'And you'll be a famous opera singer!'

'Too late for that.' His face ever so slightly tightened.

Oddly, Eli dismissed her request for a picture of him from his youth, as she had requested of all the Club members, proposing simply that he didn't have any. 'The others will give you. Plenty.'

Suzy was disappointed, but didn't pursue it. He compensated by readily handing over to her the bulging folder that contained his full collection of Far Right material. 'Take it all. I'm glad to get rid of it.' She explained how she was planning to integrate the literature into the project and Eli beamed.

Having vacated the salubrious surroundings of the bathroom, Eli returned to bowing before his precious record collection, engrossed in the careful process of selection.

'For a day like today, I think we should hear from the Barber of Seville!'

Suzy was delighted that she recognized the song, doubly so because she was certain it had not been gleaned from any television commercial.

'An opera with a happy ending,' he announced. 'Unusual.' He began to sway, giving Suzy another image for the burgeoning collection. She shifted him to the swirling music-themed picture above his mantelpiece – 'I don't know what you're going to do with all these photographs.' 'Ssssh!' – then on to the bookshelves for a next.

'Pick out a book.' Eli pondered his selection. 'Any one.'

'For you, Shoshana, poetry!'

'And try not to pose!' Suzy positioned the book in his hand. If only she could get him to stop puffing himself up, distract him in some way. 'What do you like most about the Club?'

'It's a good place to wait to die, no?' he replied casually.

Suzy lowered the camera. 'Why do you say that?'

'Because it's true. The Club is for people who don't live their own lives any more. There's nothing terrible in that. It's what happens to everyone.'

Yet Eli himself contradicted that very observation.

'You are here to give us our memorial. It's good. Everyone loves you!'

'Except Lionel,' Suzy corrected.

Eli was surprised.

'He thinks I'm a spy.'

'Well, he's a bloody fool!' Eli's face flashed red, yet his previous expression was quickly rescued by a turn in the music.

'Ah!' Eli saluted his music system. 'This is *una voce poco fa* – a little voice within my heart. Very famous.' He began to hum, then soon engaged the song, gently at first, allowing his voice to warm, slowly building its force as he tracked the swell of the sound.

Suzy was enthralled, and it occurred to her how irrelevant it was that she couldn't understand the language. The emotion *was* the language. It was something she had identified in the Yiddish conversation class. And it was precisely how Terry understood the language of photography.

Emotion was creativity – creativity was emotion! The insight exploded inside her.

8

Terry was in the foulest of moods, caused or aggravated by a dire cold about which he was in obvious denial. Otherwise, why would he have still come in?

He began the session with a recap on the notion of constructive criticism.

'Go home!' suggested Megan, doing what she did best, saying what everyone else was thinking while taking the consequences alone.

'In your opinion,' Terry replied.

He started with Megan's work. Her somewhat arty black and white mood piece of three young women staring out blankly yet with a hint of defiance, was passed around then stuck up on the whiteboard.

'First of all, forget about what you know about Megan's project. Concentrate on what you *see*.'

Megan herself was the first to stick up her hand, much to Terry's irritation.

'Megan, you'll get your chance. No one's said anything yet!'

'I just want to explain it was taken outside the Refugee Centre, where the three were protesting about local . . .'

'Megan!' Suzy had never seen Terry lose his temper before and she dreaded the thought that this first occasion would be in the context of constructive criticism. 'Let's get this straight. In here, we let our pictures do our talking. Now come on. Somebody!'

Suzy was anyway struggling to concentrate on the task. She

had spent the previous afternoon going into early evening on the conveyor belt that was Fabulous Faces, photographing one after another of the fabulous, and not so fabulous. She was finding it hard to readjust her perspective away from a plethora of rouged lips and dark smoky eyes.

'Salvo! Where are you when I need you?' Terry was obviously desperate.

Salvo promptly raised his chest. 'I see hope.'

'Hope?'

'Yeah. The way the women are staring, *above* the camera. The faces convey optimism. Quiet! Young faces. They're looking up, life is looking up. And the way that one leans forward – confidence.'

'Does anyone else see hope?' Terry sneezed and bless yous followed.

Brian put up a hand in solidarity.

'Other comments!' He scanned the room. 'So far we have *hope*. Anyone for *faith* or *charity*?'

Terry tried to stimulate discussion by focusing on the set-up of the shot – the use of light to create an 'ambiguous atmosphere'; the way the strong vertical lines worked to suggest imprisoning, the dynamic between each character – but he ended up providing most of the answers along with the questions.

The group did start to warm with Jo and the Hare Krishnas, an energetic colour shot taken during a religious service. However, Barry described the overall tone as aggressive which, given the subject matter, had Jo baring her teeth. He then compounded his crime by saying that the image lacked a centre, which he failed to justify, certainly as far as Jo was concerned, who pursued him relentlessly for an answer, or an apology, through lunch and beyond.

At least Jo was heartened by Terry's response to Barry's bland gaggle of models, caught in the 'agony of getting dressed'. 'If a portrait looks like a portrait, then it's failed.'

Nick introduced the class to the world of rowing, showing a close-up of an exhausted face peering in from the edge of the frame.

'It's scary,' said Nina.

'Does that surprise you, Nick?' Terry asked. Nick shrugged.

'If it's what you wanted to achieve, you've succeeded. If it's not, you've failed.'

Terry went on to describe the shot as 'too staged', which infuriated Nick, before sneezing again. Suzy noticed how the number of sympathetic 'bless yous' had rapidly declined.

Gareth's Aids Hospice was the most moving. His subject Stewart was holding a guitar. The only indication of his condition was the fact that he was in a wheelchair, which in itself conveyed a disturbing sense of foreboding. Megan was agitated by the image, asking whether it was right to use such pictures, even with permission. 'Isn't this exploitation?'

'What about your refugees?' said Jo.

'That's different. I want to help them!'

A melee ensued which Terry steered into a debate on society taboos, and the issue of parameters. He used war photography as the supreme example – 'The observer is never just the observer.'

It was Suzy's fate to follow. She couldn't think how people

would respond to her image of Eli-cum-Pavarotti. It now seemed so caricaturish against what she perceived to be the far more significant works of her peers. Yet she also stood by it. She had divested Eli of his body, and the bleached-out background ensured all attention was on the face, and the sense of performance that animated it. Eli was staring directly at the camera, inviting the viewer in, his stretched face conveying a powerful sense of energy. She picked on this depiction because she could hear him loudest in it.

'Wow! This is bold, very bold,' said Jo. 'But is he laughing or bawling his eyes out?' Suzy sank.

'It's scary,' said Nina, repeating herself from before.

'I don't understand the image,' complained Salvo. 'I see this man, a big man, with a strong expression, yes, but there's nothing to explain what's happening. No clues. I'm confused. For me!' He raised his hand in apology. 'Suzy. Sorry.'

'Why apologize?' Terry said. 'Maybe Suzy *wants* you to be confused. Confusion can be useful. So what's going on in this shot? In what way does the shot work?'

That last sentiment gave Suzy hope. No one appeared to want to contradict it.

'There's an *implied* narrative here,' Terry went on. 'And that's what pulls you in. It's a performance, but we can't go beyond that. Why is he caught in this fantastic pose? It's an iconic image. Don't you want to know? I'm dying to know!'

Suzy allowed herself to lean back in her chair.

Terry concluded on a busy fish-gutting scene of Nina's. 'Look how much information we're being given here.'

179

Iconic image! Suzy loved Terry, even at his worst.

'It's disgusting,' announced Jo, unable to contain herself. Nina had chosen Billingsgate fish market as her community, creating an instant strain in her relationship with vegetarian-turning-vegan Jo.

The Granary became refuge for many a bruised soul.

9

'How do you spell the name?'

'L-I-E-B-O-V-I-T-Z' Suzy enunciated carefully, while nevertheless failing to budge Gloria's conclusively inconclusive look.

'Maybe they changed their name,' Gloria suggested. 'So many people did. Binicowski became Bennett, Gradowicz became Gradon. Before long, it was hard to meet any Jews!'

The remark made Suzy wonder about her own surname. It surely didn't begin life as Green.

Gloria was trying to be encouraging, although her concentration was far more on finishing table preparations. It was now laid out magnificently, glasses and cutlery aligned with military precision on a crisp white tablecloth. At its centre were two curving challahs, the knotted loaves that Jewish tradition required as part of the Friday evening ritual that inaugurated the Sabbath. Suzy considered the chairs beyond the three rewarded with table settings and wondered who might have constituted brisker custom of earlier times.

'This is my grandfather.' Suzy presented Gloria with the

photograph she had inveigled from her mother, the one of him in celebrated childhood.

'My dear. How old do you think I am?'

And quickly the other in early manhood.

'Sorry. Can't help you. Show them to Becky when she gets here. She's older than me. But don't you *dare* tell her I told you that!'

Suzy also fashioned new photographs – Gloria fussing in her kitchen; standing proudly matriarchal by a sideboard parade of family photographs; kissing Cary, her much adored pet poodle; delicately stretching out her arms to mirror the pose of the ballerina image behind, the living room's most distinguished painting. 'My late husband bought it in an auction,' she hurriedly said as if he might enquire later whether his effort had received due recognition.

The Gloria of her apartment was an amended version of the original. The same basic characteristics were there, but their order reversed. To the fore was a certain gentility, a marked gracefulness in contrast to the assertive Club organizer. This was also conveyed through costume, her plain yet elegantly conceived dress gathered neatly at the waist only made its appearance on the Sabbath. Gregariousness was fortunately the hinge in both personas.

Photographic possibility doubled with the arrival of Becky, announced in colour as well as sound. Her heavy winter coat in a dazzling shade of red commanded the doorway.

'No. She's not invited a student!' Becky teased.

Suzy could tease back. She photographed Becky all the way

181

through her taking off her coat, despite Becky's irritation, and through sorting herself in front of the mirror, to even more irritation. 'Will-you-please-stop-that-young-woman!' Suzy did at the very point Becky finally felt prepared to indulge her.

'I wanted natural shots.' Suzy explained.

'I don't *do* natural,' replied Becky firmly. 'I haven't done natural in years!'

Suzy anyway had to move fast because she was running out of time.

'You're not photographing in front of the candles,' Gloria had definitively ruled. '*Es Pust Nisht*. It's not done. That's another Yiddish expression for you. I'm giving up my smoking.' She tapped her chest. '*That's* commitment!'

Suzy's final image involved engineering these two formidable ladies into an embrace. She was reminded of Terry's observations on the special dynamic introduced in placing one subject next to another. Gloria was the taller, Becky the bigger. Gloria had placed one arm around the back of Becky, while Becky herself had deployed both arms in a circular sweep, one hand peeking from Gloria's shoulder, the other assertively across her front. Yet it was Gloria who was looking at Becky, an affectionate kindly expression, while her companion gazed assertively camera-ward, far more concerned with her public.

There were three sets of Sabbath candlesticks primed on a side table. Gloria went first, setting candles ablaze on the most ornate, covering her eyes to recite the blessing. Becky followed on the second, less distinguished set.

Gloria didn't actually ask Suzy to light the third, but the expectation was obvious. Suzy was nervous that she might stumble over the words, not having conducted the ritual herself. Yet it was something she had once been taught in Sunday school, something she had watched her mother routinely execute on those Friday nights that Grandpa visited. As she stood by Gloria and Becky, she suddenly felt it was something she wanted to do. Suzy struck the match and brought her assigned candles to flame, raising her palms to her face and reciting the blessing with an unexpected thrilling fluency – '. . . *asher kidishanu bimitz'votav, vitzivanu, lehadlik ner shel shabbat*' – blessed art thou, God of the universe, whose commandments have sanctified us, and who has commanded us to kindle the Sabbath light.

'*Gut shabbes*!' announced Gloria in best Yiddish intonation. Having ushered in the Sabbath, these three East End daughters of Israel now hugged. Suzy thought of that song, the one Jo had forced her, Nina and Megan to dance to on Sports Night. 'The sisters are doing it for themselves!' momentarily blasted through her brain.

The inevitable chicken soup arrived with a flourish. Suzy was suitably complimentary. Gloria declared hers a secret recipe although Becky outrageously proposed she had supplied it when Gloria returned to the kitchen.

To Suzy's delight, Becky had brought a photograph from her youth, one to which she was especially attached. Becky was in some sort of guide's uniform, topped by a military-style cap. 'Take good care of me.' Gloria had hers ready in a sideboard drawer, dressed stiffly as a flower girl from a long-ago wedding. Gloria aligned the two pictures in her hands, smiling in a satisfied sort of way, which immediately caused Becky to conduct her own comparison.

Suzy brought out her grandfather's pictures, this time for Becky's perusal, but the result was the same. 'Sorry, can't help you. Handsome man,' Becky remarked. Suzy was sure she had told her he was dead!

'It was the Blitz that brought down the old East End. Terrible, terrible times,' said Becky. Suzy had been relating her journey to her grandfather's childhood home. Becky began to share her experiences of the war; husband in service in the Merchant Marines – 'twice I thought he was a goner'; living through the German bombing – 'don't know how I got through it. Wouldn't now!'; life in the tunnels of the Underground – 'hot soup never tasted so good!'

She talked about all the people relocated to the country who, after the war, had no homes to return to.

'They didn't want to come back.' interrupted Gloria. 'They wanted better lives for themselves. Everyone did. And what's wrong with that?' The main course was continuing the chicken theme. 'As you may have gathered, I don't go in for all this nostalgia nonsense. People should live where they're happiest. As it so happens, Gerald and I were happiest here.'

Dessert brought the Friendship Club to conversational prominence.

'It's like one big family,' Gloria explained. 'You've seen it for yourself. We have our arguments, just like families. But no one's allowed to fall out for long. We're too small for that. Everyone counts. Even you now!' she added.

'We're getting smaller,' said Becky. 'It's really sad. We lost Ralph last year. He ran the bridge club. Such a tragedy.'

'How did he die?' Suzy cautiously asked.

'Die?' Becky stared at her. 'His kids got him into that sheltered housing in Stanmore. It's got a sauna!' It was the very place that Gloria's son was lining up for her. 'He'd have to drag me there,' she still insisted.

Suzy found a way to introduce Eli's name, reminiscing on the 'incredible' opera evening.

'Did you look at him? He's absolutely mad!' declared Becky. 'He used to get me to come round to his place. I was nervous about it, but we'd just sit and listen to his records. And him singing along! I was his audience. I pity the neighbours, I really do.'

The poodle Cary sauntered into the room with all the bearing of a prince. Gloria stood to attend to him as if he indeed was.

'He came from Romania,' Suzy said, feeding her theme.

'That's right,' said Becky. 'A refugee. From the war. But don't expect him to talk about it.'

'Why not?'

'Because of what he went through!' She pulled a face as if surprised to have to state the obvious. 'It's the same with all of them. Eli wasn't in the camps. He says where he ended up was worse than that. You know he thinks there are anti-Semites round every corner.'

'Did he have a family?'

'He had a wife.' Becky shifted in her seat while keeping her concentration on Suzy. 'She killed herself. Terrible! Just terrible. Eli almost joined her. He told me that. It was the only way to escape. Those times! And us here in the East End with the bombing.'

'What was her name?'

Becky's face furrowed quizzically. She turned to Gloria, still engrossed in the dog.

'It was something . . . unusual.'

She refocused on Suzy. 'He did tell me. What was it?' She paused. 'Rosabella. That's it! Quite a name. Rosa-bella.' She let its sound roll in her mouth. 'Beautiful rose.'

10

'I have never . . . I have never . . . I have never . . . peed in the street,' Nick announced.

Gareth and Barry immediately stood up from their chairs, followed by Nina, allowing a relieved Nick to resume his.

'What's that?' complained Salvo, feeling Nick's confession hardly worthy of the name.

'You Nina!' Suzy was trying to convey mock disgust. Nina shrugged as she joined the other sinners in gulping down the required measure of alcohol.

'Come on. A full three fingers!' Salvo was scrutinizing Barry's glass knowing how close it was to empty, as was his own, with the penalty of a next round of drinks beckoning.

'You're up, Salvo.' Gareth pushed him to his feet.

'I have never . . . I have never . . . I have never slept with my girlfriend's mother.'

'You didn't!' gasped Megan.

'Come on, you guys. Own up someone!' Salvo was swinging all around him, his smile wilting. No one had moved, except for Suzy, whose giggling had her close to the floor.

Suitably resigned, Salvo picked up his pint, carefully monitored by Barry, and was soon heading to the bar.

'I don't believe him,' was Megan's minority view. Barry suggested she ask him about his New Year. Salvo returned with drinks and toasts – the first to his girlfriend, the second to his girlfriend's mother, the third to them both! Megan scowled.

'Are you having a go?' Nick asked, with all eyes turning to Eli.

'I'm not letting him!' Suzy waved her finger at Eli, whom she suspected would be only too delighted to participate. 'You're here for research purposes only.'

Eli grinned. 'What could I have to confess to? I'm too old to remember!'

Eli was turning into a bit of a star. When he had first suggested visiting the university, Suzy was dumbfounded. It was a complete reversal of roles, and it was precisely that realization that compelled her to oblige him. If she could intrude on his world, then why couldn't he experience hers? Nick found it amusing. In fact, they all did, and so now did Suzy. She was at her most self-conscious on entering the bar with Eli. His clothing reflected his best attempt at carrying off a vaguely

187

setting-appropriate disguise, while the problem of the frame on which these hung remained. Yet no one paid them particular attention. Eli was, as odd as it sounded, fitting into Sports Night perfectly.

Indeed, he was already a personality to her classmates, visually at least, through his dissection at the first group tutorial.

'Suzy took a magnificent picture of you, Ee-li' said Salvo, mispronouncing his name yet again, making him sound like a mythic presence. She didn't recall that being Salvo's feedback at the time. Suzy just had to follow that up by mentioning Terry's 'iconic' comment on the piece, and of course Eli demanded to see it. Suzy also talked of her JFC tapes, surely Eli's very first recorded performances. 'Might be very valuable one day. Maybe even more valuable than my locks of hair!'

It was Jo who was most taken by Eli's presence. Whenever she was able to sneak from the bar, she plonked herself by his side, chatting spiritedly as if he was a local celebrity. It reminded Suzy of the strange bubble that students occupied – in the East End, yet far removed from it. She wondered how many of their class had actually made the acquaintance of local people. It made her proud of her own breakthrough. Eli *was* an East End celebrity, and he was with her!

Against the raucousness of a student bar, Suzy couldn't help returning in her mind to Becky's revelation of his wife's suicide, at a time and in a world that Suzy couldn't even begin to imagine. Rosabella! When Becky announced it, the coincidence of the rose association did freak her out, enough for her to mention it to Nick that same evening. Rosabella was such a colourful name. It sounded straight out of one of Eli's operas; so fitting to this larger-than-life character that continually confounded Suzy, now chatting and swilling beer with her classmates. Just what had Eli endured?

'Dead ants!' Suzy was tiring of Jo's one routine and refused to join her wriggle on the floor. Indeed, they collectively decided to punish her with a 'ginning', Salvo drumming the table while a gleeful Nick administered the sentence.

It suddenly occurred to Suzy that she had a way of demonstrating to Eli that students did possess a serious side. She asked Megan, now a leading light in the student newspaper, to repeat an earlier story regarding the local elections. The Student Union had decided to ban 'racists and fascists' from leafleting on campus. It was a story that was bound to appeal to him, and Eli moved next to Megan for some minutes.

However, Suzy's scheme dramatically unravelled as Megan was subsequently required to pull her underwear over her head in the cause of *truth or dare*.

Eli's own *truth or dare* was an easy one for Suzy. It was Salvo who extended it by pointing to the stage. He clearly didn't know Eli! He had mounted it long before Salvo had negotiated the microphone. Eli proceeded to belt out an incredible *Nessun Dorma* in his velvety baritone, shocking an entire room of wild students into silence. Suzy even noticed Lady Lena peeking from behind stage curtains. The applause that followed the climactic conclusion was deafening. The whole table stood in stunned tribute on his return. Salvo declared 'Ee-li' an Italian brother, and hugged him. Jo offered to manage his career and began

189

discussing a South American tour with Nina. Eli had sealed his iconic status.

For her turn, Suzy had been given what she considered an easy choice. Eli grinned as she delivered her peck – 'on the lips,' as Jo demanded – thereby avoiding the issue of the *truth* of Nick and faking orgasms.

'This is bad, extremely bad, Nick, for two reasons.' Salvo was nodding his head gravely. 'She didn't want to tell us, which means she's faking it *all* the time. *And* she wanted to snog another man, right in front of you! Man, give up this rowing shit!'

'Hear! Hear!' Suzy roundly agreed.

11

Suzy was describing Valentine's night.

'Nick took the car!' gasped Jo.

Suzy showed off her bracelet present. 'Isn't he a real sweetie.'

'And what did you give him?' Megan asked.

'A plastic boat. It's useful!' she protested against their laughter.

Megan proceeded to tell Suzy about her mother, a native of Portsmouth, and her dire warnings about sailormen.

'Nick's a toff,' declared Jo. 'Does everything to hide it – his designer ripped jeans – which means he's a huge toff. It's not fair! I'm the one who needs a rich boyfriend.'

Jo's dad was unemployed, and she feared her finances wouldn't last her to the end of the year, even with the bar work.

Hence her following up an advert for students prepared to offer themselves for medical experiments.

'Is that safe?' asked Megan.

'I'll probably be a greenish kangaroo by the end of it, but a wealthy one.'

'Get a move on!' Terry shouted from the front of the class as it snaked its way up the H-Block stairs.

The Department of Fine Arts lived on the rarely visited top floor. Its students were nicknamed 'floaters' for the way they conducted themselves, so self-consciously arty in manner and dress as to have completely alienated their Faculty partners. Nina was the only one in danger of *going over*, occasionally caught in their section of the Granary, her offence excused, just, by her foreignness. Her affair with one of the Arts lecturers remained an utmost secret, deliciously shared with every female member of the class.

Terry gathered his charges outside the life drawing class.

'They're on their lunch break, which is why we're here. We've been given special permission to make this visit. I-don't-want-you-to-touch-anything, got me? And I don't want you to talk until I say so. Just wander around, and breathe in!'

The room, with its high vaulted ceiling, was more like a small hall. Light was streaming in from large windows to the side and above, combining to create a haze effect. The floor and bare walls shared the same tones of muted white. Close to the front was a small rectangular podium no higher than knee height, across which was draped a luxurious purple cloth, made all the more striking in the stark environment. Surrounding it in a vague semicircle several layers deep were canvas-mounted easels, each assigned a palette tray of richly varied colour.

Suzy felt herself almost gasp as she entered. It was like a scene from some archetypal past that demanded to be viewed in sepia. Where were the great Parisien *artistes* with their berets and moustaches to complete the stage set?

She approached the closest easel, admiring first the exuberant clumps of cobalt, emerald and lemon pigments, the swirl of mixes across the palette. The canvass itself had been moderately worked on. Suzy followed the flow of brushwork that was summoning forth the figure of a young woman, completely naked, lying leisurely on her side. The most intricate work was around the face, which portrayed a serene, distracted attitude.

Suzy turned to a next canvass and was introduced to another incarnation of the same woman, except it wasn't. The limbs seemed longer, or maybe just more provocatively poised. What had been a predominance of blues and greens were now crimsons and browns. There was an altogether greater sensuality to the work, the face more directly engaged in its viewer. The woman followed Suzy to the next canvas, and the next – in each the same, in each so different.

'So what are we seeing here?' Terry finally asked, breaking the spell.

'Not enough,' announced Salvo, looking wistfully at the podium.

'Thank you, Salvo, for relentlessly promoting Latin stereotypes.' Terry scanned for other contributions.

'Different ways of interpreting the same image,' Suzy offered up.

'OK. Let's take a moment to remember that. What is before the artist is *objective*, what they put on the canvas is *subjective*. Recording is an act of translation, of metamorphosis. That's a good word for you Nina. Get Barry to explain it! And the artist, the artist alone, is responsible for what he or she chooses to see. It's a message you should have loud and clear by now. Here it is, perfectly illustrated for us.'

Terry put his arms along the tops of adjoining easels like he was embracing old friends. 'What else do you think I want to show you here?'

'That this *isn't* what we photographers are about,' proposed Barry.

'Why not?' asked Megan, affronted by the remark. 'We're just as good as them!'

'But we're not artists,' continued Barry.

Terry interrupted. 'If this is an "is photography art?" discussion, I'm not going to let you have it because we'll all get bored to death.' Terry lowered his arms. 'I brought you here to point up something else. About process!'

He turned to face one of the emerging images on a canvass. 'These are artists caught in the very act of creation. These students are spending hours – weeks! – agonizing over every detail: colour, shade, tone and texture. I'm showing you this because I want you to respect what *we* photographers do.' Terry scrutinized the class. 'What would we have done if we were here on a shoot? We've got a naked woman on a bed. This is your kind of thing, Barry, isn't it?' Someone sniggered. It wasn't Barry. 'We'd fiddle for a while with the lighting. Get her posed. Take some photographs. And leave. Done and dusted in a few hours.' He was now in his familiar pacing routine. 'You know what I feel? It's outrageous! What we photographers do. Don't you feel that when you come to a place like this?'

Terry secured his few nodding heads.

'We could get depressed about it. But what I want to propose is that we are actually doing *the very same thing* and, hear this carefully, taking the *very same care and attention* as these artists here. The medium is different, and that just gives us a different approach. But colour, and shade, and tone, and texture. Come on! This is our language! There's nothing flippant about what we do.'

In the Granary for the rest of that week, *spot the life class model* became a favoured male pastime.

12

It was about to be Suzy's third visit, once again dressed up pre-posterously smartly for far too early on a Saturday morning, leaving her boyfriend's bed for *shul* on *shabbes*!

For some reason, Nick was beginning to be funny about it all, with some commentary about 'your people', suggesting she was taking her commitment to the project to unnecessary lengths. Her defence was Terry's exhortations that were now being heard with every class.

'Terry's a showman!'

'He also marks our work,' she replied. 'Anyway, I'm being ethnic. It's chic, didn't you know?'

Nick had also been strange about the Far Right literature Suzy had been ploughing through for some days. 'Racialism will save Great Britain', 'The big media conspiracy exposed', 'Fight the pollution of white lands'. What Suzy found hardest to believe was that there were people out there whom she had never met, and who nevertheless hated her. She needed Nick to see this for himself, but he would only give the material the most cursory of glances.

'It's sick!' He made the remark as if Suzy was to blame.

Suzy placed herself between the twin hats of Gloria and Becky, counting a paltry tally of twelve men and five women. The men below had dotted themselves around the sanctuary space as if each was standing in for absentee rows, or perhaps squeezing themselves among the ghosts of members past, Suzy mused.

Wolfie was leading the prayers. He had set free a Torah scroll from its home in the magnificent flame-shaped Ark and was holding it aloft as he paraded towards the *bimah*. Men and ghosts stood to attention, joining in the slow rhythmic melody. Suzy sensed she could trace back the strands of individual voice to their owners – Izzy's contribution a high-pitched affair, Monty's disappointingly flat despite his nightclub-singer appearance. She certainly recognized Eli's, his voice enveloping the others in rescue.

When it came to the Torah reading itself, Eli assumed centre stage, striding onto the *bimah* with an air of appropriate solemnity. Becky furiously turned pages forward and back until Gloria whispered the page number. Eli began recounting that week's chapter in the great biblical saga and, as Suzy listened to the rendition, she began to contemplate the power of a compelling narrative. Terry had spoken of photographers as *gods creating worlds*, and she recalled a class discussion on religious iconography. Could a single photographic image one day found a religion, she wondered?

Congregants grunted their approval at Eli's conclusion, delivered in a tight crescendo. His grateful gaze swept downstairs and up, and he smiled at Suzy. Such a performance warranted far more than this small audience of aged faithful. If only there could be a rash of conversions in the area that would restore the fortunes of the synagogue, and give Eli the following he so richly deserved.

The service's end was celebrated in the Club hall. In addition to orange juice, there was wine and cake. Suzy returned to the old photographs on the wall. These must be the ghosts she had conjured up. It was the picture that caught a synagogue service in action that most intrigued her.

'It's a disgrace!' Eli was standing next to her. 'That picture was taken on Yom Kippur. The rabbi allowed it. Look at him!' He had a gentle bearded face, standing in the midst of his flock. 'Thinks he's a film star. Some rabbi!'

Suzy's conversations tended to centre on the project. Becky enquired when she would get to see the photographs of herself, and how she could order copies. Esther was concerned that she hadn't featured in enough shots. Arnold wanted to make sure

Suzy would cover the next JFC 'Come Dancing' session. She was now the official Club photographer!

Izzy had remembered to bring an old photograph for Suzy: 'Twenty-one, just out the army, and ready for anything!' Monty's proved to have a memorable association. It was taken just before the Battle of Cable Street. 'I went along with a bigger cousin. Didn't do much. Just joined in with the shouting. There were thousands and thousands of people.'

Miriam's was perfect: a bright image of her youthful, prim self taken on a day trip to Southend. 'Don't ask me when!' However, as well as that picture, she also had a batch of more recent photographs covering three generations, at least, of family. Particularly worrying was the promotion of a favoured sixteen-year-old grandson that preceded a conversation on Suzy's marital status. Suzy suspected she was going to hear of his seventeenth birthday.

Eli wouldn't say what was for lunch. Suzy speculated on chicken to silence.

As they weaved their way through the back streets of Stepney, Eli asked to view that day's takings of members' photographs, toward which he had already declared his inability to contribute.

'Monty was at Cable Street,' she said as they stared at his preposterously youthful guise. He had glasses even then.

Eli grunted in reply.

She enjoyed telling him about the impact of his campus visit, and his newly acquired 'H-Block Ee-li fan club'. 'I feel privileged to know you!' Eli started talking about Jo and Salvo in a tone that suggested they were now all part of the same gang!

He was fulsome over Nick, which Suzy thought odd given how little they had actually spoken, added to which was his revelation of the *truth* that he had once worn the same pair of underpants for twenty consecutive days! As they continued to walk, she detected her relationship with Nick sliding into conversational prominence. Eli wanted to know the circumstances of their meeting, how long they had been together. What had begun as friendly banter was turning into something more akin to fatherly interrogation.

It was when Eli raised their different religious backgrounds that Suzy decided to bring the discussion to an end. As an eighteen-year-old, she most definitely was not prepared to contemplate her children's upbringing, and the intensity of Eli's manner disconcerted her.

Suzy brought to his attention a cemetery across the street, which enabled her to speak about a Prague cemetery encountered that previous summer. What had intrigued her were the bright photographs of the deceased that were integrated into the very headstones.

Suzy asked Eli if he thought the pictures helped the bereaved to feel they were not just visiting, but actually *seeing* their dearly departed. He replied obliquely, talking of how terrible it would be to lie in an unmarked grave, as if you never existed. His tone was curiously heartfelt.

It *was* chicken for lunch. 'But not just any chicken!' Eli stressed.

It *was* just any chicken, despite the gooey sauce Eli had endeavoured to drown it in. Suzy was regretting that she had mentioned Nick's culinary abilities. Eli had gone to considerable effort with all three courses and she was suitably generous with her appreciation.

Notably absent throughout lunch was musical accompaniment, which she presumed was in deference to the Sabbath day. Without the screen of music, there was an unusual intimacy to the atmosphere. Casual words of conversation felt somehow weightier. Eli was relaxed as they chatted. He teased about how religious she looked in a skirt, complimented, then touched her grandfather's earrings. It made her realize just how close they had become.

Suzy also noticed a startling new contribution to Eli's home. He had positioned the two photographs she had presented him with prominently on the mantelpiece. Suzy admired first her single image, and then this unlikely pairing. What impressed her even more were the frames in which these were contained: thick silver affairs in such contrast to the routine images they displayed.

Suzy had forgotten how brazenly Eli had formed himself in their shot as if they were in competition, grinning triumphantly. She inspected his features, trying to re-imagine him as a young man. What would he look like if she could retouch his face, shade in the lines across his forehead, blacken his hair, trim cheeks and chin? It wasn't hard to believe he was handsome.

Having been starved of the opportunity to take photographs in the synagogue, Suzy retrieved her helpmate with relish, sliding it over her face.

She took Eli at the table, exploiting the natural light from the windows, moving in for a closer head shot. He was smiling, basking in her attentions, obligingly tilting his head.

'Why did you tell me you killed your wife?'

Eli's expression tightened. 'You don't believe me?'

'No.' Suzy snapped with the camera again.

'I didn't save her. It's the same thing, no?'

'No. It's not. Not at all.'

'It was a long time ago,' Eli said.

After yet another shot, she lowered the camera. 'Is that why you don't have any photographs?' Suzy motioned towards the mantelpiece. 'You don't want to remember.'

On that, Eli rose from his chair and left the room, leaving Suzy momentarily acutely anxious. Had she misread the situation, been too presumptuous with him? Eli quickly returned, carrying in his hands something like a small trunk. It appeared quite ancient, marked by severe bruising. He placed it on the floor, prising open its rectangular lid.

'Come!'

Suzy joined Eli on the floor.

'Can't remember when I was last in here.'

The first object to emerge was a ragged hat or cap of some description, which he carefully lowered to the floor. Loose papers followed, badges, coins, a pen, a spyglass, then a small ornamental dagger. 'Holiday souvenir,' he smirked. 'And this!' It was an elegant pearl-handled pistol, which he passed to Suzy. She held it uncomfortably while he rummaged on.

'Ha!' He was attempting to get hold of what Suzy could now see was a small photographic negative. He found several others, and a pair of entangled negative strips. Suzy was grateful to exchange the gun for them. There was creasing, and tears. The negatives were in terrible shape.

'You wanted pictures of me, when I was young!'

Suzy blew on one of the more salvageable negatives and held it to the light, identifying tantalizing shapes.

'What d'you think? D'you want them?'

Suzy certainly wanted them. She was thrilled.

13

Suzy composed herself. 'Prince Charles was visiting a Jewish Old Age Home.' It was an Eli joke that Suzy had actually found funny. 'He stopped by one of the residents. Mrs Goldberg! he shouted. Do you know who I am? Mrs Goldberg gazed up at the Prince. No, she shrugged. But if you ask the nice nurse over there, she'll be able to tell you!'

Her mother's expression hardly flickered. She appeared to be adopting a *position* on Eli, just as surely as she had her position on the East End as a whole. And their afternoon exploits in the area hadn't helped its cause.

Her mother was baffled by their visit to the huge 'Battle of Cable Street' mural, which she dismissed as lurid. And it was raining by the time they reached Eastchapel market, covering it with an unfortunate sheen of gloom. Her mother stared contemptuously at the now plastic-embraced stalls of cheap goods, and pleaded that they move on.

And they had a dramatic encounter or, more accurately, non-encounter. Of all the JFC members to come across, it had to be Lionel! As he approached, Suzy did consider that this could be an opportunity finally to win him to her cause. She had her charming mother as back-up. However, when Lionel realized who was down the street from him, he spun himself round in the most ungainly fashion, then scampered away before a word was exchanged.

'Making friends, are we?'

It was down to Nick to save the day.

Suzy had never seen his flat in such pristine condition. All his housemates had been banished for the occasion, and Nick had undertaken a clean-up of monumental proportions. The living room was awash with candles conveying a theatrically romantic effect, although the fact that this was in honour of her mother did queer the impact. The traffic-cone goalposts had been retired. What she had thought of as the permanent debris of books and files on the floor had been tidied away revealing fresh squares of carpet. Suzy also noticed that the multitude of cigarette burns had vanished from the walls, apparently via the magic of Tipp-Ex. And, to cap it all, he had the melodic sounds of Tony Bennett wafting from his tape deck. How did he know that, she wondered?

'What a lovely place!' her mother announced, sitting on the puffed-out settee on which, just the previous day, Suzy had admired housemate Gary sitting cross-legged in his string underwear picking his feet.

'Yes, it is, isn't it,' she replied.

Even Margaret the cat had been especially groomed for the evening although, from her expression, she was as dubious as Suzy, preferring her own company in the hall.

Nick disappeared, returning in a tall white chef's hat to serve up champagne! Her mother threw a glance of wonderment in Suzy's direction.

'Where did you get this?' Suzy protested. It was all too much. She retreated to her camera.

Nick initially tried to sabotage her shots of him in the kitchen through several childish facial gestures. She recorded these 'for my second-year project', while capturing more serious poses at the moments he had to concentrate on the various simmerings on the go. Her mother posed with Nick, heads locked above each course, his cigarette-butt headgear carefully repositioned for each occasion. She also captured her mother's toast to Nick, and his toast to Suzy. She toasted the cat.

Suzy did have to admit the food was exceptional. Nick talked through his methodologies and her mother leaned in, once again spiritually reunited through an exchange of culinary manoeuvres.

In insisting that he be given no assistance, Suzy was left at various times to endure the weighty nodding of her mother.

'How often does he do this?' she whispered.

'All the time!'

A bowl of fruit completed the meal. Suzy picked an apple because it reminded her of one of Eli's stories from the war. She described how Eli and a friend went about the delicate task of sharing food. One would cut, and the other would choose. The former role was the agonizing one, with the dreaded possibility of an uneven incision. Cutting that apple took a lifetime, Eli had said.

The story momentarily silenced the table.

'Have you met this Eli character?' her mother asked Nick.

'Sure. The singer!'

'Don't you think it's odd? Suzy talks about him as if he's her best friend.'

'It's what happens with the people in your project,' Nick replied. 'If it's going well. You get close.'

'She's got him all over her bedroom wall.' That was an exaggeration. It was a JFC wall in which he was prominent. 'It's like an obsession!'

Her mother was equally unhappy with Nick's defence of rowing. 'I've never met a sailor' being her terse comment on the subject.

After the meal, Nick removed his guests to the settee. He placed his camera on a table opposite, carefully fixing its angle before setting it to timer mode. He once again reattached his chef's hat and dropped to her mother's side. However, she wanted Suzy in the middle.

'A rose between two thorns,' Suzy quipped.

14

Suzy showed Terry another – a large woman with exploding hair pouting outrageously.

'Most of them treat it like a fashion shoot. They bring in their own special clothes.'

Terry went back to a previous image and compared the two. The world of Fabulous Faces was clearly intriguing him. It already fascinated Suzy. She sensed something evocative in the images going far beyond what they simply were – an assortment of glamour shots involving primarily the glamorously deficient.

'We get a few men.'

Terry promptly handed the photographs back. 'Very interesting.' He shifted in his chair while he searched out her latest submission. 'Time for Jewish Football!'

He laid out several of her pictures along his desk, then placed against them the texts she was proposing for each.

There was a scene of Eli lighting the Chanukah menorah against words that began 'race is our religion'; Izzy dancing the two-step with Esther above 'the mongrelization of Europe'.

The incongruity of benign Club scenes against the shocking language worked perfectly, giving the combination a striking poignancy. That was at least what Suzy felt.

'These are actual quotes?'

Suzy nodded.

'Dreadful! And it really works. The concept really works. I've given you that. What I want to do today is focus purely on the photography.'

Terry slid the pieces of text to one side and picked up the pictures. He began flicking through them at an alarming speed. In getting to the end, he started again.

'You've got the ingredients, but the cake isn't rising,' Terry looked at her. 'Remember I said I'm going to push you? Guess what. You need pushing!'

Terry began stacking the photographs on his desk. 'You feel a connection with these people. An empathy. There's the Jewish thing, right?'

Suzy nodded. She couldn't trust how she might sound if she spoke. He was building two piles.

'It's not coming through. If you'll excuse me, your work feels too much like a wallpaper catalogue. Pretty, but not . . . significant, if you get what I'm saying.' Terry raised his hands in emphasis. Suzy was getting plenty. The eye of his *Clockwork Orange* poster was at its most menacing.

'There's some sort of ambivalence here, and I don't understand why.'

Terry began to lay out along his desk the more substantial pile of images, which Suzy now realized were the ones he considered most problematic. 'Let's just talk composition.'

He proceeded to take Suzy through a litany of crimes from conceptualization to balance to resonance. And that was just composition! Throughout his remarks, Terry was careful to keep a watch on Suzy, as if checking on how she was bearing up.

'You've got great people. The potential's all here.' He spread out his hands above the assembly. 'I can really see that!'

Terry laid out next the smaller pile of what he deemed the more successful images, the ones that might yet redeem her.

'Can you see what these have that the others don't?'

Suzy rallied for the question. The answer in terms of subject was obvious – Eli.

'We've decided to give Eli a bigger role here, is that right? Just look at him!'

Suzy had been for quite some time.

'He's never the same. In any of the images. Yet there's also a consistency. You're getting something out of him that I don't see in any of the others.'

Suzy sensed what he was saying. It was simply how he was with her.

'You've done something to *yourself* here.'

Having booked darkroom C for two o'clock, Suzy spent a long lunchtime in the Granary, brooding over Terry's latest constructive criticism.

Nick tried to cheer her, reprising his own hardening scepticism over Terry's approach, which provided little comfort. Suzy wasn't sceptical herself.

Salvo was in philosophical mood. In one of his readings, he had come across the theory that every moment of time had a distinct existence that continued on. 'Isn't that the best explanation of a photograph!' Nina had made a different discovery in relation to the Fine Arts Lecturer, about which she would be coy for several hours, but she was no longer interested in slipping across to the Granary Arts corner. Jo had a first date with a bar staff colleague and wanted to borrow one of Suzy's shirts. It all served to distract her from her malaise.

Nick headed off to the gym, pecking Suzy on the cheek as he gave up his seat to Megan. She had been at the student newspaper for most of lunch, and arrived with breaking news. 'In response to the ban on racist leafleting, the Debating Society has decided to run an event on free speech.' They all tried to feign interest. 'Guess what?' Suzy wondered if she was being serious. 'They've invited Grahame Hargreaves!' Megan ended on an expression of exasperated horror.

Suzy glanced at Jo. She was equally puzzled, as were Salvo and Nina, although their status as foreigners could excuse them.

'He's that revisionist historian!' Megan turned her exasperation on the table. 'Thinks Hitler was a nice guy! He's a proud racist. Big BPP supporter. You *must* have heard of him.'

'What's going to happen?' asked Suzy.

'Everything! The shit will *really* fly.'

In darkroom C, Suzy's thoughts turned exclusively to an assignment which she viewed as quite astonishing. What she believed to be the remains of Eli's early life had been entrusted to her care. And she had been given the incredible task of resurrecting them.

Her first disappointment came with the very first stage of the process. She soaked the negatives in treated water, both for cleansing and to separate the entangled negative strips – except they failed to detach. She called in Mork, then Clara, who both concluded that the only course of action would be to cut them apart, with the inevitable sacrifice of at least two of the negatives. Suzy could only proceed with Eli's permission.

However, prints were feasible from the ten single negatives, although one was torn, several badly creased, and another substantially lost to a fog. Nevertheless, Suzy experienced growing excitement as she waited for them to emerge from the drying cupboard. She quickly placed them onto a lightbox, using a magnifier to make her initial scrutiny.

Suzy found herself among a fascinating array of people. It was clear from their features and manner of dress that she had entered a very different world. They were all formal shots of various configurations of people, and varying ages. A couple of images contained substantial props – in one a group had formed themselves around a car, in another the backdrop of a house loomed.

Mork helped her experiment with exposure times, and she was finally able to print off an acceptable contact sheet from the single negatives. They examined the sheet together with Mork identifying which could be improved upon, and which he considered beyond redemption. Suzy thought of herself as a doctor attending sickly patients, with Mork the duty consultant.

After Mork left, Suzy returned to the central conundrum. Which one was Eli? There were several possibilities – the son figure seated between the older man and woman; several of the men crowding the car; any of the three children. These were the ones Suzy settled on for first prints.

One of the selected negatives was creased, requiring Suzy to use a clamp to flatten it out in the enlarger. What eventually emerged were three fairly proficient productions. The first contained the couple and a boy – the woman in drop-waisted dress and string of beads, the heavily bearded man in thick double-breasted suit with stomach extending towards the viewer, the boy in shorts and neatly combed hair harnessed in between.

The car scene produced a gaggle of young men in shirts and braces, swarming around the vehicle as if inviting the viewer to play guess the owner. The final photograph was of three children seated along a wall, one at least a girl, each competing to produce the more outrageously fashioned pose.

Suzy wondered for how long these people had languished in Eli's Romanian trunk. Surely Eli would tell her who they were. Would he tell her everything? She now felt even closer to him.

15

Eli was in a peculiar, restless mood. Suzy wondered if the photographs were its cause.

She was eager to show him what she had produced from the negatives. They were seated towards the rear of the coach on a Club outing, with Eli determined to be at his most boisterous. He kept poking Wolfie awake, stealing Miriam's boiled sweets, and then joined Monty at the front to sing a Yiddish duet. How Monty kept his balance was particularly impressive although, with the atrocious weather, they were crawling in the traffic, at the pace of a royal procession.

'This is me here. Me with my parents. Me and some friends.'

'Slow down!' Suzy pleaded. Eli had rapidly located himself in all three of the prints. It now was so obvious. In the shot of the three children, he was the one on the left, a handsome boy with dark romantic features. The shot of him by the car revealed how his features had largely survived the transition to adulthood.

'Shall I tell you the story of this car? We had family in America. And they would send us pictures with their letters. Grand ones to show us how successful they were in the *guldene medina*, the land of gold. So we pretended that this was our car, in golden Romania. Crazy, no?'

And then Eli was on his feet again. Suzy quickly obtained his permission to use them in the project – 'Sure. Didn't I find them for you?' – before he moved down several rows to oversee Izzy and Becky as they played cards and growled at each other.

Suzy stared at his parents in sympathy. She particularly enjoyed meeting up with his mother, a resilient-looking woman whom she had learned through Eli had such earthy wisdom to dispense.

Gloria sat with Suzy for a while. She spoke about her concern for an absent member. 'Lionel never misses an event. He's a real trooper.' Suzy couldn't help but feel quietly delighted.

When Eli returned, Suzy swiftly got in her second request, that she cut the attached negative strips.

'Cut away.' Eli glanced again at the pictures.

'So how do you like Romania? Shall I tell you about the wonderful new democracy there? They want to rehabilitate Antonescu. The great anti-communist martyr who ran the most evil fascist government in wartime Europe. Did you know that Romania was the only ally of Nazi Germany to initiate its own extermination programme? They even disgusted the Nazis with their methods. Can you believe it? Now they call him a great Romanian patriot!'

Suzy had a related topic of her own. She brought up the

Debating Society meeting involving Grahame Hargreaves, whose name was now plastered across the university as the opponents of his visit campaigned. She had hoped it would get Eli to sit with her but it had the opposite effect, sending him up the aisle ringing out the news.

The bus drew up outside a large building, its facade obscured by the formidable rain shower.

'Come on now. Let's get you all inside!' They had been met by an energetic young woman wrapped in a raincoat, who briefly boarded the bus and then, perhaps lest anyone be tempted to remain, took up position at the bottom of the stairs under a large purple umbrella. Assorted hats and coats spun in the air in a flurry of activity. Izzy covered his beret in protective cling film. Wolfie was given the honour of embarking first having insisted upon and, in the end, paid for the transportation. Suzy followed Becky as she struggled down the stairs, making a swishing sound with the plastic of her rain mac.

'Don't let growing old catch you by surprise,' she advised as she launched herself into the rain.

Despite the conditions, Gloria had placed herself next to the young woman, as if to stress she was only acting through delegation.

Suzy did her best to cover Monty and Becky with her umbrella, receiving a good soaking as her reward. Soon, the full contingent was regrouping in a large vestibule inside the building, coughing and shaking off the rain in what was once the renowned Whitechapel Great Synagogue.

Suzy started taking shots, capturing the fading biblical motifs that could still be traced along the walls, the ceiling's intricate geometric pattern, the marble stairway like great arms twisting upwards at either end. A board with large modern lettering declared the building's current purpose as the *Whitechapel Community Arts Centre*.

'Gather round everyone!' The woman introduced herself as Simone, impressively first name only, the Centre's administrator, which Gloria quickly confirmed.

'On behalf of Whitechapel Arts, we're delighted to welcome such honoured guests.' Becky nodded. 'It must be a special experience to come back to a place that many of you will remember as a living synagogue.'

'It wasn't *that* long ago,' Becky whispered.

'I had my bar mitzvah here!' Wolfie shouted.

'Is that what closed it down?' teased Izzy.

Monty guffawed, giving Gloria the pleasurable opportunity to assert her authority, restoring quiet in the ranks.

'The building hasn't changed that much,' Simone continued. 'The original features have been largely retained. It's extremely important to us that we respect the memory of what this facility once was.'

The word facility sounded odd, Suzy thought. It was a *shul*!

The guide went into a brief history of the site, demonstrating an accomplished command of the facts – founded in 1893, cornerstone laid by Lord Rothschild. Its style she described as a 'pastiche of orientalism'. Famous members included politicians, entertainers, a boxer or two.

'This was the heart of the old Jewish East End. There were

twenty-three synagogues in Whitechapel, and the Great was the biggest and finest of them all.'

'I had my bar mitzvah here,' Wolfie repeated, this time in a whisper to Suzy.

'Just down from the synagogue were the famous Odessa Steam Rooms.'

'*Odesser*,' corrected Esther and Becky in unison.

Becky turned to Suzy. 'The *Odesser shvitz-bod*. Why is she telling us our history? We should be telling her!'

'I feel like a ghost,' Esther added.

Simone ushered the group through large panelled doors. The impact of the massive sanctuary silenced everyone. The structure was unquestionably that of a synagogue. A huge blue Star of David bestrode the glass dome high above, the rain feverishly playing on its exterior in a low rumble of sound. The same blue was dominant in the stained-glass windows along the side walls depicting festival scenes. The upper tier containing the women's gallery encircled like an ornate ribbon. Great pillars soared from floor to ceiling. And still proudly manifest at the sanctuary's bow was the elaborate Ark topped by exotic arabesque towers.

But there was a newer purpose to the space.

'This building is still serving the Whitechapel community, just as its founders intended.' Simone was grinning.

The sanctuary floor was filled with jagged hulking pieces of dramatic sculpture. Where once there would have been pews, heads of the faithful bowed in prayer to the Almighty, now stood rows of human-sized figures, each fashioned into strangely menacing shapes. A number of the group remained close to the entrance as if unnerved by the scene. Suzy took a shot of Gloria standing in complete bafflement before one of the images, an agonized green form with exaggerated limbs poised to overwhelm her.

Simone must have sensed the tension because she became oddly evangelical, talking up the heroic efforts of the local council to preserve the building.

'All these works are by local artists!'

The ghosts weren't happy. The murmuring noise of the rain against the dome seemed to be providing its own commentary.

Suzy began circling the room to capture the moment. She saw Wolfie holding up battered prayer books that had been left to languish; a sculpture appearing to lash out at Izzy as he endeavoured to pass; Miriam staring down forlornly from the women's gallery.

But it was Eli. Suzy noticed him marching towards the Ark at the sanctuary's end. The great bull-like head of some sort of Minator figure was standing fiercely on its steps, the leader of this mutant assembly. It was a grotesque piece that seemed positioned deliberately as a provocation, as if the pagans had stormed the Temple.

Suzy caught Eli just as he picked up the head.

'You mustn't touch the exhibits!' Simone was anxiously looking around for Gloria, but she had retreated outside.

'I'm sorry. I have to ask you to put it back. *Please put it back*!'

16

'How did you expect Eli to react? Burst into tears?' Nick said.

'No!' Suzy replied indignantly.

They were in Nick's bedroom, Suzy lying on his bed in order to ease the sliding on of another pair of his trousers.

'You're using his photographs to provoke him.'

'You're trying to provoke me!' Suzy was struggling to wriggle trousers above feet.

'Anyway, it's what we're supposed to be doing. Getting to *the essence of character, emotional truth*.' She attempted to mimic Terry's voice.

'Well, you know what I think about all that crap!'

The group tutorials were fuelling rising disaffection in the ranks. Nick was still smarting over Terry's latest comment about his pictures 'failing to cohere'.

'What's the point of all this?' Nick went on. 'All this' was a photographic essay on subverting identity that Terry wanted by Friday. 'He's been out the game for too long. He's lost the plot.'

'You're so wrong!' Suzy tried getting up, but rolled instead.

'Those who can't, teach.'

It was an image Nick couldn't resist. 'Stay just like that!' Then Nick caught another as she managed to engineer herself into a vaguely standing position. Suzy turned up the trouser legs, then strode in best manly fashion to the mirror, Nick's bright red Manchester United top aglow beneath her face.

'That's good.' Nick leaned against the wall, capturing these twin male Suzys indulging in mutual curiosity.

She then returned to her rummage in Nick's cupboards. Suzy had come up with the idea after seeing Gareth's essay photographs. He had applied extensive make-up in order to turn his face completely white. He had then pulled off a double exposure, transposing an image of this new white identity onto one of his former black self. The prints he had produced of these two echoing figures were eerie, and extraordinary.

Suzy assessed various items of clothing before settling on Nick's Lycra rowing uniform. Manchester United was abandoned for the lure of the sea.

'Anyway, Eli gave *me* the negatives, remember? I didn't even know they existed.' She was on her feet again. 'He wants me to do this. He's teasing me.'

'And you're teasing him back.'

That really annoyed her. 'You've got it so easy with your project. All you're doing is snapping your rowing chums!'

Suzy was back at the mirror.

'I've never seen Lycra sag like that,' Nick noted.

'That's because you've got such a big bum!'

Nick caught her in full glare, taking several others before bringing the photoshoot to its end. He went kitchenward to brew deluxe coffee. Suzy switched on the bedroom television, because it was there, landing herself ironically enough in a cookery demonstration. Suzy wondered if she was watching a tape. It was swiftly switched off.

Instead, she returned to perusing his wall filled with the photographic trophies of his six months of Far Eastern travel. Suzy focused on a group of richly decorated faces engaged in some sort of festival, and it made her think about Terry's essay assignment. Surely these people were manipulating their identities – colouring, tattooing themselves in order to become new forms of being.

There was a very different style of photograph in the collection that puzzled her – a night sky lit by a bright moon. It was a mundane idea, and the composition flawed, the moon far too prominent to allow the eye the pleasure of seeking it out.

When the coffees arrived, announced with relish as 'Bolivian cinnamon', Suzy challenged Nick on the image. He smiled.

'I was in Thailand. It was late, very late, after a big big party. I'd smoked . . . whatever. Just lying on the roof of this minibus, staring up at the night sky. It felt so intense. We were out in the country. No artificial light. Nothing. Just an enormous thick black sky and this massive shining moon. I was on the roof looking up, and I suddenly felt like I had been turned upside down. I was now on top of the moon and it was pulling me in. It was such an amazing feeling.'

Nick handed Suzy her coffee and took a first sip of his own.

'You know what I did right after I took that shot?' He giggled. 'I climbed inside the bus, so the roof would stop me floating away. Because I knew that, if I went up to the moon, I wouldn't come back. I'd stay up there for ever!' He caressed the picture with his free hand as he finished talking. 'It's a photograph of heaven.'

Suzy moved away, and began taking off the rowing outfit, followed by the rest of her clothes. She had restored herself to full femininity, standing naked in front of Nick, enjoying its effect; his embarrassed, excited expression.

'What are you doing?!'

'I want you to take a picture of me, just as I am. I want to see how you see me.'

Nick shook his head, while picking up his camera.

'Smile for the camera.'

'Get on with it. I'm freezing!'

17

'She smells of fish, doesn't she?' Jo had interrupted her comments on her search for work over the Easter break as Nina entered the Granary.

'Stop persecuting her!' said Suzy. Nina moved towards the Granary service counter, oblivious of her vegan adversary.

'I can't believe what you said about her project.' Jo had described Nina's fish market imagery in class that morning as 'obscene'. What galled Jo even more was that Nina was talking about manning the university crisis helpline.

'How would you have felt if it was a pile of freshly sliced-up bodies?'

Jo herself had emerged relatively unscathed. Her triangle of meditating Buddhist priests had launched Terry on an address on the photographer's mission to bring visual 'wholeness and unity' to a chaotic world. Although he had also threaded into his praise the word 'clichéd'.

Suzy's pictures from the Whitechapel Great Synagogue were both of Eli. She had managed to capture two astonishing images, both with the Minator head in his hands – Elijah, the wrathful prophet smashing the idols. Salvo's feedback on Eli's portrayal appeared to reflect more his enthusiasm over their meeting on Sports Night. Nina was effusive, and she was sure that Terry was essentially pleased more on the basis of what he *didn't* say.

Most striking was Gareth's latest portrait of Stewart in the Aids Hospice. He was propped up in bed, yet wasn't sitting quite straight. Suzy fixed on the flowers in a simple glass vase by his bedside now past their peak, heads gently lowering as if they also knew. Terry picked up on how Gareth's own shadow could just be made out clipping the corner of the bed, subtly informing the viewer of his presence. He left the class to ponder Gareth's motives.

Megan rustled through her salad while detailing latest moves to prevent Grahame Hargreaves from participating in the Debating Society meeting. 'At the moment, unbelievably, he's still coming!'

'Why all the fuss about this one guy?' Nick responded, waving his sandwich.

Suzy looked at him.

'It just gives him what he wants,' he continued. 'Publicity! I'd let him come, speak to the three and a half fascinated students, and go.'

'He's not some sort of legitimate academic with funny views!' answered Megan. 'He's a racist who wants to deny people their rights because of the colour of their skin!' Megan turned to Suzy. 'What d'you think?'

Suzy paused. She had read enough of his quotes off the vast protest literature by now to know precisely what Hargreaves stood for. It was language that she had become all too familiar with through her project work, wading through Eli's folder of hate. It was with Eli in mind that she replied: 'I'm not political. You know that. But this isn't politics. Not normal politics anyway. By letting him speak, it gives what he says credibility. People are more likely to believe it.'

'Exactly!' Megan was delighted to have an ally confirmed.

Nick shook his head. 'Both of you are so wrong.' All smugness to the fore. 'Normal people wouldn't be taken in by such crap. But if you make a thing out of it, then people *will* start being interested.'

'So it's all the fault of the protestors!' Suzy had never covered this ground with Nick, not properly, and was flabbergasted by his tone. 'Has it ever crossed your mind that *you* might just be wrong for once?'

'Suzy. You're not seeing this objectively.' Nick paused. 'It's bound to matter more to you.'

Suzy had another darkroom session booked. She wouldn't miss him.

Suzy now considered herself something of an accomplished darkroom performer. She savoured the special thrill of being involved in the photographic act at every stage; that it was in *light* and *dark* that the mysteries of her craft were fully realized.

Eli had given Suzy permission to cut apart the negative strips and she sought out Clara's advice for the delicate operation. She used a pair of the sharpest scissors, and carefully cut around the strip's embrace, ensuring that, in the end, only two of the negatives had to be sacrificed. She bathed the survivors, depositing them to dry while she worked on a current film.

The timer buzzed. Suzy extricated the strips and patterned them on the lightbox. Her excitement demanded she quickly print off a contact sheet.

Of the first strip, one image could be immediately discounted, having surrendered to an impenetrable fog. The theme of all the next was 'young Eli on bicycle'. He was far too concerned with maintaining his balance on the contraption to provide any edifying pose for the camera.

It was the second strip that Suzy seized on. The first portrayal had Eli in a smartly turned-out suit standing rather stiffly alongside two women – one definitely older, the other possibly younger. There was sufficient similarity around the eyes, the shaping of the mouth, to suggest mother and daughter. The older woman had a substantial figure, enhanced by the way her dress lay like a construction around her. The younger was more delicately composed, topped by a straw hat held at a jaunty angle, casting a faint shadow across her face, introducing a hint of intrigue.

The three were reunited for the next image down, this time as the centrepiece of a larger grouping. Curiously, Eli was the only man present, providing the contrast against a feast of women, all captured relatively naturally as if in the precise moment of assembly. Suzy could almost hear the chatter as the gathering coalesced around the threesome, each contained in the same clothing as before and evidently in the same location, some sort of gardens. Suzy was witnessing an occasion.

The final picture was a climax. The younger woman was now on her own, standing on a small ornamental bridge that spanned a picturesque pond with lilies geometrically at anchor. She had dispensed with her hat, causing her hair to fall neatly around her shoulders. It could have been an early fashion-shoot image. And it was this picture that provided Suzy's first print. She had produced four by the session's end; one of Eli on the bicycle, and all three taken in the gardens. Suzy played with exposure times for some while before she allowed herself to feel satisfied with the results.

Suzy named the woman on the bridge. She called her Rosabella.

18

The woman sitting directly opposite Suzy had her eyes closed. Her head was tilted back, as if wrapped in some alluring private communion. It was an unusual sculpted face; her dark skin naturally without blemish, dramatic eyelashes and brows, lips prominent and full. Suzy marvelled at this unprecedented access, free to scrutinize a fellow Tube passenger without self-consciousness, her guard of sight surrendered. Suzy raised her camera.

'Leave her alone. She's sleeping!'

There was something distinctly unpleasant simmering between Nick and Suzy. He was angry with her for being so emphatic about taking part in the demonstration. The attempt to ban Hargreaves had failed. Suzy was angry with him for saying he wouldn't give up his precious rowing practice to join her.

The morning began in an exclusive West End gallery. Suzy was keen to visit an exhibition by the celebrated American photographer, Mort Macintyre. He was renowned for his ability to take the most mundane of subject matter and, through its very ordinariness, capture astonishing imagery – a glistening neon sign advertisement, traffic lights at an empty street crossing, a dog peering from a car. What Suzy also relished was the setting, the gallery's clean white walls and hushed reverence, that photography *deserved* such treatment.

'Arty farty,' was Nick's assessment. It was their next argument. Suzy couldn't understand why he was so keen to deny photography its place as an art form, just because it wasn't his chosen path. 'You're diminishing us all!'

Nick was soon moving them on to their next stop, skirting the grand Trafalgar Square as they walked up from Charing Cross Station. He was talking about Easter plans. Friends were taking a cottage in the Lake District and he wanted Suzy to join him, and them. She had two problems: the more substantial was the festival of Passover, and the requirement to be home for the two Seder nights of her two families; the second was money. Even with her Fabulous Faces income, Suzy was still struggling financially and she didn't feel inclined to ask her father to increase her allowance. Indeed, she was hoping to work for him over the break.

'I'll pay for you.'

That wasn't what Suzy wanted him to say.

Their conversation was amusingly interrupted when they were approached to take a picture for a group of Belgian tourists. Nick deferred to Suzy. 'She's the photographer.'

They were returning to the National Portrait Gallery because it now featured that year's winners of the Ronald Marsden Portrait Awards. Terry was demanding everyone go, especially since second years were expected to compete in it. However, Nick wanted to revisit the main exhibition space first.

'So what do you see?' Nick asked as they stood before a striking sporting image.

Beyond the physicality, there was concentration, tension, and an almost unbearable uncertainty in the swimmer's face. She could not fail.

'I see all that!' Terry had taken to calling Nick's work 'good journalism', and it wasn't in the context of flattery. Some sort of unacknowledged duel was now being fiercely played out between them.

Suzy left Nick to his contemplations in order to wander back to the genteel world of the nineteenth century. The artist Walter Francis was the first personality to attract her attention, through a dramatic self-portrait which displayed haughty flamboyance. It was imagining the process that so intrigued Suzy. Here was an artist applying paint just beyond his fingertips in order to realize a wholly fantastic self, destined to become his eternal stand-in.

In a next room, she was met by an eerie sight, that of a death mask taken from the Duke of Wellington. She couldn't resist placing her hands on the cold smooth marble, apologizing to the Duke as she felt his eyes, sliding down to his mouth and chin. She was reminded of the cemetery she had come across in Prague, where photographs of the departed were encased in the headstone. Suzy wondered if this was the essence of photography, essentially a death-defying act. Then she realized that it was surely precisely the opposite. Every picture was by definition a lost moment. A photograph *confirmed* death.

Suzy returned to Nick, and the vivacity of their own century. He was discreetly engaged in an illegal act, breaking the strict prohibition on photography to catch a bashful Bobby Charlton. Suzy reflected on the perils of excessive adoration! She paid a visit to the image she recalled selecting for Terry's earlier identification assignment. Whoever Barbara Lee was, for Suzy she was a woman whose allure lay in her startling self-confidence. Yet the way she now presented herself, Suzy feared she had been too hasty, failing to read a definite conceit. It was in the angle of the head, how her eyes stared out dismissively.

However, the model that was Terry's choice, the one he himself had taken, had grown in stature. Beyond the obvious integrity of the piece, Terry had captured a passion and enthusiasm that were surely his own. If Suzy could choose again, she would go with Terry.

Nick and Suzy reunited for the two rooms that celebrated the

Marsden award winners. The diversity of portraiture on display was staggering, reflecting formidable inventiveness. Suzy found herself being drawn to the more disturbing imagery, which conveyed the richer narratives. There was a little girl standing alone in a playground surrounded by slides and swings, icons of happy childhood, yet she was lost to an anxiety that was crushing her face. It was a heartbreaking picture. Suzy imagined herself behind the camera for the shot, and was suddenly seized by the shocking notion of photographer as abuser. She was relieved when Nick motioned that they head out.

Her head was still in the National Portrait Gallery as Suzy strode up the stairway for the next Fabulous Faces session. The infinite potential contained within that small area defined as the human face was truly astonishing.

Suzy sat in her routine position in front of the camera, watching her white-coated colleague Zandra deliver her finishing flourishes with brush and pencil, and started to contemplate what would be the implications if she applied her education within the context of Fabulous Faces. If she was to consider herself a photographer rather than picture-taker, if clients were *subjects*.

Throughout that session, Suzy made a point of chatting with each customer, enough to provide some basic indicators on personality. She then worked more thoughtfully on arranging each sitter, for the first time manipulating the lighting, ultimately delivering images that went far beyond the simple frontal portrayals of a make-up mask.

Even in Fabulous Faces, Suzy could be a god!

19

Eli was highly agitated when he opened the door to Suzy, holding a glass of what appeared to be whisky. His breath confirmed that.

The mood in his flat wasn't helped by the screeching violins, which she made him turn down. Eli waved at her leaflets pushed through his letter box that morning, latest electioneering pamphlets of the British People's Party that declared its mission to win 'the new battle for Britain'. Suzy studied their attractively designed logo of entwined British flags.

'Read it!'

Suzy started to. She was waiting for the searing hatred, which so characterized the other material, except there wasn't any. The articles talked about jobs, and housing, and healthcare. It was all so *reasonable*.

'You see what they're doing. This is their new tactic. Clever, no? People won't see what's behind it!'

She made Eli sit down on the sofa while she rustled in her bag for the tape recorder.

'Why are they allowed to do this?' He then started garbling something about Grahame Hargreaves.

'There's going to be a massive protest,' Suzy reassured. She moved to give him back the leaflets, but he insisted she keep them.

'For your project. Show the people! Shoshana. You see what's happening, don't you?'

'What's happening?' Suzy pushed the microphone closer.

'They're getting strong again. Little by little. All over Europe! People forget. The young don't know. It's starting to happen just like before!'

Suzy noticed that the small trunk of Romanian memorabilia was still in the living room, slid into the window bay. The envelope she had given him containing the first set of negative prints was on the mantelpiece, propped behind the silver-framed picture of the two of them. Suzy had brought the second set, but was now unsure whether she should present it.

'Come on! Take my picture. I want you to take me like this.'

So Suzy did, capturing his distressed state which slowly abated as she continued shooting.

Eli replenished his glass in the kitchen, returning to the sofa.

'Have you brought the other negatives?' Given his casual attitude towards the previous set, Suzy was surprised that he had even remembered. Still she hesitated.

'I know.' He motioned with a hand. 'I know what you've found.'

Suzy drew the envelope from her bag and handed it over. While Eli examined each print, Suzy captured more of him. His expression turned into an oddly fashioned smile, then his whole face seemed to shrink inwards. Suzy just kept taking him, one after another.

'I haven't seen you for such a long, long time.' Eli was talking softly. 'Do you know who this is?' Eli held up the woman on the bridge.

'Rosabella,' Suzy declared from behind the camera.

Eli squinted at her. Suzy realized that it was the first moment his wife's name had been uttered between them, and it was she who had introduced it.

'No.' Eli shook his head. 'You're not pronouncing it properly. *Rosabella*.'

The *R* had a *ch* attached to it. The *e* sounded more like an *ay*.

'Say it, Shoshana.'

Suzy did her best, repeating various Rosabella permutations until Eli was satisfied.

'*Krasavitsa*. Wasn't she beautiful?'

She was beautiful, ringletted hair around shoulders, a demure, dark alluring look.

'It was your wedding?'

Eli nodded. 'Two hundred and fifty guests! A big, big party. The biggest wedding in Burchani that year. For Rosa's mother, everything had to be the best. They were much wealthier than my family. A not so best son-in-law! That's her in the picture. She had these taken. And more. Lots more.'

Eli got up to prop the picture next to Suzy's own on the mantelpiece, Rosabella now also his audience. Back on the sofa, he started talking about how they met, but he didn't stop there. He was telling Suzy their whole story. He was ready now, finishing his whisky, talking without breathing.

In the war, they had been deported to Transnistria in the Ukraine, a place where Romanian Jews that 'were lucky enough' to escape the executions were sent to die – 'a slow death by hunger and disease'. Eli and Rosabella had the slimmest of chances that they might yet get visas for Palestine. If not, they had made a pact to kill themselves. Eli obtained cyanide pills. 'There were no restrictions on Jews buying poison for themselves!' They became separated, Eli taken off to a work camp. 'We had nothing to give each other. I cut a long curl from her hair.' Without him, Rosabella gave up hope.

'Then, death was easier than life.'

By the time Eli heard of her suicide, the tide of the war was turning. Some Jews were even being returned to Romania. He couldn't bring himself to join her. 'I've left her alone all this time!' His expression was one of utter devastation. 'She always told me it was her biggest fear. That I would leave her, and we would never meet again. But I couldn't go with her. Just couldn't.'

He peered up at her on the mantelpiece. 'Forgive me, my dear sweet Rosa.'

And there was shuddering and tears.

'Do you understand now?'

Suzy did understand. And she had sealed it all inside her camera.

'I was always heading for just one place – England. The home of the greatest man alive – Winston Churchill!'

Eli appeared determined to tell Suzy everything about his past. It felt as if a dam had burst open and his whole life story was tumbling forth in one vast sea of emotion. He spoke at length about his religious upbringing, forbidding parents, two younger siblings – a family that perished one afternoon along with two thousand souls, all from the same village, as were their Romanian executioners.

Eli arrived in Britain completely on his own. He ended up in

the East End because he was settled there by a Jewish aid organ-
ization. 'I started a refugee from Fascism. Then I was a refugee
from communism!'

He knew no English. 'I asked people to teach me words.
I collected them. Made up phrases to help me remember.
'The-cheese-in-the-moon.' Eli recited. 'The-milkman-with-the-
milk. I had to have the very best pronunciation. I was going to
meet Winston Churchill, no?'

'In the Gymnasium, everyone studied German. Would you
believe it? That was in the 1930s. You know what? It saved my
life!' He paused, then corrected himself. 'And this face.' He gripped
his chin as if his features were a commodity. 'I had a good face.'

Eli explained how he was able to pass himself off as a non-
Jew. How he had been 'blessed' with that ability.

'You could tell who would make it just by their face.' To
illustrate the point, he then began a deeply macabre exercise,
assessing each JFC member in order to indicate who would have
survived, and who would have perished. 'Becky – no. Gloria –
yes. Izzy – certainly not! Monty – perhaps.'

'What about me?' Suzy asked. This self-appointed angel of
death sized her up.

'You, Shoshana, have a good face. I told you.'

20

Suzy cried for most of the train journey. She didn't care what
people thought. She was heading back to BC with Eli's amazing

life swirling inside her head. And Rosabella on her wedding day, standing on a bridge over a pond, her life drawing to a close.

She didn't find sleep that night, and missed class the next morning. She arrived at H-Block just after lunch, successfully finding an available darkroom in which she locked herself, working furiously throughout that afternoon.

She got to Terry just as he was leaving his office, showing him the hurriedly produced first prints from the evening before.

'Wow!'

He unlocked his office. Took her inside.

'Will you look at these!' Terry carefully examined the contact sheets. 'They're incredible!'

Suzy knew they were. She knew it from the moment she had positioned Eli in her camera lens.

Suzy started to describe what had happened, but found herself hesitating. It was partly lack of sleep, partly the emotional impact of having to revisit that terrible story. But it was mostly that she felt somehow *privileged*.

'What's the matter?'

Suzy couldn't find the words.

She didn't say anything about it on the phone to her mother that evening. It was just good hearing her voice, her warm talk of Suzy's return to Leeds for the Easter holiday. She would have preferred to stay over at Nick's, but he had a so-called rowing club committee meeting after gym, with the downing of large quantities of alcohol the main agenda item. She couldn't face him in that state.

Eli called her. Bizarrely, he was talking as if their previous encounter hadn't happened. He wanted to discuss Grahame Hargreaves, when the meeting was taking place, what the protest would entail.

'Eli!' Suzy finally felt compelled to interrupt him. 'Yesterday. Everything you told me.'

'Sad life, no?'

Suzy returned to her BC room. She decided to give these latest depictions of Eli pride of place on her packed JFC wall of photographs. She started playing with the arrangement of images, then moving to construct a chronological row of Eli shots. She began with the old negative prints: Eli as a child between his parents, the teenager pushing along a bicycle, the young adult on the brink of marriage, then Eli as he was today – performer, joker – but more truthfully a devastated soul.

It was the long gap in between – from young adulthood to this old man. Suzy thought about all the years he had lived alone, the absence of family photographs on his mantelpiece, and she was crying again.

Terry asked Suzy to lead with her latest Eli photographs at that following day's group tutorial.

Those who had met Eli were shocked by the portrayals, as Suzy still was herself. There was something so raw and elemental in their animation and anguish. It also felt acutely private. The uninhibited honesty created a mood of sensational trespass.

It was Barry who raised the point, whether these were overly intrusive. The issue had been raised before, but now incredibly

Suzy was the target. She carefully listened to Terry's restated defence although, for the first time, she felt less certain. What she found herself thinking was not just how she had foisted herself into his world, but also its exact opposite – how he had been propelled into hers.

Gareth followed, with Stewart presented in two contrasting compositions. In the first he was in a chair in front of a television, a red and white football scarf swathed around his neck. He was leaning forward intently, eyes and mouth extended. In the second, Gareth had put himself *inside* the image. Stewart was in his bed and Gareth was feeding him from a tray. It was extraordinary.

'He had been given his meal. The nurse had come in and left. It was a real struggle for him.'

Terry encouraged intrigue in the class's response.

'So why did you decide to photograph it?' Megan asked.

'I was helping him. I wanted to show that.'

It was as Megan pressed him that Gareth clarified: 'I wanted to show that, as a gay man myself.'

Suzy surprised herself in not being surprised. There was something about Gareth's earlier work that had already sparked the thought. Here, he was using photography to demonstrate a true empathy in the most straightforward and unashamedly public of ways, and it struck Suzy as deeply heroic.

Terry concluded the class with grave words on the approaching holiday, and the need to begin 'wrapping up' the project narratives.

Suzy went over and hugged Gareth as the chairs scraped at the class's end.

'Why did you do that?' Nick asked her.

'He's done a brave thing. Can't you see that?'

In the Granary, Suzy told Nick definitively that she wouldn't be joining him on his Lake District holiday. She blamed it on the Passover holiday, but that wasn't her reason. Part of it was the thought of being reunited with Nick's illustrious friends, the Eves and Howards, and talk of horse riding and geography studies at *proper* universities – twenty-four hours a day of it.

But the more significant reason was Nick's refusal to attend the Hargreaves protest. That Wednesday apparently represented some vital rowing occasion. Suzy couldn't believe his priorities. It was what she repeated at the table.

'Just because they're not yours!'

He was such a tall, strong man – and she felt abandoned by him.

21

Suzy sat for a moment of final plotting with Megan and Jo after class that Wednesday. Nick bade his farewell, adding in a limp good luck. Suzy might have reciprocated. After all, he had hours of splashing ahead of him.

Megan and Jo became the first to whom she revealed Eli's story, including his wife's suicide.

'It's awful! And to blame himself like that. God! It's another world,' said Jo.

'Eli doesn't think it is.'

236

'What?'

'Another world. He thinks it's still this world.'

As they walked towards the Union building to join the demonstration outside the Debating Society meeting, Suzy pondered that word – *debate*. It rested on the assumption that there were two points of view of equal integrity – racism was as intellectually valid as anti-racism – with the truth implicitly lying somewhere in between. Suzy had left her camera behind that day. She wasn't coming to onlook. She was coming to protest!

'Nazi scum – Out! Out! Out!'

They could hear it before they witnessed it – an army of student agitators taking up position. The university authorities had set up metal barriers creating a corridor of rage on either side of the main path leading up to the Union. Suzy, Megan and Jo wriggled through to the front, securing a panoramic view of the proceedings. Suzy briefly regretted the absence of red carpeting to complete the effect. A number of stewards stood beyond the barriers, overly distinguished in bright yellow jackets, scanning the crowd with undisguised boredom. *Bloody students!* she could see in their faces, a sentiment no doubt shared by the clump of meandering police gathered around the entrance.

There had been speculation that British People's Party supporters might mount a counter-demonstration, but they had so far failed to materialize. The banners protruding above heads were all of one hue, slick ones from various political groupings zealous to exhibit their anti-racist credentials – the Socialist Forum, the East End Labour Alliance. Others were more crudely formed, with one putting forward a simple proposition which, what it lacked in intellectual rigour it made up for in the force of the language: 'Hargreaves is a Fascist Fuckhead!'

Soon a large sheet was being unfurled. Its words declared 'The East End Remembers Cable Street – They Shall Not Pass!' in striking red letters. Suzy thought of all those thousands who had once stood up to the menace of the Black Shirts. She imagined a teenage Monty manning the barricades. And now Suzy herself was part of that tradition. She was *proudly* an East End Jew.

As the time of the meeting approached, with the BPP failing to materialize, vilification became exclusively directed at those hapless students who had chosen to attend the debate, presumably on the assumption that their sympathies were suspect. A barrage of jeers accompanied each cluster along the pathway, some choosing to walk defiantly with heads aloft, others scurrying along like accused entering a courthouse.

A number in the crowd, evidently frustrated by the lack of contention, turned their abuse on the stewards, and then the police. It quickly came to an end when someone shouted 'down with exams!' causing huge amusement. Propriety was restored when a television van drew up.

By the formal start of the event, Hargreaves himself had still to make his appearance. A rumour started circulating that he was already inside, smuggled in through a back door, and it was clear that some demonstrators were beginning to make their way inside. Suzy, Megan and Jo were soon following.

The Union auditorium was packed, brimming with noisy

bustle. A student in bizarrely formal attire – suit and tie – was seated centre stage. A podium was to his front, with twin sets of empty chairs on either side. He looked nervous, scraping one hand with the other, as if a hesitant bridegroom poised to walk down the aisle.

Stewards were situated at various strategic points. Suzy caught sight of Salvo and Gareth waving from a far-off section. Being on the student newspaper, Megan had been able to reserve seats close to the front. No one was sure what was about to happen, but there was an acute sense that something dramatic would.

Hargreaves entered last, walking behind the three other speakers, greeted with an uproar of sound, an odd concoction of cheers and jibes that reverberated wildly around the hall. He was a strangely weedy man, taking his seat with a mannered, absent-minded air. Suzy imagined how she might have composed Hargreaves's face to reflect the perniciousness of his creed, yet it was disappointingly featureless. And then she realized that Hargreaves was the more sinister for it, the menace heightened through his very blandness.

As the noise persisted, the prematurely besuited student rose to his feet. His attempt at silencing the audience consisted of the delivery of some sort of pompous address. Suzy caught brief bits of it, something along the lines of 'the importance of every opinion being heard'.

'Nazi scum! Out! Out! Out!' struck up from the auditorium's west side. Some in the audience started barracking the protesters. A scuffle broke out prompting stewards to swing into action, working in a sweep from the left, frogmarching designated troublemakers from the hall. Suzy would need to act swiftly.

Hargreaves himself was remarkably calm. Suzy stared directly at him, willing all her disgust and contempt to ooze from her. In his proud bearing, she sensed a satisfaction, as if this was all some form of saintly suffering. Suzy carefully lifted from her bag the tray of eggs.

As planned, Jo attempted to cover Suzy's actions, walking to her front as she slid along the aisle. Then unexpectedly, Hargreaves himself stood up, which appeared to act as a signal, for the churning tumult of noise suddenly died, as if someone had sucked from the room all its swirling venom.

Suzy turned her gaze to where Hargreaves himself had turned, to what had transfixed everyone in the hall, to the grotesque figure standing feet from him on the stage. He was draped in a long white sheet that was splattered with bright blood red. It was smeared across his face, dripping from his hands. Suzy focused on the shocking lustre of the colour. It was an utterly fantastical image. The man was holding a card that proclaimed just one word –'Auschwitz'.

'Eli!' Suzy screamed. 'Eli!'

They would release Eli into her custody as long as Suzy guaranteed to take him immediately off campus.

The stewards had placed Eli in a side room while they resolved what to do, and were clearly relieved to have someone prepared to claim him. He looked such a forlorn figure, sitting alone among scattered chairs. Suzy guided him to his feet, helped him ease the gruesome sheet over his head, stood with him in an empty men's bathroom while he washed off the remains of what he revealed to be cow's blood.

They walked back to his flat largely in silence.

'Did the meeting continue?' Eli asked.

'No,' replied Suzy. 'It didn't.' She paused. 'You won!'

'*We* won,' he corrected.

And as they walked, Eli told Suzy another of his wartime stories. How he had once come across a man, standing alone in a forest clearing. He didn't speak or anything. Just stood there, covered from head to toe in bright blood red.

Nick would have been expecting Suzy at Sports Night. It was the last of the term. But she stayed with Eli, in his flat, listening to his stories.

PART 3

SPRING

1

Suzy worked on the project throughout her train journey, using the full extent of the table to spread out her contact sheets and prints, careful to contain a parallel mess of piled-up Far Right quotes on the adjoining seat, which she was continually testing against various images. She enjoyed the inquisitive stares of her neighbours. Yes, she was a photographer.

However, the effect was somewhat compromised by the ticket collector's cruelly loud request to see her student card. Suzy could imagine a time when she would tire of it. She thought about that other of society's discounted populations – the Old Age Pensioners. Students and OAPs; that eternal relationship – Suzy and the JFC!

As the train drew into Leeds, the hallowed Leeds United Football Club to her left, the great blackened steel arches that marked the station's entrance embracing her, she caught herself feeling pleased to be back. It was a warm and reassuring sensation, intimation that maybe she didn't need to travel so far away after all.

Her mother was at the station as expected, high on the platform to pounce her welcome. Yet she looked tired.

It wasn't long before her mother was asking about Nick. He

had been angry with Suzy for not showing up at Sports Night, had even telephoned to BC. When she told him the next morning about Eli, how she had spent the evening with him after the events of that afternoon, Nick had pouted like a ridiculous child. The farewell had been brief.

Neverthless, as usual, Suzy didn't say much and, unusually, her mother didn't pursue it. Suzy wondered if that was indicative of a certain relief. The fact that her mother liked Nick in itself meant very little. She liked Bob Monkhouse, and Ian Botham. In truth, Suzy had never been clear what rating he had received from her mother, although she suspected her inscrutability provided its own message. The fact that Nick was not of the nice Jewish boy variety was an essential ingredient that had drawn her to him in the first place. And now strangely she found herself looking forward to coming home.

However, Suzy resolved that she mustn't let their situation consume her. Her LNU priorities lay elsewhere, in the completion of the project with the short third term looming, the final deadline mere weeks away.

'So I've got you all to myself!' her mother declared. She was wrong. Suzy had brought with her Eli and Becky, Gloria and Monty, Wolfie and Miriam. She hoped her mother would make them all welcome.

What was Easter throughout most of Britain, was firmly the holiday of Passover for a small, determined enclave concentrated in the environs of Alwoodley and Moortown. And with Passover came housecleaning, the purchase and preparation of special foods, the organisation of the Seder meal that launched the festival. Returning for Passover was more a form of enlistment, with Suzy deputed to operational spheres that ensured a deep reacquaintance with the kitchen.

As she scrubbed vegetables, she found herself imagining her Friendship Club comrades going through the similar rituals of preparation. She had received her invitation to their own communal Seder. Suzy considered how her relationship with the Club members had been so completely transformed over the course of the year. Unlike her fellow students, transplanted on a three-year tenancy, these people were the authentic East End. They had welcomed her with such enthusiasm. She couldn't imagine saying goodbye.

Eli telephoned shortly before the festival began to extend holiday wishes. He talked about 'being asked' to lead the JFC Seder service, and Suzy enjoyed hearing him returned to his boastful best. He expressed his thanks to her. For what Suzy wasn't precisely sure, and she reciprocated, hers being for his tremendous help with the project. They could both be grateful.

'Have a good Passover, Rabbi Eli!' she ended on.

'And you, rebbetzin Shoshana!'

Suzy's first Seder night was with her mother and what had become a familiar small cast of regulars – her mother's sister, Bernice, who behaved with the imperious air of an aspiring royal personage; her ambivalent escort and husband, Maurice; their singular son Julian, who made a point of growing by several inches each year, and acted as if his brain was similarly spacebound.

Maurice began the service. Until he had become unwell, that role had been the prerogative of her grandfather, whose earrings once again adorned Suzy in tribute. She recalled the Seder service two years before, when they had sat around his hospital bed. With a mighty effort, her grandfather had managed to start them off with words of Hebrew blessing. In weeks he would be dead.

Maurice's recitation in Hebrew had the same faltering manner as his English. Everyone took a turn in the proceedings, mostly rendering the text in its English translation, each contributing to the retelling of that defining saga of the Jewish people, the exodus of the children of Israel from Egypt, the journey from slavery to freedom.

Suzy contemplated the extract read by Julian stating that Seder participants were obliged to feel as if they had personally endured that extraordinary journey, that retelling was a re-experience. She thought about it in the context of photographic narrative. Does the reading of a photograph constitute a re-experience?

Suzy was given the dubious pleasure of reciting the horrors of the ten plagues. The terrible vengeance wrought by God upon the Egyptians for refusing to let the Israelites go. Locusts, darkness, boils, and then that terrifying finale – the murdering of every first-born child. Freedom had come at such alarming cost. Had that also to be re-experienced?

Suzy shocked her mother by suggesting they go to synagogue the next morning. There were far smaller numbers than the Rosh Hashanah masses, which made the whole occasion feel more intimate. Yet this congregation still far exceeded the meagre attendance of the Gates of Peace. The familiar core of faithful was there with their intense devotional manners that Suzy usually found so intimidating, but which she now chose to view more benignly. They were after all the keepers of the flame.

In his sermon, the Rabbi spoke about the meaning of Passover, and how that great journey to freedom might be understood today. He talked of Jews living as minority communities across the world, and that condition being one of 'brokenness'. 'Jews are a fractured people,' he proclaimed, making it all sound so courageous.

The second Seder night saw Suzy reassigned to second parent, and second family. Her mother had set up her own second night tradition, meeting up with another area divorcee, her boyfriend, and – 'thank goodness!' – no children.

'Doesn't he have any friends to introduce you to?'

It was the sort of remark Suzy missed making. She enjoyed reacquainting herself with one of her mother's withering 'none of your business' looks. There were parameters to this sisterhood for both of them.

Baby Jennifer greeted her at the door, Charlotte projecting the poor creature from behind. 'Hello big sister!' Charlotte unfortunately mimicked in baby voice. Jennifer herself appeared not the least interested, grimacing as her sibling slipped inside, far happier to return to the anonymity of her mother's shoulder.

The service was a solo affair with the exception of the *Four Questions*, traditionally recited by the youngest and, with Jennifer excused, remaining Suzy's assignment. Father assumed responsibility for the rest, head bowed towards the ancient book, mumbling through the text as if ensuring his boredom with the ritual was shared. The baby did make an intermittent contribution from her bedroom upstairs via the crude but highly effective method of voluble screaming. Charlotte would swiftly leave the table and, as her father continued, Suzy sensed a growing discomfort, facing his abandoned child alone. She was sure his reading quickened.

The next time Jennifer cried, Suzy volunteered. She managed to placate her through the shaking and squeezing of various toys, and her own soft words. Suzy remained with her for a while, captivated by the firework display of facial contortions. It reminded her of another of Terry's aphorisms – if only the photographer could capture just one-hundredth of the complexity of people!

Suzy also helped Charlotte serve the food. Her father remained steadfast in his chair as if satisfied that he had fully met his duties for the evening. Charlotte complained about her lack of time to prepare the food, then asked about her meal of the previous night, which sounded to Suzy as if she was comparing her culinary skills with that other Mrs Green. She was tempted to make plain that her father didn't leave because of her mother's cooking, dear Charlie, he left because of *you* – whatever her father might persist in claiming.

After the meal, the front door of the house was symbolically opened for Elijah the prophet. His filled glass was the table centrepiece. Suzy read the explanation of that ritual closely, how Elijah would herald the coming of the Messiah, and the door was opened to express yearning for that time. She wondered if her Eli might yet wander in!

Her father's remarks to Suzy that evening were as usual largely administrative. He needed something from her for his tax return, and there was a question on her accommodation for next year, about which she hadn't even begun to think. He could offer her only three or four days' work in the shop that holiday. As cutely as possible, she asked about picking up a new pair of sunglasses and he waved his hand, which Suzy took as a yes.

'How's your mother doing?' It was that question again, the one that he would never dare ask her mother directly. He'd lost that right. Yet she knew it was still important for him.

'She's fine.' Suzy provided some brief elaboratory remarks, mainly on her work at the school. In truth, Suzy couldn't really say how she was doing, not any more. She had left her just as he had done. They were now accomplices.

Charlotte was the more expansive with Suzy, asking about her London life while managing to avoid any reference to the course itself, the very notion of which appeared beyond her. Suzy never really regarded herself as being in London. She lived in the East End. London was what happened next door.

'We're so looking forward to visiting you one day,' said Charlotte.

And yet they hadn't.

And so Suzy talked at length about her studies: Terry's spectacular teaching, her colourful classmates, the amazing JFC, her friendship with Eli, her fall-out with Nick. She answered all the questions she could imagine they might have eventually made it round to asking. It really wasn't that hard.

Suzy finished on whether they would be venturing down for the end of year show. Her father was non-committal, glaring at her with that vague 'don't you understand!' expression that Suzy had never really understood, as if they were equally at fault.

It was getting late.

'What was our surname before it was Green?' Suzy asked.

Her father was perplexed. 'I think a great grandfather changed it. Something unpronounceable!'

And he didn't even know his own name.

2

Suzy's work on the project began in her bedroom, the first images introduced to the walls being the period shots that the JFC members themselves had provided for her opening collage. Her ambitions expanded with the conclusion of the Seder nights, and she rapidly came to occupy most of the dining-room space, her photographs initially smothering the surface of the table before crawling up the walls aided by Blu-tack, with firm assurances given to her anxious mother.

Suzy had amassed a substantial number, and her last shots of Eli created whole new possibilities. What she had to accomplish was the awesome task of completing a sequential, engaging narrative that fully exploited the interplay of text and visuals. It was on the latter that Suzy now focused.

Terry had given her the idea of approaching the undertaking *images up* – exploring linkages on the basis of immediate emotional resonance, rather than the more usual methodology of building obvious visual connections. She wanted to try to trick herself out of being overly analytical, using the power of spontaneity to place her compositions against each other in unexpected ways.

Suzy started using a large notepad to keep track of the various permutations as they continually evolved across the pink wallpapered walls of the dining room. Different scenarios were allowed to settle alongside each other while she assessed their merits. She even enlisted her mother in the process, gaining the reaction of a fresh pair of eyes, each time making careful record.

The sensory experience was enhanced with the replaying of her collection of interview tapes, the most dramatic being her last with Eli. The emotion was even clearer in hearing his voice in isolation. The comment on his wife's suicide, his obvious guilt, was still so heartbreaking. It made her think how strong he was, just to keep living.

Most troubling was listening again to his reference to a *good face*. Suzy stared along the wall at each JFC member as his voice pronounced on their fate: Becky, Gloria, Izzy, Miriam – life or death. It was chilling.

Her mother grew concerned that she was becoming too wrapped up in the project. 'This is supposed to be a holiday. You're being obsessive again!'

Suzy was realizing just how much the project really mattered to her. It wasn't just her course mark. It had become something far more, and not just about proving herself as a photographer. 'Who *are* these people?' her mother had protested as the Jewish Friendship Club took over her home. A remarkable, irresistible gang. That was what Suzy was so determined to portray.

However, Suzy did want to spend time with her mother. They went shopping in Leeds city centre, Suzy once again featuring her mother in various shots which she threatened to turn into an essay, updating her original course application to a 'Return to Home Truths'. And she took her mother to the cinema.

Suzy had heard about the French film *Au Revoir les Enfants*, relating a true story of Jewish children taken into hiding in France during the Second World War. Her mother wasn't keen on going because such films were 'too upsetting'. Suzy nevertheless persuaded her, and they shared tissues throughout. Suzy had never witnessed a cinematic exploration of the Holocaust before, and she found the graphic portrayal of the terrifying situation faced by people not that much younger than herself both moving and shocking.

Nick phoned from the Lake District. He was having a 'fantastic' time, when it stopped raining. Some new pub games had been learned. He was thinking about going down to London for the Oxford Cambridge boat race, some sort of Rowing Club reunion whose purpose Suzy suspected would have very little to do with the race itself.

She talked about the film, its affect on her, how it made her think about what would have happened to her in such circumstances.

'I would have protected you!'

Her immediate reaction was to doubt that. What about Hargreaves! she wanted to shout back at him.

And she and her mother even managed to get drunk. Opening the bottle was her mother's suggestion. The second was Suzy's. They were on the sofa, giggling like teenagers. For some reason, her mother was talking about how she lost her virginity. If it weren't for the wine, Suzy would have been completely discomfited.

'It was with your father!' her mother protested. 'You know I wanted lots of children.' She was straightening herself. 'He would only have the one. Told him he was being selfish. *Not yet*, he kept saying.'

Suzy stared at her mother, trying to read her face as she watched it sharpen.

'I could see how much it bothered you, being an only child. It wasn't right. *Not yet*! Now it's too late – for me. Not for him!'

'Let's change our name,' Suzy interrupted. 'Let's go back to Liebovitz.'

'Hey. You never were a Liebovitz!'

'Can't I be now? I'm bored with Green. Don't you want to keep your family name going? How am I ever going to be a famous photographer with a name like Suzy Green?'

'I *hate* your bloody photography!'

It was said with such venom. From nowhere. Suzy was stunned, as indeed appeared her mother. She started shaking her head. Suzy couldn't speak.

'Dear! I just, I always thought we'd be close!' Her mother

took her hand, playing with her fingers. 'You know. Mothers and daughters.'

'We are close!' Suzy spluttered.

'We *were* close. Until the divorce. Then you hid yourself away – with that . . . contraption of yours, that *he* bought you. You don't *tell me things*! I'm your mother! Why not? Why not?!'

Suzy put her mother to bed that night. She was like a little girl – cuddling, clawing Suzy on the stair.

Suzy slipped her into bed, kissed her forehead.

'You know, I'll always love your father,' her mother mumbled. 'You know why? Because of you. Because we made you.'

A bulky envelope arrived for Suzy. The writing was unfamiliar, the letters of the address distinctively indicated with childlike precision.

The inside contained a mass of newspaper cuttings – speculation on growing support for the BPP in the local elections, planned anti-poll tax demonstrations and police fears over public safety, an attack outside a pub on an Asian youth. It made the East End sound like a war zone. Each article was carefully highlighted in yellow highlighter pen lest the viewer's eye wander. Despite her Leeds sojourn, Eli was keeping up her education.

He didn't actually include a message. His only words were in the form of small scribblings allotted to several of the articles. The exact address of the pub where the attack occurred was written beside its picture. In another, the name of the local BPP leader quoted was circled. Eli had doodled with the letters of his name, bits of Devlin reassembled as both *EVIL* and *DEVIL*.

Suzy thought of Elijah fighting with the Devil over the soul of the East End.

Suzy found a tattooist that afternoon. The pain was intense and, through gritted teeth, she accepted it as the sensation of ceremonial. A far lesser creation than Jo's swan, but Suzy's own, the smallest of roses, bright bright red, high on her left shoulder. A *shoshana*.

And Suzy *did* feel different, just as she had so hoped.

First to learn of the outbreak of flora on her arm were her Leeds friends, meeting up again in the Cherry Tree pub. Suzy discovered that she had neatly enhanced her arty bohemian reputation. Marcus wanted to touch it. Lawrence bought her a drink in its honour. She surprised herself by finding this reunion more satisfying, and she realized that her previous resentment was in truth probably more to do with herself than any of them. Suzy was recognizing the benefits of reaching some sort of mature equilibrium – neither world, Leeds nor university, need necessarily be at the expense of the other.

Nick telephoned again, full of the joys of the aftermath of a London weekend that had as its highlight the brief sighting of two boats rounding a bend. Suzy told him about the tattoo.

'For goodness sake! Why?'

He made it sound like an act of self-abuse.

She did it to feel different, and to make a point. To herself, and to the planet. She was Shoshana. Shoshana Liebovitz.

3

Her mother was annoyed with her for going back to university early. Yet it was only by a few days. Suzy justified it in terms of stealing a march on her classmates, having free reign with the department's equipment, the joys of the choice of darkrooms.

'I thought I'd have you for longer!'

Her mother would be down for the end-of-year show – 'wouldn't miss it!' – despite having endured an extensive preview throughout her house.

'You've got your dining room back.' Third term was a short eight weeks. 'I'll see you soon!' Suzy was saving the news of the tattoo until then, carefully leaning from the train window to ensure her sleeve didn't ride up.

As the train moved off, they exchanged last words along the platform, her mother quickly emotional. 'Love you, Sooz!' Suzy was matching her tear for tear.

As tradition dictated, Suzy waved for as long as she could still make out the shape of her mother on the platform, watching it thin and fade. Miriam had once said that parents love their children more than children love their parents. It wasn't true. They just love in different ways. One day she would feel able to tell her mother that.

There was something distinctly uncomfortable about arriving on a student-free campus. Suzy felt strangely ill at ease walking in an unprecedented quiet up that last stretch of dimly lit road towards BC, watching her shadow repeatedly fade and revive under the streetlights. The hall that would normally be bubbling with student mischief was filled only with a palpable silence, as if some plague had wiped out all the inhabitants in one deadly strike. At least Sir Aubrey Bernard had survived, his bust still greeting at the entrance. Perhaps he might be glad to have lived on in such a fashion after all.

Life did finally manifest itself in the presence of an elderly security guard with whom Suzy exchanged words, unusually heartfelt. She picked up her post from the pigeonhole and headed to her room, where her first action was to switch on the radio, turning it up loud.

The envelope that stood out was inevitably the yellow one. It didn't have a postmark, implying it was hand delivered. The greeting card inside, in matching yellow, stated a simply conceived 'welcome home'. She knew Eli would be expecting to see her, and she was looking forward to seeing him, but her early return reflected a more pressing concern.

The bright stillness of the LNU campus that next day struck Suzy as altogether invigorating. When she emerged from the Underground, she swiftly donned her new sunglasses successfully purloined from her father's shop over the holidays. She soon found herself being entertained by young skateboarders enjoying the freedom of the university's empty pathways, carousing in a way that bolstered Suzy's sense that she was walking in springtime. She marched into the photography department like a factory owner, amusingly disregarding the sharp 'oh God, not a student already!' expression of the duty secretary.

As anticipated, Suzy had the pick of darkrooms. She settled herself in the most spacious, and therefore most prestigious – darkroom A. In an act of supreme decadence, she spent that whole morning deliberating over the same picture of Eli. She was playing with different ways the image could be cropped, and their impact on the composition's energy, while also experimenting with different types of print papers.

It took a while for her to answer the knock on the door, carefully battening down any light-sensitive material. Surprisingly, the interloper proved to be the great man himself, Terry, who had similarly sneaked back early to develop some of his own private work. These were being put forward for a national photographic prize, and he invited her next door to render an opinion. Suzy gushed with the honour.

His work was breathtaking. The theme was *landscapes of Britain*, and Terry presented Suzy with a number of stunning colour compositions – sweeping meadows of rich greens broken by stone walls, curving and twisting like veins; cockles being dug out of mud flats, beached boats like languorous sunbathers looking on; great soaring cliffs in a dawn mist as if capturing the very moment land first raised itself from the oceans.

'What do you think?'

'They're completely wonderful.'

She quickly straightened herself, and followed that up with her best attempt at a considered Terryesque critique. He then shocked her by suggesting lunch.

Across the street from H-Block, over matching tuna salad

sandwiches, Terry was remarkably expansive. It was when he mentioned that his wife was a model – 'photographer and model. Bit clichéd, I know' – that Suzy immediately knew she had already encountered her.

'She's your photograph in the National Portrait Gallery!'

Terry was impressed.

'I knew it! There was something about how you took her. How she looked at you.'

They lived in a small apartment block in Bethnal Green, giving Terry one stop less than Suzy on the commute to university, although he preferred to walk – in theory at least, he added before tackling tuna slipping from a corner of his sandwich.

The pause gave Suzy the opportunity to contemplate the full triumph of the occasion, and whom she might call with the news. She cursed the fact that they were so unlikely to be spotted. The camera would have to bear witness, and she cajoled Terry into posing, shuffling her chair round to his while the café owner readied the machine.

In discussing the course, Suzy revealed to Terry how she had never looked forward to any class in school, and now she was terrified of missing just one. 'I never imagined you could actually enjoy learning.' It wasn't flattery. It was true.

'That's because you've found your vocation!' Terry said. 'There's a part of photography that can't be taught. It's either inside you, or it's not. A *visual instinct*. I think I've got it. I know you have.'

Terry brought up Eli's name. His status on campus had soared since the Hargreaves meeting. Terry asked a variety of questions about his background, making Suzy feel like his publicist. However, it gave Suzy the opportunity to raise something that was bothering her, which directly arose out of the Hargreaves affair. She wanted reassurance that she herself wasn't giving a *platform to hate* by using extremist material in her own project work.

'What! You think you're all of a sudden promoting racism? Don't be silly! You're exposing it. Holding it up to ridicule.'

He even paid for her lunch. Suzy was returning to the darkroom, while Terry headed off to track down wife and daughter and 'pretend I'm a new man.' She thought about the photograph of his wife, and the rapport of love that this image so obviously revealed.

'Don't stay in there too long,' he advised. 'You'll come down with darkroom fever!' Terry squeezed his eyes and crouched in illustration.

Her crush was now seismic.

Suzy called her mother that night. She had news that Eli had telephoned trying to locate her. 'I told him you were in London, and he put the phone down!'

Suzy called him later. He was clearly angry that she had not yet been in contact. Having been back barely twenty-four hours, she found this highly unreasonable. However, Eli did sound authentically anxious, over what he wouldn't elaborate, despite her pressing. 'I need to see you,' was all he would say in that familiar insistent tone that made resistance sound like betrayal.

Suzy agreed to meet up with him that Sunday. 'No, I'm not going to synagogue tomorrow!'

Friday saw a trickle of bedraggled students rolling into BC for a weekend of post-vacation decompression before the start of term.

Suzy phoned Nick's London number, appreciating his latest answering machine message – 'Go away, I'm getting pissed in the Lake District!' The fact that she wasn't sure when he was returning said everything about the current drift in their relationship. She called because she didn't want their first meeting to be under the glare of the class but, more especially, the idea of spending that weekend on her own was making her feel quite queasy. She longed to bump into familiar faces.

Suzy spent some time indulging the art gallery that was her BC home. She primarily restored a number of the JFC prints that had accompanied her to Leeds, but also introduced several images sneaked from her Fabulous Faces work. It had occurred to her that this was her very first proper professional job, and rightfully deserved recognition.

Suzy ate by herself that Friday night, going to the Bombay Parlour that was the local curry house, stopping on the way to pick up the flimsy companionship of a newspaper. The weightier press led with matching images of Soviet tanks ominously rolling into Lithuania. However, Suzy went for local interest, sampling the *East London Chronicle* which, in between gulps of vindaloo, offered up fevered coverage on the approaching local elections. Suzy speculated on the number of articles being subjected to Eli's yellow highlighter.

4

Suzy excused an early night that Friday by setting her alarm. She did some work Saturday morning, asking forgiveness before the photographs of the Club members for disturbing them on *Shabbes*. By lunchtime, she had settled on truancy as her next assignment, taking herself off to admire the exuberant textile displays in the sarı shops around Brick Lane, where Jo had already been measured up. From there she went on to Spitalfields market, by which time she had resolved to compound her crime, gleefully extending her escape to the rest of the day.

She caught the Tube to Bond Street, justifying her outing by seeking out the prestigious Mayfair galleries that were her ultimate aspiration. As Suzy marvelled at the works on display, she made sure her camera swung from her shoulder, although she did wonder how a CV launched by Fabulous Faces would be received.

In the absence of any alternative, Suzy stayed on in the West End for that evening. Supper was fast food consumed on a park bench in Leicester Square in the company of a diminutive Charlie Chaplin. She then kicked around Covent Garden and Soho, the places that, from Leeds, were assumed to be her regular haunts. There was a bustle and brashness here that was definitely out of sync with the East End. She took pictures of a world to which she didn't really belong.

On the train journey back, Suzy was able to scrutinize a couple lost to music, their attachment literally conveyed through the twin earpieces of a Walkman; subdued football supporters, a scarf trailing along the floor as if loyalty had been sorely tested; ravers in uniformly tight luminous trousers beginning their evening with handbar exercises.

A drunk got on the train a couple of stops from Leyton. He announced himself loudly, walking up the train as he begged for money. Suzy stupidly had her camera out of her bag.

'Want to take my picture darling?'

Suzy held her gaze rigidly on the floor, feeling his presence swaying above her, staring at the ragged blackened trainers on his feet.

'Take my picture! Come on darling. Look at me. I'm gorgeous, I am. Look at me!'

She just prayed for Leyton.

'They're going to win seats, here! In Poplar, and Mudchute.' Eli was squashed into his sofa, jacket riding high up his back, Suzy seated in an armchair opposite. An empty whisky glass lay at his feet.

'So what if they do! The world isn't going to come to an end. This isn't Romania!'

Suzy noticed that the picture of Rosabella was still next to her own, exactly as he had first placed her on the mantelpiece.

'Don't you see, Shoshana? The fascists are going to be discussing health, and education – of children! – along from Cable Street!'

'Eli, will you please put some music on!' Suzy was finding its absence oppressive.

Eli searched in his jacket and dramatically whipped out a passport, which he proceeded to wave in front of her. 'I always carry it. A Jew must always have a suitcase packed. It's our fate in the world.'

'Music, Eli – please!'

He got up and shuffled across to the music centre. A delicate, thin voice introduced itself to the room.

'Which one's this?'

'It's *Manon Lescaut*. By Puccini.'

Suzy was glad for the company. In tune with the sound, Eli assumed a more subdued air, as she had hoped. Suzy then launched into an exposition entitled 'Leeds holiday highlights', rendered with as much colour as she could muster. Her description of her Seder nights led her to enquire about the JFC's own. The question appeared to fluster him.

'How was your performance? No doubt up to your usual high standards.'

'I didn't go.'

'Why?' Suzy was bemused. Eli had been the main billing.

'I wasn't feeling well.'

Eli had sounded well enough when he had called her just before the festival began.

'It must have been a big disappointment. Not to go.'

He shrugged.

Suzy resumed her upbeat tone as she brought up the year project. She gaily referred to her foreboding over the approaching deadline, how her priority was now on the intricacies of presentation.

Eli asked about his negatives, when she would return them. Suzy had given him prints, but had kept the negatives while still working on the opening collage concept. She would return these soon.

'You haven't brought your camera!' The absence of her constant companion had just dawned on Eli.

'I don't need to now. That's what I'm telling you. I have plenty. Too much! It's now all down to the final selection. Getting the flow and the story right. Don't worry, you'll be in lots of pictures!'

He stared at her curiously, as if that wasn't the point. The voice through the speakers was light, ethereal.

'Are you angry with me?' he asked her from nowhere.

Suzy was dumbfounded. She scrutinized his face to see if she could discern any hint of commentary, but his expression was utterly blank.

'No! Why would I be?'

He didn't answer. Suzy thought about pursuing it, but changed her mind. There was something in his demeanour. She wondered how many drinks he had enjoyed before her arrival. Suzy had never felt uncomfortable with Eli before, and this new sensation worried her far more than any presumed cause. She wanted to shake him out of his gloom, which made her think that she may well be feeling angry.

'When I'm done – if I get done! – the first showing is going to be at the JFC. I want everyone to see it. Bet you'll all give me the hardest time. You'll be my toughest critics!'

She paused. 'Eli. What's wrong, Eli?'

267

His whole being had suddenly crumpled. Eli put his hands to his face just as he convulsed into tears. Suzy immediately went to him, held him. 'What is it? Eli! What is it?'

Eli turned to her and Suzy was shocked by his appearance. His face was red and contorted, eyes bulging. He was staring out at her, and there was such bleakness in that face. He put his hands on her arms, and moved his head towards her. Suzy immediately realized that, incredibly, he was attempting to kiss her. She just managed to avert her face as he leaned in. Then she started to struggle, feeling the strength of Eli's arms bearing down, the stench of alcohol choking the air.

'Eli! What are you doing, Eli?' she barked at him. 'Stop it!'

Eli released her suddenly. Suzy rushed to her feet while he slumped over.

'I'm going to go now.' She talked in a numb calmness. 'I'm going to go.'

5

Suzy felt a wave of relief as she re-experienced the routine of seating herself in the semicircle of H-Block Room 208.

She had spent the last twenty-four hours in anguished confusion over her encounter with Eli. It had spun and spun in her mind. She was exhausted by it. Suzy had called her mother as soon as she had returned to BC, and the immense effort to conceal her distress had drained her even more. 'Suzy, you have a good week. Don't work too hard!' Her mother had ended the call successfully oblivious.

'Are you OK?' Nick leaned from his seat, staring into her. It was what she so needed to hear from somebody. Salvo began spilling photographs above them, talking feverishly about 'best ever' work. They would talk after class.

Terry surveyed the room, and then enquired after several missing students, Jo and Nina included, but no one had special intelligence. He wasn't happy.

'Where's Jo?' Megan whispered to Suzy. She didn't know.

'Six weeks,' Terry intoned, referring to the looming deadline for the project, which he then cruelly reduced by a week in announcing he wanted to review fully completed displays in tutorial prior to submission. 'After that, I can't help you!'

Suzy couldn't think about the project, nor much else, only Eli. Could she find a way of dismissing it as a moment of folly by an old man with one too many drinks inside him? It was the conclusion she most dearly wanted. To phone him up and share another Eli joke, this time with him the central character. She recalled that last disturbing expression of Eli's, and the sensation that accompanied it, that he wasn't actually *seeing* her.

Eli had telephoned that evening. His name was carefully spelt out in both blue and green on the two messages awaiting her when she returned to BC. Suzy was instantly on the phone to Nick.

Nick drove over to BC that night. He had responded as Suzy had hoped. This time she detailed what had happened more honestly. It spilled forth, the incident thickened out with tears.

Nick focused on whether Eli had hurt her physically. He hadn't.

'Did he actually kiss you?'

'No.'

As Suzy heard herself out, she found her frustrations turning inward. This was her project. The handling of relationships was down to her. Terry had repeatedly stressed the sensitivities involved. Had she failed?

Nick wanted to call Eli, visit his home, confront him in some way. Suzy wouldn't hear of it. He then proposed she raise the matter with Terry, yet Suzy hated the idea of going to him with what she now feared was an admission of failure. Terry was the last person she would want to know of it.

'Eli telephoned to apologize,' Suzy said. She was sure of that.

'So what! Listen. Whatever you do,' Nick held her to emphasize the point, 'don't call him back! Not yet.' He was adamant that it would send the wrong signal. 'Promise me.'

Suzy promised.

She decided to skip the next day's class. There was such dazzling sunshine streaming into her room, inviting her out to play. It was the sort of spring day that bestowed on the season its archetypal image, and it was how Suzy longed to feel. She would escape Terry, and projects, and constructive criticism, *and* the East End. She would set off to do what she loved most – taking photographs.

She got herself to the Tower of London. From there, she hopped on one of the open-roofed tour buses, establishing

herself forthrightly centre front. Her progress began with St
Paul's Cathedral, then on to Trafalgar Square, Buckingham
Palace, the Houses of Parliament, Piccadilly Circus. She caught
street sellers draped in souvenirs, tourists chasing guardsmen, a
cavalry of police, cruising river barges, vast gardens and grand
squares.

Suzy was claiming every postcard image of London ever conceived, taking in all the sites that the tunnelling commuters of
the Underground were condemned to miss. And there was such
grandeur to the city, shining with glorious expectation. She
hunted London all day long.

Evening brought Suzy to Nick's door. She couldn't face
returning to BC after such a day. He wasn't back yet, but housemate Euan invited her in. She sat in Nick's bedroom for a while
amongst the paraphernalia of a boy, confirming that they truly
were a different species. She switched his television on, then
off. On his wall, she touched his prized photograph of an Asian
moon in a night sky, an irredeemably bland shot that drew from
Nick such emotion. It made her think about the inscrutability of
photographs, that their impact was essentially a singular experience.

Nick was the last one home. By that time, three bottles of
wine had been consumed among the four of them – three housemates and Suzy – and a raucous game of football was under
way, with Suzy in goal between the traffic cones. Nick was soon
signed up, and a fourth bottle opened. The cat, designated referee
for the match, was the only one left with any dignity by the end.

Suzy took great pleasure in revealing her tattoo to the house.

It annoyed her that she hadn't yet dedicated serious time to showing it off.

'Why a rose?' Nick asked.

'It's my name!' she slurred. 'I told you!'

Suzy was waiting for Nick to suggest that she stay over. Their difficulties over Easter seemed so long ago. Perhaps he felt it was understood, but she didn't want to presume. In the end, it was Euan who impishly made the offer, which Nick swiftly adopted.

They lay silently in each other's arms on Nick's bed for some time, mesmerized by the late night sumo wrestling on Channel Four.

'I wonder what a sumo wrestlers' class would be like?' Suzy said.

Nick put a hand to his cheek as he contemplated. 'A squeeze!'

Suzy burst into laughter. It was an exquisite sensation, and she allowed her whole body to wriggle and heave under the effect.

One of the players bounced ignobly to the ground. 'They're really ugly, aren't they?' said Nick. 'Sort of grotesque!'

'If I could just get a few of them along to Fabulous Faces,' Suzy giggled.

'Do you think I should go?' Nick asked in an oddly serious tone. He turned to Suzy and assumed a model's pout. 'What d'you think of me, really? How fanciable am I?'

'D'you want me to really show you?' Suzy rolled from the bed. 'Stay just like that!'

Suzy found her camera and steadied herself to take a number

of shots, with Nick on the bed adopting a series of increasingly exaggerated modelesque poses.

Suzy lowered her camera. 'Remember what you told me on New Year's, that you loved me?'

Nick nodded and smiled.

'I'm telling you a secret now. You mustn't tell *anyone*! I liked it.'

6

There were phone messages from Eli throughout that week, but Suzy resisted answering. There was her promise to Nick and, anyway, it would have been too soon for her.

She found it bizarre continuing her work on a project in which he so predominated. Suzy kept finding herself returning to that face, asking him again and again to explain himself. The excuses she formulated in his defence were many – drunkenness; depression; misplaced fatherly affection; an inexplicable emotion getting the better of him; or was it all just some misunderstanding?

Suzy needed all of these if only to stop the matter undermining her concentration. She was so close to finishing the project, delivering her inaugural exhibition as an aspiring photographer, and it was precisely these images of Eli that were to be her hopefully memorable *first impressions*.

Curiously, Eli's name figured routinely in several conversations with classmates. Following the Hargreaves affair, his profile had been dramatically enhanced, and Salvo was 'desperate' to book Eli for a second Sports Night performance. However, it was Megan who was pressing Suzy even more. She had taken several shots of Eli at the Hargreaves event. The one Suzy was most taken by was of the two of them squaring up like aged gunfighters. She noticed in Hargreaves's face what she hadn't observed throughout the whole episode, a flicker of alarm. It was Eli who had finally unnerved him. He *had* won. Megan was involved in a campaign to get out the student vote for the May elections and she planned to invite Eli to a campus talk. Suzy stalled on her advice.

That week also brought news that stunned Suzy – Jo would not be returning that term. Her parents' financial situation had deteriorated. She didn't want to put them under that pressure any longer. Suzy and Jo spoke through tears on the phone.

She arrived at Gloria's that Friday night exhausted, longing for the restorative powers of chicken soup.

Becky was already there, dressed immaculately. 'No camera?'

Gloria seemed tired herself, happy to be left to make final preparations in the kitchen while Becky and Suzy chatted in the living room. The poodle was left to carry word between rooms.

Becky was talking about her husband Jeffrey because it was his birthday. He had passed away over ten years ago. 'There's not a day that goes by when I don't think about him. I loved him but, you know what? I don't think I liked him that much. Sounds funny, doesn't it?' Her expression was exquisite – a blend of melancholy and puzzlement. Suzy regretted not being able to capture it.

Gloria emerged for the candle lighting, ushering in another Sabbath of peace and Suzy followed Becky in kindling a last pair.

As the blessed chicken soup arrived, Gloria declared a 'Suzy's news' moment. Between slurps she obliged, providing a report of her latest Leeds visit, although it now seemed an age ago.

Suzy asked about upcoming Club events. 'Isn't it Yiddish conversation again?'

'If it goes ahead,' announced Gloria sternly.

'Didn't you hear about our Seder night?' Becky quickly followed with obvious relish. 'There was a fight!'

'It was a disgrace!' Gloria continued. 'Eli says he's never coming back. Never coming back! Again! Remember all that fuss last time, Becky.'

'He's a real *meshuggeneh*!' Becky confirmed.

'Was Eli at Seder night?' Suzy was trying to grasp their remarks. 'He told me he was too unwell to go.'

'Good! I hope that means he's ashamed of himself,' said Gloria. 'You know what he called Wolfie? Just because he tried to calm him down. I will certainly *not* repeat that language in front of the candles.'

'What was he arguing with Wolfie about?' Suzy asked.

'No, my dear. Wolfie was trying to stop them, bless him. It was Lionel. Eli was screaming at Lionel of all people! Who wouldn't say "boo" to a goose.'

'What was the argument about?'

'He *slapped* Lionel!' Gloria gulped. 'Across his face. On Seder night. Well I tell you, this time we're not having him back. Eli loves being the outrageous one, but this is just too much!'

Gloria stood up from the table. 'Suzy, you came at just the right time. You saw us at our best. I don't think the Club can go on much longer.' It was delivered with a resigned sadness.

As Gloria disappeared into the kitchen, Becky leaned across to Suzy. 'They were arguing about you.'

'Me!'

'Don't understand myself. That's anyway what Wolfie said. It was something about you.'

7

Nick shocked Suzy, on two counts. He was prepared to forgo his beloved rowing for a Sunday outing, and would risk his car in the venture.

They settled on Brighton, just in case Nick started pining for water. The sun peeked through the clouds on several occasions on the journey down, justifying Suzy's flaunting of her new sunglasses which, in her vest top, neatly complemented her arm's proud bright red rose insignia. 'How arty do I look?'

Nick took Suzy's hand as they weaved in and out of the fashionable shops of The Lanes, before moving on to the extravagantly decorous Brighton Pavilion, their visit taking in a sectioned-off wing which, in characteristic form, Suzy was able to blag their way into, camera waving away the official.

Suzy surprised herself with how comfortable she felt with

Nick. It was as if they had been returned to the very beginning of their relationship. They were both trying again. Suzy needed his company.

They walked along the beachfront armed with ice creams, and up the pier. Nick squeezed them into a photo booth, which Suzy dedicated to the theme of *see no evil, speak no evil, hear no evil*, with the final fourth image improvised as *try to avoid as much evil as you can*. While they awaited the results, Suzy considered the terrifying implications of a mechanical photographer.

'What would Terry think? Where's the *emotional engagement*? This must be the end of the world.'

Nick presented the pictures to Suzy. 'Can you see how this quite exceptional photographer drew out the essence of your soul!'

Supper was illustrious seaside fish and chips devoured against a pinky sunset. Suzy reminisced about childhood day trips to various esteemed Yorkshire resorts.

'Why did your parents separate?' Nick asked.

Suzy laughed, almost choking on a chip. It was the question that had dominated her teens.

'My mum will tell you that my dad simply decided one day he was no longer in love with her. That it was a typical male my-life-has-ended midlife crisis sort of thing.'

'What would your dad say?'

'He would say it was none of your business!'

'What do you say?'

Suzy hesitated. 'Their lives overlapped less and less. That doesn't happen by accident, does it?'

Nick shrugged.

'Do you think you could be happy with the same person your whole life?'

'If it was the right person. Why not?'

'Dad was seeing Charlotte as soon as they separated. He says there was nothing between them before, but she was his assistant in the shop. They saw each other every day.'

Suzy threw the food wrapping into a bin next to them.

'Not long after my birthday, the one where my dad bought me the camera, naturally enough I went out on little adventures with it. I was in town, and I saw the two of them. Nothing unusual in that. They were walking down a street. Dad stopped by a shop window, and Charlotte started straightening his collar.' Suzy paused. 'I followed them for a bit, taking pictures. I felt like a detective. After, I threw away the film.'

Suzy revealed more on the journey home. It had been an acrimonious divorce. 'Lots of blood on the walls!' She spoke mainly about how close she had been to her father. 'He told me once I looked just like my mum, and I knew what he was saying. He couldn't get beyond that! As if I wasn't my own person. He's crap at understanding people. All the presents he ever got me were things *he* liked. Even the camera!'

The temperature that Monday morning was borderline, but Suzy still hadn't exposed her rose on campus so she decided to don a sleeveless T-shirt and give the weather the benefit of the doubt.

She had unsuccessfully tried to persuade Nick to pick her up from BC in his car, emboldened by its outing on their day trip. Anyway, he appeared to have lots of time on his hands. He was still managing to avoid the library in what was becoming a monumental display of indifference.

Suzy's library seat was calculatingly *decorated shoulder to entrance*. She was working on the collage of old photographs that would introduce her display. Here were Izzy and Gloria, Monty and Miriam, all deporting themselves in the guise of youth. Several would have been close to her own age and she tried to imagine them as contemporaries, playing dead ants at Sports Night! Yet she stopped herself lest she undermine the very purpose of her project. She had fashioned these people as extraordinary. They were icons of the East End.

In laying out the images in various patterns, Suzy was trying to coax them into a visually striking mix, still unhappy with her earlier attempts. Her guides were tone and contrast. She was also having difficulty identifying the best image to anchor the piece at its centre, and it was for that purpose that she enlisted Megan.

She had joined Suzy sometime mid-morning, taking a seat opposite after showering the library tables with lurid green leaflets rallying her student comrades for the approaching elections. Shamefully, Megan failed to notice the rose until she had shifted round to Suzy's side, giving out an alarmed 'what's that!' as if Suzy had a diseased arm.

Megan scanned the images, then began to shift them around, at one point placing Eli on bicycle to the fore. But it was another that she kept returning to, sliding to the heart of the constellation the one non-JFC personage in the collection – Rosabella on the bridge. Suzy had added her picture to the collection on a whim, and now she was being promoted to centre stage. Megan was right. There was something in the characterization that lifted the whole display.

Suzy was now obliged to reciprocate, Megan seeking her opinion on the interpretation of a piece – two refugees, an older and younger man, sitting carelessly in an unemployment office.

'Can't you see? There's huge resentment here!'

Suzy couldn't see. There was anxiousness, and solemnity, and plain boredom. Megan was so obsessed with getting a message across to the viewer. Ambiguity seemed to unnerve her.

In class that afternoon Suzy received various responses to her rose, the most creative being Salvo who licked it. She didn't ask him what it tasted like. Nick arrived late, panting as if to emphasize his post-gym condition.

The session was devoted exclusively to what Terry described as 'the science of sequencing'.

He projected five very different pictures onto the wall, all from what appeared to be the same fire scene: a row of firemen grasping hoses, a scattered row of fire engines, exhausted firemen with blackened faces sitting on a grass verge, the building being gutted by fire, close-ups of anguished spectators.

The task was to propose an order for the shots, and soon the class itself was ablaze with suggestion.

Terry used the terminology of *establishing shots*, and *transitional shots*, and *pacing*. He explored the interplay of composition, colour and mood in the building of an effective narrative. Suzy wondered which projects were causing him greatest concern.

Later that afternoon, Suzy took her rose off to Fab Faces where Zandra delivered a robust endorsement. 'So when do I get at the rest of you?' she added, twitching her fingers menacingly.

8

The policeman entered just as Salvo was finishing a lengthy exposition on the theory of aliens being time travellers.

Students shrunk back to create a path as the policeman marched through the crowd, and one sensed a collective sobering. Various shapes of cigarette were stamped out on the floor. Huddled groups silently formed.

Having made his way onto the stage, the policeman announced through the microphone the name of the person he wanted to interview.

Soon, the captain of the netball team had joined him, with the G-strung 'policeman' wriggling ridiculously on top of her.

'Never, ever do that to me!' was Suzy's comment to Nick as the act progressed.

'I know. What a waste of good fruit,' Nick gravely assessed. Salvo nodded uncertainly.

'You boys!'

'What d'you mean? It's a *male* stripper!' retorted Salvo, full of indignance.

Nick had several new pub games acquired from his Lake District holiday, the last involving an increasingly complex series of hand movements that had to be performed in correct sequence. Punishment was a brutal four fingers of beer which ensured copious amounts of alcohol were consumed throughout its playing. Barry was sticking to water, which informed everyone what he was on that night.

Suzy was rescued from a latest game and further retribution by Nina who pulled her into the crush of the dance floor, where they found themselves among a crowd illuminated by an impressive array of fluorescent decoration round necks, arms and waists. Nick sauntered off to his rowing fraternity and river gossip.

Lady Lena made her entry in characteristically vicious mood. The cricket team had lost for a second time in consecutive weeks and their humiliations were extensive, concluding on a drenching that involved a variety of dubious-looking coloured liquids, gleefully administered by the rugby club. Suzy found herself splatted when she danced too close to one of their surviving number.

Not so incredibly, the next voice at the microphone proved to be Salvo's.

A great cheer went up from his classmates, all equally in the dark as to what he was up to. 'Get them off!' Barry shouted. The idea of Salvo as a next strippergram was as plausible as any other.

'Ladies and gentleman! It's coming. This summer. The 1990 World Cup!'

A massive cheer reverberated around the room at its mention.

'England! England!' was now being chanted, led by the football teams. Nina groaned.

'The World Cup. In the Holy Land. The land of the greatest team on Earth. Italy!'

Chanting turned to boos and hissing.

'Please. Please! We Italians want England to do well, but not too well!'

Suzy was now giggling. It was pure Salvo. She couldn't imagine what havoc he was about to wreak.

'Italians gave the world so many fine things. Fine food! Fine wine! Fine women!'

He was a strippergram, Suzy concluded. She was now trying to identify any Italian women in the audience.

'What about fish and chips!' was shouted close by.

'And opera!' Salvo finished.

Suzy inhaled.

'The theme for this year's World Cup is a piece of wonderful opera – "Nessun Dorma"! And here! Tonight! At this famous venue of Sports Night! At the London New University Student Union! I give you the *Lu-ciano* of Lambeth, the *Pav-erotti* of Poplar – singing for us "Nessun Dorma". Please everyone, a big loud student welcome for the maestro himself – *Eeee-liii*!'

A huge cheer erupted. Suzy was stunned by what she was now witnessing. Salvo and Eli were embracing by the microphone. He was wearing a jacket with a handkerchief spilling from a breast pocket in a colour neatly complementing the cravat bustled around his neck.

'Good evening!' he announced through the microphone, to

yet another voluble cheer. Suzy was mesmerized. The man at the centre of such huge ambivalence was suddenly before her, and at his most glamorous. What brought her out of the trance was the sensation of a hand gripping her arm.

'Come on. Let's go!' It was Nick, speaking in an aggressive earnestness.

'Why? Let's hear him. I want to speak to him!'

'No. You mustn't do that!' Nick was insistent, spinning her around and away from Eli. The tone in his voice suggested he possessed a far greater degree of sobriety, which finally swayed her.

They wrestled through crowds whose attentions were all to their behind, where Eli was punching out the song with all the vigour and passion with which Suzy was so completely familiar. His voice swooped and swirled around them as they made their way. He was Suzy's friend. She wanted to tell everyone. This was *her* Eli. She had found him.

'He's singing to me,' she told Nick proudly. 'He's singing to me!'

9

'Ee-li was standing by the bar. I thought maybe you and Suzy had brought him!' Salvo was confused by Nick's manner. 'He wouldn't come to the table. I insisted he must sing for us!'

'Why did you leave?' Salvo then asked. 'I brought Ee-li to see you after. He wanted to see you.'

Suzy turned to Nick.

'I wasn't feeling well,' Nick replied.

'He was really great. Magnifico! He did an encore – twice. You should have seen Ee-li's face when Lady Lena kissed him! That man is a star.'

'He's called Eli not Ee-li,' Suzy said.

'I wonder how long he had been there,' Nick thought aloud after Salvo left.

Suzy *was* bothered by it, but far less than Nick. Indeed, she had significantly mellowed in her attitude towards Eli since the events in his flat, and it was a position she was eager to maintain. Suzy realized that she had been most affected simply by the shock of what had happened, far more than anything that Eli had actually done, and in truth he had *done* very little. That shock was wearing off. What she wanted now most of all was to be able to speak to him and just put the whole matter behind them. It was a question of finding the right context.

She had hoped they would re-establish cordial relations in the relaxed public circumstance of a next JFC event. However, she had now learned that Eli had apparently left the Club and, even more distressingly, over an issue that was somehow linked to herself. Indeed, if she took Gloria literally, the Club itself might close. It horrified her to think that she might be the cause of bringing to an end the very thing she was attempting to exalt. Suzy desperately wanted to calm whatever situation was fomenting around her.

'You know what he was doing, don't you? Our good friend

Ee-li.' Nick leaned across for emphasis. 'He was spying on us!'

And Nick wasn't helping.

Suzy wasn't sure which of Terry's various eyes she found the most disconcerting – there were his own which he would peer from whenever he felt he was being misled or hoodwinked, and there were those other eyes forever on guard in his office: the eyelashed *Clockwork Orange* version leering from the poster, or the lopsided glare of Man Ray's *Object of Destruction* from the shelves. She thought about this constant of *seeing*. Suzy had chosen a profession that provided endless possibility, and for the first time she found herself thinking how exhausting that was. Would she be able to look at anything ever again without always having to *see*?

'So, d'you want the good news or, let us say, points for final development?' Terry pulled himself away from Suzy's latest set of prints laid out across his desk, and down and along the floor. She was grateful to him for his circumspection. There was such little time left, and she had been putting so much effort into it.

He initially highlighted the textual aspects, and how the quotes worked against each of the photographs. 'I really think you've done something interesting, and important here. There's a real sense of your own humanity.'

Terry picked up a shot of Eli assisting Monty with his bingo card, their angled heads suggesting a comfortable intimacy, Eli's face a picture of compassion, beside a text that ended, 'drive out the muds and Jews!'

'There's something very arresting.'

Terry returned the image to the table and surveyed the full parade of shots. 'In terms of story, I'd say you have a strong beginning.' Terry liked the opening collage, which provided an evocative launch. 'And a good middle.' He picked up on some of the juxtapositions of imagery which 'effectively drew in the viewer, while the starkness of the texts maintains the tension'. 'But!' Suzy had readied herself for that. 'But we arrive at this small but significant matter of your ending. I think it was supposed to be your ending, because I ran out of pictures to look at!'

Terry stared at her. 'Where's your ending, girl?'

Suzy quickly examined her concluding prints.

'Either you didn't want the story to end – you were having so much fun! – or you weren't sure about what that ending should be, so you decided not to have one! You have to come off the fence here. You can't leave our man Eli hanging in the air like that!'

The tutorial finished with Terry reassuring Suzy that she was close to completing 'a piece of work that you and, far more importantly, that *I* can be proud of', while also stressing that she still had work to do – 'with very little time left!'

As Suzy gathered in her prints, she contemplated mentioning what had happened with Eli. Nick had repeated that suggestion, and she imagined Terry would have sensible advice for her. However, there was that other voice that argued she would simply be amplifying the problem. The end of the academic year was now so close. Why have it finish on such a note? She certainly wouldn't want it to affect Terry's assessment of her work.

Terry himself returned to the subject of Eli, as if he had intuited what was on her mind. He mentioned him in the context of a further observation.

'Did you notice how Eli changes?'

'What d'you mean?'

'Look at him in this one.' Terry put his finger on an early depiction. 'And then this one. And here!'

Suzy could see there was something in what Terry had noticed, but it wasn't clear to her precisely what that was.

'He seems to get . . . slimmer, doesn't he?'

Terry was right! There was something about his physical appearance, how it seemed to change through the display.

'And he just *looks* a lot tidier,' Terry added. 'See his clothing! Was that deliberate?'

10

Suzy was thrilled to be back among them all again. It made her realize how attached she had truly become. Two-gun Wolfie shuffling across to hug her, Miriam with more pictures of growing grandchildren, Izzy sporting a latest beret.

'Where have you been?' 'Are you too famous to visit us now?' 'Take my photograph, I've just had my hair done!'

Suzy was required to exchange greetings carefully with each member, with Miriam sticking like a barnacle to her side. She felt like a potentate receiving her subjects, moved by the intensity of the reception, but also swamped by it. True to form, it was only Lionel who chose to maintain his distance. She caught his glance, and it contained such a strange pained expression. Suzy was reminded of that mysterious argument with Eli to which she herself was apparently linked.

When Suzy spoke with Monty, she asked after Eli. He had visited Monty the previous week and was in fine mood, Monty reported, although remaining adamant that he would not come back to the Club.

'Eli can be very stubborn,' Monty remarked.

'What happened on Seder night? Was it something about me?'

'It's always something about *him*, believe me!'

Gloria called the proceedings to order, arranging members in a circle of seats by the stage. Eli's absence could be palpably felt. He was such a room-filling character. The gathering felt suddenly so small.

'Shalom, Shoshana!' Gloria began the Yiddish class by acknowledging her return.

Suzy nodded, feeling her tattoo wriggling under her sleeve, now and forever marked as this Hebrew rose.

'*Du host undz oysgefeylt*,' added Izzy, also addressing her.

Wolfie turned in the next seat. 'He says we missed you. It's true!' Heads nodded.

'We love our girl!' added Becky, twinkling at her. And Suzy loved them.

As the class began in earnest, Suzy was absorbing once again the special sounds and intonations of this singular language. She imagined herself seated next to her grandfather, introducing him to the members, he and she joining in the fevered conversation. It cascaded around her for the hour-long session. Miriam read out from a heavily taped book a story of shtetl village life by Sholom Aleichim. It led to a discussion, which led to an argument. Esther recited a poem, gently swaying to its rhythm, and the event ended on the 'Song of the Partisans' rousingly led by Arnold, Beatrice producing a guitar in accompaniment.

It struck Suzy that there had to be very few contemporary stories in Yiddish. Why would there be? It was a language whose own narrative was closing. No one talked of shtetls and partisans any more.

Suzy so wanted her project to be one of celebration, and yet there was that competing emotion. The image that came into her head was of a language and its people locked in a passionate embrace, spinning off into a great darkness. Suzy had joined the Mohicans in their death chants.

Over especially watery orange juice, Wolfie reprised the Sholom Aleichim story in English for Suzy's benefit, something about a woman in the village who feels compelled to assume the persona of every person she meets.

'How does it end?'

'She carries a mirror. So she can always remind herself who she is.'

Eli's name came up in the context of the Hargreaves meeting at the university. Izzy wanted to hear Suzy's version.

'He talks like he was this big hero. As if he stopped the event by himself!'

'Actually, it was true.'

'Did you see what he was dressed like?' Becky interjected. 'Covered in blood like that! It was terrible. He's a certified *meshuggeneh*!'

Suzy hadn't known that the incident was covered in the local press, with the article carrying his photograph. Suzy thought of the pleasure Eli must have derived, circling his very own image with that yellow highlighter.

'D'you want to hear his latest?' said Izzy. 'He wants us all to march from the East End to Parliament. At our age!'

'He's got himself all worked up,' Monty added. 'He'll calm down after the elections. That's when he'll come back to the Club.'

'He told me he's never coming back,' Izzy countered. 'He's not come to shul. We didn't get our minyan last week. Wolfie led the prayers. It was awful. He sings like he walks!'

Suzy felt a new presence closing in on her side and turned to discover it was, surprisingly, Lionel. He was staring at her with his usual intensity, which up that close was completely unnerving. What did he want?

'I'm sorry,' he quietly declared.

'What is it, Lionel?' Becky fortunately intervened, while glancing at Suzy in a way that suggested *leave this one to me*.

What transpired via a three-way conversation was that Eli had accused Lionel of upsetting Suzy and, astonishingly, had demanded he leave the Club. Lionel's arrival on Seder night – 'Gloria called me three times to make sure I was coming. I haven't missed one, ever!' – had provoked Eli's wrath, leading to the altercation, and Eli's stormy departure. Lionel was clearly still disturbed.

'You can take my picture if you want.'

He looked such a sad figure. Suzy felt dreadful. Eli must have picked up on something she had casually mentioned.

'Men living on their own,' remarked Becky afterwards. 'If only the world was run by women!'

Suzy didn't stay much longer. Izzy offered to escort her back to the station, filling what had once been Eli's role. She couldn't help but sense his presence on that walk.

Suzy chose an empty carriage for the short journey back. She was anxious over the thought now gnawing at her that she may indeed have somehow wronged these people. Lionel had been correct to be suspicious all along. Suzy was an intruder, a stirrer of troubles. On that train home, she apologized to Lionel, and to the others, and to Eli. She was truly sorry. It was never her intention. They must surely recognize that.

11

'You were never like that!'

'Let me see yours!' Salvo retorted to Nick.

Terry had asked for volunteers and as usual it was Salvo to the fore, his chosen photograph beginning the class.

Terry had expressed concern that a suitably non-specific 'some students' were losing sight of fundamentals. As a result, he had made this enigmatic demand, that everyone bring one photograph from the past that was, for whatever reason, especially meaningful. He had not been prepared to elaborate.

Nick passed Salvo's contribution on to Suzy. She carefully examined this younger Salvo, an undeniably attractive boy of about eight or nine looking the model of good mannerliness. Suzy wondered if the deceptiveness of the camera was that day's lesson! Salvo was standing by a wall, astride of which sat an older girl with braided hair, already identified as his sister. She had a hand stretching down, ruffling his hair. Her features were quite different to Salvo's, far squarer of face. It was a charming image, if utterly mundane. Suzy in turn passed it forward, and the picture continued its journey round the class before coming to rest on Terry's whiteboard.

'So tell us why you picked this one, Salvo.'

'It was the last time my sister lived at home with us.'

Salvo instantly secured the class's attention. His expression conveyed an uncharacteristic sensitivity. Suzy turned to the whiteboard and sought out the little girl in the photograph. She appeared perfectly content.

'Came back for visits, but never stayed over. It was a form of Down's syndrome – genetic or something. She died when I was eleven. I could have had it, or my brother. But it was just her.'

Nina put her hand on his arm. Faces turned to Terry willing him to move the discussion on.

'How do you feel when you look at her in the picture?' Terry now enquired, causing much astonishment.

'Angry!'

Nick's contribution was a picture of a much younger self dressed in cricket whites standing awkwardly by his father on a school playing field. Nick spoke about the significance of some cricket match until abruptly halted by Terry.

'This is an image of a father and a son. Talk about that,' suggested Terry.

Nina's photograph was of a long stretch of beach, with a cottage obscurely featured on the horizon – the cherished memory of a holiday home that had once been a summer routine. Terry pressed her on its importance and she revealed how it had been sold when her father lost his job.

'What happened to your father?'

'He got a new job. Not as well paid as before. We had to move town, which was hard. Saying goodbye to friends, and my cousins.'

Suzy had brought a family picture. She was standing between her mother and father while her grandfather towered behind, a hand reaching across to hold Suzy's. She knew precisely what age she was, for the gathering was in honour of her bat mitzvah – the day as a twelve-year-old girl she was confirmed into the Jewish faith, an event relentlessly centred on herself, and which she surprisingly enjoyed in a bashful sort of way.

She liked the shot for a number of reasons. Certainly, for the remarkable Barbie Doll straightness the hairdresser had managed to pull off, somewhat spoiled by the ghastly safari outfit she had been so determined to wear, with evidently no regard to posterity. More importantly was the sense of family celebration at an innocent time when no one would have predicted its demise. Grandpa looked vigorous, her parents at ease with each other. It was an image now overlain by so much that it was hard to recall there had ever been such a time. Yet that reality had constituted Suzy's childhood, and here was the proof.

Terry asked her to say how she felt about the photograph now, and she spoke about the ceremony representing her becoming a woman. How the years that followed had brought such change, and how her father hadn't really been there for her. 'He would try to help, but he didn't know how. He didn't really know me any more.'

Terry thanked her.

Gareth's contained a bustle of relatives and a gaily decorated room. He talked of a party, and the rush of exhilaration he had suddenly experienced. 'The room was full of black people, and it dawned on me that I wasn't black any more. Being black was a given, so it didn't matter. I felt so completely free!'

Megan brought the review of photographs to an end, and a climax. She presented herself as a nine-year-old skating furiously round an ice rink, dressed in a distinguished uniform of bright orange leotard, tiny skirt and tights. She explained how her mother had insisted she attend the weekly lessons, despite an intense loathing. The rink filled Megan with fear, being so small among far more accomplished older skaters whizzing menacingly around her, many from the rough neighbourhood schools she had been taught to be wary of.

As Megan related the story, it was clear how upset she was becoming. It didn't stop Terry quizzing her further on the photograph's significance, despite an overwhelming discomfort in the class, causing her finally to disclose the later discovery that her mother would 'meet a man' there.

'She didn't care about my shitty skating!' On that, Megan rose from her seat and rushed from the room. Nina followed. Suzy was going to join them but felt that might make it even more of a scene.

The classroom was now awash with emotion. Terry's response was simply to let the mood silently fester until Megan and Nina returned minutes later.

'So what am I doing?' he asked. Terry surveyed the photographs on the whiteboard. 'Isn't what's here utterly incredible! Just think about what we've been *privileged* to listen to.'

He lifted a picture off the whiteboard and waved it. 'Just small, flimsy bits of paper? But what emotions they contain! Wow! Right? Wow!'

Terry surveyed the class. 'Think hard about your work, and think about what you've heard today!'

Some of the students were incandescent afterwards. Megan described Terry's actions as 'turning the class into a therapy session' which he had 'no right to! He's not a counsellor! What would have happened if he'd really screwed someone up?'

Nick wholeheartedly agreed, although more annoyed by the implied criticism of the class's work. 'What does he want from us?'

Suzy couldn't see what all the fuss was about. That was the tenor of her contribution round the Granary table, backing

Salvo's relaxed defence of Terry. Suzy knew exactly what he was doing, and what lay behind his challenge. Her concern was far more over how she could ever hope to live up to it.

12

The envelope was waiting for Suzy in her BC pigeonhole that morning.

She felt the package's odd lumpiness, and suspected she was taking possession of another batch of yellow highlighted articles on *the march of fascism*.

Instead, what she found inside was the pressed head of a rose wrapped in a slip of paper, one edge of which was rough as if torn from a book. Its reverse contained a poem. By the BC entrance, Suzy began to read:

> *Thy wooing shall thy winning be*
> *See, see the flowers that below*
> *Now as fresh as morning blow;*
> *And of all the virgin rose*
> *That as bright Aurora shows;*
> *How they all unleavèd die*
> *Losing their virginity!*
> *Like unto summer shade,*
> *But now born, and now they fade.*
> *Every thing doth pass away;*
> *There is danger in delay:*

Come, come, gather then the rose,
Gather it, or it you lose!

Suzy arrived at the riverfront just as Nick was emerging from
the clubhouse. The first shot of him was astonishment combined with joy.

'I knew you'd come back one day!'

She took him clambering into the boat with the rest of the
crew, pushing off, the careful positioning of the boat at the
centre of the river. Suzy tried to imagine the tension as the crew
waited for the cox's signal. And then – go! The boat surging
through the water, mighty oars like pistons, determination and
anguish on every face.

The crew spent that whole session on the single task of per-
fecting their starts. Suzy sat on the riverbank watching each
rehearsal – the careful emphasis on technique, the crucial inter-
dependence of each crewmember – admiring the gentle amblings
of river life, breathing in the late spring air.

She even caught herself empathizing with Nick and this
strange passion of his. Suzy recalled Nick's lyrical description of
that special moment when all eight rowers performed a perfect
stroke, and how the boat would respond, lifting itself through
the water. She so wanted that to happen, and that she might
capture it. There could *just* be something grand and marvellous
about this sport after all. It wasn't kicking a ball in a park.

In watching each start re-enacted, Suzy reflected on the fact
that, in terms of her project, she had to work on her finishes!
Terry's critique was a fair one. Suzy knew she hadn't found a

satisfying way of drawing the JFC story to a close, and she wasn't sure why she was struggling with it.

Eli! What was Eli doing?

The session ended on the ceremonial of the cox once again conveyed to the river. Another crewman was similarly dispatched in honour of a birthday, successfully pulling in Nick and a second perpetrator in the process. Suzy captured a beautiful image of him emerging from the river, his hair flattened and lopsided, his Lycra outfit clinging to him with even greater vigour.

'It's a Fab Faces emergency job for you!'

Nick approached, giving Suzy an exquisite close-up for which she paid the penalty as he pushed the camera away and put his arms around her, squeezing with malicious affection – 'Get off me, you wet git!' – which ensured that he pulled her to the ground and kissed her, his teammates cheering him on.

A towelled-off Nick eventually emerged from the boathouse, and they joined the other crewmembers at a nearby pub, although she asked that they sit separately. Nick talked about training for the final gala of the year, which would bring together the four top university teams, including the despised Southwark College. 'I hope you'll be here for that as well!'

Suzy asked Nick how rowing could ever establish itself as a spectator sport given the fact that you could only glimpse such a small part of the overall race.

'But that's what you're so good at. Using your imagination!'

Suzy felt hugely relieved to be in his company, away from campus, away from the East End. It occurred to her that maybe she shouldn't break the moment by revealing Eli's letter. Yet she also knew how desperately she needed another perspective.

Nick read the poem in silence, rolling the rose head in his hand. She couldn't read his expression. Suzy cursed herself for hesitating over getting in touch with Eli. If only she had just met him again, once, cleared the air, she was convinced she would have resolved everything. Nick's view was emphatically the opposite.

'How could you even *think* of meeting him?'

Eli had sent her a love poem. That's what Nick asserted. 'You're the rose, right?'

It was Suzy's own conclusion, yet she had prayed that he might have come to a different one, the meaning misconstrued through the old-fashioned language, the elaborate tone. But Nick saw it in the plainest of terms.

What had she done!

Nick was firm over what she must do now. 'You have to take it to Terry!' If needs be, Nick was also prepared to have words with Terry – and Eli himself, the very notion of which Suzy instantly dismissed.

'Why is Eli acting like this?' Suzy asked him.

'I don't know! I'm sure there's nothing to worry about.' Nick touched her hand. 'He's just being what he is – a weird old man.'

Suzy didn't reveal to Nick everything of her own feelings. In truth, she was worried. It was the rose more than the poem. When she had first held it in her hands, she experienced an immediate rush of an incredible sensation that was undeniably *fear*. It was an emotion she would never have imagined ever associating with Eli. She had always been so comfortable in his company. Eli was this caring, jovial, larger-than-life, grandfatherly figure.

Suzy was fighting it, yet fear had stubbornly fixed itself inside her head.

> *Every thing doth pass away*
> *There is danger in delay*
> *Come, come, gather then the rose*
> *Gather it, or it you lose.*

13

Terry had circulated a roster of appointments requiring students to present him with their project work in a 'fully completed state'. He ended the note on 'no evasions or excuses accepted. Ladies and gentlemen, *your time is up*!'

Suzy would now galvanize herself for this final great effort. In so doing, she was determined to push to the back of her mind all doubts and distractions. She just hoped that Eli would leave her alone until the project was completed. She promised to get everything straight with him then. Suzy was moving into the familiar single-mindedness tinged with panic that had seen her through her every exam.

It was Megan who revealed that the second-year arts students were on assignment, releasing their lair on the top floor. 'I checked it out!'

The white brilliance of the life-class room once again claimed the most immediate impact. The easels had all been crushed to one side creating an expanse of clean space, daylight streaming in through the twin portals of overhead and side windows. Soon the territory was apportioned, with Nina and Nick at the far end, Megan and Suzy occupying the centre ground, Salvo and Gareth closest to the door.

Suzy carefully laid out her photographic finalists along the floor in their current order of hanging. She would now engage in yet another attempt to tame this monster that her display had become, with special focus on that elusive conclusion. In the process, she also had somehow to reduce the pictures to a last sixteen.

It wasn't long before various noisy consultations were taking place across the room. Suzy was hauled over a number of times by Megan, who repeatedly used the word *disaster* as if daring Suzy to agree. Having her own disaster to contend with, Suzy strained to sound sympathetic. At that moment, she was far more interested in receiving than giving.

The collage of old photographs that opened Suzy's piece garnered high praise, although Gareth found it odd that Rosabella, whom he agreed was 'fantastic', didn't feature in a later contemporary manifestation. 'Isn't that the point?'

Suzy presented several permutations on finales to her colleagues, whom she fully assembled for the purpose. Her main problem was her enthusiasm for two compositions, both visually striking, yet she sensed out of sync with the established narrative. That was also the collective view.

Nina and Salvo were having difficulty understanding the extremist texts beneath the pictures, so Suzy began reading them out, experiencing a growing self-consciousness as she continued.

'Nice people!' said Megan.

'Are they from real sources?' asked Salvo, shaking his head.

Gareth was puzzled by her approach. 'Are you saying this community exists because people hate them? That's very sad.'

'It's about defiance in the face of such abuse,' Suzy shot back at him. 'It's about celebration!'

Gareth appeared unconvinced. Suzy turned to the others and there was a brief moment of silence that was the hardest feedback of all.

Salvo quickly expressed pleasure that there was so much of 'our friend Ee-li, and so impressive!' He then talked about bringing him back for another Sports Night performance.

Nick expressed surprise that Eli was so prominent. It was the first time he had seen the display in its entirety and, when he turned to Suzy, that surprise had soured to disdain. She explained, more to Nick than anyone else, the exigencies of focus.

'He's the obvious one,' said Nina. 'Just look at that face! And look at what you've made of him!'

Suzy joked about Terry's remark on how Eli had 'smartened up his image' over the course of the project.

'Absolutely!' said Megan. 'Eli must have started seeing a new woman as you began.'

Like a jolt, Suzy came to the painful realization of just who that new woman was.

*

She began as soon as she got back to BC. Suzy rapidly pulled from the wall all the images of the Jewish Friendship Club she had so carefully built up around her. She couldn't bear to see Eli staring down at her, inside her bedroom. She packed the photographs into a box, dispatching it deep into her cupboard.

Suzy called her mother and discussed her day.

14

'So how are things?' Terry asked.

Given the fact that they were sitting in his office at Suzy's special request, he already had that answer. The silence was merely Suzy attempting to find a suitable point of departure.

'Is it about the project?'

'It's about Eli.'

Terry leaned back. 'Our opera-loving political agitator!'

Suzy would start from the beginning. The slow build-up might also serve to relax her. She reminded Terry of how she had first come across the JFC. How the Club received her so warmly. How she came to know Eli.

Suzy talked about Eli's fascination with the project, his repeated offers of help, their growing friendship.

Terry put a hand to his chin and started tapping his mouth with his fingers. It made her wonder where he thought she was going with this.

Suzy spoke of their regular contact, the East End tour, her

taking him onto campus, his performance on Sports Night, then onto the drama of the Hargreaves protest.

She thought hard about how she might begin to steer her remarks towards the problem. So far, she hadn't really said anything. It wasn't his eccentric ways, nor his peculiar forebodings.

'I think he's taken our friendship the wrong way!' she finally blurted.

'In what wrong way?'

'He's being . . . affectionate, like he might be thinking it's more than just a friendship. I know he's an old man!' Suzy scrambled in her bag. 'He sent me this.'

Terry read the poem carefully.

'My name in Hebrew means rose.' Suzy felt dreadful. She was telling tales out of school.

Terry asked when she had first noticed that he was behaving oddly towards her.

That was difficult to say. In a sense he was always odd towards her, because that was Eli. A certain oddness was integral to his character, and that was precisely why Suzy found him so intriguing. Had found! And there were moments of strangeness that weren't necessarily strange. The bouquet of roses was for her birthday, and roses were in recognition of her name. Eli had called her in Leeds on Christmas Day because he had been telling her so much about Romania, and here was the communist regime miraculously imploding. Eli sent her cuttings because they formed the very basis of her project.

As Terry continued, what Suzy felt he was really asking was could she have realized earlier and taken some sort of action. It was the sort of question that she feared most, that it might just all be her fault, that she had handled herself badly.

'I'm not accusing you of anything, Suzy.' Terry leaned towards her. 'I'm trying to understand.'

Terry was now scrutinizing her with a puzzled expression. Mentioning that he *wasn't* accusing her merely served to underline that suspicion! Suzy had gone to Eli's home, many times. She had drunk his coffee and listened to his interminable opera. They had gone on trips together, and she had brought him onto campus. Where were haircuts in her project brief?

But she had gone to Gloria's for Friday night dinners, visited Izzy, and Miriam! Isn't that what the project required, what Terry expected of them – to get involved? Can you get too involved?

Suzy left Terry's office more confused than she had entered, added to which was a festering anger. They were 'both' going to watch the situation. She would tell him if anything 'of a similar nature' occurred again.

Terry made the summation, which was essentially that Eli was an eccentric man being true to his calling. With the project now virtually finished, Suzy was no longer in his life, and the situation should accordingly resolve itself.

As Suzy walked along the corridor, she continued his questioning in her head, and then returned to her own. Had she been naive? Not naive about Eli, naive about what the assignment entailed. For the first time, she found herself directing her frustrations towards her dear leader, Terry. Well, she hadn't been *attacked* by Eli, or anything like that!

Nick was waiting for her by the Granary entrance. 'How did it go?'

'We're going to keep a watch on things.'

'What does that mean? Isn't someone going to speak to him?'

Suzy squinted. 'Eli hasn't committed a crime you know!'

As Suzy headed back to BC that night, she realized how much she now just wanted the year to come to an end. She longed to tear up her student card and lose herself in thoughts of summer. She was talking to Jo about Glastonbury, Nick about a holiday abroad, and her father about work that would earn her the means to make it all possible.

If only Jo was still at BC. It felt so lonely without her. Suzy had thought about staying over more at Nick's place, but he was so rarely there himself. Nick was being dutifully protective, yet Suzy remained just one of his priorities.

She called Gloria to discuss the project preview that had been promised the Club. Suzy had become concerned that some members might be upset by her approach. She explained the nature of the controversial language included.

'Of course we want to see it! After all this time. It's *our* show, not yours!'

Suzy wasn't sure if Gloria fully understood, and she repeated the point in a different formulation, which received the very same answer.

Suzy also took the opportunity to ask about Eli.

'Monty is trying to get him to apologize to Lionel. Until he does, and sincerely, he's not coming back. And I don't care what happens to the shul!'

Gloria's resolve hadn't wavered, unlike Suzy's own.

15

Suzy showed Nick the latest phone message from Eli. He had found more negatives.

'He doesn't give up, does he!'

'Have we been getting too serious here!' Terry's voice boomed overhead. 'What d'you think?' He scanned the class. 'Salvo!'

'Yes! Definitely. We should have a clown.'

'I thought we had one, Salvo.'

Giggles circulated.

'We *have* been getting too serious,' Terry continued. 'On this rare occasion, I'm with Salvo. This project business! Deadlines. Fear. Panic. I feel for you guys. I really do!'

Terry went to the whiteboard and started applying photographs, all of them portraits of some description. 'So we're going to have some fun today.'

'Is there booze?' was asked from somewhere.

'I want you to come forward and look at these pictures. Come on! Out of your seats.'

A whole assortment of people – ages, colours, demeanours – were portrayed, all singly composed.

'Now I want you to pick two people. Any two.'

Suzy was about to choose a cute little boy munching on a pear, except Nick swiped him before she could act. 'Oi you!' She quickly grabbed an older man idling on a park bench, her second a ballerina dramatically mid-flight.

'OK. Back to your seats. Has everyone got their two? I said just two, Barry! What I want you to do is first of all decide who these people are. It has to derive from whatever you see in the photograph.'

'Can I pick another two?' asked Salvo. Terry glowered at him.

'This one's just like my mother,' said Nina, holding up a severe-looking woman peeking from a window.

'Can we please do this silently?' Terry pleaded.

Suzy first examined the man in the park. He was turned out in a smart suit suggesting he might be on an office break. Early sixties perhaps, certainly older than her father, yet retaining a certain youthfulness despite being completely bald, perhaps around the eyes. What was more telling was how his circumstance was depicted; the fact that the photographer had chosen to reveal the full length of the bench, and he alone to one side. His head was turned towards the bench as if there might have just been someone beside him, or might be soon. The ballerina was caught side on, revealing the full ark of her body. She was either running or jumping. Because the image was cut off at the ankles, it was hard to tell which. Suzy thought how strange that was, her feet being so central to her craft. It made her appear somewhat bereft. Nevertheless there was tremendous energy in the pose, her young face thrusting forward, too busy with the task in hand to deign to acknowledge the viewer.

'Now I want you to imagine there's a relationship between these two people,' Terry announced next.

Salvo gasped as if he had been tricked.

'I want you to use your *imaginations* to describe that relationship, telling the class.'

Nina went first, holding up her woman in the window. Her second image was a second woman, attired in an evening gown, exquisitely poised at a dressing table. Nina proceeded to weave an intricate tale of sisterly rivalry, one ending up with a successful career but unhappy private life, the other vice versa.

'Why did the mother prefer the younger daughter?' Megan asked. Most people were confused.

'Which one is you?' Salvo enquired.

'The rich one, of course. Trust me. She's not so unhappy!'

Gareth presented his two young men as a story of gay love that ends with the CIA operative betraying the Soviet diplomat. Salvo related a fantastical saga based on teenage friendship that began with the World Cup, and somehow managed to end on aliens and time travel.

Suzy felt her own contribution timid in comparison. She made her man on the bench a regular visitor to the ballet, the ballerina his fantasy figure that had transfixed him. He had asked her to meet him in the park. She agreed, but stayed only briefly, and from then on rebuffs his attentions.

'Why would the ballerina meet the guy? Sounds like a creep!' announced Megan.

'Maybe he wants to help her – offer her a ballet school scholarship, or something,' Nick proposed.

'Isn't this from an opera?' proposed Salvo. 'A lonely man who returns night after night to see the same woman perform. It's one by . . . *somebody*. Isn't it?'

'Let her tell her story!' said Terry.

'That's the story.' Suzy shrugged. 'That's all I came up with.'

'What happens next?' asked Nina. 'You can't end it there!'

'It's opera. Somebody must die,' declared Salvo nonchalantly. 'Does she have consumption?'

Nick's teeth-in-pear boy became an everyday tale of rags to riches. His mechanic father wins not only the custody battle, but also a million pounds on the horses and they move to Spain.

'Why not Italy?'

'Maybe he should marry one of Nina's sisters.'

'Maybe he should marry Nina!'

'Maybe he should marry me!'

'OK! OK! Thank you everyone, I think, for your enthusiasm.' Terry rapidly brought the class to an end. 'Some healthy imaginations at work, I'm pleased to say!'

Terry caught Suzy's eye as she filed out. 'Everything all right?'

'Yeah. Everything's all right.'

16

The anti-poll tax demonstration had become virtually a class outing. Its route was, after all, down the length of the Mile End Road, passing along the very front of H-Block.

Inevitably, it was Megan who brought the event to everyone's attention and, in deference to her inside knowledge, Suzy and Nick decided to team up with her. 'Flexibility' was her watchword for the day.

The vast Mile End Road had been cordoned off since mid-morning. It stood in an unprecedented silence, as if following some massive evacuation. Steel barriers lined its flanks separating pavement from roadway, in front of which small clusters of police were gathered. Far greater numbers were in vans hidden away up side streets. Suzy captured several of these until she was aggressively waved away. Nervous shopkeepers stood in doorways, a few beside boarded up premises. Shoppers scuttled along as if under curfew. The quiet fed an air of nervous expectancy. The barbarian hordes were about to descend.

Nick, Megan and Suzy settled themselves initially by the police station down from the university because it was evident that this was some kind of operational centre, and the brisk ebb and flow of uniforms provided the next shots.

Dramatically announced by a lone piper, the first demonstrator lines appeared around one o' clock. Smartly besuited types led from the front, clearly taking their responsibilities with utmost seriousness. Suzy presumed these to be the local worthies – politicians, trade-union officials. Behind travelled a veritable army; couples, teenagers, mothers with children, the elderly, all snaking their way to a rigorous drumbeat. A host of colourful standards were being carried aloft. Suzy noted the banners of housing associations, political parties, trade unions, environmental groups, all competing for primacy. Some simply proclaimed their provenance, others referred to the cause for which they had been roused, the 'community charge' – known universally as the *poll tax* – that great symbol of evil for the government's opponents. It was as if every strand of East End life had come onto the streets. Suzy wondered if she might yet witness a Jewish Friendship Club flag!

Many students joined the growing ranks of spectators lining the route, cheering on the spectacle, some clambering over the barriers to join the procession. As the crowds grew and Suzy continued to manoeuvre for shots, she inevitably found herself separated from Nick and Megan. She was moving up the Mile End Road feeling like a child in a sweetie shop, gobbling up such bountiful imagery. And then at a next junction, she slid herself between the barriers, into the stream of people.

Being right at the heart of the noise and bustle was heaven! Suzy captured face-painted children waving streamers, a row of self-proclaimed anarchists with rubbery Thatcher masks, a cardboard cruise missile being carried for Nuclear Disarmament, mock convicts in poll-tax chains. An elderly man was holding up an image of a 'Tory Wall' being torn down Berlin-style. It made her reflect that she was in a scene reminiscent of the great seas of people assembling in every East European capital. And all the time, that relentless drumbeat, whistles and cheers.

Suzy was largely ignored as she weaved. There were several gestures made in her direction, not all friendly. One protester in a bright clown outfit insisted he would not let her pass unless she took his picture. He then asked if she had heard about some 'trouble' at Stepney. It was a rumour that had flashed down the column, causing increasing anxiety. The only confirmation came in the form of a new edginess in the ranks of the police monitoring from the flanks. Their numbers were swelling and Suzy imagined the vans she had witnessed earlier now emptying.

A group of protesters separated themselves from the main procession and Suzy promptly attached herself as they headed down a side street. The action had clearly infuriated the police, who were in close pursuit. At a next crossroads, a row of police had formed across the street, except remarkably their dress was now that of *Star Wars* extras – faces behind shiny visors, thick protective jackets, shields and batons. With loud-hailers, the demonstrators were being instructed to return immediately to the main body of the march. The stand-off was electrifying.

Missiles quickly followed jeers. Mounted police moved in. Suzy engineered herself to the edge of the group, fastening herself to a horse's side as its rider sought to push the crowds back from the junction. She momentarily considered how unjust this was – that it was the horse going face to face with the tumult, its master sufficiently removed from the immediacy of confrontation. A phalanx of eggs was slung from somewhere near, several landing on their intended target, smearing the policeman's tunic as he menaced with his baton, turning the scene briefly into comic farce. Someone made a grab at the horse's reins. The police rider lunged forward and there was a struggle. A shopping bag was launched over the animal's head, causing it suddenly to rear, legs flaring like fangs. Suzy dropped to a crouch to capture the shot.

What happened next, Suzy couldn't precisely recall. She was

certainly knocked to the ground, a searing pain down her left arm confirmed that. There was a scrum of people around and over her. Then someone was guiding her to the pavement, and she was being asked if she was OK.

The police had charged and there was chaos. Men and women were being wrestled to the ground and frogmarched away. She wondered if that might yet be her own fate. In seconds it was over.

Suzy just sat on the street kerb until the noise subsided. She noticed a Thatcher mask trampled into the road. It was such an inviting image, and it brought to mind her camera. She stumbled to her feet, clasping her arm, feeling sore all over. The camera, more accurately its remains, was yards from her and it was a grievous sight.

Several policemen approached and ordered her home.

Nick found her in her BC room. She was stripped to the waist, bathing a bruised and throbbing upper body. He wanted to know what had happened. Should she go to hospital? No bones felt broken, but she was far from OK.

Suzy had experienced a huge fright. All she could think about was that massive black horse darkening above, and her helpless beneath. She'd thought she was going to die.

Nick picked up what had once been her mighty Weston TT camera, now exposed as nothing more than a small squashed box.

'You get too close, Suzy!' he said. 'You get too close.'

17

Suzy was now furiously immersed in a race to finish the year project. She didn't actually break for lunch, stealing into the Granary for a takeaway sandwich, resisting the blandishments of Nina and her art friends. The pressure was partly self-imposed, as a way of galvanizing herself in the face of what she now had to endure – a massive loss of heart over the whole enterprise.

Suzy had spent most of that day working on framing. Contrary to Terry's advice, she had decided to place the texts outside the frame, using them as, in effect, provocative titles as opposed to something more integral to the images themselves. She had even shocked Terry by proposing to drop them altogether. 'What are you saying? It's too late for that. Just hang on in there. You'd lose the whole energy of the piece!'

It was precisely that energy that she now found so troubling. Suzy had become convinced that she was giving credence to extreme and dangerous views. In exploiting them, she was in fact perpetuating their power.

The second-year students had already started to install their own project work in studio two, and Suzy ended a long and difficult day by seeking solace in these displays of her elders. Terry had teasingly talked about several second year 'stars', and Suzy was keen to come to her own opinion.

On entering the studio, what struck Suzy initially was the sheer inventiveness. She moved under a mobile of tiny cloud images to a row of striking depictions of appalling industrial pollution composed in the form of joyful *wish you were here*-style postcards. A massive bull-like human head poked from a corner like a totem, adjoining a series of bizarre portraits entitled 'The camera tells the truth' – a middle-aged woman in a wheelchair clutching skis; a baby attempting to drag a huge black briefcase; an elderly man in a fluffy dressing gown brandishing a handgun; a teenage girl in a pinstripe suit cradling bricks.

Suzy crossed the floor to what appeared to be a perfectly bland display, scenes of nondescript East End wasteland and back alleys. The text revealed that these were all sites where the victims of Jack the Ripper had been discovered, transforming the images into something quite terrifying whose power rested completely on the response of the viewer. It was as unsettling as it was brilliant.

Daylight was beginning to extend its reach into the evenings, for which Suzy was grateful. Indeed, the rain shower that had marked her journey to the Tube station had vanished two stops east, and she was able to walk the last streets to BC under a bright umbrella-free sky.

Having lost the distraction of the project, Suzy was again reunited with the full force of the dull throbbing pain that had commandeered her left arm. She wondered whether the bruising she had examined at length that morning could by now look any better. The tattoo of her right arm was a trifle against this far more imposing 'tattoo' down her left. Megan was merrily encouraging her to sue the police, with the promise of, if not fortune, at least fame in the student paper.

The story of the demonstration, more especially the rioting that ensued, achieved wide media coverage and impressive notoriety, reaching as far as Leeds with even her mother raising it. 'Are you OK?'

Suzy was particularly irritated that what would routinely have been a ridiculous question was on this occasion so apposite. Her mother would have asked Suzy if she was OK if there had been a train crash in Birmingham! Of course, she couldn't bring herself to give her that satisfaction, delivering the routine response that her mother *was* being ridiculous.

Jo had also called to find out if Suzy had witnessed the riot, annoyed to have missed out on the drama. Suzy was able to relate a deeply first-hand account that made Jo all the more envious. 'Wow! You really were in the middle of it!'

'*Under* it!'

Jo's own news concerned a job in a photography shop, looking all bright-eyed at the professional photographers she was now encountering. Jo confirmed that she would be making her grand return to H-Block for the end-of-year show reception. She agreed to join Suzy and Nick for a night out in London town afterwards, made somewhat less enticing by the inclusion of her mother also travelling in that day.

Once again, it was the sculpted features of Sir Aubrey Bernard welcoming Suzy to BC. She wondered what he would think of being memorialized among a student fraternity that was barely aware of his existence, and cared even less. What might have seemed a form of preservation was merely affirming the reality of his condition. His vital face was a museum death mask.

The hall of residence at exam time had assumed a subdued air. The students Suzy met in the corridors shared the look of the besieged. Yet liberation was almost at hand. Suzy's first year of studenthood was about to receive its own memorializing on the august walls of the photography department. It made her contemplate how unfair that was. Examinations for most students remained a private affair – papers handed in, discreetly assessed, scores individually advised, while her efforts were to be scrutinized by the world; all her fellow students, lecturers, friends and family, the reception notables. Sized up, evaluated, whispered about, criticized, condemned – all those eyes bearing down. Suzy had to prove herself to so many people and, after a year of work, she now had mere days.

In arriving at her room, Suzy found herself strangely wrestling with the door. The obstacle proved to be an envelope slipped under it, which she had inadvertently wedged even tighter. Suzy managed to dislodge the letter and, fighting back a growing queasiness, took it inside.

There was nothing on the envelope to indicate either destination or origin. She sat on the bed for some moments, then quickly opened it. What she saw first was a neatly typed note on plain white paper: *Have more negatives. Need your help. Please call me. Eli.*

Various yellow highlighted newspaper articles followed. Suzy read one headline ANARCHY IN THE EAST END! in reference to the anti-poll tax riots, another addressed the same event from the perspective of the local elections and a rising tide of disillusionment, a third spoke of nationalist riots in Slovakia, and

Hungary. Suzy wondered how Eli had managed to talk himself past the security guard. He had found her room.

Suzy felt something else inside the envelope, turning it over to let two photographs drop onto her bed. One was from Eli's past – her print of him with Rosabella before their wedding. The other a contemporary shot – Eli and Suzy on their East End tour.

Suzy stared at Eli's face in both. Despite the years between these images, he carried the very same exaggerated satisfied smile.

18

'Them over there,' Suzy proposed.

'Not another *workers build the new London*,' Nick drearily replied from under his baseball cap.

'If we can't take workmen any more, it's going to be a quiet day!'

Suzy and Nick had decided to venture into the new Docklands development. Suzy had noted that a photographic excursion was long due, and Nick had wanted to visit the area for some time. She managed to borrow the one Hasselblad from equipment, and was enjoying the challenge of mastering its controls. Her project would have to spare her this day.

They had arrived after what proved to be a remarkably brief journey by bus. Remarkable in the sense that Suzy was struck by how the shortest of distances from the heart of the East End could culminate in such a contrast. They had entered a forest of slickly new buildings – Gotham City style-skyscrapers and curving highways – arriving at what appeared to be a central square, plonking themselves down on a bench beside a lonely outpost of lawn on which a pair of giant metallic sculptures gently grazed.

It was a cool day, yet not cool enough for the obligatory bare-chested workmen carousing to and fro. Suzy hadn't received one wolf whistle, which she pleaded was because of Nick's presence.

The real action was behind the square where the lumbering skeletal beginnings of vast structures roamed. There was something truly awesome about the scale of the undertaking in what had once been a massive complex of docks, and then derelict wasteland as the East End's servicing of the river dissolved into redundancy. Suzy had expected to come across a scattering of modern office blocks. This was a whole new city under construction.

Architectural photography held little appeal for Suzy. She remained committed to ferreting out the human stories amongst the steel and concrete. She would most certainly have to explore from the inside the buildings already open for business, enabling her to capture security guards, cleaners, a variety of office workers in modes of attire that had to be linked to some sort of caste system. She even came across an internal shopping parade neatly leading to a station entrance. Suzy was discovering how much of this reinvented Docklands life had been designed to exist safely on the inside rather than out, as if ambivalent towards its East End patrimony.

'Its fantastic!' was Nick's assessment.

'Fantastical,' Suzy's amendment.

A change of direction brought them to a complex of more human-scale construction surrounding a body of water that would have once formed part of the old docks. Indeed, it was the waterways criss-crossing the locality that were the only vestige of the area's original designation. A small yacht conveniently ambled up a channel, the perfect image for the front of the glossy sales brochure, they agreed.

As they continued on, heading down towards the Thames, they found themselves leaving the Docklands site, returning to the more familiar East End of terraced houses in neatly preserved rows. There was something distinctly robust about the old corner shops, the red, white and blue bunting of the local pubs, as if this was the front line against an alien neighbour, this latest immigrant moving in next door.

Suzy and Nick were in Mudchute and Millwall, names that made Suzy uncomfortable because she had only heard of them in the context of Eli's ranting. Suzy even caught herself telling Nick that they were entering the heartland of the BPP, as if she really knew of such things. They certainly saw no evidence of it. Those windows that displayed election posters primarily conveyed the utterly benign features of Neil Kinnock.

Soon they had reached the river, Nick putting his arm round Suzy as they stared out by a park wall. The Thames was like a huge expanse of playing field. Scurrying river boats danced before the village of Royal Greenwich lying on the opposite bank in all its picture-postcard splendour. Suzy felt herself gulp. London was a city without end.

'I'm not going to live in the East End next year,' Suzy announced.

Nick was shocked. 'But what about all this roots business? Feeling so at home.'

'I was just being silly. Romanticizing.' She turned to face him. 'I really like the area, but I've had a year of it. A year's enough.'

'Let's get a place together!'

Suzy laughed.

'What's funny?'

'You are!' She pulled his baseball cap over his face, which he huffily restored.

'I've not been very nice to you.' Suzy stared at him. 'Haven't you realized by now I'm a complete bitch!'

Nick smiled.

'I'm so different to you.'

'No you're not,' Nick replied. 'You just like thinking you are.'

Suzy pulled his cap down again. 'Don't touch it!' She raised her camera.

They managed to locate the entrance to the grand Victorian pedestrian tunnel to Greenwich. Nick raced her under the Thames to the other side, letting her lose! Suzy blamed the poor performance on her recent injuries.

To demonstrate his seafaring credentials, Nick *had* to inspect, at length, the *Cutty Sark* in its Greenwich moorings. As they walked past the glamorous Royal Naval College, Suzy suggested that he might want to investigate switching courses. 'I'm thinking of the uniform!'

They arrived at Greenwich Park, slowly meandering their way up the hill to the Old Royal Observatory. The exhibition inside headed 'Time starts here!' explained the significance of the facility, why the creation of longitude was such a vital break-through.

In the courtyard outside, a brass strip on the ground marked the meridian. Nick posed on one side. 'The end of the world!' Then with a flourish hopped across. 'The beginning of the world!'

He enlisted a passer-by to take the two of them bestriding time. Suzy wondered on which side she truly was.

Ice cream refreshed them, sitting on a grassy bank near the building. Eli's latest letter was produced not long after. Suzy hadn't mentioned it previously because she hadn't wanted Eli to dominate their day together. He had only dominated hers. The letter had been burning in her bag until that moment.

She showed Nick the typed note with its brief reference to negatives, then the newspaper cuttings, and finally the two photographs.

'This is his wife. Rosabella?'

Suzy nodded.

'What age is she in the picture?'

Suzy didn't know. 'Young.' She shook her head.

'I feel like he thinks I'm in his debt,' Suzy said. 'Like I owe him something!'

Nick gazed at her solemnly. He then stood up, delivering above Suzy a whole range of graphic epithets ending with Eli's name in a display of anger and frustration that far surpassed Suzy's own. It sounded almost therapeutic.

He spoke about harassment and how they should call in the police. He then changed tack, proposing he pay 'the freak' a personal visit. And then he turned on Suzy, towering above her as he fired questions. Why was she alone with him so often? Did she have to visit his home? Who had suggested he cut her hair?

'I asked you what you thought, lots of times!' Suzy got to her feet herself, matching the tone of his indignance, then bettering it. 'I didn't *want* to bring him to Sports Night, remember! Tell me exactly what you think I've done wrong? Tell me! I wish someone would!' She turned skyward – 'what did I do wrong?' – and then finally came the tears.

Nick pulled Suzy to him and held her.

'It's so unfair! I didn't ask for this.' She was speaking in shudders. 'I was just being friendly. Is that so bad? That was all it was. To them all. And they were friendly to me.'

Nick kissed her forehead, stroked her hair. 'What does he want?' he whispered.

Suzy calmed herself. 'It's what he doesn't want.' She breathed in deep, then again. 'He doesn't want me to finish. Eli doesn't want me to finish the project.'

19

Suzy found herself facing an unprecedented challenge. She was losing the ability to assess her photographs dispassionately.

Suzy had long ago made the decision, with Terry's prodding, to put Eli at the heart of her project, and now she had to stare down the very man who had become her central anguish. She hadn't spoken to Eli for several weeks, and yet she felt she was talking to him all the time.

Part of her wanted to excise him completely from the display. What especially saddened her was how she was now questioning her relationship with this entire community, and yet Suzy knew she mustn't allow Eli's behaviour to poison all her feelings. She could still trust her judgement.

Suzy was committed to previewing her project at the Club, and her thoughts turned again to how they might receive it. She had fashioned the work in the context of protest, in the process defining this group in juxtaposition to its supposed enemies. But that was never how they defined themselves. Suzy had imposed that on them, and only now was she fully appreciating why. *She had absorbed Eli's world view*. Suzy suddenly realized that the project not only featured Eli, it had been conceptualized by him! And now Suzy was about to inflict that on the rest of the JFC. No! No!

A day originally set aside for project completion was transformed into a desperate one of reconstruction, purely for the benefit of the JFC. Suzy locked herself in a darkroom surrounded by sheaves of contacts, frantically working through them to identify what she considered the most edifying images. The Club would get its very own display.

Suzy received her customary warm welcome. Gloria asked about her family in Leeds, and Miriam manoeuvred Suzy into asking about her family. Izzy clasped her hands, then clasped her face. Becky wanted to know what she thought about the 'shameful' poll tax riots and whether it was true that 'they were all students'. Suzy could certainly vouch for a wounded one!

She left them to their orange juice while she went to work, fixing her fourteen prints, the majority freshly manufactured, onto a section of wall. She had decided not to include the collage piece, which was a key feature of the university show. It meant they could keep the complete display for as long as they cared to. It was Suzy's farewell present to the JFC. She placed the photographs deliberately close to the older synagogue ones to demonstrate this was a latest update.

Suzy had a vague notion of how she wanted to order them, conscious of Club hierarchy as much as how the compositions worked alongside each other. As she had one final play with the sequencing, she thought to herself how with this, her very first exhibition, she had managed to dispense with an entire year's worth of education. The images were reasonable considering that they had emerged from essentially one long day of preparation. But where was her *establishing shot*? What *narrative journey* had she set for the viewer? Where were the clever *interplay of contrasts*, and *climactic visual moments*? Terry would never speak to her again if he found out.

Gloria mounted the stage and brought the gathering to attention. With embarrassing lavishness, she welcomed Suzy, and her display. 'The culmination of a year of hard work.' It was hardly that! In attempting to appease, Suzy may have simply betrayed the members in a different way. The work was substandard. They deserved far better.

'It's wonderful!' announced Miriam.

Suzy felt ashamed.

'I thought you said there was going to be some sort of wording,' Izzy unfortunately recalled.

'I changed my approach.'

'And our old photos that we gave you?'

'Changed a few things.'

Suzy quickly eased herself away from the work as the members encircled, retreating to the pictures of the synagogue's past alongside. She was once again drawn to the one taken on Yom Kippur, all faces angled in the same direction, even the rabbi's. Suzy tried to calculate where the camera would have been situated for the shot. It had to be somewhere above the Ark, the very object of their devotions. It was as if God Himself was the photographer!

'Eli says you stole pictures from him.'

Suzy turned to face Wolfie. 'He said what?' Wolfie was leaning in on his twin sticks.

'He says you took some pictures.' He spoke matter-of-factly, as if he himself didn't particularly care.

Suzy thought quickly. 'I *borrowed* some negatives,' she replied. 'He let me have them. I'm giving them back!'

Wolfie nodded. 'It's none of my business. Just thought you should know.'

'Did he say anything else?'

Wolfie shrugged. 'I saw him in the bagel shop. I asked if he was coming tonight. Acted as if he didn't know anything about it. He still says he's never coming back, but he's said that before!' Wolfie swivelled himself sideways, moving the sticks in a way that perfectly demonstrated his mastery. 'I always thought you two had a special thing for each other. It's just as well he didn't come.'

'Why?' Suzy asked.

'Why? He isn't in any of your photographs!'

It was true. Suzy couldn't bring herself to include him. She had rationalized that it might have caused upset, given his fall-out with the others. That was her cover.

Suzy was soon on the receiving end of extensive feedback. Izzy thought he looked 'very distinguished'; Miriam wanted ten copies of a dancing pose for assorted family round the globe; Monty had had himself described by Esther and wanted to know what he had found so funny; Becky complained about her hair, but thankfully not much else. Even Lionel appeared grateful. Suzy had been delighted to come across an image of him, which she suspected was her only one.

'You've done us proud,' said Gloria. 'I never realized you were so good. You'll be famous one day. I promise you!'

Mounting the stage for a second time, Gloria brought the assembly once again to order. She announced the implications of that night's event, namely that Suzy would no longer be attending the JFC 'on business that is! We are conferring on you a special Jewish Friendship Club life membership. You can come along just as you please.'

Suzy imagined herself proudly flashing her JFC membership card as she promenaded down the Mile End Road. Suzy was now officially part of this singular community – an authentic East Ender.

'We'll expect to see you here regularly.' Gloria embellished her previous remark.

Becky took Suzy's hand and they ascended to the stage together. Becky then presented her with a gift. It was a necklace with a small silver Star of David. 'For she's a jolly good fellow!' struck up, delivered with varying degrees of vigour.

Suzy found herself genuinely moved. She had made firm friendships. They had enabled her to reconnect with a part of her being that she hadn't properly acknowledged. That was what had drawn her to the JFC in the first place – she was convinced of that now – and that was the promise they had kept.

Gloria insisted Suzy say some words. She wanted to speak.

'Thanks to all of you from the bottom of my heart. You made me feel so welcome right from the beginning. I've enjoyed talking to you, photographing you, dancing with you! And I've even picked up a *bissel* Yiddish!' She paused, taking a moment to marvel at this incredible band of people. But it was catching Becky's expression. Suzy could feel her own eyes filling.

'I feel privileged to have known every one of you. You will always be my East End family.'

Afterwards, Suzy didn't feel in any rush to leave. At the evening's end, she was sitting with Gloria and Becky in an empty hall.

'Don't know what will be in a few years,' Gloria said. 'I don't imagine we'll still be ballroom dancing, do you Becky?' She let out a great laugh. Becky smirked. There was a sharpness to her words that made Suzy feel deeply sad, and yet there was that other emotion, like a gratitude. Suzy had been blessed with the opportunity to provide this record. It was what Terry had once said, about the project being unique.

'Will you still visit us?' Becky asked. She sounded like a small child. Suzy couldn't bring herself to answer. She thought about the impact of her presence, and something she hadn't previously really considered – the impact of her absence.

20

Suzy became a virtual recluse for those few days before the concluding tutorial with Terry, even resisting Nick's attentions to uphold the purity of her single-mindedness.

She permitted herself only one actual reprint, stealing into the darkroom to produce a tighter crop of a particularly troublesome composition. She worked on last adjustments to each text and image collaboration, ensuring she wrung out their full potency. And she fiddled with framing.

However, Suzy focused mainly on her ever-problematic ending, experimenting with a range of formulations, finding herself repeatedly distracted by the conundrum of Eli. It was as if resolving the project had become intertwined with resolving their relationship. His face stared out at her from so many of the photographs. Yet these were all her images! She thought of herself as a Baron Frankenstein having to face down his monster. She wanted to shake Eli, shout at him. What was this bizarre claim on her? He had helped her with the project for which she was grateful. He must know that. And now the project was over. Why couldn't he just leave it at that?

Her hermit-like existence was partly inspired by that very concern. Eli was familiar with the university. He had even located her room at BC. Every corridor she walked down, every street she crossed, rekindled the thought that he might just be there, waiting for her. Ironically, she had taken to carrying his negatives on the assumption of that very eventuality. It was what a part of her wanted most of all, and what she most feared.

Suzy had talked through with Nick whether she should contact the police, but when she summed up what had been the nature of his 'crime', it amounted to so very little. He had tried to kiss her and had immediately stopped when asked to. He sent her material relevant to her project, and an obscure poem on love. He had returned two photographs she herself had given him. The rational side of her could easily dismiss it all as inconsequential. And did she really want police banging on this elderly man's door? Had it come to that?

The saddest of news put the whole matter into perspective. Aids patient Stewart had died. Gareth announced it in class. He had been with him just two days before. Stewart was having difficulty breathing, and Gareth had told him not to speak.

Terry commented on how tired Suzy looked when she came into the studio. She told him in no uncertain terms whose fault that was, and he smiled.

They were meeting in a studio to enable Suzy to lay out her completed project display on the floor. Terry had chosen studio two, the one that contained the amazing second-year projects. Suzy's work stretched to just under the cloud mobile, and she found herself repeatedly glancing up at the surrounding work. It was added pressure that she didn't appreciate.

Terry marched along the side of her work before crouching by the opening collage. He began with a relatively innocuous remark on framing. He then proceeded to review every one of the sixteen shots, carefully reading the texts, reflecting also on the interplay between the pieces. Terry employed such delicious phrases as *underlying unity*, *the accumulation of effect*, *plotting energy*. He mentioned *empathy*, and *commitment*, and *passion*. Most significantly of all, it concluded on warm congratulation. Suzy beamed through her weariness.

Nevertheless, Terry did have criticisms, which turned out to be several. Beyond small technical deficiencies, he highlighted what he felt was a 'lingering ambivalence'.

'I'm still not convinced that you're being consistent here. You don't need to have a clear-cut ending. This isn't a Hollywood film. The important thing is that you're always in charge. Don't expect your viewer to solve your problems for you.'

Terry led Suzy to the second-year display that she herself had found the most striking, the one that contained the locations of Jack the Ripper's victims.

'This photographer is completely in control. Not just of the work, but also of the imagination of the viewer.'

He refrained from making further comment. The purpose of

the exercise was to confirm that her project was up to submission standard. His ultimate feedback would be delivered in the form of her mark.

Suzy began to pick up her pictures from the studio floor, Terry brooding from behind.

'How is he?' he asked, pointing to one of her Elis.

'Haven't seen him.'

Terry looked at her curiously.

Suzy might have chosen to bring him up to date. But the project was over. Done with! She had successfully managed that – in every respect. That was what she had laid out before Terry. This was all her responsibility, and her achievement, from beginning right to the end.

'So who comes to the show reception?' Suzy asked as she collected up last photographs.

'Everyone from the Department. The whole faculty will be there, and the Dean. All student years. We normally get some graduates who've gone on to better things. Useful contacts! And we should even have a few gallery owners on the lookout for new talent. Remember to brush your teeth!'

Suzy slid the pictures into her bag. 'Will you make sure they see my work?'

Terry screwed up his face. 'Planning not to join us?' he guffawed. 'Are your parents coming?'

'My mum. Just hope she gets here on time. She's catching a lunchtime train. My dad said he'd try, which means he won't try enough.'

Before they left the studio, Suzy handed Terry a photograph.

It was one of the two of them when they had shared lunch before the start of term.

'This is so you'll always remember me!'

Terry poked her arm. 'You know, I'm going to keep this.' He examined the picture closely. 'I think we should get the guy who took it onto the course, what d'you think?'

Suzy assessed the picture with an air of mock contemplation. 'Absolutely! Huge potential. I've never been taken better!' And they laughed together along the corridor.

As Terry reached his office, he turned to her. 'This Eli business. I'm sorry.'

Suzy shrugged. 'I know.'

21

Nick had coaxed her into attending. It was the last competition of the season, his final opportunity to play on her sense of girl-friendly duty.

The afternoon was glorious. The sun blessed the day with its unremitting presence, coating the water with a dazzling sheen. Boats surged like rockets through the becalmed waters. Suzy tried to follow their exploits, but more blessedly allowed herself simply to laze on the riverbank, enjoying the tickling of the warm grass beneath.

She had company. Nick's recruitment drive had extended to Megan and Salvo, although all three were proving hopeless supporters, constantly in confusion over which boats, and at which moments, they should contribute their cheer. The other distraction was Salvo's extensive picnic, more liquid than solid, which meant that, as time went on, they became ever bolder with their acclaim, but far less discriminating. Even the ducks garnered their applause.

Both Megan and Salvo had come armed with cameras, which they deployed in bursts. With Suzy's own well and truly deceased, she had nevertheless resisted borrowing one, and it felt such a release not having that burden. She would leave the *seeing* to her comrades.

Terry's final project evaluations were compared, swiftly. They compared summer plans at length. Megan had managed to get some assisting work with a photographer and anticipated a summer of weddings and christenings. 'We don't get bar mitzvahs in Norfolk!' Salvo was 'dreaming' of Italy, but desperate to travel. Suzy had some ingredients of her own in place, the most dramatic being her joining Nick for at least part of his grand European tour. But at that moment she principally just wanted to go home and sleep, for a very long time.

Wild riverside revelry was taken as a sign that Nick's team had pulled off some momentous victory. Every team member ended up in the river over the course of the celebrations, which kept Suzy and the others at a safe distance. A drenched but delirious Nick came over at some point. He joined the picnic, finishing the wine, wringing out the river from his shirt. The gallant LNU knights of the Thames had thwarted the evil doings of Southwark College. Lady Lena was sure to be proud!

It was on account of Lady Lena that they gathered that evening.

'Piss off!' Salvo was sentenced to buying a second round, having failed to find someone else prepared to own up to peeing in the shower.

'You deserve it. You're disgusting!' were Megan's words of consolation.

Sports Night had not witnessed such crowds since Freshers. Being the final one of the year, there was the promise of even more outrage than usual, with Lady Lena circulating a proclamation beforehand demanding the presence of every student, on pain of unspecified violence.

She was soon on stage in all her grotesque radiant splendour, her arrival greeted with even more vehemence than usual. The outfit was a cross between Madonna and Lady Di. She haughtily scanned the audience, expressing her welcome tinged with the disappointment that such a 'disreputable rabble of misfits' had shown up.

Soon, LNU sporting legends of the past year were bowing and scraping before her, receiving the accolade of the crowd, being asked to consume a pernicious-looking brew as their dubious reward.

'Be humble!' Lady Lena announced as a limp hand acknowledged each.

Nick swaggered as he paraded on stage with his teammates. The wicked intent of the drink was confirmed first hand, with Nick hoarse on his return. He had nevertheless escaped the fate awaiting the rugby contingent with its less distinguished record, stripped to their underwear and led through a series of excruciating challenges involving assorted kitchen implements.

The live band moved everyone onto the floor. Even Lady Lena deigned to go on a rare walkabout among her subjects. Suzy had never seen her up close before, and she was even more disconcerting – darting grey eyes behind silvery face paint and enormous bouffant wig. It was the way she carried that air of brutal indifference. The Lady was a brilliantly malicious creation.

Nick spent some time with the rowing club. They were administering a whole series of ginnings, with Nick receiving as well as giving. Suzy had never seen him consume so much alcohol and feared the consequences.

Its impact was obvious when Nick ventured onto the dancefloor. While his verbal abilities were largely intact, his bodily coordination was seriously compromised. He was pirouetting and gliding in all sorts of ways denied him in the tightly confined space. In spinning perilously close to the rugby club wall, Suzy watched helplessly as he was captured for trespassing, his punishment 'the bumps'.

She tried to intervene but Nick waved her away. Suzy was left to look on as a gang of rugby players repeatedly launched him into the air to a count. Nick was laughing at first, then stopped. 'Seven! Eight!' their voices boomed. In contrast to the glee of his tormentors, Nick's face was now ashen. 'Eleven! Twelve!' Were they going to stop? Somehow Suzy managed to force her way into the circle and demand they let him down. She felt like an angry mother facing down local hoodlums.

To jeers and scowls Nick was abandoned on the floor, lying still for some moments.

'Are you OK? Nick! Shall I get you some water?'

Nick appeared to be anything but OK. He finally stood up, but was shaking. Suzy prodded Salvo into following him into the bathroom.

As Suzy sat with Megan, they began to notice something ominous writhing towards them along the floor. An oozing white foam was slowly filling the room, dancers now merrily wading and splashing in the gunk. Suzy just thought how dreadful the whole occasion now felt. She decided it was a maturity thing. Sports Night was for first years drunk on escape from home. Suzy's first year was drawing to a close. She despised students!

It was Megan who first noticed the figure standing above Suzy. He delivered a small package. 'Some guy told me to give you this.'

'What guy?' Suzy immediately rose to her feet while the messenger vanished into the swamp, leaving her with a surge of anxiety.

There was nothing written on the outside, which was in itself indicative. She swung round, twisting in every direction. Suzy couldn't see Eli but assumed he could see her from somewhere in the crush of people – watching, teasing.

'What is it?' Megan was baffled by Suzy's sudden state.

She quickly opened the package to deny Eli the pleasure of a lingering suspense. Something dropped into the swelling foam and Suzy scrambled to the floor, grabbing hold of something oddly soft wrapped in material. She wiped off the foam, finding in her hand two locks of hair tied with colourful bows.

'Get Nick! Please get Nick!'

Megan rushed to extract Nick from the bathroom. For what seemed an eternity, Suzy was left at the table completely on her own, sitting amid a manic swirl of student celebration, yet utterly frozen. She just stared hard at the floor, concentrating on the patterns forming and breaking in the river of foam, praying that she be left alone until Megan and Nick return. If only God would please grant her that. Part of her wanted to flee from the room but she knew, whatever the direction, Eli would be there.

'Where is he? *Where's that bastard*?' Nick was wild. 'I'm going to find him. I'm going round there right now!'

'No. No!' Suzy held Nick tightly, marshalling all the adrenaline now raging inside, fixing her eyes on him. 'Just stay here! Stay with me. Please Nick! Just stay with me!'

'What's going on?' Megan was pulling at Suzy. 'What is it!'

Suzy went back to Nick's that night. Sleep was impossible.

In the quiet of the early hours, she went into the bathroom.

Suzy took both locks of hair with her. Rosabella's was darker than her own, a long wispy curl. She played with it, twisting the hairs around her fingers, feeling its texture in her hands. She then committed both locks to the waters of the toilet, flushing them to oblivion.

Suzy then went in search of Nick's Swiss army knife, careful not to stir him as she rummaged in his room. She returned to the bathroom and removed her shirt.

For what felt an age, Suzy stared at herself in the mirror. What would a photographer make of this face? She thought of that little girl in the National Portrait Gallery, alone and terrified among the swings and slides.

Suzy turned her right arm towards the mirror, squeezing the rose tattoo between her fingers. She then pulled out the knife's blade and began scraping at the rose skin, bolder with each stroke, letting the knife sink deeper. There was pain, just as there was when she had acquired the tattoo. But this was the pain of release. The white of the basin below was soon patterned in a bright red, like fallen petals of a rich red rose.

22

Suzy was working in studio three with Nina and Gareth. Nina was repeatedly turning to Suzy with a concerned motherly expression. 'I didn't sleep well!' Perhaps Suzy should have made a remedial stop at Fabulous Faces before coming onto campus.

'What's the matter with your arm?' Gareth asked.

The bandaging had added an unfortunate lump in her shirt-sleeve.

'Is that still from the poll tax demo?'

He hadn't noticed it was the wrong arm! Suzy nodded, grateful for the cover. She then proceeded to unbutton the cuffs of her shirt, carefully bunching up the sleeves.

The studio space had been equitably divided for the end-of-year show. Suzy was satisfied with her territory on a far wall, yet facing the entrance.

It was the first time that Suzy could view the completed works of all her peers. Megan already had her refugee display fully hung, great doleful faces staring down at these classmates struggling to catch up. Nina's fishmongers were skinning and slicing their way up a side wall, but it was Gareth's melancholic portraits that Suzy kept returning to. Stewart conveyed such quiet dignity. He would live on. She knew that was why he had welcomed Gareth's attentions. Gareth had offered immortality to a dying man.

And that was what Suzy had provided the Jewish Friendship Club. Whatever became of them, there would always be this witness to a moment. Suzy saluted her Gloria, and her Becky, her Monty and her Miriam. They would live for ever.

Through the opening collage, Suzy had introduced an outsider to their ranks – Rosabella, standing elegantly on a bridge. And there was another outsider, omnipresent yet unseen, the conductor of this mighty orchestra – Suzy herself. They were all now embraced by eternity.

Nina complimented Suzy on her work, talking up the extraordinary detail she had captured with every face. They were indeed splendid and generous, in such contrast to the pernicious tracts she had forced them to escort.

Eli deported himself in various portrayals of his 'good face' that he claimed had enabled him to survive his fascist tormentors with whom he was once again placed. Yet Suzy realized that Eli wasn't really a survivor. He was a victim. The display was not a statement of defiance. It was a statement of defeat. The ambivalence that Terry had correctly observed, that Suzy herself had sensed, was nothing more than a reluctance to face up to that. Which was why she had changed her ending for this very last time. The photographic finale was now one composed as Eli had recounted the story of Rosabella, an image of his broken crumpled form across the sofa of his home. Her work was a testament to the power of hate. That was not what she had set out to do. Indeed, it was precisely what she had resisted doing. But it was the *truth*.

'Megan is our leader!' Salvo shouted, while he made ready with paper planes. She was standing at the front of the class, asking for everyone's attention.

Megan then delivered a final plea for *every* student to cast a vote in the following day's elections. Opinion poll predictions had the BPP winning ward seats in the East End, and she railed against student apathy. 'Not voting is the equivalent of a vote for them!'

Always, the mysterious *them*, Suzy thought.

'I'm a bloody foreigner. I can't vote!' Salvo declared.

Terry looked completely bemused when he entered. 'Has there been a takeover?' He let Megan finish and she returned to her seat.

'Megan's a good choice,' Terry muttered. 'Shame about the hair.'

He rounded his desk. 'So! How is my little *community* of photographers? A year of thrills and spills drawing to a happy close!'

Terry devoted the class to a wide-ranging discussion on the

key lessons of the past year. He made sure that the usual suspects were ticked off, the ones that spoke of *empathy*, *engagement*, *passion*, *risk-taking*. This was the language they had been force-fed all year long.

He spoke with such enthusiasm, yet Suzy wasn't so convinced any more. She had made the shocking discovery that the camera didn't always protect you.

Wine emerged from his desk drawer. 'Very cheap,' he assured. Plastic cups were passed around.

His toast was 'to an excellent class. And to seeing clearly!'

Salvo readied with his own toast to Terry on the class's behalf. 'To a teacher who likes to talk, from a talker who likes to learn.' No one quite understood.

Terry had another. 'To freedom across Europe!' He had been commissioned to do a follow-up to his Berlin piece for the *Guardian*, and was going to a reunifying Germany the following week.

Gareth took to his feet to toast the memory of Stewart. Suzy proposed one for Jo, and Salvo promptly added another, as if on her behalf – 'to Ee-li!' Suzy sipped uncomfortably.

Terry stopped Suzy as she headed out at the class's finish. 'Your project, Suzy. You changed your ending!'

Suzy waited for his assessment, although part of her really didn't much care any more.

'I see what you're doing,' Terry said. He was staring at her, and she so just wanted to be allowed to leave. 'It works, but it's a gloomier piece.'

'Yeah.' She shrugged.

23

Nick wanted her to stay over, but Suzy had to return to BC this final time. He offered to remain with her while she packed but she couldn't see the point. Part of her longed for his company. But she was also so exhausted. She said goodbye to him by the Underground entrance. They kissed for some time and, even with its persuasiveness, she still resisted.

The hall was beginning to empty of its student rabble. Sir Aubrey Bernard was lost behind assorted bags and cases drowning the lobby. Suzy reacquainted herself with her own mighty suitcase, dragging it from its year-long hibernation at the top of her cupboard. Clearing began with the photographs on her wall, with family first – Mum and Dad, and Grandpa. She reminded herself that she must add baby Jennifer to the collection, her sister. Suzy wasn't an only child any more.

Soon, all the walls were restored to their original bleak cream tone, and she thought of the next fresh-faced eighteen-year-old filling the space with a new batch of prized mementoes. Suzy was ready to move on. A student was in life's no-man's-land, and she was thinking more and more about the value of permanence.

Suzy telephoned her mother to confirm arrangements for the following day. She would travel straight to the show reception from the train station. Nick had agreed to drive Suzy and her mother back to BC afterwards to collect her belongings.

Her mother had booked a room for them both in a hotel near Oxford Circus. It was to be her treat. 'Two single women on the town!' Suzy's primary concern was how she was ever going to hide the residual bruising from the poll tax demo, not to mention a mutilated tattoo.

'Mustn't keep you from your packing.' Yet she did, for a long cherished pastime. 'It's shameful that your father's not coming. Baby or no baby!'

Suzy really wasn't that bothered. She would be back in Leeds soon enough. 'Mum!' she interrupted. 'Dad loves you. You know that, don't you?'

Her mother went silent. 'He loves *you* very much, Sooz. Don't ever think otherwise.'

'You're not listening to me, Mum! I *see it* in how he asks about you. He still loves you! It's important that you hear me.'

'We've known each other since we were fourteen.' Her mother paused. 'We'll always love each other.'

Suzy phoned Nick that next morning as he had requested, deliciously waking him in the process. It also gave her the opportunity of reminding him to vote, which he swore to do on his camera's life. They confirmed their meeting in the Granary just prior to the show, joining Megan and Salvo, Gareth and Nina. It was to be their very own reception for Jo, whose arrival Suzy now eagerly awaited.

In finishing off her packing, Suzy came across the box at the back of the cupboard in which she had placed all the Club photographs that had once wallpapered her room. It contained the rose poem, and the photographs returned by Eli. She jammed the box firmly into her bin.

Suzy had the delicate matter of deciding what to wear for the show reception. The idea of gallery owners being present excited her, and she explored a number of possible images, deciding in the end to mix two by putting her sedate pale blue shirt up against her most arty purple trousers. As a final touch, she added the glamour of the Liebovitz dynasty earrings, flaunting them in front of the mirror. It was to be their final East End outing of the season.

Glorious sunshine greeted Suzy as she strode from BC, patting Sir Aubrey on the head on her way out. Even Leyton High Street felt oddly Mediterranean. She managed to find the Polling Station in a school off the main road. Having delivered her tick, she went down the list to the name of the BPP candidate, scoring it through in an act of voodoo.

Descending into the Underground on such a day was surely reprehensible. Suzy stood close to the platform's edge to catch the rush of wind charging through the tunnel as the train approached. She devoted the journey to reviewing her summer holiday discussion with Nick. He wanted to include Eastern Europe in the tour, given the upheavals being played out and the photographic opportunities that this represented. Suzy relished the idea of being his guide in Prague, taking him to all the sights that the previous year had so enthralled her. Timing and cost were the two outstanding issues, both of which related to that other discussion, the one so far unresolved with her father over summer work in the shop.

Suzy had to wait her turn at Fabulous Faces. Zandra teased about her *student discount*, this free consultation in recognition of her special day. Suzy responded by continually referring to her as Sandra, recently revealed as her name beyond this Fab world.

She began by washing Suzy's hair, blow-drying it in such a way as to give full sway to her curls. 'Don't know what your problem is. I'd give anything to have hair like yours.'

As Zandra moved in on the face, Suzy reminded her that she wasn't a *Dynasty* actress. 'Understated!'

Zandra nodded. 'Don't you worry. You want the poor student look!'

She applied foundation, immediately obliterating an annoying spot, which unforgivably had chosen that morning to surface. After blusher, Zandra worked on the eyes. 'You've got great eyes. You really should make more of them.'

Suzy's features had never undergone such close scrutiny. She felt completely self-conscious.

'How long will your show be running for?' Zandra asked. She promised she would try to 'get along to see what all the fuss is about. We're the people who do the hard work. All you do is press a button!'

Zandra was moving down her face – 'do you use a moisturiser?' – choosing lipstick of a daring purple shade 'to match your trousers'.

Suzy couldn't recognize this alluring creature forming before her. She hadn't intended to get herself photographed, but it was Zandra's artistry that deserved preserving for posterity. That was her justification to Malcolm behind the camera. Zandra clapped her as she left.

This exoticized Suzy emerged uncertainly onto the street. She couldn't help turning into every mirror that she passed. It all looked way overstated to her, and she was aching to get the reactions of her classmates, especially Nick.

After a brief flirtation with shopping, exclusively of the window variety, Suzy made her way to the Underground, tunnelling back to her East End. As she travelled, she tried to get a sense of her appearance from the way people did or did not acknowledge her. She was finally wearing her very own *fab face*. According to Eli, it was also a *good face* – yet that hadn't saved him.

She ascended at Mile End Road Station. Suzy had decided to have a sneak preview of the first year show in its fully realized state and, in the quiet of her own time, appraise how her work truly stacked up against her comrades in arms. More cutely, she had heard that professionally produced name cards headed each display, just like in the galleries. She was keen to see the effect.

As she walked out of the station, she heard her name being called. It was from behind her, in a voice that was instantly recognizable. She swung round to face Eli.

24

Suzy wasn't that surprised, and there was a part of her that felt huge relief. More than she would have imagined. Eli was smiling exuberantly.

'Look at you, Shoshana!' He embraced her before she had

any time to react. Yet there was something reassuring in his unselfconscious familiarity.

She was also encouraged by his appearance. He was dapperly dressed, wearing a neat blazer and beige summer trousers. He looked the very image of a gentleman out for a leisurely stroll. Suzy found herself relaxing. This was the moment that she had wanted all along. Their meeting was inevitable. She was even still carrying his negatives in her bag in readiness. And it *could* be this easy.

'You look fantastic!'

Suzy had momentarily forgotten about her Fabulous enhancement. She explained where she had been, and the show reception that evening.

'You must be so excited! The Club is so proud of you. Your work is for all of us.'

'Have you gone back to the Club?' Suzy asked.

'Yes! Of course. All that nonsense is over with. They need me so much, believe me! The shul *begged* me to come back. They're struggling with their minyan. And you've heard Wolfie sing, haven't you!'

Eli seemed almost serene, completely at ease with himself, and with Suzy. He wanted her to join him for a coffee, urging gently. 'Allow me – in honour of your special day.' The opportunity finally to clear the air between them would certainly make it special! Suzy agreed.

As they walked to a favoured local café of Eli's down the Mile End Road towards Stepney, he regaled her with a whole new collection of jokes. 'Market stall trader Frank was telling a passing friend how terrible his life had become, how his wife had left him, his children wouldn't speak to him, his home had been burgled, his recent illness. All the disasters that had come his way. Just before leaving, his friend asked Frank what he was selling. *Lucky charms*!' Eli guffawed. And there were too many more.

Suzy found herself prepared, then even keen to bring Eli up to date with her life. She was reconnecting with him in the familiar terms that they had so recently shared. Coffee extended to lunch. She talked about the project show and the people who were coming to view it, exuding all the excitement she could finally allow herself to feel. She talked about the West End galleries she had toured and in which she longed to one day feature. 'You will, Shoshana. You will!' She talked about her mother's visit, her imminent return to Leeds, about Nick, how they were still together, her and their plans for the summer. It all just seemed to tumble forth.

Eli listened intently. He had the manner of a proud father, pleasuring in her chatter, drinking it in.

Suzy rummaged in her bag, handing over the old negatives she had been keeping for him.

'I have more, Shoshana. Better ones. I found them!' Eli stared at her. 'From the work camps. When I was in Transnistria. And some things of Rosabella's.'

'What things?'

'Amazing! Amazing! You want to see?'

And so Suzy walked the few more streets to his home. Eli spoke excitedly of a precious Caruso recording that he had just purchased. 'I will play it for you!'

351

She was shocked by his flat's appearance. It looked as if he was preparing for a jumble sale. All manner of effects – clothing, cutlery, dishes – were spread across the living room.

Suzy declined his offer of a drink. As he poured his own in the kitchen, Suzy recognized that the items laid out on his dining-room table were from his old trunk. There was the hat, tattered documents, cap badges, the spyglass, ornamental dagger.

With whisky in hand, Eli sought out his beloved music centre.

'What did you find of Rosabella's?'

'Patience, Shoshana. Patience. First of all, music.'

Caruso suddenly exploded into the room, his voice relishing its release like a genie just freed from the lamp.

'Listen! Sublime, no?'

'Are you . . . rearranging the place?' Suzy asked, rather loudly to compete with the sound. She noted how his mantelpiece was now curiously brimming with pictures. All the prints that she had ever produced for him were on display, his family reunited in his living room.

'I bought a camera!' Eli proudly announced.

And it was true! Bizarrely, Suzy beheld him holding the latest version of her very own Weston TT. He passed it to her, and she caressed the camera like the old friend it was.

'Take my picture. Go on!'

Suzy was reminded of her father on her birthday talking in similar fashion after making a similar presentation. It must have cost Eli far more than his Caruso.

'Are you taking up photography?'

'Please. Take my picture.'

Suzy obliged, moving close to allow his ebullient face to fill the lens.

He also wanted one of them together, so Suzy set the camera to automatic, positioning two dining chairs for the exercise. She stood up immediately she heard its click.

'So are you joining my course?' Suzy teased. 'You like being a student!'

'I bought it for you,' Eli earnestly said.

Suzy was stunned.

'Yours is broken, no? You need a new one.'

'No, Eli. I couldn't. Don't be silly!'

He held the camera out for her, but she refused to take it.

'Eli. No!'

He reluctantly put it down and returned to the sofa where his whisky glass awaited.

'It was a peace offering,' he said. 'That's all. You're angry with me.'

'Would I have come here if I was?'

'So why am I not in your display?'

Suzy was confused. 'What d'you mean?'

'At the Club. I saw it. There wasn't *one* picture of me!'

For the first time, Suzy felt herself tensing. 'That wasn't the project!'

She sat herself on one of the dining chairs, scanning the table-top memorabilia. She sensed there was something significant missing.

'They were just random pictures for the Club to keep. I thought you had left!'

'You *were* annoyed with me.' Eli had a strange calm about him. It was Caruso who was agitated, now a galloping wheezing sound.

'Have you voted?' Suzy quickly asked.

'Certainly! Not that it will make any difference.' Eli smirked. 'They've won!'

'Why d'you keep talking like that?'

'You really believe you're safe, don't you?' Eli now presented a smug expression. 'That's what we all once thought. What can they do?, we said.'

'Eli. You have to stop thinking you're back in the war. Can't you see what it does to you?'

Suzy was getting up to lower the music when he mentioned Rosabella.

'Before I show you, I need to explain something about Rosa, and me. So you'll understand.' Eli took a gulp from his glass.

'You know what she asked me, before we were married?' Eli's face was darkening. 'Never to leave her. I made that promise.' His voice now soft. 'I was so happy to. She was a kind, a good person, and so beautiful. Like you. She made me feel like a man, but I was just a boy.'

Suzy realized that the way Eli now appeared was familiar to her. It was exactly as she had depicted him in the photograph which she had chosen to conclude her project, when he had likewise spoken of Rosabella. He was now talking so quietly that the noise of the music was interfering with Suzy's hearing. She moved closer.

'Bodies of the dead were being thrown into mass graves. Like they were animals. Like they had never lived.' Eli seemed completely lost to a nightmare world, his face shrinking as he continued. 'No coffins, or boxes. Bodies were wrapped in rough sheets, but it was so cold. People would steal the sheets.'

'Eli. What are you telling me? Why are you doing this?'

'You have to know!' He stared at her as if the point was obvious. 'I couldn't . . . kill myself because I was weak. I hated myself for it. I should have gone with Rosa. Death is easier than life.'

Suzy stood up. She just had to disengage. The music was now pounding, Caruso bellowing from every corner.

'Take my picture. Please? Take me looking like this.'

What was he asking? Suzy was confused. Her head felt light. The combination of his words and the relentless music was making her dizzy. She moved away hoping he would compose himself. She was now beneath the swirling music painting, by the mantelpiece that held this family that she herself had resurrected. She took in his parents, then siblings, recalling the very moment she had conjured them into life. What was missing was the picture of herself. Its silver frame now contained the picture of Rosabella. Except there was something peculiar about it. Suzy lifted the image, drawing it close. The face had been tampered with, another transposed onto Rosabella's own. Suzy froze as she recognized it. It was her own face. It was she who was standing on a bridge in Romania.

'Look at me, Shoshana! Look at me!'

Suzy couldn't move, or feel anything. It was the pistol. It was the pearl-handled pistol that was missing from the dining-room table.

'Forgive me, Rosa. Forgive me!'
Then a flash.
FLASH!

25

For the record, Suzy received an *A distinction*, the only first year in the history of the course to receive such a mark. Terry wrote to her parents that her work reflected 'Suzy's exceptional abilities as a photographer. She had extraordinary flair, commitment and integrity.'

Suzy's pictures were inevitably the central focus at the end-of-year show. Her ones of Eli received most attention. The image that concluded the display was used by several of the newspapers. They took a certain macabre pleasure in presenting a photograph of the perpetrator from the camera of the victim.

Suzy's funeral in Leeds attracted hundreds. Most of her course was there – Nick and Terry, Jo, Salvo and Gareth. Even Zandra from Fabulous Faces made the journey. The traditional seven days of mourning were conducted at her mother's home. Her father came every morning to sit with her. They followed all the Jewish rituals – mirrors covered, seated in low chairs, clothing torn.

Eli was buried quietly in a Jewish cemetery in the East End, despite the tradition not to inter suicides in consecrated ground. Monty, Izzy, Wolfie and Arnold gathered. The service was delayed while a minyan formed. The women of the Friendship Club stayed away.

Monty gave the address, brief words that expressed confusion and disbelief. He asked that they should think of Eli as a sick man, another victim of the Holocaust. And he spoke of Suzy, how they were both victims.

Gloria wrote to Suzy's mother on behalf of the Club. She told of how Suzy had become family to them all, how much she was loved, their shock and sympathy.

Some members refused to go back to the Club and it soon disbanded. Gloria moved into sheltered housing near her son in Stanmore. Monty found a place in a Home for the Elderly in Hackney. The Gates of Peace synagogue was sold that spring with Suzy's photographs still on display in the hall. Miriam passed away the following year.

Suzy's mother, accompanied by her father, came down from Leeds for a special memorial event at the university. She spoke of Suzy's huge thirst for life, how that was what had drawn her to photography – her curiosity with everything. Terry paid his tribute, and Nick spoke on behalf of her classmates.

Two pictures of Suzy were placed alongside her work. The first was her Fabulous Faces image, Suzy caught on her very last day of life. Nick had insisted that one of his own also be displayed. It was taken in his bedroom. She had asked Nick to photograph her in order to discover precisely what he thought of her. Suzy was smiling – one of her wide, generous smiles that ignited the world.

Exposure was inspired by a true incident.

Michael Mail was born in Glasgow and now lives in London. In 1999 he won the UK's premier short-story competition, the Macallan *Scotland on Sunday* award. His first novel, *Coralena*, was shortlisted for both the Saltire and Scottish Arts Council book awards.

Scribner

Coralena

Michael Mail

Germany, 1972. A young woman, Sophia, awakes
in her new apartment. She is leaving her past, with
all its troubles and traumas behind. Life seems full
of possibility. At work her boss has given her new
responsibilities; here, Dieter appears as interested
in her as she is in him; untouched since the war the
flat, like her, seems ripe for renewal. She awakes,
full of these promises, and looking across the room
sees written on the morning condensation of
the inside window one word – RAGE

'Mail is a master of pace'
Sunday Telegraph

ISBN 0-7432-2062-5
£6.99